W9-BHG-330

Gold Medal: Best Mystery of 2016, Readers' Favorite Awards

Gold Medal: Best Mystery of 2016, National Indie Excellence Awards

Silver Medal: Best Novel of 2016 (Any Genre – Pacific Region), Independent Publisher IPPY Awards

Silver Medal: Best Novel of 2016 (Any Genre – Western Region), National Indie Excellence Awards

Silver Medal: Best Mystery of 2016, CLUE Awards

Gold Medal: 2016 Benjamin Franklin Book Awards (Best Fiction Cover), Independent Book Publishers Association

Gold Medal: 2017 Ariana Awards (Best Mystery Cover). Electronic Publishing Industry Coalition

What would you do if you were accused of murder?

You're not a police detective or a district attorney who can work inside the system. You're not a wealthy celebrity who can hire investigators to untangle the web of lies.

What if you had to clear your name alone?

And what if you were so shy, so uncomfortable with people that just talking to strangers was difficult, let alone asking questions?

Steve Ondelle is a very unusual murder suspect, a perfect distraction for the San Francisco Police in a very unusual killing.

He keeps a journal of these bizarre events, told in his own unique way. Using only the words and points of view he chooses to accept in the English language.

Step by step a hidden killer tries to portray him as a murderer. To escape these newly-minted lies he must first confront old truths.

This is his story.

The Fog Seller

The Fog Seller

A San Francisco Mystery

Don Daglow

SOUTH HUNTINGTON PUB. LIB.
145 PIDGEGON HILL ROAD
HUNTINGTON STA., NY 11746

Sausalito Media, LLC
Sausalito, CA

This is a work of fiction. Names, characters, businesses, places, events and incidents are either the products of the author's imagination or used in a fictitious manner. Any resemblance to actual persons, living or dead, or actual events is purely coincidental.

ISBN 978-0996781503 (Paperback)
ISBN 978-0996781510 (Kindle)

Copyright © 2015 Don Daglow. All Rights Reserved.

Published by Sausalito Media LLC
PO Box 1035
Sausalito, CA 94966

Sausalito Media is a trademark of Sausalito Media, LLC. All Rights Reserved.

Cover design by Borocki.

Printed in the United States of America.

Contents

PART I

JOURNAL ONE

"It's the same dance everywhere I go. I've done nothing wrong. They ask me questions. I'm not good with questions. They insist. I start to freak. They get suspicious. I really freak. They decide to freak, too."

She stops reading out loud, pauses to look up at me.

My heart sinks. She's seen my journals.

There's no undoing it. I should have put them somewhere safe, but now...

"I write journals all the time," I tell her. "It helps me think."

"You started this one on August 23. Back then you were just... You'd never met The Lady with the Joke Book in Her Purse."

I nod.

She runs her fingertips across the leather, absorbs the reassuring scent, the gilt edges. "Expensive," she says.

"I get the leather ones to remind myself that whatever I write has to be worthwhile. It has to matter."

She smells the binding again, then looks back at me. "And it's OK for me to read it?"

"Sure." I sound more confident than I feel, but it's too late now. Five volumes written just for me and myself. Maybe this will help her know me better.

Maybe this will make her run away for good.

But if no one ever reads the words, then why do I bother to write them?

1.

It's the Same Dance
Everywhere I Go

Thursday, August 23

It's the same dance everywhere I go. I've done nothing wrong.
They ask me questions. I'm not good with questions. They insist.
I start to freak. They get suspicious. I really freak. They decide to
freak, too.

I try to forget what happens next.

I'm doing my walkthrough on the main deck of the Ferry *Louis H.
Baar*. Above me I can hear the pinging of Luis' cowboy boots on the
carpeted steel as he gathers lost sweaters and checks that all the passengers are clear.

I hate finding purses.

This one has brass trim and looks expensive, its leather the color
of a peach in bright sunlight at the Farmers Market.

We get one or two a day. Once a month they'll call you in, ask what might be missing from a certain purse. "I don't open them to look," I always answer.

All I want is to be left alone to do my job and live my life.

I hate finding purses.

I finish my routine and head down the gangway. Fresh air supplants the vaguely musty smell of carpets and upholstery and hard years on salt water.

It's after 10:00 on a warm summer morning in San Francisco. The tourists waiting for the return trip to Sausalito are decked out in shorts and flip-flops.

I go to the little office behind the Ferry Building and give the peach-colored purse to Trish, along with a gray hoodie from the stern.

She holds the purse up by its long strap, looks at the strange vertical silhouette. I shrug. She shrugs back. She enters the trip time and logs that it was on the *Louis H. Baar*, then locks it in the cage.

The last bike-riders are descending the gangway as Luis comes up behind me with a sweater and passes it to Trish.

"*Ahórrale*, Stevie! That purse looks good on you. It goes with your big green eyes, your soft brown hair, your full six feet of super-sexiness."

He flashes his big I-love-the-world grin. I should never have told him that my ID says I'm six feet tall and I'm really 5'11 and a half.

"Am I still in first?" he asks me.

"I have to update the spreadsheet," I tell him. "More French speakers this morning, and Trish is big on French this week."

"And two more speaking Chinese!" he says proudly. Luis likes to bet on Chinese in our weekly pool. We predict the languages we'll hear on the ferry and the winner gets a free lunch.

"Yup, I've got your two Chinese," I reassure him.

"That's a lot of new scores. You writing all this down, Stevie?" He gives me his evil eye. He may be one small guy but he has enough personality for an entire crew.

"Yes, I'm writing down every score."

He nods approvingly. "Hey, Stevie, maybe nobody comes for this purse and they let you keep it!"

I ignore him and go back to help our crewmate Linh board our impatient passengers.

2.

Not French or Italian

or Spanish

Friday, August 24

It's supposed to be sunny today but the fog clings to the frigid waters of the Golden Gate, inviting us all to drift to darker moods as we ready the *Louis H. Baar* to depart from Sausalito.

All except Luis. We are barely away from the pier when he comes down the stairs to the lower deck. The woman following him wears an expensive-looking black suit with large gold buttons, and her black high heels are even louder than Luis' cowboy boots on the thinly-carpeted metal steps. The two of them walk straight towards me.

"Stevie, this lady says she's the one who lost your pink purse." He smiles proudly, folding his arms on the chest of his dark blue jump-suit.

"It's not pink," she interjects. A European accent, but not French or Italian or Spanish.

"Stevie, this lady says she's the one who lost your purse."

She's maybe 40, tightly curled dark brown hair. Very red lips, very black eyebrows. Unusual curve to the hairline on her temples.

"Did they call you?" he asks her.

"No, nobody calls me. I arrive at my hotel and realize I lose my purse. I repeat every step I make yesterday. All my credit cards. My passport." She clenches her white-gloved hands. Just one small ring silhouetted on her right ring finger.

"We turn in everything we find," I tell her. "It's at the Ferry Building."

"Which ferry building?" She swallows the r's in 'ferry' so the sound vanishes down her throat and rolls around a while before returning to pronounce the "y."

Not German. Not Russian.

Luis chimes in, "San Francisco, ma'am, only Ferry Building we got. Only big thing left from before the earthquake in 1906. Sausalito's just a pier, no nothing."

She hesitates. "All right." She stands there, apparently unsure what to do next.

"You can sit anywhere you like," Luis tells her.

"Yes, thank you," she says.

The *Louis H. Baar* has over 700 seats on three decks, and there are open spots in every cabin. But she just moves a couple of steps to her right and leans against the bulkhead. The horizon line rises and falls gently in the window beside her.

I walk off to do my chores. I have to remind Luis that Fort Point, Mission Dolores and many other "big things" in San Francisco are left from before 1906. From before the Earthquake *and Fire* of 1906.

Luis will remind me that I am the professor, and it is my fault when the student is not properly prepared.

I empty the forward trash cans and walk back towards the aft cabin once more. The woman is still there in the passageway, patiently leaning against the steel wall.

She steps forward as I approach, one hand cupped to her mouth as if to whisper something.

An old man with a walker approaches from the far cabin. He flashes a big smile and says in a loud voice, "Lucky I have this thing! Rough seas!" He laughs and brandishes the walker.

The woman in the expensive suit does not laugh. She looks impatient, frustrated at the interruption.

The old man makes his way between us, still chuckling at his own joke.

I wait for him to reach the front cabin. The woman now appears lost in thought, looking out the window at a huge Chinese container ship maneuvering in the Bay.

She does not cross the three feet between us to whisper what she was about to whisper. She says nothing.

I never know what to do when people won't say what they're thinking.

I never know what to do when people do say what they're thinking.

I get back to work so I can finish my routine on time. I empty the trash by the snack bar, pick up empty sugar packets, discover a nickel lying on the floor. I put the nickel on the counter and the trash bags by the main deck gangway.

Luis stops me as I'm about to check the rest room. "That was all English with the lady with the purse," he says. "Nothing to write down. Nobody scored nothing."

"That's right," I tell him.

"Good!" Luis says, and heads back upstairs.

In a few minutes the Ferry Building's clock tower emerges from the fog and we are ready to dock in San Francisco. Soon the engines will slow as we approach the pier, and I head for the stern to get the big aluminum hook and snare the mooring line.

The woman with the lost purse is still standing in the same spot, still leaning awkwardly against the bulkhead, still lifting one uncomfortable high-heeled shoe and then the other.

The moment she sees me she again steps forward, her expression anxious.

"Do you look in purse when you find it?" she asks

"No. We just turn them in."

"Oh. Good." Her words say she's pleased but her face looks disappointed. "You..."

She has to stop. The PA system, even louder than usual, reminds everyone to gather their belongings and get ready to disembark and that if anyone has forgotten they left their bike at the back of the boat then the place they left their bike is at the back of the boat and they should go to the back of the boat to get it.

The woman winces in silent frustration, drowned out by the long announcement on the tinny speakers. People start to crowd past us towards the gangway, anxious to exit the moment that Trish deploys the hydraulic ramp. I step back to clear the way and more people push between us.

I have to tend the line and cannot wait to hear what the woman is finally ready to say. I call out, "Sorry!" and hurry back to the stern.

Hook in hand, I snag the heavy rope, always mindful of how a taut line can sever a finger or crush a hand. Once all is secure I go to the rail and look down to see the woman in the fancy suit walking carefully down the ramp.

She glances back, once. She sees me at the railing, then turns and walks around the corner to the office. Trish will ask her questions, check the ID from the purse and then return it.

I will never know what the lady with the lost purse keeps wanting to say to me. Or why she never says it.

Or why she never sits down or takes off her shoes, even when her feet hurt.

But I will not lose sleep over it.

What will keep me awake tonight is a different question. From where in the world do people come when they speak English with that accent?

3.

Mr. Don't Ask Me Anything

Friday, August 24 (Cont.)

Luis has kids and wants to get off early, so he works 6:00 to 3:00, plus OT when Christmas or a birthday are coming. I have nowhere to go so I take a split shift on the *Louis H. Baar* and cover both commutes, with five sailings in the morning and seven trips in the afternoon.

Everyone gets what they want. Luis gets home to his family. I get four mid-day hours free in San Francisco. Trish's crew chart looks perfect in a report that no one ever reads.

Some days I go a certain place to do a certain thing. Some days I join my roommate, Liam the Fog Seller. Some days I just walk and lose myself in the City.

Today after we clear the 11:25 arrival in San Francisco I change out of my uniform and I'm off to watch them feed the penguins at the

Institute of Science. On the way I stop to ask Trish about the lady with the lost purse.

"Yeah, she came by and claimed it," Trish confirms.

"Where do you think she's from? She has an unusual accent."

Trish doesn't look up from her clipboard. "Sounded Russian to me."

"The sound of her r's is wrong for Russian. Too rolly. In Russian the letter r rolls off the tongue, but it only rolls once. Her r's roll more, like in Spanish, except they aren't from any Romance language."

"Doesn't matter," she says, still preoccupied with her papers. "We don't get points for accents, just for languages."

"True enough," I tell her.

"Is Luis still in first?" she asks me. "He lucked out with that Chinese tour bus on Tuesday."

"I have to check tonight. Where does the woman's passport come from?"

Now Trish puts down her clipboard and stares at me over her black-rimmed glasses. "You know, Mr. Don't-Ask-Me-Anything, you sure have a lot of questions of your own today."

I notice that she has cleverly phrased her question as a declaration. I am not fooled.

I say, "See you later," and walk away.

"There was no ID in the purse," she calls after me. "All that was in it was a joke book. She told me exactly what I'd find inside so I gave it to her."

I stop and turn to look at her. "A joke book?"

Trish nods, smiling. "She wanted me to thank you."

I shake my head and turn to set off again. "Crazy world," I call back to her.

"She wanted me to tell you," Trish calls back. "She wanted you to know what was inside."

I take all this in but continue walking. Why would the woman care that I know what's in her purse?

I cross the sweeping boulevard called The Embarcadero that runs along the edge of the Bay, the summer breeze gentle for now. By the time I return this afternoon the wind will be whipping whitecaps across the water and snatching maps from the hands of frazzled tourists.

Why would a purse hold nothing but a joke book? Not the passport and the credit cards she says she lost. No keys. No tissues.

No lipstick for a woman with bright red lips.

And where in the hell does that accent come from?

I reach Market St. and then turn left onto Spear. As I always do, I stop by the building where my father used to work. I say hello, tell him I'm OK.

It's not really the building where he worked. That building is no longer here. But I'm standing in the same place.

My father is no longer here. But I'm standing in the same place.

It's the best that I can do.

4.

The Tourists Turn to See if I'm a Crazy Person

Friday, August 24 (Cont.)

The California Institute of Science is located in Golden Gate Park, but they're tearing down its beautiful old art-deco buildings to build a modern glass museum. So for now the Institute is located in a drab eight-story office building on Mission St.

The next penguin feeding isn't for an hour, and most of my usual haunts from the old Institute aren't replicated at the temporary Judson Aquarium. Even Eli of the Coral Reef is nowhere to be found today.

I'm standing beside a monitor that shows a fast-motion video of the construction of the new Institute of Science. Great yellow beasts tear deep gashes in the earth, then mighty cranes erect a lattice of dark gray steel.

They've added a promo for the Gift Shop to the end of the ever-repeating tape, with eternally-happy background music. With a cry of delight, a child picks the perfect stuffed dinosaur from a shelf. "It's an allosaurus, just like the one in the show!" the girl explains.

Her mother beams at this proof of her daughter's intelligence and the educational value of the California Institute of Science.

They meet at the cash register with an ecstatic dad and brother, who have selected a cardboard airplane kit. As the music soars they joyously check out with the smiling clerk, a Chinese lady. I recognize her. Amid all the actors, she's an actual real person who works in the shop.

I recognize someone else.

Behind the happy kids with the perfect gifts is a short line of equally happy people with perfect items of their own. One of them is the woman from the *Louis H. Baar*. The Lady with the Joke Book in Her Purse.

Her hair is shorter, a perky shake-it-all-out cut. Her lipstick is glossier, her eyes brighter. She looks ten years younger, ten pounds lighter and ten miles-per-hour faster. But there is no mistaking that hairline, the nostrils. It is the same woman.

I think about this. Obscure foreign ladies do not regain lost youth and transform into suburban mothers overnight.

I turn and round the corner into the gift shop.

I am in luck. The now-famous cashier stands in front of a real line of real shoppers waiting to check out with real money. Tired moms keeping their energy up for the kids. Students from a suburban fifth grade getting acrylic-crab souvenir keychains. Two Japanese tourists with penguin hats and sweatshirts.

I pick up a $1.99 dinosaur notepad and join the line. It takes three minutes to reach the check stand.

"Hello, hello sir! Good to see you again!" she greets me.

I have to hurry, since the line now stretches back behind me. "I see you're on the video out there," I tell her.

"Yes, they shoot commercial two months ago. Nobody say nothing and they show up." She scans the back of my notepad. "Actress get sick so they have to have old lady do picture."

"You are a very good actress," I tell her.

"The director, he yell at all the people a lot."

She is handing me my change. I try my question now, the best question I can think of on short notice. "Some of the actors look too smiley. They look funny. Do they sound funny, too?"

"Oh, no, no. They not want anyone like me. They not want 'broken English.'" She takes the next mother's fold-out dinosaur book and scans its bar code, but pauses to flash me a big smile. "But I was only one can do cash register right!"

I smile back and move away, my new theory already starting to crystalize. The Lady with the Joke Book in Her Purse does not have a strange accent from somewhere in Europe.

She has a strange accent from somewhere in acting class.

* * *

Real Scientists are curious. It's what makes them work, what fuels their engines.

Right now I need someone who's curious.

The planetarium is the one place "out front" in the Institute of Science where they have Real Scientists instead of touch-screens, tour guides and interns. But the old planetarium is now rubble and most of the old astronomers are retired or relocated.

Tom, the weekend guard, says a planetarium office still exists upstairs, reached by a forbidden elevator that's guarded by a locked door. Sometimes I recognize a scientist by the vending machines. They all recognize me back.

Maybe The Guy with the Deep Voice Who Prefers Planets is here today. He likes telling stories about different kinds of atmospheres and drinks Diet Dr. Pepper from the machine on the far right, just like me. He'd help me prove my theory.

A lost purse that contains nothing but a joke book might not arouse their curiosity. But when someone creates a fictional character to get the purse back... I just have to tell this to a scientist. A scientist who can then ask his friends inside the Institute about that video.

Ask about things like who makes their videos. Who casts their videos. Which will lead to the actors who are in their videos.

I go to the dais where the lobby security guard sits ready to defend the ticket desk. "Can you call the Planetarium Department for me?" I ask.

"Do you have an appointment?" He pronounces every syllable in the word "appointment" very clearly, out of respect for those who plan ahead.

"No. I just have a couple of really fast questions."

"You can find the email link on the website. Calscience-dot-org, all one word."

Why does it have to be a new guy at the desk today, one who doesn't know I'm a regular?

Not a denizen like Eli of the Coral Reef, but a regular.

I decide that if I can't ask a scientist I'll just ask everybody, starting with him. "Do you know who creates the videos for the Gift Shop, like the one running over there?"

The new guard nods confidently. "Marketing and Communications. You can email them, too. Calscience-dot-org."

"I mean, who is the person who produces the video?"

Sometimes my voice gets intense when I get impatient. I don't mean to, but I start to get loud. Now the tourists turn to see if I'm a crazy person wandering in from Mission St.

I turn to look at the tourists who are turning to look at me. Suddenly I see a familiar face. The Astronomer Who Does Sunsets the Right Way is about to walk right past me.

She is one of the scientists I've been searching for, but all I manage to get out is "Excuse me?"

Actually, it sounds more like "Excuse me!!!"

She stops in her tracks and turns only her head to look at me, the rest of her body still aimed at the back of the building "You're the guy who likes the way I do sunsets in the planetarium," she says.

That's the one thing I ever thought of to say to her. She remembers.

"I'm really sorry to bother you," I begin, lowering my voice to a rational volume. "I need to find out who's in charge of the gift shop video. It's a long story, but there's a problem with it. Kind of."

She absorbs this for a moment, her brown eyes deep in thought. Her hair is braided tightly down her back, a river of dark brown against the pure white of her blouse. I wonder yet again what she would look like if she wore it down.

"Just ask at the shop." She smiles uncomfortably. "To tell you the truth, I hate that video."

I hesitate. I'm talking to a woman whom I'd never talk to because she would never want to talk to me. If I say the wrong thing she'll discover that she doesn't want to talk to me. Scientists are good at discovering things.

The result of all this thinking is a thoroughly stupid look on my face while I'm saying absolutely nothing.

"Sorry," I tell her. "I think someone in the video may be trying to... Not necessarily to..."

She looks at her watch, turns her back and walks away. As she goes she looks back at me and says, "This way." Her boot heels echo confidently on the concrete.

The guard, startled, rises half-way from his chair. "You need any assistance, Dr. Costa?"

She doesn't stop, just waves a friendly goodbye as we walk towards the back of the building.

5.

The Elevator You Never See

Friday, August 24 (Cont.)

The Astronomer Who Does Sunsets the Right Way, whose name is Paula Costa, takes me to the elevator you never see behind a door you cannot open. As we ride I give a concise account of The Lady with the Joke Book in Her Purse.

I try very hard to sound neither boring nor insane.

We exit the elevator and walk down a long hallway, my story still unfolding. We pass a painting of the façade of the old Institute. My father and I could be two of the tiny figures entering the glass doors behind the great white columns. I want to stop and stare but I do not.

To my surprise, it turns out that I am not the only person in the Institute who doesn't know who creates the gift shop videos.

Not the Director of Non-Ticket Revenue, who runs the store.

Not the Director of Educational Programs, the familiar face from

Channel 9's Public TV pledge weeks, who wears dark stockings to hide the long scar on the back of her left calf.

The extra-tall PR Director is at his desk, but as Paula leads the way into his office I recognize him and silently take a step back into the hallway, out of sight.

He is someone who knows me from before. Someone who knows I am not good with questions.

I don't want to remember his name. But I remember every word he said that night.

I have to get out of here before he says those words again.

If Paula has noticed my retreat she does not comment as she comes back into the hallway. "Sorry," she says. "That was strike three. I thought it would be easy but..."

"It's OK," I tell her, keeping my voice low. "I have to get back to the ferry."

"If I find out anything I'll call you." she says, giving me a card to scribble down my number. I give it to her and she hurries off.

Real Scientists are curious. It's what makes them work, what fuels their engines.

I can hear it in her voice. I am not the only one who can't stop thinking about the strange accent and the even-more-strange behavior of The Lady with the Joke Book in Her Purse.

* * *

I live below a big white 1908 house in Sausalito, a house that has two generations of garages.

The new garage is up the hill from the house, perched on a twisting street, and it holds three cars. The old garage is down the hill at the end of a driveway that no longer exists, and it holds my roommate Liam the Fog Seller and me.

I open the rusty wrought iron gate and climb the steep stone steps that lead up to my garage. Above me Mrs. Blount, my landlord, opens the curtains of the big white house to see who's coming.

Every evening at this time the gate opens and closes with a mournful squeal. It is always me. And every evening Mrs. Blount comes to the window to look down the hill at the intruder.

I open the door and switch on the lights, as I'm rushed by Zina the Wonder Dog, Liam's yellow lab. Zina is the only being on the planet who thinks that Liam and I are similar. Or at least she treats us both that way. We come and go as we please, and together we make enough money to pay the rent.

Seventeen feet of aquariums line the left side of the room, the heavy wooden rack only three shelves high because of the low walls that support the ancient oak beams of the vaulted ceiling.

The bottom shelf is four 55-gallons for smaller fish and "grow-out tanks" for juveniles. The top is a mix of twenty, ten and five-gallons for quarantine and for "fry," the tiny babies. On the middle shelf is my pride and joy, the new 210 and the two 90-gallons on either side.

The rest of my side of the garage holds a bed, a reading lamp, a small desk for my computer, a narrow closet and a bureau. There's a little kitchen at the back, and a small room in the corner with a tiny shower, sink and toilet.

Where my side of the garage is filled with aquaria, Liam's side is filled with books. History, novels, centuries of stage plays. Every work by Shakespeare with matching bindings, with his old college notes in the margins.

Liam calls it "the wall of things we needed before the Internet." But I've never seen him part with a single volume.

I open the door and walk outside so Zina can do her thing. She spends an hour or two down the hill with Mrs. Tarrow each day so she gets a break and a chance to run, and her evening trip to the stand of oak trees is a brief affair before she rushes back for dinner.

After a dinner of frozen pizza for me and gourmet kibble for Zina it is water change night for the top row of tanks. Each one matches the tropical water conditions of Lake Malawi in southern Africa. To keep it that way, even with powerful filters, I have to siphon out and replace 25% of the water in every tank once each week.

I climb the ladder, insert the plastic tube into an aquarium, squeeze the rubber ball that starts the water flowing and siphon out a bucket-full of water and gunk. Then I haul the bucket out the door and dump it in the big black plastic trash can with the valve that connects it to the bright green hose that feeds the drip lines in Mrs. Tarrow's garden down the hill.

Siphon-haul-dump. Siphon-haul-dump.

Liam likes to look at the tanks but declines to take part in water changes. He thinks of my fish as "your fish," which is fine by me.

I always think about things when I'm hauling buckets of dirty water.

I think about how every drop of water is used twice, about how the waste from the aquariums becomes vital food for the garden down the hill.

I picture how Mrs. Tarrow smiles when she tends her prize tomatoes, when she re-lives the awards ceremony last year at the County Fair with everyone applauding. At 70-something that smile of hers can still light up a cold and foggy night.

Siphon-haul-dump. Siphon-haul-dump.

I think about The Lady with the Joke Book in Her Purse, standing there with her black suit and white gloves and her painful heels.

And I think about how Paula looks when she smiles. Her smooth brown skin. The eyebrows that arch like the top of a stained-glass window. Her never-wrinkled blouses and always-pressed pants.

The way she makes children laugh when she talks about The Man in the Moon during her shows at the planetarium.

Siphon-haul-dump. Siphon-haul-dump.

Top shelf nights are always the hardest.

Sometimes dreams do come true. Like my dream that the Astronomer Who Does Sunsets the Right Way will notice me.

Today she sees me, learns my name, nods when I talk.

Today she asks for my number and says she'll call me.

I know it won't work out, because it never does. But I will still give myself permission to dream. For a while, yet, I can dream.

That's the one skill I have truly mastered. I live in the Here and Now.

Siphon-haul-dump.

The past is pain and boredom, the future is the same. Neither one is Here and Now.

If now, right now, holds joy then I deserve to feel it. Like the tiny fish that the starving man catches with his bare hands, a taste of joy renews me with the flavors of the Here and Now.

It's what's gotten me this far in this cold and angry world.

Siphon-haul-dump.

And here and now Paula smiles at me and has not yet gone away.

6.

My Grandma Says People Get Mad and Unmad

Tuesday, August 28

It is a cold and foggy morning. Commuters hunch and shudder as they wait in the long line on the dock in Sausalito, the Bay hissing at the pilings. The Ferry *Louis H. Baar*, pure white with two bright blue stripes down each side, waits calmly for her passengers.

Some days I think the stains below her windows look like tears.

I open the gate and the crowd presses forward in search of warmth. Marching shoes and boots and flip-flops sweep down the metal gangway to the floating pier, then cross the threshold to line up again at the snack bar to feed their addiction to Linh's freshly-brewed coffee.

Luis disconnects the shore power as I cross the gangway, don my bright orange parka and take my position at the stern to cast off the line. I check for kayaks and paddleboarders, then call, "All clear!" into the radio.

The engines roar and we drift backwards, dark water frothing all around us. In the distance a fog horn booms, echoing across the Bay to vibrate the deck beneath me. The air is filled with the smells of salt water and diesel fuel, mixed with the cloying scent of raw sewage from the fleet of anchor-outs clustered just offshore.

"Mr. Ondelle?"

I turn to see a Mexican kid, about 18 or 19. He's wearing jeans and a sweatshirt that's nowhere near warm enough to be out here on the stern this early in the morning.

"You're Mr. Ondelle, right?"

I hear my voice saying, "Yes."

"You don't know who I am?"

This happens sometimes with my old students. I may look the same after five years, but they do not.

I guess all this is playing out on my face because he puts me out of my misery. "I'm Tommy Gonzalez."

I compare two pictures in my head.

Tommy at 13 or 14 in middle school. Dark hair neatly combed straight up. A kid who wants to be at school, wants to do well, wants you to tell his folks he's working hard.

Tommy at 19. Hair longer now, hanging down across his forehead. A full six feet tall, but bigger across the shoulders than me. The warm brown eyes I remember so well. I should know him from those eyes.

I step forward and give him a hug, and a torrent of memories rises up through my heart and into my throat.

I pull back. "It's great to see you!" I say, hoping he sees none of what I'm feeling. "You working in the City?"

"Part time. And going to school. SF State."

More memories. "Like I always tell you, if you stick with it you'll get in."

He nods. "I remember lots of things you told me, Mr. Ondelle.

What you wrote me in my yearbook about never giving up on my dreams."

"You can call me Steve now, Tommy. I'm not your teacher anymore."

"OK... Steve." He pauses. "Dude, that does not sound right."

"How's your mom?" I ask him.

"Good, good," he says. "We still talk about you sometimes."

"Tell her hello for me, please. Tell her I still remember her tamales at Christmas."

I'm not used to having my hopes and dreams come true. But here's one of those dreams, standing right in front of me.

He starts to say something, stops, then starts again. "Are you going back to... I mean. Are you going to go study in England and do what you were gonna do?"

"Probably not."

I'm not used to talking to people who know me from before. People who actually know me.

"How come? We were all gonna come be your students again in college." He gives me that same Tommy Gonzalez smile. "What happened to 'Take arms against a sea of troubles, and by opposing end them?'"

More memories. I look across the Bay at where the Golden Gate Bridge should be. Today it's just a wall of fog.

I bring my eyes back and try to focus. "Just not meant to be, I guess. But you're doing your part. You're a college kid!"

"We all know you didn't do anything wrong, Mr. Ondelle. The people who lied about you weren't even there that day."

There, he says it.

He adds, "You didn't have to quit."

Now I can't look away, my heart breaking all over again.

My silence seems to drive him forward. "My grandma says people get mad and un-mad. If you'd stayed it would have happened. They'd have gotten un-mad."

I know better. I know they'll never get un-mad.

I know I'll never get un-lost.

* * *

When we reach San Francisco I wipe down the bathrooms and I'm done for the morning.

The temporary Judson Aquarium at the temporary California Institute of Science is one place I can almost always find a friend. And right now I need a friend to talk to.

This is not the familiar old aquarium of my childhood, with long rows of matching windows offering incredible glimpses into under-water life.

This Judson Aquarium has exhibits housed in Sears above-ground swimming pools. Big steel tanks that look like cabins from an old submarine. Terrariums perched above the tropical fish so the rising heat will keep the cold-blooded reptiles warm.

The ancient alligators I know so well are gone, off to retirement at a farm in Florida.

The sharks are in Seattle and Chicago.

At least the penguins are still here, with public feedings in a tiny theatre in the back corner.

A figure stands alone, silhouetted in the low light opposite the massive undersea-bank-vault that holds the fresh-water catfish. I can't see him clearly in the shadows.

I don't have to.

I know his shoulders are slumped and that his hands are fidgeting.

I approach and lean on the tank beside him. "Hey, Eli."

"Hey, Steve." His voice is nasal and a little gravelly. You have to get used to it.

"How you doing?" I ask him.

"I'm cool."

As my eyes adjust I can make out the features of Eli of the Coral Reef. Counting his Giants cap he's half a head shorter than me, maybe 5'6", with short brown hair. His earphones wait patiently, tucked around his neck, a sure sign the Giants aren't playing till tonight.

"You see the reef fish yet today?" I ask him.

"Not yet."

"You want to go look now?" I ask.

He smiles, finally. "That'd be cool."

The big pale-blue reef tank has just a handful of rocks and corals dotting the broad, flat steel floor.

A few colorful fish wander around the tank. They look confused, like they went to sleep last night in their own bed and woke up this morning in a strange, sterile hospital.

Eli stares intently through the small window and smiles. "How's your new butterfly project?" he asks me, his eyes still on the fish.

I give myself challenges so I won't get bored, and it all starts when we see butterflies in Sausalito that shouldn't be any closer to California than Japan. It's a long story, but I figure out that they are hitchhikers in a shipping container at a pottery shop, and I have so much fun that now I always have a butterfly project.

The Lady with the Joke Book in Her Purse is my newest butterfly project.

"Paula actually calls me back," I whisper to him.

Now he looks at me and his eyes go wide. "That's amazing!"

"I'm meeting her downstairs in... 39 minutes. We're going to the studio where they edit the gift shop video where the actress is standing in line."

"You're going there with her?" he asks, incredulous.

"Yeah. I'm afraid to go because I know I'll say something stupid and she won't want to be with me, but the only reason she wants to be with me is because I tell her I want to go so if I don't go she won't go with me."

"Uh-huh."

"You know what I mean."

Eli of the Coral Reef nods. "Uh-huh."

That's the great thing about Eli. He does know what I mean.

A column of visitors with English accents enters the room and heads straight towards us, the flood from a fresh wave of tour buses.

Eli of the Coral Reef starts drifting towards the shadows.

This, of course, is the problem.

When he's at work, Eli covers the swing shift as a security guard for an office tower down the street. He's paid well because he's the only guy who can watch eighteen monitors at the same time and never miss a thing.

But when he takes off his uniform and his badge, he goes from having super-vision to being super-invisible.

I look towards the retreating silhouette. "Hey, Eli, you see the clown trigger? It's digging at something under that rock!"

He shakes his head, then turns and walks away.

7.

A Sincere Smile and a Sneer

Tuesday, August 28 (Cont.)

Just as her voicemail from last night promises, Paula meets me at the vending machines that serve as the temporary restaurant at the temporary Institute of Science.

Beaming, she shows me a scribbled note with names and an address in her precise handwriting.

"Voila!" she proclaims. "Name and address of the studio where they did the post."

"That's great!" I tell her. "What's post?"

"Post Production. It's when they edit everything, add the music, stuff like that. And, check this out..."

She reaches into her woven leather purse and pulls out a crumpled paper, holding it up with both hands

It's an image from the gift shop video. At its center, smiling joyfully, stands The Lady with the Joke Book in Her Purse.

* * *

The address Paula carries is not a production studio. It is a small, well-worn hotel near Union Square that wants to be elegant when it grows up.

It should just be happy that it hasn't fallen down.

I approach the young man at the front desk and explain that we're looking for Avanture Video.

He gives me a sincere smile and a sneer, somehow doing both at the same time. "Go out the front door, turn right, turn right again at the alley, second door on the right."

This sounds sketchy at best, but we follow the alleyway as directed and come to the second door. A series of shiny brass plates are bolted to the wall, with weathered index cards taped alongside. One of the hand-written cards says "Avanture Video."

The door is locked. I find a buzzer and press it.

"Yeah!" says an angry male voice from a speaker I can't see. I feel Paula jump beside me.

Check that. I'm the one doing the jumping.

"We're looking for Avanture Video," Paula shouts to an unseen microphone.

The voice says nothing, but a buzzer sounds and the door clicks. I open it and we enter.

There are no straight lines anywhere. A narrow corridor with dull red walls veers at an odd angle to the right. To the left a curving stairway climbs sharply in an equally odd direction.

As we stand there a woman with short jet-black hair comes down the stairs. A brightly colored parrot decorates her tank top, and the ribbons in her hair match the colors of its plumage.

"Which way is Avanture Video?" I ask. The parrot has green and red wings, and its eye is strategically placed on her left breast.

"Green room is downstairs, studio's that way," she says, pointing down the crooked hall.

I do not ask her why I should care more about a green room than one of any other color, and we find the studio around two corners and up a gently sloping ramp. It has a heavy door and is filled with speakers, computers and flashing lights. But no people.

Paula looks around, says, "Nice toys."

We step inside to wait. A poster by the door depicts the hockey masks from each of the eleven *Friday the 13th* movies, several of them autographed in black or silver. I try to make out the signatures but cannot read them.

We hear the sounds of a toilet flushing and water running in a sink. In a few moments a tall young man with a beak-shaped nose and long muddy-brown dreadlocks comes around the corner. He enters the studio as if we're not there, swinging the heavy door shut behind him as we step out of his way.

"We're looking for Avanture Video," I announce yet again.

He glances at us, then does a double take as if he'd thought we were mannequins and has only just now realized that there are living people in the room.

"This is it," he says, and goes back to ignoring us. Sitting down at a panel, he turns and twists various knobs. He smells of cigarettes.

"We like your work in the Institute of Science museum store video, and we want to see what it would take to get the same kind of tape done for us." I am not telling a lie. Not exactly.

"They aren't tapes, they're digital files," he says, intent on a Mac screen filled with colored bars.

There are circular patterns of acne scars on his left cheek, but none on the right.

"Who was the director?" Paula asks.

Beak-nose rapidly maneuvers the mouse with his left hand, clicking and dragging in different directions. "Jack Bishop."

"Union talent?"

"Why do you ask?" He shaves the pitted side of his face more carefully than the side where the skin is clear.

"If you're not a signatory we have to find a producer who is. House rules." She sounds utterly self-confident.

I have no idea what she's talking about.

"You have to be equity if I run the board," he says. "House rules."

He glances over at me again, trying to discern if I am in fact a mannequin and that Paula is the only real person in the room.

"Local talent or LA?" she asks.

"Institute stuff was TLW. Theatre Lab West. You want a big name from LA? They all do promos here when they're in town."

"Budget?"

"Twenty K for the one you saw." He's starting to smile. Straight, even teeth stained yellow by smoke and coffee.

"And for clients who aren't dumb money?" Paula asks.

He leans back and laughs out loud, finally meeting Paula's eyes. "Jack will tell you twenty-five. Use a standard suite instead of the Pablo and you can wrap it for ten."

Paula laughs with him, reaching into her purse and pulling out the printed video frame. "This actress any good? We liked her look."

He looks at the image, shakes his head. "Lots of actors in TLW." His eyes return to the screen.

"Thanks." Paula says, then turns and walks out of the studio.

Beak-nose fiddles with his control board and ignores me.

I resist the urge to take a headset, carefully loop the cord around his neck and strangle him.

* * *

Paula has to teach a class, but as we walk back to Union Square we celebrate our impending visit with The Lady with the Joke Book in Her Purse.

"If she's playing this weekend at Theatre Lab West I'm free," she says excitedly. "Please, just get two tickets and I'll pay you back. I have to meet this woman!"

"You're getting as bad as me!" I tell her.

She writes something on her business card and passes it to me. "That's my cell. Call me the minute you find out!"

She gives me a little hug good-bye and I watch as she descends the stairs into the Union Square Garage. Disbelieving that she gives me a little hug good-bye.

I look down at her business card. At the handwritten number on the back. Even more disbelieving that she gives me her number.

I shake myself back to the Here and Now and walk the two blocks to Theatre Lab West. The first glass-covered poster by the entrance is for *Six Characters in Search of an Author*, by Luigi Pirandello. No familiar faces.

The other current production is Shakespeare's *The Taming of the Shrew*, done in *Saturday Night Fever* sets and costumes.

There she is! Gawking over Kate's shoulder as Petruchio gyrates on the dance floor, spangled with reflected disco light. She looks still younger than in the video, long wavy reddish-brown hair spilling across her shoulders. If it were not for those nostrils I would have missed her.

Quite a range of characters, this actress. Mysterious 40-something foreigner. Happy suburban mother of two. Now she's the disco princess of the 16th Century.

Only the two lead actors' names rate inclusion on the poster, but The Lady with the Joke Book in Her Purse cannot elude us for much longer.

I enter the ticket office and buy two tickets for Saturday night.

I take several long, slow breaths.

I call Paula to tell her the good news.

8.

It Serves Only You and Will Follow You Anywhere

Wednesday, August 29

Liam the Fog Seller stands atop the round concrete bench in the Powell St. BART station, 50 feet below the streets of San Francisco. He wears a black satin top hat, a tuxedo with tails, baggy black pants, a neon yellow T-shirt and a diaphanous pale blue scarf.

"Ladies and Gentlemen!" he proclaims, drawing a glare from an old Chinese woman sitting nearby. "The trains that roll through this station will take you away from this place and time!"

Most travelers ignore him. A few turn to see what this crazy man is doing.

"Yes, the train *takes* you away," he pronounces. "It severs your ties with this spot, this piece of San Francisco, leaving you with ephemeral memories and a longing in your heart!"

A man wearing a 49ers jacket snorts at this, but does not turn around to watch him.

"So how do we resist? What force can still connect you to your city, your dreams, your memories, even here in the ceramic purgatory of this underground BART station?"

"Your heart!" answers a woman who has approached to stand in front of him.

Liam the Fog Seller smiles down at her. "Yes, my dear, exactly! Your heart is the link that reaches out to the world!" The woman beams. Liam looks back to the waiting passengers. "And how does the world respond? How does it reach out to hold you on the hilly streets of San Francisco?"

Liam pauses, letting the question hang in the air. Then he reaches into his tuxedo pocket and pulls out a small glass vial with a bright blue label.

"The fog!" he whispers. "It is the fog of San Francisco that grounds you in the real world! Up on the streets the fog is cold and lonely. But when you carry it close to your heart, look, you can feel it! It's warm and reassuring!"

Some chuckles. The man in the 49ers jacket laughs out loud. Liam is starting to get to them.

He always does.

"Above us the fog comes and goes, pushed and pulled by great forces of land and sea. But here, inside this tiny vial, it serves only you and will follow you anywhere!"

More laughs.

"Ladies and Gentlemen, I personally collected every molecule of this fog high on the hills above San Francisco Bay. I do not set a price upon it. Drop whatever you wish in the box and I will give the Fog to you, for anything or nothing. I wish you safe travels and warm embraces! Thank you all very much!"

He waves his top hat with a graceful flourish and a few people applaud. The woman who called out, "Your heart!" and two other travelers approach, dollar bills in hand.

His half of the rent. From hundreds of little vials of foggy air that he does in fact collect high on the hills of Sausalito and then gives to all the people who smile when he makes up reasons to buy something that they can have for free.

The threaded vials and caps cost $45 for a box of 144 – triple what he'd pay if he'd just settle for plastic instead of glass. The labels and ink from our computer's printer add three pennies.

The fog is free.

Tonight Liam the Fog Seller will board the *Louis H. Baar* for my last voyage home. Go for dinner in Sausalito on the street they just call "Bridgeway." Stop at the little restaurant where you can watch your burger go round and round over the spitting flames of the charcoal grill in the front window. Sit beneath the elephant statues in the park, have a chance to think.

I'll think about how in three days Paula and I will see The Lady with the Joke Book in Her Purse. How we'll try to go backstage after the show to meet her, to ask what's really going on.

I'll think about how I can somehow get through this date with Paula without acting like a fool and scaring her away.

One of these days I'll learn to be like Liam.

The process should be well underway by the time I turn 102.

9.

Another Lost Boy
Without His Medication

Friday, August 31

"Maybe you can take this Paula girl to lunch at a romantic café or something." Luis wears his dark brown cowboy boots, the ones that match the muddy water around the pier. He taps his heels on the deck in time to a song I cannot hear.

"I'm taking her out to dinner before we go to the play tomorrow night," I tell him. "That's hard enough."

I watch the churning water as the engines thrust into reverse and the boat slows its progress. The mooring rope awaits me, dangling from a metal boom.

"Stevie, you finally asked her out! *Bravo, ese!*'"

He is in a rambunctious mood and I don't want to tell him that it is Paula's idea that we go out to dinner before the play.

"How long you been telling me about the beautiful Astronomer with the Sunsets? It's been like a year you been making up poetry about her!"

"Don't confuse fantasy with reality."

"Stevie, it's like I always tell you. You gotta be ready for the day when God gives you..."

"I know, I know."

Luis lowers his voice. "See, Stevie? You dreamed about her and now she likes you. Maybe she'll bring back all those words you never..."

I cut him off. "Once we find The Lady with the Joke Book in Her Purse it will all turn into nothing."

"Don't think all negative like that, Stevie. She might..."

"It's just a game to her," I tell him. "A riddle. 'Can you find the lady who pretends to have a foreign accent and has nothing but a joke book in her purse?'"

"Stevie..."

"It's a treasure hunt that's fun for a few hours. But then we solve the puzzle and she moves on and it all amounts to nothing."

"Hey, you have your butterfly problems to solve so you don't get bored," he says. "Maybe Paula likes hard problems, too. Maybe she wants to find a guy she can do hard problems with, somebody who's like a scientist but he's not like all the other scientists 'cause he hunts like a butterfly and stings like a bee!"

Why won't he leave me alone? "Please, let's just drop it," I tell him.

"Stevie, Stevie, Stevie..." he clucks at me, even though he knows I hate this. "Leti always says you're the nicest guy we know. '*El guapito tranquilo*,' she calls you. You just gotta let the ladies get to know you."

I ignore him and snare the heavy line, looping the thick rope over one steel cleat on the deck and then the other.

Luis keeps pushing, apparently determined to upset me. "You should talk to Liam. Have him take some of that confidence and shoot it into the ol' Stevie."

I stop ignoring him and meet his eyes. "Are you trying to piss me off?"

"Stevie, you had so many bad breaks. This is finally a good one! You just act sexy like Liam and you'll..."

"The only person I want to act like is myself." I turn and head downstairs to help Linh stock the snack bar.

* * *

My original plan for lunch is to hang out with Liam, but I'm still too angry at Luis for saying things he knows I don't like him to say.

When I feel this way I come to Golden Gate Park. I let the pathways take me where they will, drifting west. I savor the walls of tall trees that surround me, avoid the dead ends where the loud and angry men hold sway.

I need to keep walking. Luis knows better than to say that Paula could ever really care for me. To say that if I just act like Liam everything would be OK.

I am so angry that I yell at the top of my lungs. At the sky. At the sun. At the ground.

At myself.

Sometimes a jogger hears me and stares, then looks away. I know what they all think. "Another lost boy without his medication."

As I near the ocean I'm starting to feel better. I can hear the wind and surf, and the traffic on the Great Highway, where Golden Gate Park meets the Pacific Ocean.

But then I see a ruined house beneath a broad palm tree and I realize my mistake. I am not by the tulip garden and the majestic North Windmill. I am near the southwest entrance to Golden Gate Park, the very place I most want to avoid.

It is too late. Before me is the old South Windmill, a landmark once visible for miles, the Keeper's House boarded up at its side.

With its wooden cap rotted away and its massive arms long missing, the windmill of today is a rounded concrete bunker. Windows sealed, doors tightly locked, it sits in pools of shadow behind a chain link fence.

I can hear my father's voice here, telling stories from his father's time.

How the wooden tower reaches halfway to the moon when you stand at its base and look up.

The color of the flowers and the scent of the sea breeze.

How the majestic canvas sail creaks and the bearings groan as the housing swivels with the wind. How the great spars, each carved from the trunk of a massive tree, sweep majestically in the afternoon breeze off the Pacific Ocean.

I can still hear the emotion in his words as we stand in this very spot, as we look at this same empty shell. How it isn't right that such a beautiful place is allowed to fall into disrepair and waste away.

How it isn't right that a father can fall into disrepair and waste away.

I am worn down, empty. I cannot find the breath to scream more fury at the sky. I slump down on a bench and scream silently instead.

*　*　*

Siphon-haul-dump.

Friday is middle-row water change night for my aquariums. Zina, Liam's dog, watches my every move, ever hopeful that something I spill will be good to eat.

It is not easy teaching her not to drink from the dirty buckets, though she has finally mastered self-restraint.

Siphon-haul-dump. Siphon-haul-dump.

Pail after pail of water goes into the big barrel, through the hose and down the hill into Mrs. Tarrow's garden. Her vegetables like Friday nights.

I know that soon I will find The Lady with the Joke Book in Her Purse. Find out why an actress brings a prop onto the Sausalito Ferry, leaves it on board, then comes back for it again and points herself out to anyone who'll listen.

And, just as surely, I know that with the chase complete I will somehow sabotage things with Paula and she'll be gone.

Siphon-haul-dump.

Change the water every week, provide good food, give them rocks to hide in. The fish grow, pair off and breed. More tiny, brightly-colored fish appear. The cycle repeats.

Perfect balance.

The balance I can never find in life. Close enough to mean something. Not so close that I scare someone away.

I do not want to scare Paula Costa away.

If tears skipped down my cheeks some would fall into the bucket, and from there into the barrel, and from there they'd flow to Mrs. Tarrow's garden.

10.

I Wish Real Audiences Were Like You

Saturday, September 1

After seeking Mrs. Tarrow's advice I have settled on wearing my suit, with a white shirt, my only tie and my good shoes.

I look in the bathroom mirror. All I see is an older, even more awkward version of the school pictures my mother keeps in the old wooden box.

Late in the afternoon I walk down the hill and take the ferry into the City. Sitting and fumbling, a nervous passenger on the *Louis H. Baar*. On my own boat.

Alonzo kids me about dancing at the clubs, then asks for help on his choices for the language pool next week.

After the initial rush to the snack bar Linh comes over and tries to distract me from my worries, something she understands because she worries a lot, too.

Paula picks me up at the Ferry Building and we drive towards Union Square. We park in the underground garage and walk two blocks to the restaurant, where our dinner will cost two days of pay. Her high heels click as confidently on the sidewalk as her boots do on the Institute's concrete floor.

She wears a black dress with a white pearl necklace and a black wool overcoat or cape – I can't tell which it is without staring but it has no buttons. I do catch myself staring at her hair. The braids are gone and it pours across her shoulders, glistening chocolate over the pale gelato of her skin.

We stand in line at the front of the restaurant, waiting with elegantly dressed couples who'll be attending dramas, dance or musicals nearby. To set the mood the walls of the dining room are covered with theatrical masks from around the world. I recognize *Kabuki* from Japan, *commedia dell'arte* from Italy, the half-mask from *The Phantom of the Opera*.

Paula points to the face of a fiercely snarling Japanese warrior. "Looks like he didn't like the food," she whispers.

I look at the other masks, seeking inspiration for a clever reply. But I'm too nervous to be clever, so I just smile.

Our turn comes and a young man in a tuxedo leads us down a wide, sweeping staircase. As we descend our arms touch and Paula takes my hand and holds it.

I don't know what to do. I hold her hand back.

Probably too tight. I hate this.

I love this.

Once we're seated I try to think of what to talk about so she won't see everything I'm feeling. I tell her how my butterfly projects come to be called my butterfly projects when a butterfly from Japan lands on my orange parka in Sausalito. She laughs.

I ask how she's able to talk like a video producer when we visit Avanture Video.

Paula smiles the way she does when she asks children if they want to see the Crab Nebula. "Whose voice do you hear when we play the videos in the planetarium?" she asks. "Or I guess I should say, 'when we used to play them.'"

I have to think for a moment. "On the Mars program it's the morning news radio woman. On Expanding Universe it's... it's the weather guy on Channel 7."

She laughs. "I wish real audiences were like you."

"I'm not a real audience?"

She reaches out and touches my hand. "You're way better than a real audience."

I pretend not to react to this even though my heart races. "So... Are you saying they're professional announcers?"

"Uh-huh. In Fort Collins I was able to do the VO myself, but here it's different. Every word has to come from union announcers, from AFTRA."

"And you're not in AFTRA."

"No. I have a B.S. in Astronomy and an M.A. in Communications, but I'd have to get a job in TV or radio to join the union. Doing planetarium shows doesn't count."

"So that's why you know about post and editing suites and digital files."

She takes a sip of water, looks for the waiter. "That's right."

"Is your doctorate in Astronomy, too?"

She laughs uncomfortably. "I'm afraid I don't have a doctorate. I'm the black sheep in the flock."

I try to cover my surprise so she doesn't see it. I fail miserably.

"I know," she says. "Everybody just assumes I'm Dr. Costa because I work at the Institute and teach part-time at SF State. But I'm just plain old Paula Costa."

Without planning to do so I manage to say, "You certainly don't seem plain to me." Which, I realize after saying it, is probably one of the better things I could be saying right now.

She apparently agrees, because she smiles. "The irony," she says, "is that the lady with no Ph.D. is the one pushing Dr. Bresham to put more science and less schlock in this last show. I told them that Blackman Planetarium is not Disneyland."

"It's better," I say confidently.

"Well I won the battle and lost the war," Paula says. "The new planetarium will be 98% Hollywood, 2% Hubble."

My heart sinks. The old planetarium is one of the few places I can remember almost always feeling happy.

"Bresham finally took me aside last week and told me to stop with the Hollywood crap or I might end up without a job."

"That's not fair!"

"You have to fight for what you believe in. But, as my mom always said, you also have to know when to stop."

"Sounds like Mrs. Tarrow, my neighbor."

A new smile, one I haven't seen before. "My mom worked three jobs to help me go places like Space Camp so I could follow my dream. I wanted to be an astronaut. When I realized I was more likely to find a job on Earth I changed my dream to joining the NASA press corps or teaching science."

"Lots of teachers in my family, too."

She examines me for a while across the table.

I have no idea what to say so I say nothing. Instead I pick up my menu and read through it a second time, even though I've already decided I want the ravioli with four exquisite artisanal cheeses.

Paula does not pick up her menu a second time. Instead she says, "May I ask you something?"

Here it comes. The place where things go terribly wrong. I'm not good with questions.

I try to stay calm. "Sure," I tell her. Too loudly. I sound like a rubber band is lodged around my throat.

She smiles at me. She hears it, too.

But she asks her question anyway. "Why is it that you talk so readily about the present and the future, but never about the past? I've never actually heard you use the past tense."

Scientists are curious. They notice things.

"Just kind of my thing." I say. The bottom of the menu informs us that the restaurant charges an automatic 18% gratuity on all parties of eight or more.

"What happened? What made you stop using... an entire part of the English language? How long have you done this?"

Scientists are naturally inquisitive. They don't mean anything by it, they're just born that way.

"In high school. It..." I search for the right words. For some reason I am not freaked out by her question. Luis would be proud of me for still sitting here, not walking away.

I find some words. "Not thinking about the past... Staying in the present just helps me focus. On the right things. It keeps me in the Here and Now."

She hesitates. "So you haven't spoken a word in the past tense since high school?"

"Oh, I still mess up sometimes." I try to smile.

Paula's chin rests on the palm of her hand. Her nails are red. I have never seen her wear polish before. Her hand on the planetarium pointer always jumps to the right point in the sky.

She shakes her head and just says, "Amazing."

"There's a time about six years ago that would make you laugh," I tell her, "and quite a few times back when I... It takes a while to get it right."

Why am I telling this woman things that I never tell people? The kinds of things that always make people freak and go away, so I never say them?

She looks at me, laughs, and just says the one word again. "Amazing."

11.

The Taming of the Shrew's Saturday Night Fever

Saturday, September 1 (Cont.)

As it turns out, we will not see The Lady with the Joke Book in Her Purse tonight.

Before the curtain opens a melodious female voice asks us to turn off our cell phones and then announces, "Ladies and Gentlemen, tonight the role of Bianca will be played by Daria Haudmill."

There is a strutting Petruchio with a New York accent and a defiant pose to go with every line. A Kate with a *Sopranos* dialect and eight costume changes.

But tonight there is no Lady with the Joke Book in Her Purse.

All that work, all that digging, and now the actress isn't here. I look over at Paula, but her attention is on the stage.

I open my program and in the dim light run my finger down the cast list. It says, "Bianca............Candi Bonham"

I lean over and whisper in Paula's ear, "Her name is Candi Bonham."

She whispers back, "Yes."

At the intermission she sips chardonnay and I drink Italian spring water because it's the only water they have. We try to decide if we should laugh or cry.

An hour later the band belts out *The Last Dance* as the Taming of the Shrew's Saturday Night Fever dancers frolic atop a glowing, flashing disco floor. A phalanx of rhinestone-covered actors moves in impossible unison behind the gyrating Kate and Petruchio.

Paula is on her feet, dancing, laughing and clapping along with the music. The rest of the audience goes along.

I stand beside her, clapping. I hope she does not notice I'm not dancing.

I am not good at dancing.

We cheer with the rest of the crowd as Kate and Petruchio take their bows and the curtain falls.

We sit there talking as the audience retreats. She thinks this Petruchio is all-dancer, no-actor. I agree.

Paula turns in her velvet chair, arm draped across the seat back, looking into my eyes. Her long dark hair has subtle highlights I've never seen. Anywhere.

She thinks this Kate is nowhere near as assertive as Shakespeare intended her to be.

"You'd make a good Kate," I tell her. "No one would think you're not assertive."

"Most men don't smile when they tell me that."

I don't know how to respond, so I just keep smiling.

Finally an usher, a tall, thin woman with a small birthmark on her chin, comes forward to tell us we have to go. She appears to relish this opportunity.

"How do we get backstage to see Candi Bonham?" Paula asks, sweet and matter-of-fact.

The usher looks us over and hesitates, the way she'd examine a gift basket from a neighbor with a nagging cough.

"We met her at a performance she gave at the Ferry Building," Paula adds.

Apparently the usher doesn't realize that Candi Bonham is not present and accounted for tonight. She warms up a few degrees. "I'll take you back and see if they'll let you in."

Backstage every corner is filled with crates, cases, racks of costumes. At one place the hallway widens and a long counter below a mirror is covered with bags and boxes, small tubes and plastic tubs, all over-lit by banks of bright round lights. Chairs are twisted at all angles the full length of the counter.

But no one is here.

The usher is as surprised as we are. "There's a room back here, but the whole cast wouldn't..." Her voice trails off as she reaches for the knob on a metal door.

As the portal opens we see the sequined cast of The Taming of the Shrew standing uncomfortably in the crowded room as they listen to an unseen man.

The man now sticks his head into the opening. "We're having a meeting here," he growls.

"Sorry!" The usher releases the door, which swings shut.

A moment later a different man emerges and confronts us. He is Chinese American and is wearing a dark blue sport coat, a deep blue tie and a contrasting shiny gold badge clipped to his pocket.

"What're you guys doing here?" he asks us bluntly, waving the usher back to her post.

I am not good with questions.

I start gritting my teeth.

"We came backstage to see why Candi Bonham was out tonight," Paula answers.

"You guys friends of hers?"

"We saw her do a street performance on the ferry and wanted to come see her," Paula tells him.

"So you're friends of hers?"

Paula hesitates. "More like acquaintances."

"So you won't be that upset to hear she's dead."

Our mouths gape open. My stomach goes into free fall.

"Can you both account for your movements yesterday, last night?"

Paula thinks a moment, still stunned. She nods.

The man looks at me. I get that feeling again but swallow hard. "Most of it," I say in a measured voice. "Except for a walk in Golden Gate Park."

"We'll need statements from both of you. I'm gonna have you wait here for a few minutes till they finish up inside."

Paula has now caught her breath. "What happened?"

The officer's phone starts ringing and he reaches inside his jacket. "She and Supervisor Giantonio were found shot to death in her apartment."

Paula and I look at each other but don't say anything.

I can see the exact moment when the thought starts to form in her mind. "Exactly where in Golden Gate Park do you take those walks, Steve?"

And then, "How long have I known you and just how weird are you, anyway?"

She doesn't say any of this.

She doesn't have to.

12.

Take the Ferry Last Friday

Saturday, September 1 (Cont.)

It's too late.

I can't take the ferry home.

Only one last bus serves the lost and weary of Sausalito this late at night, and it delivers me to a quiet, empty corner in the heart of town.

Of course Paula doesn't drive me home. No one wants to be alone with a man who's searching for someone who turns up dead.

I climb the long way up the hill, the cool breeze now a cutting wind, and I know this segment of my life is about to end.

My foolish thoughts that this chapter might be followed by another chapter that holds the same friends, the same anything...

Foolish, Steve. I say the word again with every step. Foolish foolish foolish foolish foolish.

I wish that I could go back and take the ferry last Friday all over again. That I could be miles away when Candi Bonham arrives with her not-quite-Russian accent.

I wish I could go back and ignore the peach-colored purse, turn in a lost sweatshirt and get on with my life.

The street is dark but I know the way. I open the wrought iron gate at the base of the old stone steps and the hinges squeal mournfully. Even this late, my landlord Mrs. Blount looks down from her lofty window in the old white house to see what's going on.

Paula will not want to see me again.

The police will most certainly want to see me again. To tie up loose ends. Fill in a puzzle piece. Eliminate possibilities.

I will become a ticket out of the front-page scrutiny of the case of a murdered politician. A teacher who quits his job after being hounded by rumors. A guy who's so strange you can suspect him of anything.

My fingerprints so conveniently on the victim's purse. I know what will happen next. The stage prop will be compelling real-world evidence, found with the dead San Francisco Supervisor and his actress paramour.

It's the same dance everywhere I go. I've done nothing wrong. They ask me questions. I'm not good with questions. They insist. I start to freak. They get suspicious. I really freak. They decide to freak, too.

I try to forget what happens next.

13.

What Happens After the Train Comes and You Go

Fourteen years ago, as seen from Sunday, September 2

It is very long ago. But it is still like right now to me.

If I back away and stay quiet I know that eventually it will be over.

"What did you do with my vodka?" Screaming at me isn't working so she goes to her cold threat voice. She pushes back unkempt gray hair to stare me in the eye.

"Nothing," I say. "I don't touch your things."

"Like hell you didn't! You went through the drawers in my bureau!"

"I told you, I was just looking for my books. You said you'd give them back on Saturday." I am telling the truth.

She gets that gleam in her eye, the joy at having another needle to probe beneath my skin. "If you don't tell me what you did with that vodka I'll burn those books!"

"I'm telling the truth!"

She looks at the fireplace. I can see her mind working. The newspaper she needs to start a fire is out in the recycling, behind the garage. It's a rainy night. Winter. She's wearing a long, dark orange quilted robe, thick but not thick enough to hold back the wet, cold air outside.

So she slaps me, hard, across the face.

I am surprised this time. I whirl around with the blow as a fingernail slices across my ear.

I rub the side of my head and look at my hand. I am not bleeding.

She sounds more drunk now, more frustrated. "Tell me what you did with that vodka!"

I can tell that she is starting to lose steam. The self-pity will start soon. Things will either get much better or much worse quickly.

"You took it so you and your friends could drink it, that's what you did!"

I know better than to answer now. There is none of her left to reason with.

I stay silent.

"You think you're so smart. You think I'll forget about this in the morning and you can take our liquor and swill it with your friends!"

I stay silent.

I shake my head. I'm cold. This isn't our living room and that's not my mother. It's...

"I'll ask you again. Why did you get off the train at UCSF, walk down the hill to Golden Gate Park and all the way to Ocean Beach when that same N Judah train would take you within three blocks of the exact same spot?"

I stay silent.

"Have you taken your medication?"

"I don't take medication." For some reason this question is easy to answer.

The Captain shakes his head. "I know a good doctor you can talk to."

He walks around the little room, his right hand rubbing at the center of his forehead. A long, straight scar runs from the base of his ring finger half way across the back of his hand.

"Tell me about something unusual you saw in your walk in Golden Gate Park last Friday. Something you wouldn't see every day."

I think about this. "When I... After..."

I'm not good with questions. I stop, take a deep breath. Start over.

"There's a little café at the turnaround for the N Judah, just south of the Park. It's where I take the train back if I'm short on time. People sit and eat and talk outside on the sidewalk at little tables, even if it's cold and foggy."

"Was it foggy when you were there on Friday?"

"No."

"What was unusual at the café?"

"You ever hear someone say they're about to recite a poem, and talk about the poem, then talk some more, and then never actually recite it?"

He gives me a funny look. His red and black tie has a small spot near the tip.

"You were there and you heard a guy do that?"

"You never know for sure. If you're waiting for a train you never know what happens after the train comes and you go. To the people who don't go on the train. Their world stops and your world keeps going."

"Steve, do you ever give a straight answer to anything?

"I'm not good with questions," I tell him.

"Yes, I think I get that." He stops, rubs his forehead again. "So if I have someone go out there and talk to people at that café who were working last Friday they may confirm that there was a guy there who said he was going to recite poetry but took forever to do it."

"Yes."

"Would they remember seeing you?"

I shrug.

"Any other suggestions?"

I try very hard to think. "You can ask people at the old South Windmill if they remember seeing someone sitting on a bench with a black sweatshirt over his head."

"Would that have been you?"

"And you can ask rollerbladers on Martin Luther King Drive if they remember a man screaming at the pavement. Or maybe the clouds."

"Uh-huh."

"Between Crossover Drive and Sunset, mostly. But a last little bit west of Sunset."

"You are good with suggestions."

"People say that," I confirm.

His cell phone rings and he answers it. "Kreitzer. Uh huh. Uh huh." He looks at me and gives an exasperated sigh. "What the hell is a sumo-trophy demon something?"

"*Pseudotropheus demasoni*," I correct him. "It's a fish from Africa. With blue and black stripes."

He sighs again as he listens, then looks at me.

"Our Lieutenant Li apparently loves your whatever-it-is Demonzoni. And the big one with spots like a giraffe."

"Tell him thank you." After I say this I realize it sounds sarcastic but I cannot take it back.

Kreitzer either does not notice or does not care. "OK. OK. Thanks." He hangs up, turns to me and starts reciting selected sentences from a script he knows by heart. I can see him sorting through the mental index cards, deciding which ones to include.

"Steve, I'm going to have someone drive you home. Lieutenant Li says he and the officer from Sausalito P.D. locked your place back up, returned the keys to Mrs. Blount and it's secure. I appreciate your cooperation and that you saved us the hassle of getting a warrant. If we don't find anything relevant to the case your computer and your personal files will be returned to you within a few days. Do not leave the area without calling me. If you have any more... suggestions for me please call the number on my card."

"Thank you," I tell him. I feel overwhelmed with relief. He's letting me go home. He hands me the business card with the number I can call with any suggestions.

This time the phone on the battered table rings and he answers again. "Kreitzer."

I stand up, take my black wool jacket from the back of the chair.

He looks over at me, surprised. "We won't be driving you home after all. Amanda Tarrow is here to pick you up."

* * *

Mrs. Tarrow's dark red 1986 Volvo station wagon smirks at me with its crooked radiator-grill grin as we emerge into the late afternoon shadows and cross Vallejo St. A blast of cold air sweeps down the hill and I shiver and zip my jacket up around my neck.

She has parked in a "Police Only" spot. There is no ticket on the car.

In her black velvet Chinese shoes she is barely five feet tall, but there is something about Mrs. Tarrow, even at age 70-something, that feels big. I worry about her thin frame and barely-there weight, yet everything about her suggests health and energy.

I always tell her she is a collection of contradictions.

She says the same thing about me.

The moment we're in the car she pats me on the knee and says, "Dear, don't you ever go into a police station again without an attorney."

This surprises me. The second largest picture of Jack Tarrow on her mantelpiece shows him proudly wearing his dress uniform as a Captain in the SFPD. It's the one at the left. A plain wooden frame. Oak, with a matte finish.

As usual, she reads my mind. "Jack always used to tell me, 'God should send the Guilty in for questioning alone. But the Innocent should bring their lawyers.'" She shakes her head and laughs, her short silver hair flaring like a square-dance skirt.

"How do you know I'm innocent?" I ask her. I think I already know the answer.

But she sits and thinks about this for a long time, until I wonder if she has trouble hearing me over the sounds of the evening traffic. Or if she has decided not to answer me at all. We enter the Broadway Tunnel and I can't clearly see her face.

Finally, we burst back into the glare of the setting sun. "How do you know I'm innocent?" I ask again.

She looks over, her pale blue eyes like iridescent opals. "Steven, you are capable of a great many things. But I believe you are incapable of hurting anyone other than yourself."

14.

What Is It You Don't Want Everyone Here to Know?

Monday, September 3

Alonzo is our Gandalf, the senior member of every crew. He is the ferry man's ferry man, a full 6'3 with a voice like the guys in the movie trailers.

He handles the heavy hoses of the bunkering barge like they were strands of Christmas lights. His reassuring tone transforms uptight passengers into mellow friends. He knows every operation of each vessel in our fleet, and for the last 20 years he is the one who trains every new recruit. Including me.

Alonzo usually works the run from Larkspur, but if he meets us in Sausalito's morning darkness we all know it will be a good day. He must be in his fifties, but there is no crease or wrinkle in his dark brown skin.

Luis says that wrinkles are afraid of him.

"How you doin', Professor?" he asks me on this very good morning. Alonzo likes to call me Professor.

"It's a very good morning, Alonzo," I tell him. Nice to have you here."

"Nice to be alive, Professor!" he says.

We're entering Chamber of Commerce time in San Francisco, the Indian Summer when the fog stays outside the Golden Gate. The passengers cluster on the outside decks to feel the sea breeze in their faces.

It is the final sailing of the morning when Luis joins me on the stern as we depart from San Francisco. He's been trying all morning to get me to talk about being inside the police station without asking me a question.

I am not helping him with this.

"I recorded the news and bought the papers," he is saying. "Nobody said nothing about the police arresting anybody."

I carefully coil the mooring ropes and set them back in place. Luis looks around again to see if anyone can hear us.

"The Chronicle says the police talked to one guy and you were cooperative."

"Who says it's me?"

"Stevie, don't give me that bullshit, man. I'm trying to help."

I duck through the door into the cabin and head downstairs to do my chores.

"*Un día pasará cuando yo no estaré aquí para ayudarte!*" he yells after me. I don't understand every word of his rapid-fire Spanish, but as usual I get the gist of it, that I should appreciate him.

* * *

As I walk by the little office on my way to lunch I see Trish and step inside.

She has not recognized Candi Bonham from her pictures on the news, does not know that The Woman with the Joke Book in Her Purse is dead. But to get a spontaneous answer instead of a suspicious stare I still must make my questions sound as trivial as my other butterfly projects.

"Hi," I tell her.

"Hi."

I ask, "What is the title of the joke book in the lady's purse?"

She looks over at Linh, who is turning in receipts from the snack bar. "The quiet one is turning into Sherlock Holmes," Trish tells her. "Now he wants to know all about the book."

Linh, who is quiet herself, smiles and continues working.

Trish looks back at me. "Actually, I'm afraid I don't remember."

She has to remember something, since to know it's a joke book she has to read it. "What about the cover?"

Trish smiles. "It had a well-dressed man on the cover. I liked his suit."

"How do you know it's a joke book?"

She sighs dramatically. "It had a bunch of quotes on the back saying it was hilarious and funny and... hilarious."

"Can you tell me one of the jokes?"

Trish gives me a very serious look. "OK, Steve," she says. "I'll make you a deal. I'll tell you what I read inside the book if you tell me why you ask lots of questions but you'll never answer any. You never talk about your life before you came to the District. What is it you don't want everyone here to know?"

"Trish!" Linh murmurs. She looks over at me, biting her lip.

"See you later," is all I tell her. I walk away.

There can't be that many joke books with men on the cover wearing suits that Trish would like.

* * *

The book department in the big box store is sandwiched between the kitchen appliances and the lawn furniture, with golf equipment just across the aisle.

I examine each book on the shelves labeled "Humor." The only people wearing suits are Oprah Winfrey and a robot.

A man approaches, wearing a big box store polo shirt, khaki pants and a copper anti-something bracelet. "Do you have a joke book with a man in an expensive suit on the cover?" I ask him.

He smiles, then turns his head and looks around the store. His dark brown hair is starting to thin in back.

"Is it a new release?" he asks.

"I don't know," I tell him. "I don't know the title or the author, just that a man in a designer suit is on the cover."

"No one beats our prices on this week's hottest new titles. Hard-cover or paperback?"

I try to think. Would a hardcover fit in that oddly-shaped purse? "Paperback," I stammer. "Actually, I don't know."

"We have double discounts on top hardcovers. Is it a best-seller?"

"I don't know."

"We carry all the best-sellers," he tells me, "including 93% of the titles that people enter the store with a specific intention to buy." He turns again to look for something.

"So you haven't..." My question peters out.

He turns back to meet my eyes. "Did I handle that OK?" he asks in a low voice. "You threw me off for a minute but I remembered to keep smiling and stay on-message."

Now I glance around the store, trying to see what he's been looking for.

"It's in the "O" of the "Coffee" sign in the café, isn't it?" he asks me. "That's where the camera's hidden."

"How do you spot something that small?" I ask him.

He smiles proudly. "I didn't. I just watched your eyes and you showed me where it was."

I shake my head. "I have to work on that."

"Don't worry," he reassures me, a friendly hand on my back. "I won't tell anyone I spotted a Customer Delight Agent."

"Thanks," I tell him.

* * *

Liam the Fog Seller stands on a plastic milk crate across from the ticket machines in the Embarcadero BART Station, one long stairway down from the busy streets above.

"Ladies and Gentlemen!" Liam calls out, startling a short middle-aged man who is struggling to buy a ticket on a machine with a vandalized display screen. "I have written a poem, a sonnet for San Francisco, and it goes like this!"

The travelers continue on their courses, ignoring his literary intentions. Liam recites:

What flows like lava over every rock band's stage?
What swirls and eddies at a diva's feet?
What does Godzilla's mouth project in rage,
While he scorches all of Tokyo with his heat?

From where do zombies march to munch their neighbors?
From where do vampires rise to suck our blood?
From where do villains charge forth with their sabers,
To nip the rebels' challenge in the bud?

What makes our San Francisco famous,
As it ponds and pours 'cross rocking skiffs?
What claims our wand'ring hearts and tames us
With the beauty of the Bridge on rocky cliffs?

Still stumped? Don't Google, text or stand agog.
This potent stuff of magic is... the fog!

A scattering of applause from across the floor. One level down a Muni light rail train pulls in, making the ovation sound louder.

"Thank you, thank you," he goes on, pulling a glass vial from his tuxedo pocket. "Now if you are not a rock star nor a diva and do not happen to have your own supply of fog, I can solve your problem!"

"Oh, this one's a diva all right," a woman says as she walks by with her friend. They both laugh at this and Liam laughs with them.

"In this vial is your very own personal non-pasteurized, completely pure and natural San Francisco fog, which I have myself personally captured in the hills above San Francisco Bay. Drop something in the box or not, but either way step right this way to get your very own, very personal San Francisco fog!"

A few people clap as he bows and sweeps his big top hat to the floor in gratitude. A couple approaches him for a vial. I watch as they drop a dollar in his box.

More money to keep a roof over both our heads.

On the last voyage home tonight Liam will replay the day, honing his presentation. Refining the moves he's learned from Leonard the Human Statue. By the time he comes back from walking Zina he'll have new material and will start practicing it on my fish.

Fish are far more attentive than people. It's just one of the reasons I enjoy their company.

15.

How Can You Have a Lighthouse Without a Light?

Tuesday, September 4

I am once again shrouded in my orange parka. This is the 7:20, the first trip of the day, the run of the efficient morning people. The go-getters anxious to advance at work. The get-outers unwilling to waste a moment of their vacation.

As we slow to approach the pier a woman with a St. Louis baseball cap asks me about the tower above us on Telegraph Hill.

"It's called Coit Tower," I tell her.

"Who was Mr. Coit?"

"Mrs. Coit. It's her idea, her money behind the Tower."

She gives me the familiar "You sure talk funny" look but does not say it out loud. Instead she asks, "What purpose does it serve?"

"Its purpose is to honor volunteer firefighters, so it's supposed to look like the nozzle on a fire hose." I tell her. "And if you go up to the top there are really cool views."

"That's all? It's not a lighthouse? Does it have bells?"

"No."

"It looks like a lighthouse. Does it have a beacon?"

"No."

"How can you have a lighthouse without a light? Damnedest thing." She wanders off, shaking her head.

Apart from the fog this first voyage of the day is uneventful, everything routine.

But as I reach the railing at the stern I can see that the pier we're approaching is not routine. Three uniformed police and a very tall well-dressed bald man stand in a tightly knit group, looking up at me as we pull in.

My stomach tightens its Gordian Knot. Three uniformed police are not here just to ask me questions. I've done nothing wrong, but they're taking me to jail.

Do I look at them? Not look at them? Ignore them? Walk down to meet them after I clear my duties?

The passengers are heading towards the stairs. One thin man in a purple running suit remains on the aft deck, aiming his video camera over my shoulder at the Ferry Building clock tower. He is oblivious to the panic screaming through every nerve ending in my body.

I decide to get it over with. I'm an innocent man. Innocent men walk up and look people in the eye.

I head to the gangway, my hands shaking in my pockets, and follow the legion of passengers down the ramp.

I freeze again.

The officers have stopped Luis and are handcuffing him.

I hurry down the gangway and approach them.

The big plainclothes cop with the shaved head is supervising the emptying of Luis' pockets. He waves me away with an oversized hand.

"Keep moving, sir. Please. Let's give this gentleman some privacy."

"But you're making a mistake. He's Luis Deverro."

"We know that, sir. Now please move along."

"You can't want Luis Deverro. He's the one who..."

"Sir, the gentleman is being very cooperative. We need you to be very cooperative and move along."

They want Luis Deverro.

"It's OK, Stevie," Luis says. "They found a gun in my locker and they want to talk to me about it."

"A gun?" I can't make sense of it. "You hate guns. You wouldn't even buy one after the break-in!"

"I found it and I didn't have a chance to turn it in. It's OK, Stevie. They'll straighten it all out."

The big cop looks at me and smiles without showing any teeth. "All right, sir. You no longer have to move along. We'll move along instead."

They turn and walk off, carefully leading Luis by the arm.

"Do you want me to call Leti?" I ask him.

He looks back over his shoulder at me and smiles. "No, I'm OK, Stevie. I'll be home for dinner."

16.

Sometimes They Shoot Them, Sometimes They Don't

Tuesday, September 4 (Cont.)

Instead of calling Leti I call the number on the card that Captain Kreitzer gives me.

"Kreitzer," barks the voice that answers the phone.

"This is Steve Ondelle. You still want to hear my ideas on The Lady with the Joke Book in Her Purse?"

Only the slightest hesitation. "Hell, yes."

"Luis Deverro wouldn't do anything wrong."

A pause. "You have something to tell me?"

"Yes," I tell him.

"Go ahead, I'm listening."

"Luis hates guns," I tell him. "I don't know why he wouldn't turn in this one but he hates guns."

"How do you feel about guns, Steve?"

Many memories. "I'm afraid of them."

"In what way?"

I take a deep breath. He's asking me questions again. I want to stop talking, go for a walk. But that won't help Luis.

I compromise by walking up Market St. towards Drumm, the phone held tightly to my ear to block out the sound of the buses and the old railway cars.

Deep breath. "I'm afraid of guns because when you grow up in a family where there are guns in the house and you think someone might use one someday, then you're afraid of guns."

"Who did you think might use a gun in the house?"

"How many questions will I have to answer in order to get you to let an innocent man out of jail?"

"Depends on your answers. You want to come on ever and we can sit down and talk?"

I walk through the shadow of a building shrouded in gauze and scaffolding, shiver for a moment in the cold breeze. "If it's OK, I like this better."

"OK, suit yourself. Who did you know who might use a gun?"

Deep breath. "My mother."

"OK." He thinks a little. "You thought your mother might use a gun. Why did you think she would use a gun?"

At Drumm I cross to the sunny side of Market, lost amid the lunchtime crowds.

"Steve," Kreitzer repeats, since I'm not saying anything. "You said you're afraid of guns because your mother had one and might use it. What did you think she would do with a gun?"

I lean left to avoid a kid on a skateboard. "You know when you watch TV and someone is acting crazy and pointing a gun at people and you don't know what's going to happen and sometimes they shoot them, sometimes they don't?"

"Yeah, I know what you mean."

"Well, the people they're aiming the gun at, the people in the room, they're never going to forget that. You know. The ones who don't get shot."

Silence.

"You still there?" I ask.

"I'm here. How many times did this happen?"

"Just a few."

"You ever own a gun?"

"No."

"You ever fire a gun?"

"No. Wait... Yes. Just a BB gun."

"God..." He groans out loud and mumbles something I don't hear. "Do you realize that the gun we found in Mr. Deverro's locker is the weapon that killed Supervisor Giantonio and Candi Bonham?"

My stomach goes into free fall again.

"You still there?" he asks.

"Yes. I just can't believe... This is..."

"To tell you the truth, we were interested in your locker, Steve. Just as you told me they would be, your fingerprints were on the purse at the murder scene."

"That's why I tell you things."

"We got the warrant for the entire office because you could have stashed something anywhere."

It's the same dance everywhere I go. Accusations, questions, suspicions. I've done nothing wrong.

I force my focus back to the phone. "Luis doesn't have a lock on his locker. All he keeps there is his lunch and a little bottle of Tylenol."

"I know. Anyone who was in the office could have put the gun there. Including you."

"Yes. He trusts me completely."

"Steve, do you remember everything I told you about the right to have an attorney present when I talk with you?"

"Yes."

"Do you want to stop talking and get an attorney?"

"No. I'm OK. It's Luis I'm worried about."

Another phone rings in the room with Kreitzer. "Hold on," he says.

The sound in the phone switches to a soft hissing tone, punctuated with an occasional beep. I cross Front St. and continue walking up the broad sidewalk of Market. A man with a drum set made of plastic buckets is feverishly playing in time with a boom box blasting a Michael Jackson song. A small circle of people stand and watch him.

When I get far enough away from the drums to hear again Kreitzer's voice is back on the phone.

"Steve, you still there?"

"I'm here."

"That was the Lieutenant who just drove in with Luis."

"The bald man with the left nostril that's been cauterized?" I ask.

Kreitzer snorts. "Yes, that's the one."

"He'll tell you about me. I keep trying to tell people that Luis can't be the man you're looking for."

"He told me," Kreitzer answers. "The thing is, Luis told the officers he found the gun on the ferry and he was the one who put it in his locker instead of turning it in. He says he was busy and put it off and then wasn't sure what to do."

It makes no sense. "Luis would never keep a gun. I know that's what he's saying, but he wouldn't."

Captain Kreitzer stands and starts pacing. I can tell from the screech his chair makes on the old linoleum tile and the sound of his hard rubber heels as he walks. "You know what I think, Steve? There's one way I can explain it."

"How?" I ask him.

"I think Luis is just the kind of guy you say he is. Honest man, hates guns. But I think he didn't turn in the gun because he knew you'd been in here with me. He knew your fingerprints were on the purse, and he was trying to protect you."

"I... I guess that's possible. He always tries to... The lady being murdered is freaking us all out. Luis likes to try to take care of me."

"So I've got one more question for you, Steve, if you can handle it."

"Go ahead," I tell him.

"Luis is willing to risk going to jail to protect you. What are you willing to do to protect him?"

17.

When Everything Wouldn't
Be Wrong

Wednesday, September 5

What we do has consequences. I accept that.

If I don't pay my electric bill the heaters on my aquariums will stop working. My fish will die.

I pre-pay my electric bill one month ahead.

I don't like consequences.

But sometimes consequences have the wrong address on the envelope.

Last night Captain Kreitzer drops all the charges against Luis and has an unmarked car drive him home. As he predicts, he's there in time for dinner with Leti and the kids.

This morning our vaunted GM George Grainger takes his turn.

He fires Luis, takes his job away. We sail on time at 7:20 AM without him.

"This is all wrong," I tell Alonzo, who arrives to cover Luis' shift. "The police made a mistake."

"Tell him to call Tom," Alonzo says. "If it's wrongful, he can fix it. That's why we have the union."

"I guess."

"It'll be OK, Professor." Alonzo claps a big hand on my back and we head off to man our mooring lines.

I wish I felt as positive as he does.

* * *

Leonard has to work each day at lunchtime, but I need to talk and I always know where to find Eli of the Coral Reef. It is a beautiful, cloudless morning but I feel only gloom as I walk up Market St. The wind at my back feels harsh and cold.

How can you feel so sorry when you've done nothing wrong? I already know the answer.

When everything wouldn't be wrong if you weren't there.

When you know you have to do something to make things right.

When you have absolutely no idea what to do.

As I approach Grant St. a small crowd is listening to a man with a powerful, deep voice singing an old spiritual. Some watchers clap along and stomp their feet.

It is The Prophet of Market Street. He's singing more these days.

They call him The Prophet because sometimes he'll answer questions about the future for the people who're passing by.

Sometimes the people even ask him first.

Like every song the Prophet sings, it sounds like it's written just for him:

When the storms of life are a-raging, stand by me
When the storms of life are a-raging, stand by me
When the world is tossing me

Like a ship upon the sea
He who rules the wind and water, stand by me.

In the midst of tribulation, stand by me
In the midst of tribulation, stand by me
When the hosts of Hell assail
And my strength begins to fail
He who never lost a battle, stand by me.

In the midst of faults and failures, stand by me
In the midst of faults and failures, stand by me
When I do the best I can
And the world misunderstands
He who knows all things about me, stand by me.

By the time he finishes The Prophet of Market Street has drawn a crowd that responds with enthusiastic applause. He returns to sitting quietly on the sidewalk.

I drop a dollar in his Styrofoam cup but do not wait to hear what he has to say.

* * *

Not long ago it would take me an hour to ride the N Judah Muni train to Golden Gate Park and the old Institute of Science.

Now it takes just a few minutes of walking to reach the tired gray walls of the temporary Institute. Those walls enclose many of the same people, many of the same things.

But it does not feel like home.

I open the big glass door and walk inside.

Past the promotional video where the late Candi Bonham still beams at her purchase from the Institute gift shop.

Past the guard station where Paula Costa first agrees to speak with me.

Past the door you cannot open that guards the elevator you never see.

A tour group surrounds the coral reef exhibit as a docent extolls the wonders of the Judson Aquarium that will open next year, when they won't be here to see it. I begin my search for the reclusive Eli.

I find him sitting cross-legged on the floor in a distant corner, studying the delicate waving tentacles of a colony of anemones. He looks like a Buddhist monk, deep in meditation.

I approach and sit beside him.

"Hey, Steve," he says, still watching the anemones.

"How's it going?" I ask him.

"I'm cool."

I just blurt it out. "Luis can't come to work with me on the *Louis H. Baar*."

Eli turns to stare at me, his mouth open. "What?!"

"Luis gets fired this morning because he finds the gun from the murdered Supervisor and Candi Bonham and he doesn't know what to do so he doesn't turn it in and then they find it and they fire him."

Eli takes off his Giants cap, runs his fingers through his hair, puts his cap back on again. "That was... Why didn't he turn it in?"

"Probably to keep from getting me in trouble."

Eli just stares at me.

"It's my fault, Eli. If it weren't for me Luis would still have a job."

He shakes his head. "You're not the one who found a gun and didn't turn it in."

"But if I'm not on the *Louis H. Baar* then there's no one for Luis to try to protect, and he still has a job."

Eli stares down at the concrete floor. "You can't... It's not your fault, Steve."

"It doesn't matter that it's not my fault," I tell him. "I still feel like it's my fault."

He looks back up at me, shakes his head again. "I spend too much time regretting my own mistakes," he says. "I learned that it doesn't help when I regret everyone else's."

18.

A Few Surviving Flecks of Glitter

Thursday, September 6

I finish my morning routine and set out to join Liam for lunch before he goes up to Union Square to sell his fog. It is the second day that we sail without Luis, and despite Eli's wisdom I don't like the conversations I've been having with myself.

I'm just exiting the Ferry Building when a voice calls out behind me. I don't have to turn around to know who it is.

Captain Kreitzer walks up, shakes my hand, indicates that I should keep walking as he falls into step with me.

"Luis has no job," I tell him angrily. "All because of that arrest on the dock right in front of everybody."

"I know," is all he says. He's wearing a different dark gray sport coat than the first time we met, but still wears the same red and black tie.

"He has a wife and two kids who depend on him," I tell Kreitzer. "Can you call the GM and get his job back?"

Kreitzer keeps his eyes on the traffic as we cross the Embarcadero. "I'll see what I can do."

"Seems like if a guy loses his job because of you, 'I'll see what I can do' isn't much of an answer."

"I didn't put the gun in his locker." Kreitzer shoots me a look. "I have another question for you,"

"I'm not good with questions."

"I need to ask this anyway."

I look at him but say nothing.

"How much do you know about Tommy Gonzalez? The grown up Tommy, not the kid."

My heart sinks. Another friend caught in the meat-grinder.

"I'd see some tough kids in my classes. Tommy's not one of them."

"He knows you, knows that you're not good with questions."

"Every student I ever taught knows that. Everybody who works on the ferry knows that."

A cluster of people are gathered ahead of us in Justin Herman Plaza at the foot of Market St.. They're clapping and chanting, but I can't make out what they're saying. Kreitzer stops to listen and I stop and wait as well.

"Hey hey! Ho ho! Triangle has got to go! Hey Hey! Ho ho! Triangle..." Fifteen people stand in formation in front of the empty fountain.

A thin, bearded young man with a bullhorn raises it to his lips and the chanters go silent, huddling behind him.

"Everybody!" he shouts. "Everybody listen up!" He wears a white T shirt that depicts a crossed-out red circle over a triangular blueprint.

"Just one mile from here they're ready to break ground on SoMa Triangle, a project that will displace over 800 peaceful residents of San Francisco!" he shouts. The crowd boos.

"There are 147 errors in their Environmental Impact Report, but they think the Board of Supervisors will approve the project!"

The protestors turn back to face the crowd, and now they're wearing cardboard masks with the faces of different people.

"Who are they?" I ask Kreitzer.

"They look like college kids."

"No, I mean the faces on the masks."

Kreitzer snorts. "That's the Board of Supervisors."

"Why are the developers so confident?" the young man shouts through the bullhorn.

One protester steps forward. His mask bears a face I recognize: the late Supervisor Gerry Giantonio.

Suddenly someone slams two slats of wood together, the sharp crack like the sound of gunfire. People jump, and the man with the Giantonio mask collapses on the pavement.

"Because Supervisor Giantonio was murdered one week ago!" the leader shouts. "One less vote to save the homes of 800 seniors and low-income people!"

I consider calling out, "And Candi Bonham! She's a victim, too!"

But I know it will not help.

"Why are we here?" the young man shouts rhetorically.

The people behind him turn to face the crowd again, and now they all wear identical masks of the slain Supervisor.

"We must all be Gerry Giantonio!" he exclaims. "We must all speak out to save these peoples' homes!"

A man in a track suit is taping the event, and the bearded leader stares into the camera. "Are you with us, San Francisco?"

The small crowd cheers. The protesters resume marching in a circle and chanting, "Hey hey! Ho ho! Triangle has got to go!"

I look at my watch. I should get going.

"About Tommy Gonzalez," Kreitzer starts again.

"You're not going to get him kicked out of school, are you?"

Kreitzer ignores this. "His sister, she interned at a law firm last summer."

"Lizzie?"

"Yes, Elizabeth Gonzalez."

"Hey hey! Ho ho! Triangle has got to go!" the protesters chant in front of us.

"She's a good kid, too," I tell him.

"The firm gave her a great review," he says.

"So why are you asking about Tommy? Besides the fact that he knows me?"

"Tommy did some odd jobs for them while his sister was there. Packing files, moving boxes. The firm is Moth Auerbach Jefferies."

This means nothing to me. I just look at him.

"Moth Auerbach Jefferies represents SoMa Triangle," he says, then points to the protesters. "If these guys are right about the murder of Gerry Giantonio, then Tommy Gonzalez is the only link we've got between you and the SoMa developers."

"Hey hey! Ho ho! Triangle has got to go!"

"And you're the only link we have to the murder of Candi Bonham," he adds pointedly.

My head hurts. But not as much as my heart.

* * *

The letter is over-scented with lavender. I hold it up to my 210 gallon tank, the brightest light in the room at night, so I can read it. My big *nimbochromis venustus* swims over to take a look, his giraffe-spots glowing on his yellow body. He has a bright blue face and is approaching the size of my hand.

The *venustus* is not like people. He asks me questions, but always the same two things: "Is that something to eat?" and, "Are you feeding us now?" A hundred times a night. No words necessary. If you see him come to the glass you understand.

Every fish in every tank asks the same thing, "Are you feeding us now?"

These are questions I know how to answer. Yes or No.

Never, "I don't know." Never, "Well, if you look at it one way..."

The envelope that holds the letter is addressed to me, in delicate, precise handwriting, slanted at an odd angle.

Zina sniffs it and recoils, the powerful scent overwhelming her delicate nostrils.

"Too much, huh, Zina?" I ask her. She looks at the envelope as if it has just tried to bite her. I stop for a moment to scratch behind her ears and she settles down beside me.

I carefully open the letter. Inside is a Hallmark card. On the front is a picture of a brightly colored bouquet and the inscription "Thinking of you" in flowery script. A few surviving flecks of glitter twinkle in the light.

I open the card and a folded piece of paper falls to the floor. The factory-printed message reads:

Though we may not be together,
Our memories of times past
And of all our wonderful friends
Will keep us linked in each other's hearts...
Forever.

Below it is a note in the same slanted handwriting: "Candi left this cell bill and I thought I should give it to you since you were trying to help her."

It's signed, "Mimi from TLW."

I pick the piece of paper up from the floor, unfold it. It is indeed a copy of Candi Bonham's phone bill.

Why would someone at Theatre Lab West think I'm trying to help her?

Why would anyone think she can be helped at all?

19.

There are Lots of
Different Kinds of Lonely

Saturday, September 8

It wouldn't be so bad if there were a building where my father's office used to be. But this spot on Spear St. is a void, a gap left in the glass and marble walls to create a narrow patio.

So I can't visit where he'd sit on the second floor, can't look up at the window that stands in for his office window. All that remains is thin air, surrounded on three sides by office towers.

I never know where to go in this elegant void to try to talk to him. Today I'm tucked into a front corner, away from the windows of the copy shop where frightened people print yet another hundred resumes.

I lean my head against the gray steel gate that will roll out at night to guard the entry. "Dad, I'm doing my best," I hear myself say. "But wherever I go something just seems to go wrong."

The metal surface is hard and cold.

"I'm just lonely. Very very very lonely."

There are lots of different kinds of lonely.

Don't-want-to-be-by-myself lonely. Mad-at-myself lonely. Can't-stop-thinking-about-someone lonely. All-these-billions-of-people-in-the-world-and-I'm-still-alone lonely. How-can-people-treat-people-that-way lonely. I've-screwed-up lonely. I'm-going-to-die-alone lonely. I-can't-sleep lonely. Don't-want-to-be-alone-but-don't-want-to-talk lonely. I'll-never-have-kids lonely.

Now it's time for A-friend-is-in-trouble-because-of-me lonely. Maybe two friends.

I want to call Paula, but after leaving too many messages I know she isn't returning calls from the strange man who's been looking for a woman who's just been murdered.

She-isn't-calling-back lonely.

I run my fingers along the metal gate, feel the cold surface against my forehead. "Dad, I know you can't talk to me but I need you right now."

If he were still alive my father wouldn't know how to react to all this. He'd say something like, "Well, we all go through tough times."

He's not alive, so he can't even say that. But still I talk to him.

It's the best that I can do.

"I have to find some way to get Luis his job back," I say after a few minutes. Maybe more than a few minutes.

"He hasn't done anything wrong except try to help me. If Leti – that's his wife – if Leti has to get a job that's... She needs to be home with the kids."

The cold metal gate says nothing. The wailing of distant sirens echoes faintly down the street.

"The guys on the radio keep arguing about how Giantonio's death will swing the vote on this big construction plan in SoMa, but I don't care about politics and projects. I just have to find a way to get Luis his job back and to keep Tommy safely enrolled in school."

I have no idea how.

Neither does my father.

20.

You Sausalito People
Sure Are Different

Tuesday, September 11

R-r-r-r-r-rip! Across the room from us, a middle-aged man in a faded Raiders jersey angrily rips up another envelope, his long, scraggly red beard shaking with his wrath.

"You sure you don't want to sit at the computer?" I whisper to Luis.

"No, you drive," Luis whispers back.

I run through the listings, looking for a daytime job that doesn't require a degree. Luis is a sharp guy and has experience as a deckhand, a painter, and in park maintenance. We should be able to find something that will sustain him for a few weeks.

Outside the windows of the Sausalito Public Library the twilight has grown discouraged and been replaced by darkness.

"I'm looking for a DVD about belly dancing," says a deep male voice from the other side of the partition.

The unseen Librarian hesitates only an instant, her voice even and respectful. "Yes, sir. So you're looking for... Is it... instructional?"

Luis looks at me and raises his eyebrows playfully.

"That would be perfect!" the man responds.

"Let's see what's available," the Librarian says.

We hear the sounds of jingling keys and footsteps.

"You Sausalito people sure are different," Luis whispers.

"We Sausalito people are trying to help you find a job," I whisper back. This site is getting us nowhere, so I try another.

"Sherlock Holmes is at my side," Luis says.

"We'll get you back on the *Baar*, but for now..."

"Don't worry, Stevie. They'll figure it out."

R-r-r-r-r-rip! The red-bearded man mumbles something as he tears and re-tears another envelope. His forehead and cheeks display constellations of bright red freckles.

I wish for the hundredth time that Kreitzer's detectives would bring back my computer so we could do this at home.

"How about... Expediter at a recycling center," I read aloud softly. "Must be physically fit and able to lift large barrels." Luis gives me the thumbs up and copies down the address.

"Drivers for Staging Company," I whisper. "Deliver furniture, window treatments and décor to model homes."

Another thumbs up from Luis. "Window treatments. If anyone needs their windows treated, I'm the man."

"OK, I give," I ask him. "What are window treatments?"

"Stevie, you have so much to learn. Window treatments are curtains and blinds and... other stuff."

"Where do you learn these things?" I ask him.

He smiles. "I'm married."

R-r-r-r-r-rip! The man with the red beard shakes his head violently, his long scraggly hair spraying across his shoulders. "Never!" he mutters. "Never, never, never!"

* * *

Liam likes to leave me notes.

This one is taped in the usual spot on the front of the 210- gallon, where the giraffe-spotted *venustus* keeps trying to read it from behind. It says:

Hang in there, Steve.

Once the cops figure out who really killed those people
life will go back to normal. Luis will get his job back,
maybe find an even better one. Tommy will be OK.

Paula could wander back, too.

I throw the note in the trash, take Zina outside, then start the water changes for the tanks on the bottom row.

Liam is more upbeat than I could ever be.

But far less realistic.

21.

Would Tourists Prefer Albert Einstein or Abe Lincoln?

Wednesday, September 12

"So then I get this letter," I'm saying. "Actually, it's a card. And it's signed by someone named Mimi at Theatre Lab West. And inside it is a copy of last month's cell phone bill for The Lady with the Joke Book in Her Purse."

No response.

"So I take the card and the bill and I put them in a plastic bag in case they have fingerprints on them and I bring it to Kreitzer at the police station, and he gets this big smile and he says 'Very interesting' over and over. But then he tells me to wait and he actually gives me a copy of the card and the cell bill to take with me."

I pause as some tourists walk by. They look up at the bronze statue of the World War I general, and I pretend to listen to the person on the other end of my cell phone.

"Uh-huh," I say to no one. "Uh-huh,"

It is a beautiful, sunny day in front of the new de Young Museum in Golden Gate Park, across the plaza from the site of the old Institute of Science.

The Institute of Science, where they have the basement with the snack bar and one time my father lets me have an apple turnover. I think about it every time I have an apple turnover.

One of the tourists says something about the statue to his companion, speaking in French. The other man nods and they move on.

I only eat apple turnovers in places where I can remember being with my father.

And every time I eat one I remember him.

"So now I'm sitting here with a dead woman's phone bill, I've never met anyone named Mimi, and it just feels... bizarre. I feel like I'm violating her privacy. And I feel like Kreitzer is giving me copies because he wants me to do something with them. But that's his job, he's the police detective."

A young couple in shorts and matching black leather flip-flops approaches and looks up at the statue of the confident general.

"Hello!" the statue proclaims loudly, doffing his hat.

The woman lets out a little scream. The man jumps.

"Welcome to the Spreckels Museum of World Art!" the statue says as it bows to them, balanced perfectly on the stone pedestal. "I recommend the Maori masks exhibit from New Zealand!"

Having recovered their wits, the couple look up at Leonard the Human Statue and laugh. I think the woman really means it.

I know that the man really doesn't.

"How do you do that?" she asks. A small group of visitors forms around them.

"My parents decided to have me bronzed instead of my baby shoes," he replies. She laughs again, and this time the crowd laughs with her. A little blue-eyed boy wearing a Boston Red Sox shirt stares up at Leonard, his mouth half open in disbelief.

I drop a dollar in the beret to show them how it's done, and a scattering of coins and another dollar follow.

The woman opens her purse, finds a dollar and places it in the hat. "You're very good!" she tells him, and leads the way up the museum steps. Her husband follows without looking back.

"Thank you, thank you very much," Leonard says. "We Men of Bronze absolutely adore silver... although twenties and hundreds are lovely, too!"

The woman looks back over her shoulder. "I'm going to tell the bus driver about you!" she calls out, laughing.

"And I'm going to tell all the Rodin sculptures about you, sweetie!" he calls back, and blows her a kiss. Then he turns to me and whispers, "Three more and I'll break for lunch." The confident general reassumes his pose.

This is what makes Leonard the Human Statue unique. I've watched him work a corner for two hours without repeating a line. Liam can do improv, too – Leonard says he's really good – but I could never think the way that they do.

I resume my bored phone listener pose, picturing how Paula would look leaving the now-demolished Institute after a day of planetarium shows.

"I wish Paula would call me back," I tell Leonard.

The weathered general confidently stares across the field of battle. He does not reply.

* * *

If you want to spend time with someone who has to work while everyone else is eating lunch. the least you can do is bring him a good meal.

I take the sandwiches from the brown paper bag and hand the ham and cheese to Leonard, keeping the tuna for myself. I distribute water bottles and the oatmeal raisin cookies.

"Thanks for getting this, dude," Leonard says as he takes a huge bite of his sandwich. "I gotta go back to Union Square. The construction here is killing the crowds."

"Uh-huh," I agree as I take a bite of my sandwich.

"But I guess I don't have to tell you that!"

I shake my head. "It'll get better when the new Institute opens."

The human General Pershing statue sits on the curb behind the granite base of the much larger bronze General Pershing statue, where the shrubbery offers us some privacy for lunch.

"Thanks for listening to me ramble." I tell him. "Helps me sort things out."

Leonard has already finished half his sandwich. "If I got bored easy I couldn't do this job."

"I guess not."

He takes a long drink of water and starts on the cookie. I am barely half way through my sandwich.

"Maybe I should go back to the Wharf." Leonard says.

My mouth is full so I just nod and say, "Uh-huh."

He takes the last bite of his cookie. "Sorry. You didn't come by to listen to me bitch about the crowds."

"No worries."

Leonard perks up. "Hey, I know a guy who teaches part time at Theatre Lab West. We can go see him next week and see if he knows anyone there named Mimi."

"That'd be great," I tell him.

"So what do you think, Steve?" he asks me. "When I go back to Union Square. Would tourists prefer Albert Einstein or Abe Lincoln?"

22.

You Can Overdose on the English Language

Six years ago, as seen from Saturday, September 15

I could teach it from memory right now, the whole project from start to finish with the same students, as if we were frozen in time.

"Who wants to start?" I ask the class.

Maria's hand shoots up. I know she'll do a great job but I want to get some of the shy types to participate first.

Tommy Gonzalez hesitates, raises his hand. He wears a checkered shirt, ironed to wrinkle-free perfection by his mother before she sends him off to school.

"OK, Tommy, what is Shakespeare really saying in the 'To Be or Not to Be' speech from Hamlet?"

"It means, he's saying you have to decide when to stand up to people. Sometimes it's not worth it and you need to just let things be.

Other times you just got to go out and do something, you can't just sit there."

I nod in agreement. It's something that a kid from the barrio can readily understand.

Felipe speaks up. "Why we have to read this stuff, Mr. Ondelle? My brothers never had to read Shakespeare."

The class knows what's coming next. Even Felipe knows.

I cross to where the blackboard has a lighter background because it's erased only once a year. I point to the "Professor Polymirth Plan" written there:

1. Graduate from high school
2. Graduate from college
3. Take over the world

"If you're going to take over the world," I recite, "you need to graduate, and you need to earn respect. This is the most famous speech in literature, but most grownups can't tell you what it means. When you teach them what Shakespeare is really saying they'll respect you, and then they'll help you take over the world."

Felipe rolls his eyes but says nothing. They've heard it all before and they'll hear it all again as I try to build up the confidence they deserve to have.

"All right, who can tell me about the end of the speech, the last ten lines?"

I'm surprised to see Jenni raise her hand, and Maria flashes me a dirty look for not calling on her.

Jenni conducts an invisible orchestra as she speaks. "It's like, if you're so scared of dying that all you can think about is dying then you're never going to do anything because you can't think about anything else so you're not doing anything else because all you're thinking about is not getting killed or whatever,"

Once again, I have to agree that she's right.

"So at the end, it's like he's saying, you guys all think I'm all brave and everything but I'm not 'cause I'm just standing here talking and I'm not doing anything."

"Mr. Ondelle!" Maria raises her hand emphatically.

I shake my head. The classroom is moving, rocking gently. But it's not an earthquake, it's too...

"Mr. Ondelle! Mr. Ondelle!"

That isn't Maria's voice. It's Jenni Mathis again.

Only she's not an 8th grader any more. She's 19 and a passenger on the *Louis H. Baar.*

"Mr. Ondelle! It's so good to see you!" Jenni gives me a big hug. She's with a girl I don't know but I can see in the friend's eyes that she's heard the story about the strange Mr. Ondelle and his sudden departure.

"What's up?" I ask her. I'm about to go about my chores downstairs, but there's plenty of time for that.

"Well, the big news is that my mom finally left my dad after all her complaining and just like making everyone miserable."

A bitter taste in my throat. "I'm sorry, Jenni."

To my surprise, she's all smiles. "Hey, it's great by me! Since I was like fourteen all she can do is criticize me! I can't wait to get my apartment even though living with my dad isn't all that bad, but my trust fund only pays for school and books, you know, and I really want to live in the City, because it's like so boring up in Marin, which is why we didn't want to just go shopping there, so we decided we could just take the ferry and I thought we might see you and now we're here and we see you!"

All of that on one, maybe two breaths. I've always liked Jenni, but you can overdose on the English language at the rate that she injects it into your brain.

I see her on the *Baar* about once a month, and for now I show no signs of lingering health effects.

And her father. One of the ringmasters of the circus where the grand finale features me walking away from my job and my dreams.

Jenni begs him to stop, tells him he has everything all wrong, but he ignores her.

I have not seen his face in five years, not until Paula walks into his office at the Institute of Science three weeks ago and I almost walk in behind her.

Carl Mathis. Now that's a name for Kreitzer to add to his Inquisition.

She goes on. "It's funny, cause I was thinking of you because after a few weeks with my dad I thought about how like I'm half of *The Odd Couple*, like we studied back in the day."

I laugh with her. My God, she remembers that class.

Before I can comment she goes on. "I mean, at least my mom didn't like cheat on my dad and then tell everyone on Facebook, like Sandi Garcia's boyfriend."

"That was fu... It was really bad," her friend says.

"Mr. Ondelle, you'd never say anything mean about anyone on Facebook." Jenni tells me.

"I'm not on Facebook."

"You have to try it! I'll be your first friend!"

"Thanks, Jenni. If I ever join Facebook I'll friend you."

Liam likes Facebook. To me it's everything I remember about attending high school that I'd rather just forget.

"OK, that's a promise! First Facebook friend!" Jenni proclaims.

I raise my right hand. "I promise."

I neglect to say that she'll be a grandmother before I follow up on this little vow.

23.

Not Much Space In Between

Monday, September 17

Luis and I have it all planned out: two nights a week I help him with his job search for an hour before he has to hurry home to kiss the kids good night.

It has been a lousy Monday. The union grievance over his termination has been rejected, dismissed without discussion. The Local says they've played their only card, and the lawyer at the Community Network tells Luis he's out of options.

I have suspended the language prediction game, at least for now. Without Luis chirping at everyone about how he's going to win each week the process has lost its joy.

For the rest of this month Luis is helping his cousin on a big landscaping project, but after that he needs to find a job. Tonight we're working on his resume.

It's the best that I can do.

Liam and I don't have a good place for two people to work, with one wall of aquariums, one wall of books, one wall that's the kitchen and not much space in between. So Luis and I sit at Mrs. Tarrow's big oak dining table with a pad of paper and freshly-sharpened pencils.

Since we are guys and not to be trusted, Mrs. Tarrow places a pad on the tabletop and covers it with a bright red tablecloth.

Smart lady, Mrs. Tarrow.

I've printed out an article from a website about how to write a resume. It is written by a lady named Marta who has a nice smile and seems to know what she's talking about.

Mrs. Tarrow sits in the living room and reads, but I know she is using her super-powers to listen so she can help if needed.

The printout says that the summary at the top of the resume should list Luis' best qualities with dramatic words.

Luis bats his eyelashes at me, clearly enjoying this. "Tell me, Stevie, what are my best qualities?"

I refuse to take the bait and start making a list. Reliable... Hard-working...

Luis looks at the printout and reads it out loud. "Don't use the first word you think of, since this makes you sound ordinary. Look for powerful, less common words that pack a punch."

I rub my forehead. Under the table Zina shifts her weight so her head is on my foot and her thigh is pressed against Luis' ankle.

"Maybe I should work with Liam instead of you on this, Stevie. He sells fog to people. He uses all sorts of fancy words . Why can't I have Liam help me with my resume?"

From the living room I can hear Mrs. Tarrow chuckling.

* * *

Luis is on his way home, Mrs. Tarrow is finishing off the kitchen and then on her way to bed. I'm exhausted but there are water changes to do, and I've already missed too many nights to let myself off the hook on this one.

I step around Mrs. Tarrow as she wipes off the countertops and grab myself a glass of ice water. A few gulps before I climb the sixteen steps to my garage will wake me up again.

A piece of paper is secured to the refrigerator door by a magnet that's shaped like a sea lion. The page is covered with Mrs. Tarrow's graceful handwriting:

Knows Steven not good with questions.
— Ferry? School? Classmate?
Knows Steven's routine, could plant gun.
— Ferry rider? Crew?

"Take it down if you like."

I turn around and look at her. "I really doubt it's someone from the ferry," I say, pulling down the note.

"We must never assume," she says, sitting at the breakfast bar. More Jack Tarrow wisdom. "And if you'll be so kind, I'll have my amaretto now."

I grab the tiny crystal glass, add the requisite single ice cube and pour the dash of amaretto, then bring her drink and the note to the counter to finish reading.

Had motive to kill Supervisor Giantonio, or
Had motive to kill Candi Bonham
— SoMa Triangle project? Other?
Hired Candi to drop purse to get fingerprints
— Not experienced in evidence

"This explains why Kreitzer wants to ask about Tommy Gonzalez," I tell her. "He fits the first two categories."

"But none of the others," she says.

I wince. "Kreitzer has records of him doing summer jobs for a law firm while his sister's interning," I tell her. "Turns out they represent SoMa Triangle."

She looks at me, frowns, takes a microscopic sip of amaretto. But says nothing.

At the bottom of the list she has written in the two names I already know will be there:

Carl Mathis
Tommy Gonzalez

"Carl Mathis belongs on this list but Tommy Gonzalez doesn't," I growl. "Mathis hates me and Tommy loves me. And Mathis works in PR at the Institute of Science where they hired Candi for a video, so he fits the 'Knew Candi' blank, too. It all came together for me talking with Jenni yesterday."

"You should call Ken and tell him."

I nod. "Last night. On his voicemail."

All she says is, "Good."

"Why do you say 'Not experienced in evidence'?" I ask her

"The fingerprints on the purse. The killer went to all that trouble but the woman who runs the office..."

"Trish."

"Trish. If her fingerprints were on top of yours it verifies that she touched it after you did, which verifies your story and doesn't place you at the murder scene. The killer was in a hurry or inexperienced. Or both."

I let the ice cold water flow down my throat. It tastes bitter. "So I'm being dragged through all this for nothing. I'm not good with questions so they think I'll hang myself."

She leans forward, looks squarely at me. "In a high-profile case where there's pressure for a quick arrest, a suspect who's..." She stops, re-orders her thoughts. "Someone who's not good with questions can draw a lot of resources. It can buy the killer time while the trail goes cold."

"So Luis loses his job for nothing." I stare down at the ice in my half-empty glass. "And why doesn't Kreitzer say he knows I'm innocent?"

She sighs. "I'm sure he has his reasons."

I console myself with more water, then wave my glass towards the note. "Is this one of Jack's methods?"

"Jack put notes on the fridge and he'd read them over and over and keep adding things," she explains. "He called them his charts."

"I wish Kreitzer were doing this stuff," I tell her.

"Oh, he is, my dear. I'm sure of it."

PART II

JOURNAL TWO

She reaches for the stack of notebooks by my bed. "I finished the first one," she says. "You left a lot of blank pages at the end."

"Sometimes you need a fresh start," I tell her. "I mean... Someone's trying to make it look like I'm a murderer. Luis loses his job because of me. A woman I hope will care about me isn't even speaking to me."

She sighs and shakes her head.

"Not the time to write another chapter that's just like the last one," I tell her.

"Where were these? I never saw them before."

"In my drawer. By the bed."

"Is it OK for me to keep reading?"

I pretend not to hesitate. "Sure."

"Some of it... It's hard for me now. When I read it."

"I know."

"But I want to keep going."

I nod. "Whatever you want to do."

She takes the second journal, runs her hand across the cover. "You want to go sit in the garden? It's warmed up outside."

"Sure." I hold up two books. "Which one shall I take? I'm in the mood for old school poetry."

"You have to take them both," she says confidently.

"And why is that?"

"Robert Browning and Elizabeth Barrett Browning. Those two should never be separated."

I have to admit she's got a point.

24.

The Cowardly Lion Walking
Beside the Tin Man

Tuesday, September 18

The late-summer sun warms my face as I walk down Geary St. towards Union Square to meet Leonard the Human Statue for our lunch with his friend from Theatre Lab West, Paul Strapp. With a little luck, in just a few minutes I'll know the last name of Mimi from TLW.

The lunchtime flood of office workers spills into the streets, with students and tourists mixed into the downtown crowds. I'm walking behind two girls in their late teens or early twenties, one carrying a bag labeled *A Draught of Naught*. As they walk their heads bob in soft conversation, the communication easy and familiar.

The way it never seems to be for me.

They veer around the grizzled Prophet of Market Street, who sits cross-legged on the sidewalk behind a Styrofoam cup. Today there is no singing, no spiritual.

As the young women pass he looks up, then raises his voice. "I hope you choose love, girl," he says. "New York is a cold and lonely place."

The girl closest to him looks back, just for a moment. Her face is confused, almost panicked. Then she turns and hurries off.

I pull a dollar from my pocket and drop it in his cup as I walk by.

He looks up, meets my eyes, but says nothing.

I see the light up at Kearny is about to turn yellow, and I hurry to cross the busy street in time.

* * *

The heroic statue of Abraham Lincoln stands in contemplation of the Macy's store across the street, a thick book held tightly in one hand.

As I approach I can see the smirks of people on the nearby benches. They're waiting for me to pee my pants when Lincoln comes to life.

I look across Union Square, take out my cell phone and pretend to dial. After a moment I say, "Hi, honey. I hope you're ready to go to lunch soon, because I'm starving."

A man and woman approach, carrying ice cream cones in honor of the warm September weather. They walk up to the statue and I can hear the woman saying ."...for a sec and see if the guidebook has any stores where they don't think people are made of money."

She screams, a short high-pitched wail, as Lincoln comes to life and stares over her husband's shoulder at his ice cream. The 16th President lustfully licks his metallic lips.

The crowd on the benches laughs. The woman shrinks back and blushes.

Leonard-as-Lincoln looks down at the melting ice cream and intones, "Four scoops and seven drips ago, our forefathers..."

A big laugh. I laugh with them, and drop a dollar in the hat at Lincoln's feet.

On cue, more people step forward and the hat begins to fill.

* * *

Union Square remains busy and Abraham Lincoln is on a roll, but the moment 1:25 comes Leonard the Human Statue hops down off his pewter box and proclaims he's ready to walk over to Theatre Lab West.

We cover the two blocks to the theatre at a casual pace, passers-by staring at the walking Lincoln statue and pointing him out to their children. A guy in UCLA sweatpants with a USC sweatshirt hurries to turn on his camera and capture us on video to show his friends when he gets home. Leonard smiles and tips his top hat to the camera as we walk by.

I feel like Dorothy walking beside the Tin Man.

No, that's not it. I feel like The Cowardly Lion walking beside the Tin Man.

And Dorothy isn't returning my calls.

We enter the theatre and approach the ticket window. Traditional gold masks representing comedy and tragedy are sculpted into the ornate molding above each lobby door.

"Where would I find Paul Strapp?" Leonard asks the woman behind the glass. She seems completely oblivious to the fact that she is speaking with Abraham Lincoln.

"Go out the front door, turn left. Two doors down is the academic entrance. Go downstairs," she recites. "Don't know the room number but if you ask someone they'll tell you."

"Is Mimi here today?" I ask, from behind Lincoln's left shoulder.

The woman gives me a puzzled look, as if I were speaking a foreign language.

"We don't have any Mimi's here," she says decisively.

"You're sure?" I ask her.

She gives Abraham Lincoln a disappointed look, and he tips his hat and leads me towards the door.

We follow the path as described in search of Paul Strapp. Leonard stops at the bottom of the stairs and looks around.

"I said get me another goddamn drink!" a female voice demands from an open door nearby.

"Don't you think you've had enough?" another woman asks.

A man says, "We're celebrating. Bill's coming home."

"Get me the damn drink!"

I feel a bead of sweat as it makes its way down my forehead.

"I'll do it," the man says.

"You're making it worse. You know that," says the second woman. She sounds like a college student trying to strike a mature tone.

The drunken voice bellows, "Go home, Emily! If you're going to ruin our night, just go home!"

I tell Leonard I'll wait in the lobby and climb back up the stairs.

* * *

Despite being 6'2, blonde and athletic, Paul Strapp is a nice guy.

"I remember some students who liked to go down to Mondo Mia's for a drink after a show," he tells us between bites of his roast beef sandwich. "But a Mimi..."

Leonard looks at me. We know what's coming, and the disappointment is already etched in Lincoln's craggy face.

"I'm afraid I've never heard of a student here named Mimi."

I feel like screaming, but instead just rearrange the fries next to my untouched turkey sandwich .

Strapp rubs his oversized hands together as if he were washing them in a sink. "I even looked in the last couple of years of school directories, just to make sure," he says. "Sorry to let you down."

What else could TLW mean? If Mimi isn't from Theatre Lab West then where is she from? The Lost World? The Linens Warehouse? The Lucky Wonton?

Those Lying in Wait?

We start our walk back up Powell St. towards the theatre. "It's time to give up the search for the mysterious Mimi," I tell them. "I just have to screw up my courage, find a quiet place to talk and call all those numbers on Candi's phone bill. It's what Kreitzer wants, but it's the only way I can prove Luis is innocent and get him his job back."

We've reached the front door of the theatre. "I can help you with the quiet place to talk," Strapp says, waving his hand for us to follow.

Leonard says, "I'll come along and help," and I flash him a grateful smile.

Paul leads us through the lobby to a door at the back labeled "Staff Only." We walk down a long wide corridor, then turn left into a short, narrow hallway with two doors on each side. He knocks, then opens the second door on the left and leads us in.

"The part time faculty share this office," he tells us, pointing to the ancient gray steel desk. "Just don't get me in trouble."

25.

I Don't Know Exactly How to

Get to Milpitas

Tuesday, September 18 (Cont.)

Leonard sits down at the desk and I pull out my copy of Candi's bill. He takes my cell phone, puts it on speaker and gives me a wink. I read off the first number to dial, which turns out to be the B of A customer service line.

The next is a dry cleaner that has nothing waiting for Candi Bonham. I dutifully write down the connections in my little notebook.

On the third call a woman answers and Leonard, still in his metallic Lincoln makeup, goes into action.

"Hi, my name's Abe Penny," he announces happily, "and I'm calling to tell Candi Bonham that she's our prize winner for the Trip to Anywhere from KPWN Radio. Is Candi Bonham home?"

The woman on the other end hesitates. "You must have the wrong number. There's no one named Candi here."

"Wow, that's too bad," Leonard says, "because for Candi to claim the prize we have to talk to her. Maybe someone else there knows Candi or has the right number?"

"No, I'm sorry."

My heart drops. This one is going nowhere.

"I see, I see," Leonard responds. "Did I dial the right number? Is this the Bonham residence?"

"Actually..." The woman starts to giggle. "This is a public phone at the Ferry Building. Is there a way that I can win the Trip to Any-where?"

"Sorry," Leonard says without an ounce of sadness in his voice. "Thanks for listening to KPWN!"

The next number is the answering service for The Lee Agency, where everyone is doing lunch and cannot possibly come to the phone. Could an agent have helped Candi get the gig as The Lady with the Joke Book in her Purse? Leonard leaves an unexplained request for a return call and my cell number.

Next we reach The Dizzying Heights Hair Salon in Pacific Heights. I write it down, shake my head so Leonard will apologize for calling a wrong number.

Then we hit another phone booth, this one close by, near Union Square. "Are those the only two public phones left in San Fran-cisco?" Leonard asks me.

I shrug. Why would Candi be collecting phone booths?

The next call rings forever and Leonard is about to hang up when a woman's voice answers. He goes into his Candi-has-won-a-trip-to-anywhere spiel.

I shudder as I think that what Candi actually has undertaken is a trip to nowhere.

"That's... that's great!" the woman says. "But Candi doesn't live here anymore. She moved out last year." A New York accent softened by a few years somewhere else.

Leonard shoots me an excited glance. "Do you have Candi's current daytime contact information or where she works so we can award her prize?"

He reads back the phone number as she gives it to him. It matches the cell phone number on the bill. The ex-roommate must be living in a monastery to have missed the news of her friend's murder.

"Great," Leonard says. "And may I please have your name, so we can thank you on air for helping your friend?"

"Julia Wong, W-O-N-G."

"Great, Julia. Thanks so much."

"Sure," I hear the voice on the phone say. Then she adds, "So is this the radio station from the desert with the DJ who wrote that book Candi talked so much about?"

It takes all my will power not to scream the words "Book?!!"

Leonard takes it all in stride, meeting my panicked eyes. "We are in fact that very station, Julia. And if you can tell me the third word on page 47 you'll win a McDonald's Gift Certificate!"

Leonard the Human Statue is good at improvisation.

Julia moans sadly, and her voice gets softer. "I don't have one," she explains. "I just remember the picture of Che Guevara on the cover. Candi had it with her the last time we had lunch."

Leonard erupts with joy. "Julia, I'm going to call that a right answer, because Che Guevara is indeed on the cover of the book. Just give me your address and we'll have that gift certificate on its way."

"Actually," she says, "I can come down to the station this afternoon to pick it up. I'm off this week."

Leonard hesitates for only a moment. "Julia, I'm afraid that only our transmission tower is in San Francisco. They moved the studios to Milpitas four years ago to save money on rent."

I don't know exactly how to get to Milpitas. Maybe Leonard thinks that Julia Wong doesn't know how to get to Milpitas either.

"But Julia, one of my staff members is in San Francisco tomorrow at lunchtime meeting a sponsor. You name a spot that's convenient for you and I'll have him meet you there and give you your prize."

She hesitates a moment, then says, "Oh... OK. Let me think... How about Stella's on Columbus at 12:30?"

Leonard looks at me and I nod that I can do it.

"Let me just write this down, Julia, and I'll pass it to him. His name is Steve, he's about 6'1..."

I resist the urge to interrupt and say "Five-eleven and a half."

"He has short dark brown hair and green eyes, and don't let him talk you into buying him lunch with your prize."

She does not laugh. "OK. OK, I'll look for him there at 12:30."

When he hangs up he gives me a broad smile. "Now you have a big decision to make," he says.

"What?" I ask him.

"Exactly how big a McDonald's Gift Certificate did she win?"

26.

All the Parts That Sound Completely Insane

Wednesday, September 19

North Beach is San Francisco's Italian neighborhood, the birthplace of Joe DiMaggio. All that remains of that long-lost era is a row of Italian restaurants, tourist shops and a church along Columbus Avenue and a few small side streets.

It is 12:25 and I stand uncomfortably by the door at Stella's, waiting for Julia Wong.

I have no idea what I'll say when I meet her, apart from "Here's your McDonald's Gift Certificate." Do I tell her that her ex-roommate is dead and give her Captain Kreitzer's number?

All I know about Julia Wong is that she has a Chinese name, an American accent, and that she is Candi Bonham's ex-roommate.

Do I just hand her the paper and leave, having learned nothing? No closer to knowing who would murder two people and try to make it look like I'm the killer? No closer to bringing Luis back to his job and protecting Tommy from becoming Kreitzer's next victim?

The lunchtime crowd munches on small salads and sips from big paper cups, crowded together in the long, narrow room. Two black-booted motorcycle cops savor oversized cookies; one has a scar on his elbow that's shaped like the coastline of Peru. A nun sits by herself in one corner, reading a newspaper.

On two occasions my hopes rise as possible Julia Wong's enter the shop. Each of them orders, then leaves without looking for her McDonald's gift certificate.

A woman in a gray business suit keeps looking at me. A large brief-case with an ornate brass buckle sits beneath her tiny table, and the nail on her right index finger is broken. She does not look like a Julia Wong and I maintain my vigil at the door.

The street outside is full of tourists, drawn by the fabled Indian summer of San Francisco.

"Steve?"

I turn around. It is the woman who has been watching me. She has short, light brown hair and very green eyes.

She reads my mind. "Julia couldn't come. My name is Debbie. She asked me to get her prize."

My heart sinks. So this is the latest dead-end.

"Here," I say, and I hand her the half-hour-old $20 McDonalds gift certificate. "Tell her congratulations."

"Thanks. I will." She hesitates, smiles, and goes back to her table.

I should walk out, since I'm supposed to be meeting the radio station sponsor. Unwilling to give up, I step forward and join the line. I always feel strange in coffee shops because I don't drink coffee.

I'm not going to follow her like some stalker. There's no point in talking to her since she's Candi's roommate's friend, not Candi's roommate.

But I still don't leave.

Debbie drinks her coffee and reads a book called "Virginia's Promise."

As I reach the front of the line she puts the book away and gathers her things. I buy an apple juice and find myself walking to the exit with Debbie right behind me. I hold the door for her.

"Thanks again for bringing me the prize," she says.

"Sure," I tell her. Then I blurt out, "Do you know Candi Bonham?"

She withdraws a step. "Why do you ask?" .

There is no going back. "She's... she's dead," I stammer. "A murder victim. Three weeks ago."

She looks back through the window at the crowd inside. "Why are you telling me this?" Her voice is trembling.

What have I gotten myself into now, frightening innocent people?

I pull out Captain Kreitzer's card. "This is the police detective's card, the one who's investigating the murder. If you or Julia could, you know, talk to him. I just thought..."

To my surprise she lets out a long sigh of relief, waving her hands in front of her face as if to clear a nest of spider webs.

She reaches into her purse and pulls out a business card of her own.

The two cards match.

"So much for the career of Debbie Milovich, ace detective," she says and laughs uncomfortably.

Suddenly I get it. "There is no Julia Wong," I tell her. "You're Candi's ex-roommate. You're thinking our call might lead to a suspect in the murder, so you use a false name and ask to meet in a crowded public place."

She nods, embarrassed. "I called Captain Kreitzer and he said it was probably nothing, but he'd make sure there were officers around."

I look at the two big motorcycles at the curb and the two big policemen just inside. "I'd say he's doing a good job of it."

She holds out her hand. "But I'm still shaking anyway."

"I'm sorry."

"No, I'm... I'm glad I'm not the only one who's trying to help Candi."

"Can we sit down for a minute and start again?" I ask her.

She nods.

* * *

We split a coconut pastry that is neither a cake nor a cookie but is nevertheless delicious. Debbie orders coffee and I sip my apple juice.

I give her the short version of my story, leaving out all the parts that sound completely insane but leaving in all the parts about Luis but leaving out almost all the parts about Paula. No point in getting more upset.

"You're from New York?" I ask her, although the accent I noticed has now disappeared.

"We moved when I was in high school. I have to think about it now to, you know, get my New York self back." She smiles. "It was the only way I could think of to make Julia Wong sound different on the phone."

She plays with her half of the coconut cookie-cake, demonstrating the ability to break off and eat a single shred at a time. "Candi and I only shared the apartment for six months, last October through March of this year. Then she told me she was getting more gigs and that she could go back to living on her own. We had a month to month deal, so that was it."

I try to eat a very small piece of the dessert so that my half will last as long as hers. I lack the same dexterity and simply create a pile of crumbled flotsam.

"I'm a paralegal for Troy Barahal Clifford and Diaz, so our schedules were pretty different. She'd started dating a man she said was very exciting, but he never came over and that's all she'd say." Debbie shakes her head. "Seems pretty obvious now who was the mystery Romeo."

"Supervisor Giantonio."

"He'd have the bucks to help her with the rent, too."

I nod as if I know how many bucks Supervisors have.

Debbie leans forward, lowers her voice. "Candi... she did a lot of things to make money. I told all this to Captain Kreitzer. Acting was her first love and what she really wanted to do, but actors... She did some modeling, and she liked that, and she worked the booths at conventions and stuff. Way more exciting than what I do, handling documents in divorce cases."

It's like me and Liam. He has the romantic job. I have the one that pays the bills.

"And she had her certification in massage," Debbie adds. "She made money that way, too."

"What about the book?" I ask.

"It was next to her purse when we had lunch. I still go to this hairdresser she told me about, and we..."

"Dizzying Heights?" I interrupt.

"How did you know that?"

"The phone list. Sorry, go on."

"It's OK. So, we ran into each other there and I hadn't seen her in months and we grabbed a bite to catch up."

"So, you know why the book is so important."

"Not till you explained things just now, but Captain Kreitzer asked me about it. Candi told me that a woman hired her to promote the book. The author's a local DJ."

"Phil Steen. Google makes books easy to find once you have the description you gave us. What about the woman?"

"Candi didn't say much. Just that she was..." Debbie hesitates. "She was very masculine. In her clothing and... Just the way she was."

Our first hint about the person who hired Candi. It's a woman. She may be gay. Or it may be a man who wants to look like a woman who's gay. Or a woman who's straight but is trying to look gay. Or she just has a deep voice. Or she smokes a lot. Or...

"Sorry I can't tell you more than that," Debbie is saying, as she plays with the last crumbs of our dessert. "But that's all Candi told me. It's all we have to go on."

I pick up my apple juice, decide I'm not thirsty and put it down again. I look across the little table at Debbie and shrug. "It's the best that we can do."

27.

He Makes Some Kind of a Muted Barking Sound

Thursday, September 20

I am manning the stern with the mooring hook as we approach the Ferry Building on my final morning trip. I look down at the landing and my stomach drops.

Captain Kreitzer is leaning on the railing, looking out at Yerba Buena Island and the Bay. He looks up at me and waves.

Without thinking I wave back. The way you do with your father when he picks you up after a game.

We secure the *Louis H. Baar* and I walk down the gangway to see what bad news he has for me today.

He shakes my hand as I walk up and says, "Have time to go for a little walk?"

"Sure." What else am I going to say?

He shoves his big hands in his pockets. There is a tiny tear below the waistband on the right hand side of his sharply-creased pants. Probably caused by shoving his big hands in his pockets.

"You know, you really should leave the police work to the police," he tells me. "Your little stage play with Debbie Milovich could have turned out very badly."

I nod. "Is that why you give me a copy of the cell bill with all those numbers?"

He makes some kind of a muted barking sound without opening his mouth. "Never know what you might remember or recognize if you keep looking at it."

"Uh-huh." We're walking west toward Fisherman's Wharf. We pass a run-down warehouse with a sign that says the building is the new magnetic north for Venture Capital.

"I've got another name to bounce off of you, see what you remember," he says.

I give him my best skank eye look. "You're not going to bring up Tommy Gonzalez again, are you?"

"Already brought him up. This is a new name."

"Someone else I know is innocent?"

"That's why I ask you about them," he says simply. "So you can tell me if you think they're innocent."

I don't have a good comeback for this so I say nothing.

"Name is Thomas Festane. Tom Festane."

I chew my lip. The name means nothing to me.

"I don't know him," I say. "Or I don't remember him."

"He had a stepdaughter in your classes," Kreitzer says, looking down at his narrow notepad. "Nina Rodgers."

"Nina I remember. Why is he a suspect?"

"Not a suspect. Just a person of interest."

"Because he could be a professional killer."

"This wasn't a professional job. Efficient, but not professional."

I wait to see if he'll tell me more. He doesn't.

"Why is he interesting?"

"He had the chance to learn about... what you're like."

"And...?" I ask him.

"He has ties to SoMa Triangle, the big office and condo project that Supervisor Giantonio opposed."

I feel myself smiling. That does sound interesting.

Kreitzer keeps going. "Tom Festane is an attorney. He worked at a big San Francisco law firm called Moth Auerbach Jefferies for eight years. Their biggest client is TZD Development, the company that's building SoMa Triangle."

"But you said, 'he worked there.' You're using the past tense."

"You should try it some time," he answers. "Yes, Tom Festane left there two years ago to join a fund that develops shopping malls. A fund with no known ties to SoMa Triangle."

"And...?" I ask again.

"He now lives in the City and works in Sausalito. Takes the ferry once or twice a week."

"That means I'd recognize him," I tell Kreitzer. "Not that many counter-commute regulars."

"And he'd recognize you."

"So anyone who recognizes me and has any small, slim connection to SoMa Triangle or their law firm is a suspect?"

"They're interesting."

"And because it's not a professional killer just about anyone on the ferry could be a suspect."

He nods. "The murder weapon was stolen in a burglary ten years ago. It could have gone through six different owners."

"Until someone decides they need to use it."

"Murders happen when people are angry or desperate. This one looks like it was planned, but planned in a hurry. That usually means desperation."

My head hurts. "So it's someone who knows me, who's desperate about something, who has access to a stolen gun, and who rides the ferry."

"That's about it." He turns and we start walking back in the other direction. Neither of us says anything, and I wonder if he's thinking what I'm thinking.

We carry 467,000 passengers on the Sausalito Ferry last year.

That's a lot of suspects.

* * *

Eli of the Coral Reef never takes his eyes off the newest inhabitant of the big steel tank.

"They just subdivided *abalistes stellatus* and *abalistes filamentosus* into separate species," he tells me. "Should have done it years ago. It's obvious this one's a *stellatus*. Look at his tail!"

"Uh-huh."

Eli peers up at me from under his Giants cap. "So what happened after you shared the coconut cake with her and you spilled crumbs all over the table?"

"Nothing," I tell him. "Once both of you you know what the other person knows there's not much to talk about."

"What are you going to do now?" he asks me, his eyes back on the cautious newcomer to the temporary reef.

"Kreitzer already has a copy when I call to tell him about the joke book from The Lady with the Joke Book in Her Purse, so..." I shake my head. "Yesterday I'm all excited because I think I'm making progress and now it feels like I'm getting nowhere all over again. All I can do is try to help Luis get a new job."

"So have you ordered it from Amazon?"

"The book? It has to be at a store somewhere in The City," I tell him. "I don't want to wait for it to come in the mail when I can hold it in my hands and buy it on the spot."

"Have you ever ordered anything from Amazon?"

I give him a disappointed look.

He smiles and recites back to me, "I like to hold it in my hands and buy it on the spot."

"Exactly."

"I don't blame you for feeling that way about mail-order books," Eli says, looking up at me. "I feel the same way about mail-order fish."

28.

The Note is More of a List
than a Letter

Friday, September 21

Captain Jack Sparrow and I stand patiently in line at the sandwich truck on Market St.

"Don't worry about it," I tell Leonard the Human Statue, who is decked out in full costume, makeup and wig as the Caribbean's most famous pirate. "Making rent is the most important thing. And I've used up all the numbers on the cell bill."

He kicks at an imaginary rock on the ground. "I hate doing data entry."

"You're smart to take that six week gig," I tell him. "Then you can relax and not worry about money till January."

He grimaces. "I have to wear a tie."

I try to swallow a laugh but fail miserably. The image of the uncatchable Captain Jack Sparrow chained to a desk transcribing customer signup cards cracks me up.

"Sorry," I tell him.

"Are you ready to apologize to Bobby?" the young woman behind us says to her little girl.

The child in her arms smiles and says something like "Anana ma ma ma." She's still in diapers and doesn't appear to understand any of what her mother is saying.

The aforementioned Bobby stands beside her, his bright green flat-billed cap twisted off-center above his narrow face. He grins. Long, scraggly brown hair crawls like ivy down his back.

We reach the window and order our tuna sandwiches, the most pirate-style item on the menu.

"It's just till the end of next month," Leonard says, "But it feels like forever."

The girl behind us grasps her baby daughter's chin, forces her to meet her eyes. "Listen to me. You can't be mean like that to Bobby or Mommy will have to punish you."

Bobby grins again, a thin line of teeth showing between narrow lips.

I shiver.

The little girl smiles, rubs at the tattoo of an hourglass on her mother's forearm. "Ma ma ma ma ma!" she babbles.

I thrust a twenty through the window and pay for both our lunches, ignoring Leonard's protests that it's his turn.

It's the best that I can do.

* * *

Finally.

Lieutenant Li finally brings back my computer, my little file box with my bills, the sheaf of letters from my father.

It is exactly four weeks since the arrival of the peach-colored suede purse in my life.

My story of Debbie Milovich and Julia Wong has inspired Liam's thinking. As usual, the note taped to the front of the big aquarium is more of a list than a letter:

Thoughts for Steve:

Kreitzer is using you and Candi's roommate, suggesting you chase down leads.

Must have laughed when his amateur detectives detected each other.

Do you keep pursuing this?

Nag Kreitzer to call, admit mistake, so Luis gets his job back and you can move on with your life.

Whoever Mimi is, she's trying to use you, too.

Whoever sent Lady with Joke Book in her Purse was trying to use you, too.

Is Mimi on their side or on yours? Her own?

Can any of them still use you if you decide not to play?

Seems like the first time in two years you haven't been bored.

But may be dangerous.

Cheers,

Liam

I think about all this as I vacuum gunk from the left-side 90-gallon into a bucket and then carry fresh water to the tanks.

Liam has a point. If Kreitzer can get Luis' job back, why should I try to find the woman who says she works for Phil Steen?

Siphon-haul-dump.

I want Paula to stop being afraid of me. Kreitzer is a police captain.

When he solves the case she'll know I'm not a... Not someone who could kill someone.

She probably already knows that now.

Siphon-haul-dump.

Or maybe I'm just kidding myself and she'll never see me as a regular guy.

I'll never see me as a regular guy. Why should she be any different?

29.

Oh, Just a Murder Weapon, That's All

Tuesday, September 25

It is a glorious late summer day, the calm surface of San Francisco Bay glowing in the sun as we slice through the water.

Picking out Tom Festane as a regular on the *Louis H. Baar* is a process of elimination. The smiling face from his LinkedIn profile guides my search.

He turns out to be the guy who calls Linh "young lady" when he buys his coffee each morning. Dark hair in a perfect part, his shirt bright white and his tie an even brighter yellow. As advertised, we see him about twice a week on the counter-commute route to Sausalito.

If he remembers me he shows no signs of it. I remember him only because of Nina actually liking this latest stepfather and her stories of the ones who have preceded him.

I am wondering where Nina is today and how many more stepfathers she's experienced when a different former student appears at the bottom of the stairway. It's Tommy Gonzalez, Festane's teammate on the Kreitzer suspect list.

"Hey, Mr. Ondelle, I wanted you to meet my friend Rebecca," he says. The girl with him smiles and extends her hand. I can tell they are more than friends.

"It's great to meet you," she says.

"Very nice to meet you, too, Rebecca." I shake her hand.

"Tommy says you're the best teacher he's ever had," she says. She has long, dark straight hair, big brown eyes and a wide smile. She looks good next to Tommy, even if I have a hard time adjusting to him as an adult.

"So when is Lizzie coming to visit me here on the ferry?" I ask him, trying to change the subject. His sister is one of my first students, from my rookie year at school.

He shakes his head. "She likes to drive. She isn't even a lawyer yet but she wants everyone to see her BMW."

"She's real tall now," Rebecca adds. "She looks like a model."

"You could still be our teacher again, you know, our professor," Tommy says, with that look in his eye.

He needs to move on, but I do not say this because it would break his heart.

"You never know," I say instead.

"Tommy told me the story," Rebecca says. "It was so unfair."

I flash back for a moment to the image of Tommy's mom, literally trembling with fear, speaking to the Board of Education and defending me, all through a Spanish translator.

I shake my head to drive away the image. I adore Tommy, but he has to get out of the past, live in the Here and Now. "Stuff happens," I say. "Imaginations run wild. Nobody's fault."

"Not true!" Tommy says, surprising both Rebecca and me with his vehemence. "Those parents lied!"

How can I make him stop?

"Remember what you taught us, Mr. Ondelle? About Shakespeare? How "To be or not to be" really means "Is it time to stand up for yourself?""

God, he remembers that day.

"Those parents lied. The kids all told the truth, but they made up reasons to attack you when all you did was teach us and be our friend."

He looks at Rebecca, then back at me.

"I'm still your friend, Tommy. Always will be." It's all I can think of to say.

Tommy's shoulders slump. "You can't change the past, but it still pisses me off. I know you had your reasons. I... I just wish we all stood up against a sea of troubles." Rebecca puts her arms around him, leans up and kisses him on the cheek.

It makes me feel good to see someone love this kid that way.

* * *

"OK, I've been reading up on what this Marta lady on the Internet says about job interviews," I start out. "We'll just do the first three questions tonight."

"What do I win if I get them right?" Luis asks.

I ignore him and read out loud, "Always respond with clear, concise answers. Never lie, but use every question as a chance to present relevant experience, a personal strength or other persuasive content."

"So keep it short and say lots of good things about yourself," Luis says.

"Exactly," I tell him. "OK, Question one: What made you want to apply for this stock technician job?"

"I need a daytime job."

I know this is not a good answer and so does Luis. I look down at my printout. "OK... and how about relevant experience, a personal strength?"

Luis straightens the pad of paper he is using to take notes. He has had four interviews in two weeks, but no job offers.

"I... I can climb ladders, move big boxes. I work hard and I'm always on time."

"Good!" I tell him. "Question two: What's your favorite thing about your last job?"

Luis' eyes light up. "I liked helping the passengers. I liked the people I worked with."

"Great answer." Mrs. Tarrow says. She's finished loading the dishes but will not press the button till we're done. Her old dishwasher is louder than her old Volvo.

"Question three: why did you leave your last job?"

Luis sits, thinks for a while. Finally he says, "I lost my job because I was busy and I waited too long to turn in a lost item."

I look over at Mrs. Tarrow. It's the truth.

Of course, the next question will always be, "And what is the item?"

Oh, just a murder weapon, that's all.

How do we twist that answer to present relevant experience, a personal strength or other persuasive content?

Maybe I'll write to Marta the job-hunting expert on the Internet and ask her the answer to that one.

30.

The Best Pots Come from a Kiln

Wednesday, September 26

Each evening after we tie up for the night I take the long concrete stairway that leads from downtown Sausalito up the steep hill to our street. Much of the year I make the climb in darkness, my little flashlight struggling with the shadows on the dark stairs. By the time I reach the top my legs feel heavy and I'm breathing hard.

But not tonight. In the lingering daylight of late summer the steps fall away behind me, unnoticed, forgotten.

Under my arm is the joke book from The Lady with the Joke Book in Her Purse, my prize from today's search of a little bookshop on Filbert Street. The title is *How Much is That Strange Man in the Window?* And the author is Phil Steen. Its cover portrays Che Guevara as a tall, thin model posing in an expensive designer suit.

It also has something to do with why Candi Bonham and Supervisor Giantonio are dead. And why someone would want my fingerprints on the purse, and why the gun would appear on the *Louis H. Baar*.

And why Luis has no job because of me.

I open the wrought iron gate, looking up to see my landlord Mrs. Blount appear on cue at her window high atop the old white house. Tonight it does not bother me.

On my way up the steps I meet two runners coming down the hill, a popular shortcut for the locals. I step aside and they wave their thanks.

I approach the door and fumble with my keys, anxious to open a can of tuna and devour both it and the book.

"Steven, would you like some dinner? I made spaghetti and Zina wanted to wait for you down here today." Mrs. Tarrow stands at the bottom of the sixteen steps, recycling buckets in each hand as she prepares to open her kitchen door.

I let out a deep breath.

"Sorry I surprised you," she calls up the narrow stairs.

"It's OK." More deep breaths. I'm dying to read the joke book from The Lady with the Joke Book in Her Purse. And there are still more tanks to clean, tanks that are two days overdue because of evenings spent with Liam in the City.

But I'm hungry and dinner with Mrs. Tarrow will do me good. The book and the buckets can wait.

I walk down the red-brick stairs, past the first rows of her garden. The tomatoes cluster on their wire parapets, ready to defend the green bell peppers down the hill.

As Mrs. Tarrow enters the kitchen with her buckets Zina rushes out to greet me, the yellow lab once again having used her charms to extend her mid-day break with our generous neighbor into a longer visit.

Mrs. Tarrow sees the book tucked under my arm and shakes her head. "Teri listened to him in the car in the mornings. I don't care for his... crap."

Crap is a very strong word for Mrs. Tarrow.

"It'll just take me a minute to get this pot boiling again," she says. Mrs. Tarrow knows I can't resist her spaghetti.

"Thank you," I tell her.

"The Board of Supervisors postponed the SoMa Triangle vote again today," she says, measuring the pasta. "I saw it on the news."

"Seems like the murder is blocking the project, not getting it approved," I tell her.

"Uh-huh." She picks up an onion, starts to peel off the skin. "So, that's the joke book from The Lady with the Joke Book in Her Purse?"

"Yes."

She meticulously cuts and cross-cuts the onion without dropping a single piece, her tiny hands confident at a task they've done ten thousand times.

Zina lies in the kitchen and watches the proceedings. Just in case.

"Jack always liked investigations like this," she tells me. "He would say, 'Someone is writing a script.'" She looks over at me. "And, whoever it was, they usually turned out to be guilty."

"Writing a script?"

She pauses for a moment, then buoys herself again. "Jack would say something like, 'Act 1, Scene 1, woman wearing gloves drops purse in front of innocent man so he'll pick it up and they'll have his fingerprints.'"

"I don't remember telling you about the gloves."

She smiles proudly. "You didn't have to. Act 1, Scene 2, the woman and her Supervisor-lover shot, off-stage, no witnesses. Act 1, Scene 3, the murder weapon shows up in a locker where you could have hidden it, again making you a prime suspect."

"Act I, Scene 4," I pick up the story. "The police ask me questions and I'm not good with questions."

Another smile. "Exactly."

"You know a lot of things about how criminals work, spending your life with a cop," I tell her.

"Jack understood a lot of things." She gathers the onion bits and sets them aside, then flashes me a smile. "But the person he understood best of all was me."

"I wish I could find someone who'd talk like that about me," I tell her.

Mrs. Tarrow deftly cuts paper-thin slices of garlic I could never hope to match. "You'll find someone, Steven. She's around here, somewhere."

"I'm not like normal guys," I tell her.

She acts as if we don't have this conversation every week when she invites me down for dinner. "You seem very intelligent and interesting and charming to me."

For some reason tonight I want to insist. "I'm not like normal guys," I tell her. "I come from… you know. My family."

She gives me her look and I know what's next. She says, "The best pots come from a kiln."

I don't talk about growing up in my family but if she thinks I'm talking about growing up in my family that's what she always says. "The best pots come from a kiln."

I don't want her to know it, but sometimes I say it to myself, over and over again.

When I feel like people are looking right through me as if I don't exist. "The best pots come from a kiln."

When I feel like everything I do is wrong. "The best pots come from a kiln."

When I feel like I really am what Paula thinks of me. "The best pots come from a kiln."

I do not want Mrs. Tarrow to know, but it is my ladder in a world where every elevator always seems to be going down.

31.

For Once He Appears to Have No Idea What to Say

Thursday, September 27

"Ladies and Gentlemen!" Liam the Fog Seller proclaims. "Welcome to Union Square!" He bows and doffs his black silk top hat.

Most of the diners at the outdoor cafes don't appear to notice.

"Yes, it's San Francisco's Union Square, where a famous logo magically transforms a $2 pair of socks into a $200 fashion statement! Where you can't see a Broadway play near the park without paying for an expensive ticket, but if you over-park you'll get an expensive ticket for free! Yes, Union Square, where everything you see is manufactured overseas by non-union labor!"

A few chuckles. Liam the Fog Seller is not discouraged when people ignore him.

Eventually some of those people laugh and give him money.

"The double-grande-sized phallic symbol behind me is not, as you may have thought, an ancient fertility obelisk. It is, in fact, a monument to the heroes of the War of 1898. Now, can anyone here tell me why we fought the War of 1898?"

Some passing tourists have stopped to watch him, as have more of the people sitting in the coffee shops. No one answers.

"Ah, so no one here remembers why we fought the War of 1898. Perhaps that tells us how important it is to be fighting wars!"

A smattering of applause. I have to leave soon for my afternoon shift, but I don't want to miss what happens next.

"So what is important to you? If the War of 1898 isn't memorable, what do you remember about coming to San Francisco? What makes you think of our fair city?"

"Some loud guy interrupting our lunch!" yells a man from a table bordering the plaza. Some onlookers laugh.

Liam laughs, too, tipping his hat in their direction. "Thank you, thank you! Now, what else will you always remember about San Francisco?"

"Cable cars!" someone yells.

"It's cold!" Several people call out in support of the fact that today it is, indeed, cold.

"Cold Cable Cars rumbling through the fog!" Liam proclaims. "Exactly!"

More smiles, more people watching now.

"Now, you can't take home a Cable Car. And you won't go home with the cold... as long as you dress warmly and drink lots of fluids! You, sir, zip up that jacket and order some green tea!"

Laughter. How can he do with a crowd of strangers what I can never do with anyone but Luis and Mrs. Tarrow?

Liam reaches into his black tuxedo jacket and pulls out one of his little vials. "This, ladies and gentlemen, this is how you remember San Francisco, with bottled fog! Yes, I personally collected this fog on the hilltops surrounding San Francisco Bay, and you can take it home as an icon of your trip to our fair city!"

A few people turn away, but most still listen.

"I have no 800 number, no infomercials, no private jet," Liam proclaims. "Pay anything or nothing, and I'll give you a bottle of San Francisco fog! I wish you all safe travels and warm embraces! Thank you very much for listening!"

As the crowd applauds, a little boy, no more than five, approaches Liam and holds out a dollar.

Liam looks down at him, hands on his hips. "I don't want your dollar," he tells the boy. "I want a high five instead!"

The boy slaps his hand and Liam hands him a vial of San Francisco Fog. He hurries back to his parents' table at the cafe, holding out his prize.

What started slowly turns into a good performance for Liam, over $20 for a handful of the little vials with the blue labels.

I'm about to hurry back to the Ferry Building when I see a young woman with long, wavy brown hair approach. "Hi, my name is Emma. I liked what you said," she says, holding out a dollar.

"Thank you, Emma," Liam says. He hands her a vial of fog.

"We lived in San Francisco when I was little. What I remember... My father worked over there, where the shoe store is now. It used to be the office furniture store." She straightens her purse strap on her shoulder. Her yellow cotton top has the letters UCD embroidered on the sleeve.

"I remember. I walked by there all the time," Liam tells her. He wants to pack up and move on, but can tell she wants to talk.

"He left when I was seven. I... I finally worked up the courage and drove down from Sacramento this morning to see if he might still be working here, or even if they knew where he might be. But it's not an office furniture store any more. Now they sell shoes." She pulls her purse strap up again.

Liam turns, meets her eyes. For once he appears to have no idea what to say. They just stand there looking at each other.

I have to get back to work or they'll sail without me.

Liam's supposed to leave on time, not make me late.

32.

A Puzzle Piece Packed
in the Wrong Box

Thursday, September 27 (Cont.)

I know I don't fit in. I'm like a puzzle piece packed in the wrong box.

Luis has a great wife, two smart kids. Luis fits in very well.

Yet here I am coaching him on how to look for a job. The voice in my head keeps saying, "Some career coach! How's that dream of being an English professor coming along?"

As much as I tear myself down, Luis tears himself down even more. "Just one of a million guys with a Spanish accent trying to feed his family," he tells himself. No high school diploma. Just another average face in another average crowd.

I know better. Mrs. Tarrow knows better. But Luis needs to remember that he knows better, too.

"OK!" I announce. "New job! Materials Handler at the Institute of Science, helping prepare for their move!"

I look at Luis to gauge his reaction.

"That's where your friend Paula works," he says.

"The very place," I confirm.

"Stevie, that's where you like to hang out."

"Exactly."

He shrugs his shoulders, reaches down to rub Zina's ears.

"I thought you'd enjoy working near Paula."

"You're the one who's in love with this girl," he says with a grin. "I never met her."

Mrs. Tarrow laughs.

"OK, OK. But wouldn't you like to work someplace where I can drop by and see you?"

"Sure," he says. "Sure."

Mrs. Tarrow looks at me and arches her eyebrows.

* * *

"I know you're not returning my calls and that's OK," I begin. "But I need to ask a favor."

The computer on the other end of the cell phone waits patiently to hear my request.

"Luis has no job because of me, because of The Lady with the Joke Book in Her Purse. You know my stories about Luis, what a great guy he is. He finds a gun on the ferry, and he doesn't know what to do, and then they find it and they arrest him but then they let him go because they realize he's trying to protect me even though I haven't done anything wrong and then the GM fires Luis even though he hasn't done anything wrong."

I pause for breath.

"Oh, and the gun they find in Luis' locker is the murder weapon from Candi Bonham. And the Supervisor."

I haven't even gotten to the point yet. I hate this.

"Actually, what I'm calling about is that I'm helping Luis find a temporary job till they sort all this out and he can come back to the *Louis H. Baar*. There are jobs for Materials Handlers at the Institute but Luis won't apply because he doesn't... Even though he's never met you, it's... he's heard me talk a lot... So I know you don't know him but I hope you'll suggest that someone call him and you know, check him out. Maybe you could put in a good word for him. He's... He's the most reliable guy I know."

I guess there's nothing else to say.

"I guess there's nothing else to say," I tell the recording.

I recite Luis' phone number. Then I add, "You don't have to call me back."

33.

It Is Time to Walk Away

Five years ago, as seen from Monday, October 1

It's been five years now, but it all still feels like it was just last week.

It is time to walk away.

I'm standing outside the big walnut doors that lead to the District Board Room. Mrs. Gonzalez, Tommy's mom, stands awkwardly in a corner. Her hands still tremble, fifteen minutes after her short speech in my defense.

The young woman who serves as translator stands beside her and talks about the weather to try to calm her down. Mrs. Gonzalez is violating the master rule of undocumented workers: drawing attention to herself. All to stand up for a teacher who has inspired her kids.

Don, the determined young president of the district's teachers union, huddles with a knot of supportive parents.

They have all come to speak for me, to praise my teaching, extol my character.

I am not used to this.

"An after-school project about famous detectives from literature, both men *and* women. What could be wrong with that?" Don asks the parents.

"Nothing!" they murmur.

I don't have to look at Mrs. Mortimer, the math teacher standing by the water fountain, to see her frown as she hears this.

She has never said a word to me about it, but she thinks something is very wrong with an 8th grader rolling up a piece of paper and dangling it from his lips to portray Dashiell Hammett's famous detective Sam Spade.

"How did a tube made from binder paper lead to accusing a teacher of selling drugs?" Don preaches. "His kids finished more books this year than any 8th grade in the County, because they learned to love reading!"

The parents clustered with him agree once again.

The kids from the Detectives project are all here tonight, all except Jenni, whose father is leading the attack. Lori and Cristina are clustered by themselves at the edge of the lobby. Jacob and David stand nearby. Cold air flows over them each time someone opens the door.

Jacob blames himself for starting this, but I tell them that bringing the characters to life is part of reading.

I hate having to wait like this. I've already made my decision, so what the School Board decides doesn't matter.

It is time to walk away.

I shake my head. I don't care anymore... I've done nothing wrong.

The door to the room re-opens and The Man with the Crooked Tie returns to sit across from me at the table.

"Well, Mr. Ondelle, we'll check all that out and talk to this Captain Kreitzer, but it appears to align with your application for employment."

"OK," I tell him, since I can't think of anything else to say.

"I just have a few more questions, Mr. Ondelle, and then we can wrap this up."

"I'm not good with questions," I tell him.

"I'll take care of the questions, Mr. Ondelle. You just keep giving me answers. Unless you want to graduate from random background checks to targeted FBI special investigation."

It's the same dance everywhere I go. I've done nothing wrong.

"So why did you pick the job of ferry deckhand after you resigned your position as a teacher? Seems like a strange career choice." His short dark brown hair is combed in the shape of an aircraft wing that projects out over his forehead.

"When you apply for lots of jobs and only one of them comes through, that job turns out to be a good choice."

He peers at me, apparently trying to decide if I'm being sarcastic or merely strange.

"You have an unusual way of speaking, Mr. Ondelle."

"People tell me that."

"You understand, these random interviews are carried out by the Department of Homeland Security to help defend America's ports, waterways and vital infrastructure."

I want to stand up and shout at him, "You idiot, why don't you just call Kreitzer's number?! This is no random interview! You get a call from a public phone on an anonymous tip line about a subversive nut case named Steve Ondelle who works on the *Louis H. Baar*. This isn't about national security! It's about a killer who's trying to divert attention to me!"

Instead of all this, I just say, "Yes. I think these interviews are a good idea."

"Are you saying you have something to tell me?"

"No. I just think it's good to make sure the ferries are safe."

Again, he appears unsure whether I am a malcontent mocking him or a grateful citizen praising his life's work.

"Do politics, the things you see on the news ever make you angry?" he asks.

"I never watch the news." I tell him.

"How about on the radio?"

"Sometimes the radio broadcasts make me angry," I concede.

He leans forward in his chair. "Tell me, Mr. Ondelle, when does the news on the radio make you angry?"

I decide to answer honestly. "When a Giants batter swings at ball four and strikes out with the tying run on second and Buster Posey on deck."

34.

Do I Look Like
I'm Up to Something?

Wednesday, October 3

I'm not like Leonard, or Liam, or even Paula. I can't just manufacture a story and march up to strangers and ask questions.

Last Friday I'd have waited the four weeks for Leonard to finish his temp assignment so he'd be at my side when I respond to a return call from a number on Candi Bonham's phone bill.

But last Friday is before this Monday. Before I'm summoned to meet The Man with the Crooked Tie who's been told I'm a dangerous psychotic working on the ferry.

Last Friday is before the double murderer who writes the script starring me as the killer sends another interrogator to the man who's not good with questions.

So when I get the voicemail returning my call to The Lee Agency, I have a choice. I can wait for Leonard and take the chance that I miss an opportunity to help Luis.

Or I can screw up all my courage and go up there and talk to them. Alone. By myself.

The Lee Agency's web page proclaims that they are the top San Francisco source for trade show hosts and hostesses. Their founder, Ms. Victoria Lee, is a very elegant Chinese woman. A press release announces that they are the official agency for exhibitors at the big CDA Show, which will take place at San Francisco's Moscone Convention Center.

I have no idea what the big CDA Show is, but I am nevertheless impressed.

If I give myself time to think about it I'll chicken out. I need to just march in there and talk to them, make it up as I go along, the way Leonard or Liam would do it. My heart is pure and all that, so the world will pave the way.

I finish my morning chores and wave to Alonzo. I walk down the gangplank. I stride past the Gandhi statue that sits behind the Ferry Building.

* * *

The Lee Agency is headquartered in a narrow, modern nine-story office building sandwiched between two old storefronts. As befits the top San Francisco Agency for trade show hosts and hostesses, they are across the street from one wing of the sprawling Moscone Convention Center.

The sign in the lobby says that the Lee Agency is in Suite 900, in the Penthouse. I get in the elevator and push the button labeled "9."

Nothing happens.

I push it again. Still nothing.

I retreat to the lobby, return to the sign. This time I notice a small red button at the lower right, next to a numeric keypad. Above it a label says, "Press button and dial suite # for access."

I have not considered this. My plan is to politely enter the office, ask to speak to Ms. Lee and then ask if she worked with Candi Bonham and see what happens.

I look at the door to Howard St. It would be easy to walk out. Kreitzer has the copy of the phone bill. He will already have made all these same calls, I'm unlikely to learn anything that a trained police detective would miss.

But Luis needs to get his job back, I need to make the murderer stop targeting me. Doing something feels better than doing nothing. Maybe Ms. Lee will tap her forehead and tell me things she suddenly remembers that she forgot to tell the cops.

I've been living with Liam too long. He's starting to rub off on me.

I press the red button and a loud dial tone fills the tiny lobby. I key in 9-0-0 and after three loud tones a louder phone rings.

"The Lee Agency. How may I help you?" asks a woman's loud-but-melodic voice.

"I'm... I'm here to ask about one of your assignments."

The front door opens and two young men enter, each carrying a stack of identical books titled *Persist or Perish*.

"OK," the voice asks me, "do you have the assignment number?"

"I, uh... no. I don't have it with me."

The two guys pass behind me, debating whether they should hand the books out themselves or give them to Glenda. The elevator door closes and they disappear.

"Do you have the location?" the voice asks pleasantly.

"I think it's Moscone," I ad lib.

The front door opens again and a young woman enters, dressed casually in a gray sweater and jeans. She stands respectfully behind me, waiting to press the red button and enter a suite number for access.

The voice on the speaker hesitates. "Are you selling something?" The tone is not suspicious or accusatory. More like "You naughty little devil, you!"

"No, I... No."

"Jen, does the man in front of you look dangerous?" the voice asks.

The woman waiting behind me laughs.

"No. Not very." She has blonde hair pinned back with a plastic tortoiseshell comb and unnaturally perfect teeth.

"That's what I thought," the voice says. "Jen, you mind bringing him up?"

"Sure." Jen looks at me, flashes the smile again and says "Please, right this way. It's the rear elevator."

We get in, the doors close and the car starts moving up before we can even press a button.

The elevator doors open on a large waiting room with a sofa and chairs scattered against the walls. A museum poster depicting Chinese opera masks of the 18th century sits above the sofa, between two images of smiling-but-serious models. The photo closest to the elevator has slipped a quarter of an inch in a counter-clockwise direction in its frame.

Three young women are in the waiting area, reading or peering at cell phones. Behind the desk is another young woman, the owner of the melodious voice in the lobby. She wears a white blouse with a stiff collar and has short dark hair.

"Di's already in there," she tells my companion. "Just go on in."

"Nice meeting you," Jen says to me, flashing her perfect smile. A buzzer sounds and she walks through a door labeled "Private."

The receptionist now turns to me. "OK, let's see if we can help you."

"Thank you," I say. "Is there a chance I could speak with Ms. Lee?"

She looks up at me, her tone again conspiratorial. "That... that is very unlikely. What are you up to?"

Up to? Do I look like I'm up to something? I look around the room. The waiting women are ignoring us. A monitor on the reception desk shows the lobby downstairs.

"We don't have any calls out for male associates right now. You're not selling anything. So you must be up to something." She smiles up at me proudly. *Quod erat demonstrandum.*

One of the women who is ignoring us giggles in appreciation of the receptionist's logic.

I have no idea what to do next.

Paula would say something responsible. Leonard would have a snappy comeback. Liam would ask for her help.

"I need to ask your help," I tell her.

She gives me the "I think I've heard this one before" look, but says nothing.

"Has Candi Bonham ever worked with you guys?"

The smile disappears. The curiosity vanishes.

"Why do you ask?"

"I'm... I'm trying to..." What exactly am I trying to do?

The "Private" door opens and a woman I recognize as Victoria Lee walks out, flanked by Jen and another young woman with another perfect smile.

Lee looks at me, then back at Jen. "This is the male model?"

Jen laughs.

The receptionist does not. "He's asking about Candi Bonham, Ms. Lee."

Now they all go stiff, suddenly suspicious.

All but Victoria Lee. "I take it you are not a police officer," she says calmly.

"No. I... But I have permission from Captain Kreitzer."

"And what kind of permission is that?" The crease in her black slacks is sharp and straight, as is her posture. Her face beneath the bangs and perfectly-styled shoulder-length black hair suggests she's 40, but her presence suggests far older.

I realize how stupid I sound. "I'm... Right after Candi does this gig on the ferry they find her murdered... My best friend loses his job because of it."

They all just stand there and stare at me.

"I'm not telling it right because it's complicated, but I'm trying to get his job back. If... If you've already given the police all the information they want, then... I guess there's not much more I can do."

Victoria Lee stands completely still for several seconds, the expression on her face both neutral and severe. Everyone now looks at her.

"Come in," she says.

It is a command, not an invitation.

"Kreitzer would of course not come see me himself," she says, once I am obediently in my seat.

"I have his card if you need it. If you have anything to share with him." Could I really have found a link that he has missed?

"I do not need to share anything with Lieutenant Kreitzer," she says. Trophies made of brass and crystal and silver crowd the top of the credenza behind her chair.

"You know him?"

"Long ago."

"He's a Captain now."

She is looking somewhere over my head, but at nothing in particular. "I know."

I have no idea what to say. As it turns out, I don't have to say anything.

"Here is what you tell your Lieutenant Kreitzer," she says. "Candi did none of her private business here."

She stops, turns to the computer, types something. Waits. Types something else.

Her posture remains perfectly erect, as if her spine were King Arthur's Sword sunk in bedrock at a precise 90 degrees.

She reads something on the screen, then turns back to me. "Candi did eighteen events for this agency last year. She was late once. Evaluations were good. Not great, but good."

The door opens and the receptionist walks in with some papers, which she hands to Victoria Lee without looking at me. The crease in her slacks is a copy of her boss, though her spine lacks the same steel blade.

Lee looks over the documents, pulls a large envelope from her desk drawer, inserts the papers, folds down the metal brad.

"Here is what you tell your Lieutenant Kreitzer," she says again. "I will give you this list of all her assignments. I will tell you that she had the look, and that because she had the look I assigned her only to the show floor, receptions and to conference hospitality. No 'gigs on the ferry.'"

I don't know what "the look" is, but based upon the expression on Victoria Lee's face it is unsavory.

"She was a Lee Associate. Even if she were freelancing, she was still part of my team. I will do everything I can to see that the person who did this to her is caught. He can send Li back here and I will speak to him. He can send you. You can have all the paperwork you want."

"Thank you," I tell her.

"But Lieutenant Kreitzer," she says, "I will not speak to him. Do you understand?"

"Yes, ma'am."

She hands me the envelope.

I stand, thank her again and turn to go. Then stop myself and turn back to face her.

"You know I'm not a police officer, right?"

"Yes," she says without looking up from her desk. "I know." She resumes working as if I have already left the room.

I leave the room.

35.

If I Find Him I'm Afraid
of What I'll Find

Thursday, October 4

Liam the Fog Seller stands by the side entrance to the St. Francis Hotel, just down the block from Union Square. A crowd of Japanese tourists has gathered on the sidewalk, waiting patiently to board a row of tour buses.

"Welcome to San Francisco! Welcome!" Liam shouts, bowing deeply to the crowd with a flourish of his top hat. Most of the waiting visitors ignore him. A cable car rattles down the hill on Powell St. and he waits for it to pass. The gripman waves.

"I have a big piece of San Francisco that I have made small just for you!" Liam begins again, pantomiming big and small things with his suddenly-delicate hands. He has miniature American and Japanese flags tucked into the ribbon on his black silk top hat.

He pulls out a vial of fog and holds it up proudly. "This, ladies and gentlemen, is the fog of San Francisco, freshly transported from where it surrounds you and swept into this vial, where you surround it and take it home with you." He pantomimes the vistas of nature and a warm embrace.

If you could see him do it you'd get what I mean.

It looks like some of the waiting tourists may be warming to him. A few of them smile.

"Thank you" he shouts. "If you would like a vial of San Francisco fog I will give you one. If you would like to drop money in the box, you may do that, too. Whatever you wish to pay, anything or nothing."

A middle-aged woman comes over, drops a dollar in the box. Liam bows, hands her a vial, thanks her, she retreats. Two more follow.

An older man comes over. He holds out a twenty dollar bill, far more than Liam can change from the dollars in the box.

Liam shakes his head. "No, thank you," he says, smiling. "It is too much. Here, this is my gift to you." He gives him a vial, extending the gift with both hands as he bows.

Another woman from the group walks over, speaks to the man in Japanese.

"Thank you!" he says, and accepts the vial of fog.

The woman guides the man back towards his wife. "Thank you!" she calls over her shoulder.

"Have fun!" Liam calls to them.

Soon every seat is filled and the doors close on the last bus in line. Liam waves goodbye with his big top hat.

"I saw what you just did," says a voice behind him.

It is Emma Hernandez, the girl from Sacramento who's looking for her father.

Emma. Who stands with her eyes locked with Liam's and does not move when I need to rush back to the Ferry Building for my afternoon shift, just a week ago today. Who seems as suddenly connected to him as he seems to be connected to her.

So many things that Liam can do that I cannot.

"That was very sweet."

Liam looks at the departing bus. "Always better to take nothing than to take too much."

She cocks her head at him and smiles.

"You back to search for your dad?" he asks her.

"I guess. I'm not sure. I'm afraid I won't find him. And if I don't try, but then... I'm afraid..." She moves her purse strap higher on her shoulder, checks the clasp. "If I find him. I'm afraid of what I'll find."

* * *

Liam sits across from Emma upstairs at Dave's Diner, a 1950's retro place that serves both the tourists and the workers of Union Square.

"Steve has gotten to know this cop who's investigating the murder of an actress who did a gig on the ferry. He could talk to the guy, ask him to try to trace your dad."

Emma shivers. "I don't want to find him... that way. If that's the only way I find him I don't..." Her voice trails off.

"I understand," Liam says.

She wears a white turtleneck sweater and long silver earrings that get tangled in her wavy hair when she plays with one of them, which is whenever she talks about her father. Now she unhooks one from her ear, uses both hands to release the beads from a stubborn curl.

"Hernandez isn't an unusual name. That makes it harder, but I can check it for you on the computer tonight."

She rests her chin in her hands. "Already tried, nothing there."

"You never know," he says. "I'm pretty good and I can get Steve to help me."

She looks right at him. "I'm not a helpless girl."

He looks embarrassed. "I guess veterinary students have to be pretty good with computers."

"Even those who bake bread for a living," she says.

Liam laughs. "How long till you're practicing medicine and we see a line of cats and dogs and race horses at your door?"

"No race horses. And I want to work in veterinary physical therapy, not as a vet. I'm completing my M.S. and volunteering at the shelter with Dr. Cosgrove so I can get more experience."

He looks at her in surprise. "They do physical therapy on animals?"

"Dr. Cosgrove got a grant to study canine elbow dysplasia this year and it's a really exciting new field. It'll take another year to get my PT certification after I finish my Master's, and Manny really needs me at the bakery so I have a steady job and it all fits into my plans."

"When you do find your dad," Liam says, "he's going to be crazy proud of you."

She smiles sadly. "If I find him."

"I lost my dad, too," Liam says. "Cancer. I was 18."

"I'm sorry."

He shakes his head. "Nothing we could do. Just watch him waste away."

Emma sits in silence for a while. "That's what I want to know, I guess. Some dads leave. Some dads are taken away. I want to know which one, which kind my dad is. Or was."

Liam looks at her deep brown eyes and I see him going places that I have never seen him go.

His burger is getting cold. We rarely spend the money to go to restaurants and he should be eating.

"Your burger's getting cold," she tells him.

He looks down, picks it up, takes a bite.

At least she's sensible.

* * *

Mrs. Tarrow raises her tiny glass of amaretto and I clink it with my half-empty water glass. "To Luis!" she says.

"To Luis!"

He has an interview next Monday at the Institute of Science. An interview arranged by Paula Costa.

Mrs. Tarrow gives me a big smile. "It was very clever of you to call and suggest that she reach out to him."

"I have to remember that just because she's not speaking to me doesn't mean she's not speaking to someone else."

"True enough. And maybe the next step is..."

I shake my head. "My luck reserves are all used up after getting Victoria Lee to speak to me."

"I can't believe you went all by yourself and walked in and said, 'I'm Steve Ondelle and I have some questions!'"

Zina raises her head and looks at me, apparently amazed as well.

"I don't want any more visits from The Man with the Crooked Tie."

"You know, Steven, every time the killer does something like this to try to incriminate you he gives... he or she gives Ken Kreitzer more to work with. They're trying to write that script about you but they keep telling us more and more about themselves. One slip and he'll have them."

"He or she hasn't made any slips yet," I remind her.

She salutes me with her glass. "'Yet', my dear Steven. They haven't made any slips yet."

36.

With 90 Dark Days Left to Go

Sunday, October 7

Eli of the Coral Reef peers down from our perch high above home plate, his scorecard balanced on his lap. It is covered with intricate notations in his miniscule yet legible handwriting, recording the result of every play and the call of every pitch.

Sometimes I'll keep score at a game. Eli prepares everything for The Congressional Record.

Behind us a short, balding guy is shooting the action on video, marking down plays on a clipboard. A couple of times he calls down to Eli, says he missed a play, asks what happened.

Eli always has an answer.

And a big smile.

"Thanks for getting these," Eli tells me again. "Great seats."

Eli won't come by himself but if you come with him he's like a kid in a candy shop, and the effect will last for days.

It's warm today, but I can feel Eli's winter coming. It starts today, the last Giants game of the year. Then, in January, Judson Aquarium shuts down for the move to its new home, closing the coral reef exhibit with 90 dark days still left to go before baseball season.

The 90 days when both of Eli's lifelines, the Giants and the coral reef, will be cut.

I keep suggesting that Eli should find a new hobby, a new passion to carry him until the new aquarium opens, but all he does is roll his eyes.

The Giants have endured a lousy season. We're 16 games out of first and the people in the stands look shell-shocked, stoic or stoned.

Eli beams at every pitch. "Look there," he says. "Crawford's moved six inches closer to second two pitches in a row and Martin hasn't changed his lead. He's setting the trap."

I look down at the Giants' shortstop. The pitch is a fastball for a called strike on the inside corner. He examines his glove and casually moves six inches to his left.

"You see?" Eli says. "Watch, he's gonna do it again." The game ticket juts proudly from his shirt pocket. His smile could light up the entire city.

And all I have to do is buy two nosebleed seats for the game.

Some days, some places, I can make a difference in this world.

37.

And the Cowboys Showed Up
at the Hospitality Suite

Monday, October 8

Leaving no stone unturned means you have to go to places you would never go. Like the Dizzying Heights Hair Salon in Pacific Heights.

I am once again flying solo and flying blind. After my bizarre welcome at the Lee Agency last week I now seem to expect that just walking in the door will move people to hand me reams of information about Candi Bonham, inspired by my mission to return Luis Deverro to his job.

Last week I dutifully hand Kreitzer the list of Candi's assignments from Victoria Lee. He examines them with barely-concealed joy, then looks up at me as if I were a toy car that turns out to have a real engine.

"How in the hell did you get her to give you these?" he asks. I sit in the old gray steel chair in front of his old gray steel desk.

"She says that even though Candi would free-lance she's still part of her team and she wants to help any way she can. She says she'll give anything you want to Lieutenant Li."

Kreitzer looks like he can't tell whether he wants to smile or to punch someone.

"But let me guess. She will still never ever speak to me."

"Something like that."

He rubs the back of his neck. "Figures." Someone has tried to write an obscenity on the old desk with the back of their shoe heel, but the only product of their effort is a crude letter "F."

"Why is she so angry?" I ask.

He shakes his head. "Sealed records." Now a small smile. "But I'll answer you the way that you answer questions for me. Let's say you bust a guy who owns a modeling agency on charges of prostitution, and you also arrest his wife."

"OK."

"Let's also say that it turns out that the venture was a little side project by the husband. The wife runs an honest business and doesn't know he's booking extra jobs for the talent."

"Seems like she's not someone who'd miss important details."

"Not now, but... As you would say, once you arrest someone for something they didn't do they're never going to forget that."

I nod. That is in fact how I would say it.

Kreitzer leans back in his chair, the old springs squealing in protest. "He pled out, we were able to keep her out of the papers and her arrest record was expunged since it was a mistake. She divorced him, life went on."

My heart jumps, thinking of Liam's note from last week. "So why can't you do the same thing for Luis Deverro?" I ask. "His arrest record is a mistake. Can't you just expunge it, too?"

"Already did, though it could be unsealed if he were arrested again."

I'm overjoyed, practically exploding with excitement. "Then you can call Mr. Grainger and get Luis his job back!"

"Already did that, too," Kreitzer says. "The guy wouldn't budge."

"What???" I realize I'm standing up, leaning forward on the desk. I sit back down.

"I suggested it three different ways. No dice."

"Why?"

"Luis admitted he found the gun and didn't turn it in. Even though we were willing to overlook it – hell, I must have sounded nuts explaining that away – your Mr. Grainger was very clear. A gun on the ferry and you're fired. He said the union backed him."

I slump forward, my head in my hands. "How am I going to get Luis his job back now?"

Kreitzer's voice has a tone I have not heard from him before. "I don't know. But I'll try to help."

So here I am, turning over more stones. Ascending the steep sidewalks of California St. to the Dizzying Heights Hair Salon, the next number on Candi's phone bill. In search of more miracles.

The salon is a modern marvel of glass and aluminum, set on the second floor of an older building that has been renovated so many times that it has lost all sense of its original design.

I press the buzzer and a young woman's voice says, "Yes, may I help you?"

"Hi, I'm Steve Ondelle," I say, trying to keep my courage up. "I... I'm sorry, I don't have an appointment."

A moment passes and the glass door buzzes to tell me I've been granted entry. The steep, narrow staircase has an undulating cast iron handrail that looks like a massive vine with leaves shaped like arrowheads. At the top of the stairs is another glass door, this one unlocked.

As I enter a tall young African American woman approaches. "Hi, Steve, I'm Savannah. I'm free right now – how can I help you?" Two other women remain intent on their clients, but I can tell that everyone in the room appears fascinated about whether I'll ask for a Number Two razor cut or just a little bit off the sides.

"I'm trying to help my friend get his job back," I start out, and the mood goes bad in a hurry. Savannah takes two steps back, glancing at the older of her co-workers.

"I'm trying to find information about Candi Bonham's activities so the police can make an arrest. Then my friend can... It's complicated, but he can get his job back."

Savannah looks back and forth between me and her boss. The older woman hesitates.

I keep going. "If Candi Bonham has visited here at all in the last few weeks and you remember anything about what she says or does... I have the business card of the police Captain who is investigating the case."

The older stylist turns to me. Her thick rubber gloves are covered with black dye, as is the rubber apron she wears to protect her sweatshirt and jeans. "Candi was my client. The police have been here already. None of us had seen Candi since June, more than two months before she died."

"I'm just..."

"Now, sir, this is a business and all of us need to get back to work."

I nod. "Thanks. I'm sorry to bother you." Savannah steps forward to guide me out.

A voice comes from the foil-covered head sitting in the chair beside the manager. "Is Candi that actress who was killed with the Supervisor?"

"Yes," the manager and I answer in unison.

The woman tries to turn to face me, her silhouette bizarre with fifty tufts of hair sticking through the aluminum foil on her head. Her face is old, made older by the cap of foil, with deep bags under her eyes and nests of wrinkles around her mouth. "She was here on my last visit. So sad, we were all sitting here laughing and a week later she was dead."

"It must have been someone else," the manager says. "Candi was my client."

"The stylist... she was the very tall blonde girl. She's been here on and off since..."

"Bernadette!" the manager growls. "The little bitch!"

"I'm getting cold here," says the younger woman's customer.

"Sorry!" The stylist runs hot water, goes back to washing the customer's hair.

"Couldn't be Bernadette," Savannah says. "She went back to school, back in January."

The stylist groans as she applies shampoo to her client's hair. "It's my fault, Jeannie. I had her cover some Saturday appointments that weekend my in-laws showed up. It was six weeks ago. Maybe Candi walked in that day?"

"Maybe the little bitch called half my clients and offered them..."

"So you never heard the story about the twin cowboys and the hookers?" The older client turns even farther towards me, a wicked smile on her wrinkled face.

Everyone in the room looks at her, mouths open.

"Is this a bad joke?" Jeannie says. "Turn around and hold still."

The woman complies, but keeps talking. "Candi told us this story about how she got assigned to work the front desk at a hospitality suite at the Vergessen Hotel for this convention, but she mixed up the suite number and went to the wrong floor."

Savannah sits down in the waiting area, engrossed in the story. Jeannie takes a lock of hair and slides it between the bristles of a narrow brush. The younger stylist is rinsing her customer's hair but hanging on every word. For the moment I am forgotten, a fly on the wall standing at the front of the salon.

"So she went to this big suite at the Vergessen, because that's where the company thing was supposed to be, and the double-doors were unlocked so she thought it was the hospitality suite and she walked in, but the place was empty so she thought, you know, that they just hadn't set up yet, and she heard voices so she walked round this corner and that's where the door to the bedroom was."

"Oh, God..." Jeannie says. She dips her brush in the cup of goop and runs it along another tuft of hair.

"Candi told us – it was hilarious! She told us the room had two identical queen beds and that each identical queen bed had an identical man wearing nothing but an identical cowboy hat. And these two identical twins were banging the brains out of what looked like two identical blondes. Or at least, she said, the blondes' boobs and butts were identical!"

No one else laughs. Maybe you have to have been there.

The woman keeps talking. "We all laughed till we cried. Of course, none of us knew that Candi... Anyway, she hightailed it out of there and found the right room and did her shift, but it was all just so hilarious."

"And then the cowboys showed up at the hospitality suite, right?" Jeannie says skeptically.

The woman shakes her head and Jeannie shouts, "Hold still, please!"

"No," the woman says. "That would just be too silly if the cowboys showed up at the suite. The story was already about as silly as any story could possibly be. I mean, if you leave out the part about Candi dying and everything."

She's right. Leaving out that part helps.

38.

I Have to Learn from Liam

Monday, October 8 (Cont.)

Siphon-haul-dump. Siphon-haul-dump.

Tomorrow I will go back to Kreitzer's office and tell him the story of Candi and the twin cowboys in the hospitality suite. I will tell him who I have talked to, what they've said.

I do not think he will find it to be as silly as any story could possibly be.

After this, I am done.

I am done calling numbers from a dead woman's phone bill, violating her privacy and invading more innocent lives.

I am done visiting places I would never visit and asking questions I would never ask. I am done clenching my teeth and then opening my mouth to speak.

I am done trying to prove I am innocent of any crime when I already know that I am innocent of any crime.

I have to learn from Liam. Break the cycle. Live as someone who deserves a life and not look over my shoulder to see who's coming to take it away.

It happens in my family. My father dies and everything comes apart.

It happens at my school. People freak over nothing and it all comes apart.

It happens with The Lady with the Joke Book in Her Purse, but this time it's Luis whose life comes all apart.

I can help Luis find a job, but I have to break this cycle. Live more like Liam and less like a victim waiting for the next attack.

Siphon-haul-dump.

Zina whimpers up at me, empathetic as always. She can tell when things aren't right.

Kreitzer has people to help him, people who know what they're doing. People who get paid.

Lightning strikes twice. Or maybe the lightning is no coincidence. The woman who will never speak to Kreitzer decides to speak to me.

The beauty shop customer who isn't there when the police stop by decides to share a silly story about twin cowboys on a sex adventure.

But this is not me. It cannot be me.

After this, I am done.

39.

By the Time I'm Back
He Will Be Gone

Ten years ago, as seen from Wednesday, October 10

In some ways it seems like forever ago. In some ways it feels like last September.

The old hand-me-down suitcase and the new blue duffel bag sit by the door.

The taxi is due in five minutes.

I look out the window at Mt. Tamalpais. I know this is the last five minutes of one era of my life. Once I walk out this door nothing will ever be the same again.

In five more minutes this will not be home. It will just be where I grew up.

My father sees my look. Maybe he misreads it.

"Hey, big guy. You're going to do great in college. It was one of the best four years of my life."

I look over, see his smile, smile back at him. He has rolled the wheelchair towards the glass door so he can see my face. Once his powerful shoulders could have propelled him with a single push. Now a few feet across the hardwood floor is a strain for his emaciated arms. He tries to catch his breath.

The day is warm and sunny, but waves of cold air keep flowing over me.

"I'm not worried," I tell him. "I'm just... I'm just looking at the mountain one last time. I'm going to miss this place, miss you guys."

"We'll see you at Thanksgiving," Dad says reassuringly.

What I don't say is that I'm terrified that by the time I'm back he will be gone. As best as I can get him and Mom to tell me, the timing will be touch and go.

"It's only ten weeks, honey," my mother says. I see in her eyes how the days are rushing by, like leaves carried off by autumn winds.

Ten weeks may be too long. We all know it. So there's no point in saying it.

The irony is that she's sober. All these years of trying to control her drinking, and she can never do it. She can't get sober for Dad, even though he's never left her. She can't get sober for me, even though I'm a little kid trapped in her wild, warped world.

"What's great is that when I looked at the calendar," she says happily, "this year, between Thanksgiving and Christmas is less than four weeks."

Now that Dad is sick there's no one to take care of her. No one to make her dinner when she's too drunk to open a can of soup. No one to pull her up off the floor when she drops down in a heap and pees herself. No one to fight with for hours every night about money, or about some past slight, or about something she imagines seeing on TV.

No one to go out and buy her vodka to save the money she'd spend calling up Imperial Liquor and having them deliver.

"I'm doing pretty well these days," Dad says. "Once I stopped the radiation I started feeling a lot better."

So she proves herself wrong. She gets sober. For the last three months of high school, for my last summer living at home with my parents, I get what's left of my real mom back.

But Fate has a mean streak. In order to return my mother, it first must take my dad.

The only link I ever have to a sane and normal world.

"You're looking better, Dad," I tell him. It's true. The radiation turns him from an active middle-aged man into an invalid in four sessions. Despite the implications of stopping treatment, he has gained a little weight and his face seems less haunted and narrow.

Maybe they're right. Maybe we'll get one more Christmas together. Maybe I won't have to rush home one night and hope I arrive in time to say a last good-bye.

The taxi sounds its horn outside, a piercing note that dies away off-key.

My mom goes to the wheelchair, rolls it towards the door so we can say good-bye. I look at the old suitcase, think about us taking it on vacation when I am a little boy, when it's too heavy for me to carry and Dad has to haul it to the car. Our last real vacation together. When I still think we are a normal family.

She comes around the wheelchair. I give her a hug, and she holds me tightly. "We'll see you soon, honey. We're very proud of you."

"Thanks, Mom," I tell her.

I lean over to say good-bye and hug my dad, and I start to cry.

I cannot stop.

He does not know what to do with this. "It's OK, big guy," he says. "You have to go off to college. It's time for you. You'd just get bored if you stayed here."

I bury my head in his shoulder, still crying uncontrollably.

The taxi sounds its off-key horn again.

My mom rubs my back with her hand, the way she does when I am very little and it's time to go to sleep.

"It's all right, darling," she says. "It's OK for you to go." She reaches out and opens the front door.

I shake my head to clear it. I realize it is not ten years ago. I am not standing with my parents. A chill runs through me from the open door.

I am not listening to her.

But I can still hear my landlord Mrs. Blount talking. I watch her nervous hands as she plays with the pearls on her bracelet, moving them like a baby with a ring of plastic beads.

"We really hate to displace you like this, but... You've got the full thirty days, we wouldn't budge on that, even when they offered us a bonus. And we've been looking on Craigslist and there are some really nice places open right now."

I am not listening to her.

"Separate places, like this. So you're not, you know. Inside someone's house." She picks cat hair from the front of her black sweater and forces a smile.

I am being evicted. Losing my garage, my house, my home.

I am not listening to her.

We're standing in place, frozen, my hand still clutching the knob of the freshly-opened door that is closing another chapter in my life. Mrs. Blount remains on the front step, her hand still worrying at her bracelet, her very black hair knotted behind her neck.

I can't move somewhere where they do a credit check because I have no credit card. Neither does Liam. They do not give Fog Sellers credit cards.

Where will I put my aquariums, my fish?

I have to have a concrete floor because water weighs eight pounds a gallon. My 210-gallon weighs over a ton all by itself when you add all the rocks and gravel.

The insurance. They all want insurance.

"We... I know that a two year lease is something you can't match... You have been very good about the month to month, but the price they offered..." Her voice trails off. She looks down at her red canvas shoes with the gold laces. The one on her left foot will come untied soon but the right one looks OK.

I am not listening to her.

Zina stands beside me, knows something is wrong. She whines softly, twice.

Liam can adapt to anything, but I have to be able to walk home from the ferry. To reset myself. To re-balance.

"Is Liam here?" Mrs. Blount asks. "I've only seen him a few times but he seems so nice. I know this is bad news. I was hoping he was home so I could tell him myself. Tell you both, I mean."

I know what she means.

"It's OK, I'll tell him," I say. Then I nod and close the door.

I look at my tanks. Over six tons of water, give or take.

Zina rubs against my leg and looks up at me with those big brown eyes, as if to say "I only weigh 60 pounds."

I kneel down and give the graceful yellow lab a hug, grateful for the warmth. She does her best to hug me back.

Liam's right. Sometimes you want a friend who lives on the same side of the glass as you do.

40.

I'll Settle for Someone
Who Can Tolerate Me

Wednesday, October 10 (Cont.)

Mrs. Tarrow looks at me across the top of her laptop on the kitchen counter. "Steven, it's no bother. I can park the Volvo on the street. It's from Sweden. It can handle Sausalito."

I shake my head. "I can't take your garage."

She shakes her head back at me, her silver hair swinging back and forth. "The garage is for the fish. Teri's old room is for you. For both of you, including Zina."

"Thank you," I tell her, and I mean it. "But we should find a place that's... that isn't a room in someone's house. Even your house."

"Steven, sometimes you can be very stubborn." She returns to scanning the website for Sausalito rentals.

There must be fifty townhomes, apartments, duplexes and houseboats we could share. And each costs far more than a ferry deckhand and an artisan street performer could ever pay.

A complex called "Moonshine River" advertises that it's conveniently close to local schools. I point out the contradiction and Mrs. Tarrow laughs, her eyes sparkling.

"Ah, Steven," she says. "We have to find someone here in town who will appreciate you."

"We only have twenty-nine days," I tell her. "I'll settle for someone who can tolerate me."

She glances at me over the screen of her laptop and continues clicking.

A half hour later we have a list of places she'll call in the morning, and she announces it's time for bed. Zina hears this, gets up and goes to the door, ready to climb the sixteen narrow brick steps back to our-home-for-just-29-more-days.

I give Mrs. Tarrow a hug, and then she puts a hand on each of my shoulders. "You know this is no coincidence," she says, very seriously. "Our friend is writing another chapter in the script. They've run out of ways to make you look guilty, so now they're trying to stress you out and make you act crazy."

I look over at where Zina stands impatiently by the door.

"I know," I tell her. "I know."

41.

Romanticizing the Dirty Backwaters of Sausalito

Thursday, October 11

How can he be so calm?

Liam sits across from Emma in a booth at Dave's Diner, just like last week. She's driven down from Sacramento on her day off, just like the last two weeks.

"Mrs. Tarrow wants us to move in with her for a little while, just till the right place turns up," he's telling her. She listens thoughtfully, her hands playing with the cord of her faded red 49ers hoodie. He has a burger coming. She's having a salad.

I feel as if I'm nowhere in the room.

"That gives us a safety net," he's saying. "Mrs. Tarrow loves Zina.

We can look around, she'll scout the online sites for us. Pretty amazing, a little old lady who's not afraid of computers."

"My mom was like that," Emma says. "Only she never had the chance to get old."

He leans forward. "You know, it's scary similar. I lost my dad, you lost your mom while we're both young. My mom, your dad... both among the missing."

She looks at the old posters on the back wall. "Yeah."

"And you have Manny and we have Mrs. Tarrow."

"She does seem like... But isn't Sausalito expensive?"

"The parts the tourists see, the houses on the hill." Liam's eyes light up. "But there are lots of other places, too. Old boats tucked in the corners of expensive harbors. Converted shacks from the old shipyards. Shipping containers that have high-efficiency wood stoves and a view of the Bay."

He sounds like he's channeling one of his books, a veritable 21st-century Jack London.

She is enthralled. The way no woman ever is with me.

After being evicted with no warning I am on the edge of panic, with less than a month to find a place we can afford that can take six tons of aquariums and a 60-pound dog.

Liam is calmly romanticizing the dirty backwaters of Sausalito. Places where six tons of aquariums could never go.

I'm living in the cross-hairs of a murderer who keeps trying to take away the life I've worked so hard to rebuild.

Liam is happily pursuing this new romance with a carefree joy that is as alien to me as inhaling fire.

The food comes and we dig in. "What's your place like?" Liam asks, his mouth half full of burger.

Emma looks out the window at the old facades of Powell St., playing absently with one beaded earring. "Not like here," she says. "In Sacramento the apartments all have two stories, stucco walls and a pool shaped like Africa."

"Your place like that?"

She smiles at him. "At least my place is close to the bakery. I can walk to work and everything smells good every morning."

They each take hungry bites of lunch.

"Manny's bakery," Liam asks, "do you have apple turnovers?"

"Sure. Manny makes great ones. And blueberry and cherry, and sometimes peach. Whatever's in season."

He shakes his head. "I love 'em all, but Steve only eats turnovers with apples in them, and he only eats them in places in San Francisco where he spent time with his dad."

She inspects the depths of her salad so she won't have to comment on my rules of apple turnover consumption, a kindness I appreciate. She spears a tomato wedge and deftly changes the subject.

I appreciate that, too.

"So would you guys live someplace like that? In a storage container?" Emma sounds like she's both fascinated and repelled by the idea.

"The one I saw actually wasn't all that bad. But we have to find someplace with a concrete pad, to hold up Steve's aquariums."

OK, so maybe I don't feel so ignored after all.

"I'd love to see them," Emma says. "And Zina the Wonder Dog, spelled Z-I-N-A, not with an X."

I already have a lot of things to deal with right now. The Lady with the Joke Book in Her Purse. Losing our home. Luis losing his job. Paula.

Liam needs to slow down, be careful or he'll just get hurt. When things start out this well the ending is always excruciating.

How can he be so calm?

"We'd love to have you over sometime, any time you like," Liam says.

"A week from next Thursday?" she asks. "I can come down next week but I can't stay because I have to open for Manny first thing Friday morning. But in two weeks..."

"Done," Liam says happily. "A week from next Thursday."

If this means what I think it does I'm going to have to change my plans. There are times when I'd just be in the way.

42.

But Not the Kind of Nuts They're After

Friday, October 12

"Carl Mathis and Tom Festane both move in the right kinds of circles to know people who can throw money at a problem," I tell Kreitzer. "Mathis is an executive for a big non-profit. Festane does big-money real estate."

"But not with SoMa Triangle," Kreitzer says between bites of his Philly cheesesteak.

"But he's worked with the SoMa Triangle guys."

"Yes, some of them." He swallows, wipes his mouth with a paper napkin, then puts the napkin back under the salt shaker so the wind off the Bay won't blow it away.

"There's one factor we haven't discussed," I tell him.

He downs three fries in one bite. "What's that?"

"The Twin Cowboys. Candi walks in on their sex adventure at the Vergessen Hotel a few days before she dies. Maybe that's the missing link. We keep looking for ties to SoMa Triangle, but maybe it's Candi who's the target, not Giantonio."

He wipes his mouth again, secures the napkin again. "We checked. No twins in Carl Mathis' or Tommy Gonzalez' families. Tom Festane's father has a twin brother, but they're both pushing 90 years old. We'll keep looking, but..."

I pick up another fry, picture 90-year-old twins in cowboy hats banging away with two blondes at the Vergessen Hotel.

Suddenly I'm losing my appetite.

"I agree with Mrs. Tarrow," Kreitzer says, half to himself and half to me. "Someone wants to keep pressuring you, so they spread the word in wealthy circles that your place would be a perfect rental. They hoped that you'd go nuts if you were evicted."

"I am going nuts. But it's not the kind of nuts they're after."

"The dad who rented the place for his kid is trying to help us backtrack where the idea came from," he says, popping another fry in his mouth. "But there's no email trail and no one's sure who talked to who."

"Whom," I correct him before I realize what I'm doing.

He gives me a look and very carefully pronounces the word, "Whom."

"Sorry," I tell him.

"The dad's in banking, real estate. So yes, Carl Mathis and Tom Festane have those contacts in their Rolodexes."

"I rest my case." I take another bite of my burger.

He switches gears. "I've got a new name for you. One that was right in front of my face."

"And..."

"We've talked about Carl Mathis, because he apparently knew Candi and he knows you. But we haven't discussed his wife, Mary Anne."

"Ex-wife," I tell him. "Jenni says they've just separated."

"I know. But nothing's been filed yet so we don't have much to work with."

"Mary Anne Mathis..." I think as I chew. "Tall, slim, always dresses for success, always looks like she ran three miles that morning. I see her on the *Baar* sometimes. But not for a while now."

"Uh-huh."

"Light brown hair, highlights, always wears it tied back." I go back to working on my fries. "Her hair stylist is left-handed."

Kreitzer starts to ask about this, changes his mind, writes something in his notebook. Then he says, "I'll tell you why she's interesting."

"Please."

"A male perpetrator needs a female co-conspirator to hire Candi and deliver the purse," he says. "A female suspect could pull it off alone."

I try to picture the elegant Mary Anne Mathis as the masculine female character described by Debbie Milovich.

"Was she at that big School Board meeting?"

"No. That was Carl Mathis' crusade."

Kreitzer nods.

"Is she working for SoMa Triangle?" I ask him.

"This confidential?"

"Sure," I tell him. Then I add, "Can I tell Mrs. Tarrow?"

"Yes, you can tell Mrs. Tarrow."

"OK."

"The mom's an attorney here in the City, works for a big software company called Talkami."

"They have a messaging app for kids," I tell him. "The one with those TV ads where the genie says, 'Open, Talkami!'"

"I don't watch much TV," Kreitzer says. "Mathis' boss at the company is a guy named Peter Polossov, whose wife just happens to own Talkami. Not to mention a few sizable buildings around town."

"So Mary Anne and her boss move with the movers and shakers and the boss' wife is into real estate."

"Yes," he says, "they move and shake with the best of them."

"But no ties to SoMa Triangle?"

He shakes his head. "None that we know of. Yet."

"Are you going to question her?"

"No comment."

I chew morosely on a fry. Our list keeps getting more names. But what it doesn't keep getting is more answers.

43.

Stories That
Don't Want to be Told

Saturday, October 13

Mrs. Tarrow and I climb out of the Volvo and look at the peeling walls of the old warehouse. She purses her lips in disapproval.

Standing on the curb is a woman in a black jacket, black leggings and black boots. She looks up, sees us and puts on her most professional smile. "Hi, I'm Barbara Brandt."

We all shake hands routinely. I realize that for one brief moment she thinks I am a normal person who does normal things like shaking hands routinely.

"Shall we take a look at the place?" Barbara asks. She has short blonde hair that curves perfectly behind each ear. Her silver earrings have eleven beads dangling inside elliptical hoops.

"This is a wonderful live-work space," she says, leading the way around a corner. "A true vintage industrial loft with operable windows and a view of the Bay." She begins leading us up some old wooden stairs.

"Upstairs..." I start out. "That... that won't work."

Barbara looks back proudly. "Amanda here told me all about your aquariums. This was a warehouse for the shipyards during World War II. This unit could hold a battleship."

We enter a doorway and walk down a musty passageway, half-lit by an occasional dangling light bulb. Barbara leads us to a door, knocks twice, waits, knocks once, waits, then opens it with a key.

Inside the room the floor is covered with piles of brightly colored clothing. Some stacks come up to our waists, a couple are taller than I am. We can barely see the window on the far side.

We are the only ones visible in the room, but I can't help feeling like someone else is there.

"It's hard right now to get over to the windows," Barbara explains pleasantly. "They've been using this space to sort used clothing. They fill up big containers and ship it overseas."

"Where do they send it?" Mrs. Tarrow asks.

Barbara laughs. "I have no idea. Now back around here..." She carefully steps between two piles of old jeans. "Right here you can see this door, this leads to a bath with a big sink and a shower. At this price it's a steal!"

I try to avoid inhaling. The place smells of things that have absorbed far more than washing can ever cleanse.

"And of course we'd give it a good old-fashioned scrubbing." Barbara pantomimes a good old-fashioned scrubbing to reassure us. "Would this be a good place for your son?"

"I'm afraid that..." Mrs. Tarrow suddenly lurches left, leans on my arm, and I feel her knees give way.

"This way!" I hold her securely, try to steady her uneven steps as I guide her out of the room and down the stairs so we can call the paramedics.

Barbara trails behind us, asking, "Are you all right?" over and over again. Mrs. Tarrow says nothing, but it feels like she's breathing and she's walking mostly on her own.

When we reach the parking lot I try to get a better look at her but she covers her face with her hands. I don't care what she says – she's going to the hospital.

A couple with two French bulldogs hurries over from across the street. "Are you all right?" the woman asks Mrs. Tarrow.

The man takes out his phone and starts to dial. "Pat, I'm calling 911," he says.

His wife takes off her jacket and moves to place it around Mrs. Tarrow's shoulders. The bulldogs pant loudly, sharing their owners' concern.

"I'm all right," Mrs. Tarrow says, taking a deep breath.

"Are they coming, Bruce?" the woman asks her husband, then turns back to Mrs. Tarrow. "Dear, you don't look well. We need to get you to a doctor."

"I'm fine," Mrs. Tarrow tells her. "I... I just needed to get out of there, get some fresh air."

Pat and Bruce, the bulldogs' owners, both shake their heads at me, their message clear: "Don't you dare not take this woman to the hospital."

And with that Mrs. Tarrow turns so only I can see her face and gives me a big wink. I'm ready to strangle her, but hide my relief so I don't spoil the show.

It appears that Liam the Fog Seller is not the only street performer who's living on our hill in Sausalito.

* * *

I know I'm repeating myself but I tell her anyway. "My stomach is still in knots after your little drama this morning!"

Mrs. Tarrow looks down at the pizza, takes another slice and carefully aligns it on her plate. "Now, Steven, you know we weren't alone in that room, and whoever was there wasn't just an ordinary squatter."

"Maybe it's more than just a vintage industrial live-work loft with operable windows and bay views," I tell her. "Maybe it's a *haunted* vintage industrial live-work loft with operable windows and bay views."

She laughs, spearing a bite of pizza with her fork. "Well, Barbara already knew that people were in there before we walked in. You heard her knock in code before she used her key."

"Aren't real estate people always supposed to knock?" I ask her.

"They knock," she says, "but not in precise patterns with pauses. Whatever was going on in there is winding down, but it's not gone yet. It may be nothing, or it may be far more dangerous than Barbara realizes. If we'd turned the wrong way we still might have opened Pandora's Box."

"Finding Pandora's Purse is bad enough," I tell her. "As far as I'm concerned Pandora can keep the rest of her luggage."

She laughs again, and I walk around to the fridge to take down her chart and return to set it next to my plate. I take another piece of pizza.

Zina sits patiently next to me. She knows which of us is the clumsy one who's more likely to drop a wayward olive.

"I haven't added a lot to the list," Mrs. Tarrow says. "Just that our friend works around wealth."

I sit back down and read through the chart again.

Knows Steven not good with questions.
— Ferry? School? Classmate?
Knows Steven's routine, could plant gun.
— Ferry rider? Crew?
Had motive to kill Supervisor Giantonio, or
Had motive to kill Candi Bonham
— SoMa Triangle project? Other?

Hired Candi to drop purse to get fingerprints
— Woman, or has female partner

— Not experienced in evidence
Moves in circles with the wealthy
Had stolen gun: Criminal record? Gang?

Carl Mathis: Parent, PR at Institute
Tommy Gonzalez: Former student
Tom Festane: Parent, ex-SoMa Triangle lawyer
Mary Anne Mathis: Parent, attorney

I look across the breakfast bar at Mrs. Tarrow. "Kreitzer agrees with us. Both of the Mathis suspects and Tom Festane have networks of rich clients."

"We're making progress."

"But I don't care what Tommy's score is," I tell her. "He's not a murderer."

She gives me a strange half-smile. "My dear, it's too soon to start keeping score in this game. The lights are just coming on in the stadium."

44.

You Can Tell That
I'm A Scientist

Tuesday, October 16

The *Louis H. Baar* is barely clear of the dock in Sausalito when the shoreline disappears in the fog. My orange parka makes a nylon-rubbing sound as I pull in the damp mooring line and coil it carefully on the stern.

A man with short gray hair and a tall woman, both layered in suits and overcoats and scarves, sit on a bench near the railing and discuss whether a man named Delsing will be good at making it rain. From the look of their tailored clothes I'm guessing that means they're discussing whether he'll be good at bringing in money.

They last about five minutes before they shiver in the cold and go inside, which. as Luis would say, is four minutes more macho than most people.

I descend the stairs to start my routine. Passengers read or doze or talk or sip their coffee and stare out blankly at the fog.

These are the hardy veterans of the 7:20. The white curtains enveloping our world do not faze them.

I hear Alonzo's heavy steps on the deck above me and it makes me think of Luis. I picture his cowboy boots and his big silver belt buckle with the brass horse on it. He tells little kids that the horse is made of gold.

"*Ahórrale*, Stevie! What you up to, man?"

As if by magic, Luis stands beside me, his grin even wider than usual. I give him a big, long hug.

"I got the job, Stevie! Materials Handler at the Institute, moving a zillion specimens to the new building!"

"That's great!" I tell him.

"You can tell that I'm a scientist," he announces proudly. "I call things specimens."

I don't say anything, just give him another hug.

He lowers his voice. "You and Paula did it, Stevie. You set it up and she got it done. Told the Biology guy she knew me and he could trust her that I'd be good."

The mention of Paula's name sets off all sorts of emotions for me. Admiration that she would speak up for Luis when she's only seen him through my lens. Sadness that she no longer speaks to me.

Luis reads my eyes. "She never met me till last week, but she stood up for me because you stood up for me. She's different, Stevie. You were right."

I give him another hug. "This is great!" I tell him. "This is just great!"

He lowers his voice. "Now you let yourself off the hook, Stevie. You gotta stop feeling so bad. The cops know you didn't do nothing, they know somebody's messing with you. I got a job again. You can stop worrying about me and take care of Stevie."

"You starting the new job today?" I ask.

"This one time I'm gonna let you shine me on and act like it's

OK," he says, that self-satisfied gleam in his eye. "Yes, I start today. I wanted to surprise you."

"Well, don't sneak up on me like that," I tell him. "You make me jump like the tourists with Leonard the Human Statue."

"Hah! Your friend Leonard is an actor. Your bro' Luis is the one with superpowers and big muscles hard as steel!"

"Just remember, Superman," I tell him, "this job is temporary. We're finding a way to get you back on the *Baar*."

Luis smiles. "I'll be OK," he says. "Whatever happens, it happens for a reason."

* * *

I watch Luis walk down the pier and through the glass doors of the Ferry Building and breathe a huge sigh of relief. We have time to get him back to his real job. Leti and the kids will be OK.

I feel a hand on my shoulder and see that Alonzo is standing beside me, watching Luis.

"He's a good man, Professor." he says.

"Better than me," I tell him.

Alonzo points to a small brass plaque riveted below the railing near the bow. "Bud would have liked you guys," he says.

I've read it a hundred times, the little plaque about Louis H. "Bud" Baar, our namesake who helped bring the ferries back to Sausalito. Alonzo is the only one left who knew him.

"Bud would have liked you guys." It's the praise he reserves for his favorite crewmen.

I wish that I deserved it.

I cycle through my chores the rest of the morning, aware that it feels like my teeth have been clenched for weeks and I have finally relaxed my jaw. A little.

Tom Festane is on the 10:00 AM sailing to Sausalito today. As usual, he brilliantly imitates someone who does not recognize me.

Or perhaps he really does not recognize me and I'm second-guessing everything I see.

We make our 11:25 landing at the Ferry Building, I change into street clothes and I'm off on my mid-day break. I cross the Embarcadero and turn down Spear St. to visit my father.

The thick fog shows no sign of burning off.

I don't care. Luis has got a job again.

The little tables in the patio where the building with my father's office used to be are all filled with people babbling happily, so I find a quiet corner at the back.

"I'm so relieved," I tell my father from behind a massive concrete post. "Paula got Luis a job working at the Institute so he'll be getting steady checks again. I've got time to clear the record and get his real job on the ferry back."

Three young guys in business casual emerge from the building's big glass doors, talking about someone named Laura who sweeps the table at poker whenever they dare to play her.

I lean my head against the pillar. Even in the cold wind that blows down Spear St., the concrete feels warmer than it has for a long time.

"I miss you, Dad."

45.

People Die from Broken Hearts

Thursday, October 18

"Who was Daniel O'Connell?" Emma asks.

Liam the Fog Seller deftly uncaps a vial, waves it through the foggy evening air, recaps it and drops it in the old blue duffel bag. "He was a writer in San Francisco. He caught a cold and then he got pneumonia and then he died."

She runs her fingers over the carved inscription on the wall above the granite bench. It says:

Daniel O'Connell
Poet
1849-1899

Liam fills another vial, and it makes a clinking sound as he drops it in the sack.

"This is cool," Emma says. "I'm glad we came here instead of staying in the City."

He nods. "We got lucky with the fog tonight, being able to come right after dinner. Lots of times the fog doesn't come in till later and I'm here with Zina at midnight freezing my ass off."

She stands up, admires the view of the Bay and the twinkling lights. "Why did they put the memorial here?"

Clink! Another bottle filled. "Because he lived in Sausalito. A few blocks that way." He uses the next vial to point north.

"What did he write?" she asks.

"He was a newspaper writer, for the *Chronicle*. And he wrote poetry." Another vial clinks into the bag.

She smiles at him and pulls the collar of her heavy red jacket tightly around her throat. "Is there any question I can ask you about San Francisco where you don't know the answer?"

Liam smiles back as he fills another vial. "No."

"How do you know all this stuff?"

"I read a lot." Clink!

"So why did he get a fancy bench and a little park up here on the hill?" she asks him. " I mean, he can't be the only person in Sausalito who died in 1899."

Another wave, another vial. "He was one of the cool kids."

"Want help with these?" She holds up an empty vial.

"No, thanks."

Then Liam surprises me. He stops, looks at her. Then he says, "Yes, please." He never accepts help with the fog.

Emma reaches down, takes a vial from the box, uncaps it, waves it through the fog in the same way she's been watching Liam do it. She drops it in the bag with a satisfying clink.

"Why was he so popular?" She takes another vial and gives Liam a smile to say, "I can beat you at this game."

He gives the same smile back. "Because he was a nice guy and the life of every party."

Clink! Clink! Two more vials go in the bag.

"Now you're making stuff up."

He flourishes a vial like a champagne flute as he fills it. "Google it if you don't believe me."

"Really?"

"He helped found this club in San Francisco that still exists today. Everybody loved to be around him, so when he died they just had to do something."

Clink! Clink!

Emma starts to read the poem carved in the back of the bench, straining to make out the words with minimal help from a nearby streetlight. "This is so sad."

Liam fills another vial, drops it in the bag. "It gets worse. They say his wife died of a broken heart a few months later."

Emma stops reading, reaches down for a vial and fills it.

"People die from broken hearts." She says the phrase in the same way you hold something in your hands at the store while you consider buying it.

Clink! "I guess so." Liam grabs another vial.

"That's not what love's supposed to be like," Emma tells him.

Liam stops and looks up. "No. It's not."

"When my dad left, my mom didn't just curl up and die."

He nods. "When my dad died, my mom... She got better. She had to."

"She stopped drinking?"

Liam shrugs. "She slowed way down. Nobody left to clean up after her."

"You were gone?"

He goes back to filling vials. "Off at college." Clink!

She waves her vial through the fog and caps it. Clink!

More vials. More clinks.

"O'Connell's wife was probably like my roommate," Liam says after a while. "Steve thinks no one will ever fall in love with him, that whatever chance he ever had is gone. When her husband died Mrs.

O'Connell figured that was her one true love, she could never find love again and she was done."

Emma looks up. I know what she's thinking. There's no way to say, "Steve's weird" without attacking me. She bites her lip.

"Maybe Steve just needs to stop being so... restricted," she says finally. "Relax. Have a cherry turnover someplace his dad could never go."

"He's a good guy," Liam says. "He just... He hasn't gotten over things."

"What about you, Liam?" Emma asks. "What do you think?"

Clink! "About what?"

"Do you think that Steve will find someone, that we all can find someone if we keep looking?"

Uncap, wave, cap, clink! "Steve wants to be loved like Daniel O'Connell. He wants the impossible."

She kneels down, runs her fingers over the mosaic in the memorial's floor. "I don't know. Maybe that's why this bench is here, why they built it."

"What do you mean?" he asks, filling another vial.

"Maybe it wasn't about poetry or popularity," she says. "Maybe what people wanted to remember back in 1899 was that the O'Connells were really in love. That's why their friends had to build something like this, so they'd always have someplace they could go that would remind them that it's not impossible. That you can have true love."

I have no idea how Liam will react to this. He is so proud of his pragmatism, his rejection of my extremes. What he calls my self-destructive quest for perfection.

He surprises me. And scares me.

He puts aside the vial he's filling and kneels down beside the mosaic, his shoulder touching Emma's. He examines the tiles that form a three-leaf clover, set in place a century ago.

"That would be really cool, wouldn't it," he says to her. "Being in love like that would be very cool."

46.

He's In the Center of the Storm

Friday, October 19

Luis and I are celebrating his new job by going to lunch at the Beach Chalet. It is an encouraging rarity in San Francisco: a relic of the old City that has been restored instead of being replaced.

We hop off the N Judah train at Ocean Beach and walk the two blocks to the restaurant. Depression-era murals of determined Californians still line the walls downstairs.

"You sit this way," Luis says, pointing to a chair as we're escorted to our table. "You can watch the bikini girls."

It is 56 degrees outside with a cold breeze and there are no bikini girls.

My Diet Coke arrives and I am ready to order the fish and chips, but Luis cannot seem to make up his mind. I know he wants the burger because he always wants the burger. But today he keeps talking about clam chowder and some kind of salad.

Luis does not eat salad for lunch. Something is wrong.

Suddenly he stands and smiles. I turn my head but can't see anything. I stand up and turn around.

Six feet away stands Paula Costa. She is rigid, immobile, as surprised to see me as I am to see her.

Luis hurries forward, takes her by the arm. "Paula! Welcome to my celebration for my new job!"

She allows herself to be brought to the table's edge. She wears a bright white blouse tucked perfectly into faded jeans, her long brown hair braided down her back.

"Come, sit down, sit down!" Luis says.

She does not sit down.

Luis looks back and forth between the two of us. His tone changes from ebullient to serious.

"Look, this is my lunch to say thank you for getting me this job. Without you guys I'd be a night janitor somewhere."

I look outside. A double-decker tourist bus with an open top is driving by on The Great Highway. The people on top must be freezing.

"Are you happy for me?" Luis asks.

I keep looking at the ocean. Luis has no right to do this.

"Yes, I'm happy for you," I hear Paula say.

"Then come sit over here by me," he tells her.

I'm still not looking at her but I feel her hesitate. Then the sound of her woven leather purse brushing against my chair as she crosses behind me and sits down next to Luis.

"Good, good," Luis says. He looks back and forth between us, then picks up the menu.

I am still looking out at the ocean. There are no whitecaps yet. They will come later this afternoon.

Luis smiles broadly. "I think I'll have the burger."

*   *   *

Paula plays with her salad. Luis is proudly telling us how he personally packs over 34,000 specimens this week and every single one is now in the right place at the new building.

I have a small cup of clam chowder. I stir the little crackers in the soup.

I say nothing.

Paula says nothing.

After a few minutes of this Luis has finally had enough. "Let me tell you a story," he lectures us. "My Aunt Josefina's best friend was named Maria."

A fishing boat is slowly going by out on the ocean. It looks like it's traveling due north, but it's probably really going northwest.

"Aunt Josefina always wanted Maria and my Uncle Eduardo to be best friends, but it never happened. They were OK together, but only around Aunt Josefina."

Silence.

Paula rearranges her salad with the tips of her fork. "And they lived happily ever after," she says, without looking up.

"No," Luis says, "They didn't. Aunt Josefina died. And her friend Maria and my Uncle Eduardo still aren't friends. But they still go to her grave together once a month and bring her flowers."

You can see the fishing boat is going northwest now, turning to go round Point Bonita. The spars on either side are uneven. You can see it's turning a little bit away from us because the spars are uneven.

"When they're there, by Aunt Josefina's grave, they act like best friends. Because they know it makes her happy."

Luis gives us both a very serious look.

Paula breaks out laughing, unable to contain it any longer. "Are you telling us you have some terrible disease?"

"No. I'm telling you that you guys should talk with me when we're at the table."

Paula controls herself and looks at Luis. "Sorry."

"I know it's... complicated," he tells her. "What happened scared you, and Stevie's... He's in the center of the storm."

Paula looks at me, actually meets my eyes before looking down again.

Now Luis turns and looks at me. "You talk to all those people on the Ferry. Why can't you talk with us now?"

Without even meaning to I say, "Sorry."

Luis smiles and leans back in his chair. "How many specimens did I move this week?"

"Thirty cabinets of eight trays with 144 specimens per tray," I answer.

"Ah, so you do listen to your bro' Luis!" he proclaims. "And what did Leti do at home this morning?"

Paula leans against him, pokes him with her elbow. "She made hand-rolled tortillas so you and the kids would be thinking all day about coming home for dinner."

"Very good, *Profesora*, very good!"

47.

The Question That Emerges
from All That Energy

Friday, October 19 (Cont.)

Mrs. Tarrow says that we have lots to celebrate tonight. Luis has a job. Paula is speaking to me again. Leonard is mere days from escaping the prison of his coat and tie. The world is getting better.

She hums happily as she boils the noodles for spaghetti. "I know it's only till you find a new place," she says, "but having you in Teri's old room will make the house feel more alive again."

Mrs. Tarrow believes that she has convinced me to stay with her, one more cause for celebration. In truth I have no idea what I should do, but for now there's no point in arguing.

"Our friend is trying to get to you," she says, "pushing you to act like a suspect by taking away your home. But you could have the last laugh if you find an even better place to live."

"My 'friend' frames me for a murder, costs Luis his job, reports me to the FBI, auctions off the lease to my garage," I tell her. "Some friend."

She turns to the salad and changes the subject. "Emma sounds like such a lovely girl. It will be wonderful to meet her."

Mrs. Tarrow beats the oil and vinegar in the little bowl, her motion so fast that the spoon in her hand is a blur. Zina sits and watches her.

"Uh-huh. I like her."

She flashes me her still-a-schoolgirl smile. "I'd say you more than just like her."

"She's Liam's girlfriend."

"I suppose."

She stops what she's doing. Puts her hands on her hips. Looks down at the salad for a while. Picks up the salad dressing to see if the oil and vinegar have blended. Starts to beat the dressing again.

"What does Emma think of you, Steven?"

So that's the question that emerges from all that energy.

"I think she'd like me OK." I watch Mrs. Tarrow's steady, determined pulses of the spoon. "But she likes Liam a whole lot better."

Mrs. Tarrow stops beating the oil and vinegar to rest for a moment, massaging her wrist. "Reminds me of someone else I know."

"Uh-huh."

"I won't mention his name but he's sitting at the counter in my kitchen."

I do not reply. Mrs. Tarrow is in a questioning mood tonight.

I am not good with questions.

Now she asks "When are you going to tell her about Liam?"

I shrug.

"You know the clock is ticking, though. Yes?"

I nod.

"What would Paula think of Liam if she met him?" she asks, still kneading her right wrist.

She is wearing the ring that is Jack's gift to her for their 40th wedding anniversary. It has a circle of eight small diamonds, and they glint in the kitchen lights as she...

"Has Paula ever met Liam?" She asks a different question since I have not answered the last one.

"No."

Mrs. Tarrow looks at the salad dressing, decides it's blended enough and pours it over the mixed greens, tomatoes and garbanzos in the big, well-worn wooden bowl. "Emma seems to think that Liam is a great person."

I can feel where this is going. I look at the door and she sees me do it.

But she keeps going anyway. "Why not bring Paula to meet Liam?"

I answer without intending to.

"Because I want someone to fall in love with me. The real me."

I hear the words come out, hear the sound waves that should only be the silent voice inside my head, and I cannot sit there anymore. I walk, then run out the kitchen door.

Mrs. Tarrow calls after me. "Steven! Steven! Come back!"

Then, from far away, "Steven, I'm sorry! Please, come back!"

I do not know where I am going. Just that my steps are taking me away from the questions. In search of silence.

48.

Mirror Images in a World Where Nothing Else Lines Up

Tuesday, October 23

It is another warm-sun, cold-wind day. I walk south on Market St., my sandwich swinging rhythmically in its plastic bag.

I pass a bus stop with a poster for the new *Hamlet* at Theatre Lab West. No more sequins and spandex from the disco-fever *Taming of the Shrew*. Just respectable, don't-make-waves-and-sell-the-tickets Shakespeare.

The interlocking letters of the Theatre Lab West logo on the poster bring back a familiar thought. Who is Mimi from TLW?

I say the name out loud to myself, "Mimi... Mimi..." Does Mimi have a stage name, so no one recognizes her when we ask? Does she appear in this new *Hamlet*?

Just past Geary St. I see a commotion up ahead.

"Fuck you! Who the fuck you think you are?!" I hear a woman yell.

Sitting on the sidewalk, his legs crossed, is The Prophet of Market Street.

She yells down at him again. "You know me? Answer me, you lazy bastard! You know me?!"

The old man looks up at her calmly. "Like I say, you got to get that off your chest, ma'am. Eatin' a big hole in you, that whole time."

The woman is heavy and well-dressed, with ultra-short blonde hair and perfect makeup. Gold bracelets rattle on her wrist as she shakes her finger at him.

"You bastard! Who the fuck you think you are to just start yelling at people on the street!" Her black business suit is a silk-wool blend with two vents in the back of the jacket.

He says nothing, just looks up at her. His dark brown hands are folded in his lap, relaxed.

A young man with a zebra-striped backpack speaks out. "He didn't yell at you, lady. He just said something and you dropped all your shit and started screaming."

She looks down at the white plastic shopping bag that still lies at her feet, emblazoned with an ad for something called *Masque de Beauté Essentielle*. A golden tube of lipstick has rolled out onto the sidewalk and now lies between her and the calm old man.

She turns to yell at the boy with the zebra backpack, but the Prophet of Market Street's quiet voice stops her.

"That baby died in the back of that car on O'Farrell St., ma'am. She ain't never gonna come find you and call you momma and help you go on like it's all OK." He shakes his head, his close-cropped silver hair like the moss on a creekside boulder. "You got to get that off your chest, 'fore it crushes your heart."

Tears streak down the woman's face. She reaches down, picks up her bag, sobs racking her body even as she rushes off.

The boy with the zebra backpack sees that she has left the lipstick on the sidewalk, picks it up and runs after her.

"Lady! Hey! You lost this!" He dodges a newsstand and a hot dog cart to jog beside her as she hurries, then holds out the little gold tube.

She pushes his hand away and vanishes around the corner. The boy stops. Confused, he looks back at the stunned group standing on the sidewalk, the lipstick still in his extended hand.

A cry of anguish comes from around the corner and the boy sees something we cannot see. His shoulders sag and he walks back towards us, his pack hanging limply from his arm.

I resume my walk up Market, try to regain my thoughts. Try to push the sound of that cry from around the corner from my mind.

It's hard to think. I keep seeing the heavy-set businesswoman's face when she hears about a lost baby, keep re-living that anguished wail.

I need to focus. "Is Mimi just a stage name?" I ask myself. "Could she be walking here, on this block, right now?"

I feel the voice behind me before I hear it.

"Not here, son. Ain't no such woman been walkin' here."

I stop and look back at The Prophet of Market Street. He sits beside his cup of coins and does not meet my eyes.

* * *

The statue they call The Mechanics Monument is not a quiet place to eat your lunch. Surrounded by a triangle of streets choked with cars and buses, the air of the tiny plaza is thick with the gritty smoke of diesel and the strange metallic smells of city life.

The statue mirrors my mood. Three heroic men struggle with a huge mechanical press, trying to stamp a piece of metal that is eternally incomplete.

I see an open spot on the top step of the statue's base and settle in to eat. I'm on the shady side so the granite's cold, but that's what happens when you get here late.

I pull my sandwich from its narrow plastic bag, a heavy lunch of meatballs and melted cheese to help me wrestle with my thoughts. I breathe in the smell of sauce and spices and take a greedy bite, feel the flavors coat my throat.

In just two weeks I will lose my home, the place I choose to rebuild my life after version 1.0 goes terribly wrong. Another casualty of the mastermind behind The Lady with the Joke Book in Her Purse.

Two identical brown UPS trucks with twin pear-shaped drivers in twin brown uniforms are stopped at the converging traffic lights where Battery and Bush both merge with Market. They are mirror images in a world where nothing else lines up.

Like Candi Bonham's twin cowboys at the Vergessen Hotel.

The UPS drivers are not really twins, of course. Just men of similar size and build who wear the same clothing and are delivering similar packages while driving identical trucks.

Are the twin cowboys at the Vergessen Hotel really twins, or just men of similar size and build who wear the same hats and are having sex with similar women on identical beds?

I take another bite. The meatballs are already getting cold after my long walk up Market St.

Eating cold food that should be hot. Sitting alone and surrounded by people. Innocent of a crime but questioned by Kreitzer, the TSA and whatever the next agency is that's told I'm a criminal.

It doesn't matter what I do.

I can forget it all ever happened, or contemplate every question of a double murder.

I can mind my own business or search every square inch of San Francisco.

I can withdraw into my own private little world, or I can contact every Mimi in California.

Either way, I remain part of someone's grand plan. The lead actor in their script, their convenient solution for the assassination of a Supervisor.

Either way, someone capable of murder will write another scene where my name is spoken, invent another story where I play a vital role. All lies, but all just credible enough when the character in question is me.

I have to find a way to make everyone leave me alone. To give me the peace I can never seem to find.

PART III

JOURNAL THREE

It is a bright, clear autumn morning. I'm almost ready to leave for work when she comes in and puts my journal on the nightstand.

"I'm ready to go on to the next one," she says. "Still OK?"

"Sure." I try to remember what I'm writing when I run out of space in that second journal. I put my old blue duffel bag down on the bed and skim the last few pages.

I look over and see her watching me. "You're at a place that's very frightening for me," I tell her.

"I am."

"It's when I decide I have to start confronting things and not just... get blown with the winds."

She gives me a funny look. "Like confronting Liam."

"Yes. And being so naïve and thinking that Luis getting a job would make everything OK."

She stands there looking at me.

"What are you thinking about?" I ask her.

"Just... there was a time there when you were out of my life and I thought I was content with that. But then I realized I wasn't content, I was telling myself I ought to be content. But that wasn't how I really felt."

I don't want to pick at that scab. I just say, "I know."

"You ready?" she asks.

I pick up my bag and head for the door. "Let's go."

49.

Like Someone's Hunting Me
While I'm Hunting Them

Wednesday, October 24

"Dr. Discus!" I call out.

A Chinese woman comes up the narrow aisle and says, "Hello! Hello! It's good to see you!"

"Good to see you," I answer back. "This is my friend Eli."

"Welcome, Eli, Welcome!" she says, then adds, "He's in the back."

Eli of the Coral Reef looks all around us. There are aquariums everywhere, with fish of every shape and size. It smells like we're standing in a forest beside a lake.

The Giants' season is over, and the long winter without baseball has begun. Eli of the Coral Reef is already starting to fade like the leaves of the trees on Van Ness Ave.

He knows every gallon of every salt water tank in every fish store in San Francisco, so to engage his mind with something new I have to bring him to my favorite oasis of fresh water aquariums.

It is the best that I can do.

I lead the way back through the long, narrow store. "Dr. Discus!"

A middle-aged Chinese man in a green cotton jumpsuit stands on a short stepladder, using a net to chase a gray-green fish around a tank.

"Hello, Steve," he says. "Damn *jurupari* dig up tank, shred plants."

I turn to Eli. "They're like big, wide mandarin dragonets," I tell him, translating from fresh water to his native salt water.

"*Synchiropus splendidus,*" Eli murmurs. I think he is enjoying this, though with Eli sometimes it's hard to tell.

"Dr. Discus, this is my friend Eli of the Coral Reef."

"Nice to meet you, Eli," he says, waving his net in a salute. "Steve say you good fish person."

Eli brightens. This is why it's so important to get him out.

"You got *demasoni* juveniles you bring me?" Dr. Discus asks me. "I got space right now."

"Not right now," I tell him. "They're feuding."

"Not good, Steve. Not good with *demasoni.*" He gives me his "Do I need to come check up on the fish I sell you?" look.

"I know. I'm watching them."

He nods seriously, and I resolve to give them an extra water change this week.

We leave Dr. Discus to the *jurupari* and do a walkabout to look in every tank. Eli spends a long time with the discus fish, which are from the Amazon basin and are shaped like salad plates with a mouth and fins. These have bright green lines like glowing iridescent topographic maps covering their sides.

"Their bodies are compressed like reef fish," Eli says, in the tone most people would use to say, "Wow, that's a gorgeous rainbow!"

One by one we inspect each tank until finally we finally reach the back of the store. I look at my watch. We have to start walking back to the BART Station soon so I'm not late for my afternoon shift. Eli has to get to work as well, take his place as Master of the Security Monitors.

"I have to go," I tell him. "Sorry."

Eli just nods, pulls down on the brim of his Giants cap and says, "I'm cool."

As we step back out into the sunlight I ask him, "Pretty good for a fresh water place, huh?"

He nods and says, "If I liked fresh water, discus would be my favorite fish."

We walk south towards the Civic Center BART station and the huge gilded dome of City Hall. A man standing next to the McAllister statue is shouting into his cell phone, but as we get closer we see that there is no cell phone present.

"Jerry, you shouldn't have done that!" the man says, holding up his invisible device. "That's not right!"

Eli and I increase our pace, ignore him as we go by.

"You make me want to kill you, Jerry!" the man shouts. "I don't care if you're my best friend! I'm going to have to kill you!"

I catch a movement from the corner of my eye. I look back.

Nothing there. Just a few ordinary people, all oblivious to our presence.

Eli looks back. "Everything OK?"

I scan the street again. No one unusual except the loud man who wants to murder his best friend Jerry.

"Ever since Leonard and I start calling the numbers on that phone bill I keep thinking I see things," I tell Eli. "Like someone's hunting me while I'm hunting them."

"Could it be the Police? To protect you?"

"I guess."

The light changes up ahead. Afternoon buses go roaring by. I look back again.

Nothing.

Eli looks back, keeps walking.

We approach Polk St. and I hear a familiar sound.

"Hey hey! Ho ho! Triangle has got to go! Hey Hey! Ho ho! Triangle..."

Up ahead a group of protesters is marching in a circle in front of City Hall. One beats a big drum in time with their chant. They wear the cardboard masks with photos of people's faces, but I don't recognize any of the images.

"I see these guys down on Powell St.," Eli says, "wearing masks and yelling about Triangle. Whatever that is."

"It's a big building project south of Market," I tell him. "Supervisor Giantonio's votes block all its approvals. But now there's no more Supervisor Giantonio."

"Oh." Eli looks at me, bites his lip.

This time the leader of the group is a young woman with long, straight blonde hair that flows behind her in the breeze.

A TV news crew has turned on its light and is about to tape her, and a second cameraman now approaches her as well. The drumbeat stops.

"We're here to say no to SoMa Triangle!" she yells. "We're here to give the victims a voice... and a face!"

The group behind her cheers, and the drummer twirls his drumsticks as he plays.

Eli and I stop to watch.

"Each face on our masks is a real person, just one of hundreds who will lose their homes to SoMa Triangle!" she shouts. "We don't need more luxury condos in San Francisco!"

The protesters behind her shout their agreement, and some in the small crowd join in.

"We don't need more towers to block the sun! We need more housing for taxpayers like these! Tell your Supervisors, say no to SoMa Triangle! Save these peoples' homes!"

I look at my watch.

Eli nods and we resume our walk to BART. "I'd hate to lose my apartment if someone wanted to tear it down," he says.

A moment later he remembers that I really am losing my place and he looks at me, embarrassed. "Sorry, Steve."

"No worries," I tell him. "I'm cool."

50.

I Always Slip and Fall
and Break My Heart

Thursday, October 25

Liam and Emma walk down Market St. together, hand in hand. Living out a fantasy I've dreamed of doing so many times, with so many women whom I've never met.

Or even someone whom I have met. Recently.

I just have dreams. Somehow Liam is able to make some dreams come true. But to make those dreams into reality he has to be a person whom I always feel like Steve Ondelle could never be.

"I loved going to that little park last week, but I'm looking forward to seeing Sausalito in the daytime," Emma is saying. "All I remember from when I was little is a sidewalk right next to the water, and my mom telling me not to climb on the rocks."

"I know the spot. I'll take you there," Liam says. "Do you remember the sea lion statue?"

She frowns. "No."

"Maybe when you see it. At high tide it's surrounded by the Bay."

She concentrates, trying to remember. "I was really little."

"Are you sure you're OK with having dinner with Mrs. Tarrow tonight instead of going to a restaurant?"

"It's OK," she says."

"Not exactly the most romantic place I could take you for dinner," he tells her.

"It's OK. It's like going to Manny and Valérie's for dinner. I do it all the time."

"Do you like the name Liam?" he asks, a little too quickly.

"You know I do."

He looks over at her. "I'm afraid it's a stage name."

"Oh." She stops walking for a moment, then starts up again. "What's your real name?"

"Steve. Steven, actually. Steven Curtiss Ondelle."

"So you and your roommate are both named..." She walks in silence as she absorbs this, then makes a weird, soft groaning sound. "Do you actually have a roommate?"

"No. Liam is my stage name and Steve is my... my birth name."

"So when you were talking about your roommate Steve and everything he's been going through, you were really talking about yourself?"

A deep breath. "Yes."

"And you work on the... You're the one who only eats apple turnovers in places that you went to with your father."

"Yes." This is not going well.

There's a red light ahead and I stop short of the corner so that the people waiting there don't hear us.

"I know I should have told you sooner. I just... I have to build up all my courage to be like Liam, and... Once I have that courage then when I meet you I don't dare let it slip away because..."

"And now you've stopped using the past tense, just like you say Steve does."

Of course she's right. "Yes."

She looks up at the tall buildings all around us, as if raindrops have suddenly appeared from nowhere on her face. But they aren't rain-drops. They're tears.

"I knew it was too good to be true," she says. I reach out to hold her but she pulls away.

"I was already scared about being around someone who knew someone who'd been murdered when it was your roommate. But I believed you'd never lie to me and it seemed like you weren't really..." Her words are choked off by tears and she wanders over to stand by the wall of the office building that towers above us. She buries her face in her hands.

"I'm sorry." I don't know what else to say without making things worse.

After what seems like forever she wipes her eyes and nose on the back of her sleeve. "Now I'm scared about the... about anything else you haven't told me. What else have you lied to me about?"

So here he is, the great Liam, arriving at the same spot where I always slip and fall and break my heart.

It all begins so well. I start to like someone. I'm strange, yet some-how they start to like me back. But then some question comes, I say something without thinking, someone else says something about me.

And the woman always asks herself the question, "Just how strange is this Steve Ondelle guy I barely know?"

And then they start looking for the door. First the emotional one, to move on. Then the physical one, to get away.

So here is the great Liam, he who can do everything that I cannot, face to face with the same script, the same glance for the exit sign. With a woman he deeply wants to stay, to love him and to not be scared away.

Maybe the great Liam is not so great after all.

"What else have you lied to me about?" she asks again.

"I haven't..." I search for words. Some random sounds come out. Then, finally, "I... The two sides of me are so different. They both speak truthfully to you, I just... I was too afraid to tell you."

"You just used the past tense again. Does that mean I'm back with Liam now?"

I take a deep breath. "It's not like a split personality, it's just... it's a role that lets me... Leonard lives that concept of getting into character as an actor and when I got to know him it was... exhilarating. The idea that if I just set aside all my fears people would listen and applaud. All the stories about me as Professor Polymirth in the classroom are true, too. I'm really shy, but in class or when I'm portraying Liam, I have permission to be... To be like I want myself to be."

She starts to walk again, still heading for the Ferry Building, and I take my place beside her.

We reach Drumm St. and stop for the light. A double-decker tour bus roars by on Market, the driver saying over the speakers, "...one of the few buildings to survive the Great Earthquake of 1906."

"'The Great Fire of 1906', that's what the old politicians would want him to be saying," I tell her.

"Is Mrs. Tarrow a real person?" she asks me, her voice hoarse. "And Luis and Leonard and Eli...?"

"They're all real. If you're still willing to come you'll meet Trish and Linh in five minutes, and Mrs. Tarrow in an hour, and I'll bring you to meet Luis and Leonard and Eli and whoever you want."

We cross the street and head towards the Ferry Plaza. To my surprise she asks, "What does Mrs. Tarrow think of all this?"

I'm not good with questions. I'm terrified by this conversation.

Must. Think. Like. Liam.

"It drives her crazy," I tell her. "Mrs. Tarrow says that if I'm a certain kind of person when I portray Liam, then I can just be that person and stop portraying."

"Yes," is all she says. She pulls the strap of her big brown leather purse higher on her shoulder.

We reach the Embarcadero and the light turns green for us to cross. She stops before we enter the Ferry Building's big glass doors.

"You have to tell me something." She looks directly into my eyes.

Oh, no. This has been very bad but now it's going to get much, much worse.

"If you talk to me... both ways, but I've only really been with Liam... What does Steve... How does Steve feel about me?"

For some reason this answer is easy, these words escape without my willing it to be. "Steve thinks that you're so wonderful, so beautiful that you could never care for someone as shy and awkward and lonely as him. As me."

She stands and thinks about this. "How does Liam feel?"

I smile, because Liam's always ready to tell you all his feelings. "I feel the same way," I answer. "But for once I'm not talking myself out of it. I gave myself permission to fall in love with you anyway."

My heart jumps. It is the first time that Liam has used that word with Emma.

The first time *I've* used that word since college. With anyone. For all these years.

I can see her heart jump too. "Love is a very scary word," she tells me. She is not smiling.

Must. Think. Like. Liam.

And then I kiss her, a very long kiss. At first she moves to push me away, but then she holds me tightly to her.

And then she pulls away and starts to cry again. "I can't do this," she says. And then, still crying, she walks the other way towards Market St.

51.

Sometimes
People Be Surprised
What They Can Do

Saturday, October 27

I don't work Saturdays but I work a lot of Saturdays.

If someone is sick or it's their daughter's soccer playoffs or they just don't feel like coming in they call me.

If I get too many hours the office or the union will complain, but we all know that it makes the schedule better for everyone. They just hassle me to say they hassle me.

It's good that I'm working so I'm in the City today. I have to talk to someone about what's happening with Emma. I'm usually the one who does all of the listening when somebody else needs to talk, but this... This is different.

It's been two days since I tell Emma about Liam and she turns and walks away. I try phone calls, texts, emails... No response.

The moment we get the all-clear I head up Market St. to meet Eli at the Institute of Science, taking long strides as I pick my way through the weekend crowds.

Ahead of me a couple walks hand in hand. The man has silver hair, while the dark-haired woman with him looks younger. They walk in step, the way people do when they've been together a very long time.

Yet again I find myself wondering if what they have is unattainable for me. Twice in two months I walk hand in hand with a woman, just as they walk now. Twice in two months I dare to think that this time things will be different.

Once I even dare to believe that Luis may be right when he says I'll find someone who loves me because I'm unique, instead of trying to love me despite my being unique.

But I am Steve Ondelle. There should be no illusions. Twice in two months I find myself alone.

Would it be different if I weren't trapped in the script written by the person who hired The Lady with the Joke Book in Her Purse?

I reach the corner where Post and Montgomery converge on Market. The Prophet of Market Street sits cross-legged in the sun, leaning against the base of an antique lamppost.

An idea comes to me. If I hesitate I won't have the courage to follow through so I hurry forward.

The Prophet's eyes remain on the passers-by. He sits beside the Styrofoam cup that holds his coins. There are six quarters, a dime and two pennies, along with one dollar bill.

"Excuse me," I start out. He ignores me.

I drop a dollar in his cup. He still does not look up. There are freckles on top of his head in the patch where his silver hair is thinner.

"Excuse me. I've met this girl, but she's freaked out because someone has been trying to make it look like I killed someone. I want to ask if this... I want to know if it all works out between us."

Still no glance. No answer.

I don't know if I'm relieved or disappointed. Part of me is terrified to ask him what will happen with Emma, another part can't wait to hear the answer.

"I mean, I couldn't kill someone. That's the whole point. Once the police catch the real murderer she can..."

Now the tired voice replies, "Sometimes people be surprised what they can do."

"That's true," I respond. "But the police know I haven't killed anyone."

Nothing happens for a while. A young woman wearing jeans and a black sweater drops some coins in the Prophet of Market Street's cup. The inscription tattooed behind her ear says, "Born to Live in Joy."

"The police know I haven't killed anyone," I repeat to him.

"Not yet, son." he says, finally looking up at me. "You ain't killed nobody yet."

"I could never kill someone!" I almost shout it at him

But he does not answer. He stares emptily at the walkers and the bike riders and the cars and the buses and the trolley cars of Market St.

I tell him again, my voice now more controlled. "I could never kill someone!"

He glances up. "No, you couldn't, son. Not unless you had to."

* * *

Eli and I stand in front of the big blue emptiness of the temporary reef tank at the temporary Institute of Science.

"Didn't bother me when you told me about Liam," Eli is saying. "Lots of species change their colors when they want to blend in or stand out."

I haven't thought of it that way.

"I haven't thought of it that way," I tell him.

"*Siganus vulpinus*," he says, glancing over at me. "Foxface Rabbitfish. They're bright yellow during the day, but go all dark and murky at night and when they wanna hide."

Liam certainly equates to bright yellow, but I wince at the image of myself as murky.

"Nothing personal," Eli adds, looking over at me again.

"No worries," I tell him.

"It'd be easier if she loved fish," Eli says.

I feel a deep sigh fill me up and then empty me out again.

After a while he asks me, "So what are you gonna do now?"

"I don't know. I mean, what do you say when someone says 'I can't do this' and walks away? I'm the person she fell in love with – I know she loves me. But..."

"Steve," Eli interrupts me. "You just used the past tense. You said she *fell* in love with you."

"God..."

"I've never heard you do that before."

I shake my head. "I guess I'm so used to talking like Liam when I'm thinking about Emma..." I look at him, my thoughts a jumbled mess.

"If I try to act a certain way in one place and act another way another place I always mess up," Eli says with a shrug. "So I gave up and just decided to act like me."

52.

Fire Your New Writer

Monday, October 29

Liam the Fog Seller stands in a narrow ray of light that shines between the office towers above the Embarcadero BART Station. The brick sidewalk vibrates as trains come and go below.

"You use detergent on your clothes and dish soap in your sink!" Liam proclaims.

Passers-by just keep passing.

"You wash your car, hose down your sidewalk and pressure-wash your deck!"

Nothing. One guy selling beaded jewelry on a rickety card table looks over.

"And where does that polluted water go? Into the Bay! At this rate the Golden Gate will be a bubble bath!"

A Fed Ex guy walks past with a cart loaded down with boxes, the wheels squealing on the pavement.

"I can't purify the Bay," Liam declares, "but I do know what has purified San Francisco for millions of years. It is... the fog!" He pulls a vial from his tuxedo.

A guy with a Stanford T-shirt is carrying a MacBook like an open pizza box. He stops to see what this weird man in the top hat and tails is saying.

"Yes, when your life is turning toxic, this little vial of San Francisco fog will remind you that Mother Earth has a way of balancing herself, all in her own good time."

He tips his black silk top hat and smiles at a passing woman whose polka dot stretch pants look two sizes too small. She gives him a dirty look and keeps walking.

"Pay me anything, something, nothing, whatever you choose, and thank you for listening!"

The Stanford guy steps up, balancing his laptop on one forearm. He drops a dollar in the box, accepts a vial of fog. "Thanks," he says. "I needed that today."

Liam tips his hat and thanks him. Everyone else keeps walking. Except one man. A familiar silhouette.

"Looks like a rough day, Steve," Kreitzer says. "Got time to go for a walk?"

Sometimes a break will change my luck, and besides, I have a question for him, too. "Let's go," I tell him, and we start off down the Embarcadero.

He clasps his big hands as he walks, rubbing the palms together. "Does the name Eve Mortimer mean anything to you?"

"I know a Mrs. Mortimer from when I'm a teacher, but her name is Madeline. Emphasis on the mad."

"Eve's her sister."

"I've never met her," I say. "Mrs. Mortimer doesn't care much for my style of teaching."

"Was she there that night?"

"At the Board lynching? Definitely. But she's a person who does all her politics in private."

He looks over at me. "Still pisses you off, huh?"

"I... Yes, it still pisses me off."

He laughs. "City Hall is full of 'em."

"But why her? She doesn't know me."

He grunts. "We've started looking for inverse motives. Someone who thought the Supervisor's murder would damage SoMa Triangle, not help it."

"Looks like it's working."

"That's what got me thinking," he says. "They couldn't get a treehouse approved right now."

"I'm ancient history to Mrs. Mortimer. I've seen her on the ferry once, a few months ago, and she pretends she doesn't recognize me.""

"Her sister lives in Novato, works in the City, but drives instead of taking the ferry. She was an investor in a project with TZD Development, the SoMa Triangle people. Put in $400,000."

"Oh."

"She lost it all."

I wince.

"Mortimer's not much of a suspect," Kreitzer tells me, "but she's the only new suspect we've got." With that, he pivots and starts walking back towards the Ferry Building. I reverse course as well.

"Just think about it," he says.

"I will."

"So I've got a question for you," I tell him.

"Sure."

"I've met this girl, and... It would... Things would be a whole lot better if I could tell her I'm not a suspect in this case. Not anymore."

Kreitzer snorts. "Everyone's a suspect. My mother's a suspect."

I think about this. "But your mother and I are not... We're not important suspects."

"You're important, all right. Somebody keeps trying to bring us back to you. That makes you very important."

"But not as a suspect," I insist.

He glances over at me. "Look, part of how you do this job is that you never assume. You deal in probabilities, but you never assume." He kicks at the sidewalk as if there were something in his path, but there's nothing there.

We walk half a block in silence.

"Screw the even and odd thing," a young man walking in front of us tells his companion. "They could win it all again next year."

"Don't talk that way, you're gonna jinx it," his companion replies.

"Bro, it's your birthday!" the first man says. "We get to celebrate! You can't jinx the Giants on your birthday!"

Kreitzer's long strides take us around them and I hurry to keep up. He appears lost in thought.

"You want my advice?" he finally asks me.

"Sure."

"Fire your new writer. I don't know who used to write your Fog Seller stuff. But you need to bring him or her back."

53.

I Can't Just Quietly Go Away

Tuesday, October 30

"Stevie..."

I say nothing, lost in my thoughts and worries.

"Stevie!" Luis says.

I look over, try to smile. I do appreciate what he's doing, using his lunch break to come walk with me for a few minutes.

"You told her, Stevie. It was the right thing to do. You should be really proud."

I give him another look, say nothing.

"It was just gonna get worse the more time you waited. Things are bad right now, but it woulda been worse next week."

I start to give him a mocking reply, think better of it.

He knows how I'm feeling. No need to make him feel bad, too.

He reaches up, puts his arm around my shoulder for a moment. "It'll be OK, Stevie," he tells me. "You'll be OK."

* * *

I bring a single white rose to the little office plaza this morning.

It is my father's birthday, and the late-morning sun slices between the buildings to shine upon this corner. Sometimes there is justice in the world.

"Happy birthday, Dad," I tell him. "I miss you."

If he were here he would be 74 today. Still a viable age. There are lots of dads who are 74 years old.

"Luis is friends with Paula now and she's back talking to me again," I tell him. "She says she'll come with me to go meet the DJ who wrote the joke book from The Lady with the Joke Book in Her Purse. We're going over there tomorrow."

A bus roars by on Spear St., cutting off a taxi that blares its horn.

"I'm moving in with Mrs. Tarrow for a little while, till I can find a new place that will take my fish and Zina and everything."

A young man in a suit and tie with a rollabout briefcase walks by, wheels clicking rhythmically on the pavement. He's staring at his cell phone as if it has suddenly turned into last year's model.

"No, I'm telling you," he implores the screen, "she took my keys, my security badge..."

A voice on the other end starts to ask him about numbers and passwords and he clickety-clacks through the front door to the office building.

I take a deep breath.

"I... Dad, it's all going wrong with Emma. She's angry with me for not telling her about Liam when we first meet and when I do tell her about Liam last week... Tommy Gonzalez, my old student, keeps telling me..."

The flush of emotion flows over me again. I think about "To take arms against a sea of troubles," how Tommy uses Shakespeare to push me to stand up for myself.

"Dad, I know I always tell you that I'm..."

I rest my forehead on the wall. Another deep breath.

"With this girl, Emma, I can't just quietly go away... I have to believe in myself and do something. But it's been five days now since I tell her about Liam and she's not returning my calls or answering my texts or responding to my emails. I... it's like trying to find the person who hires The Lady with the Joke Book in Her Purse. I know I have to do something or she'll never come back, but I have no idea what to do."

My father does not respond to this.

He cannot, because he's gone.

54.

Music and Madness for the Urban Dezert Dweller

Wednesday, October 31

The young Indian receptionist in the 10th floor office is dressed up for Halloween as a vampire, with a low-cut black dress, blood-red lipstick and plastic teeth that fall out when she tries to talk.

"May I help you?" she asks pleasantly, using one black-nailed finger to ensure that her incisors don't drop in her coffee.

"Yes," I tell her. "We're Steve Ondelle and Paula Costa. We have a 1:30 appointment with Phil Steen."

"Just one moment." She types something on her computer.

To our left is a poster with a row of cactus trees shaped to spell out K-Z-R-T against the San Francisco skyline. The caption reads, "Music and Madness for the Urban Dezert Dweller."

We continue to stand and wait. Paula's white blouse has pale blue stars in the patterns of the zodiac. The hem of her jeans meets the floor precisely at the bottom of her boot heels.

"Did I get something on my pants?" she whispers, glancing down.

"No." I answer.

Paula does a double take, points through a glass wall to a conference room to our right. On the wall is a poster for *How Much is that Strange Man in the Window?* Che Guevara smiles back at us proudly.

The door to the left opens and Phil Steen comes out. In all his pictures he is a graying, imposing 6'1" DJ with a defiant grin. In person he's barely taller than the 5'3" Paula Costa, but the defiant grin is there as advertised. He wears a Raiders jersey and jeans with big cowboy boots.

"How the hell are you?" he asks us, and we all shake hands.

Steen leads the way back through a series of three doors, unlocking each by bumping a black box with his hip.

"You can tell I'm important around here," he tells us. "The card key readers match the height of my ass!"

We end up in a studio where a tall, slim Black woman with her hair in Princess Leia buns is sitting at a mike. Steen introduces her as Mad Turner, and we all shake hands. I recognize her voice from the Honda commercials on the station that gives the weather every ten minutes.

"You're the voice from the Honda commercials on the station that gives the weather every ten minutes," I tell her.

"Indeed I am," she tells me.

Phil indicates two chairs for us to sit in. "Always a pleasure to meet two of the seven people who've read my book. We were just recording some bits for tomorrow morning."

"OK, enough nice nice," Mad cuts in. "I have to hear about how the Supervisor's girlfriend was secretly hyping Phil's masterpiece. May she rest in peace."

We tell the story of The Lady with the Joke Book in Her Purse, trying our best to ignore the fact that we're discussing the murders with a football player and Princess Leia.

"She told her ex-roommate she was doing a book promotion for you," Paula tells them as we finish. "But it seems like the real objective was to get Steve's fingerprints on the purse. Not her objective, of course, since she ended up..." Her voice drops off.

Steen shakes his head. "Wild. Wild stuff. Needless to say, I never heard of her. I called my publisher when the police were here, but... that isn't the kind of thing they'd do."

"So you know Captain Kreitzer?" I ask.

"We're just acquaintances, and I plan to keep it that way."

Of course Kreitzer would have been here

"I'll give him credit, though," Steen is saying. "He had a damn clever idea for how we could help him. He said we need to stir the pot if we want to crack this case."

Paula leans forward in her chair. "How?"

Steen gestures towards Mad. "She fleshed it out, put the outrageous in it."

Mad grins. "Starting this Friday we're doing a daily segment about how a crazed fan has been promoting Phil's book without him knowing it. We'll ask anyone who saw her to call in so we can track her down and Phil can finally thank her."

"We don't say she's dead," Steen says. "Anyone calls us, we pass it along to the detectives."

"Clever," Paula says.

Steen brightens. "In fact, our engineer Dean came up with the title for the segment, 'The Case of the Vanishing Volunteer.' Dean, meet Steve Ondelle and Paula Costa."

Steen looks through the glass into the control room, where the engineer has just re-entered.

My stomach does a figure-eight. "Dean" is the dreadlocks-laden beak-nosed engineer from Avanture Video, the first person we meet on the first day that Paula and I go looking for The Lady with the Joke Book in Her Purse.

Paula and I look in at him.

Dean looks out at us. His face goes ashen white.

55.

Neil the Super Villain

Wednesday, October 31 (Cont.)

I'm dead tired but I'm still at work, and I'm nowhere close to packing everything for the move that's now just three days away.

A cold wind blows across the dock at the Ferry Building. We're about to load the 7:55 PM back to Sausalito, our final voyage of Halloween night.

We've seen witches and baseball players and vampires aboard the *Baar* all day. But nothing like this.

I go down to pull the onshore power cable and secure the boom. Waiting at the gate is a group of at least fifty people, all dressed in fancy costumes, all wearing masks like the ones you see in pictures of Mardi Gras.

The barrier opens and they run and skip and dance and tromp up the gangway and onto the ferry. Alonzo nods at me and I follow them on board.

One group heads to the upper deck at the stern, where the heaters make it easier to sit outside. Others head to the front cabin.

The revelers keep their masks in place, and no two disguises are alike. Several have video cameras and are taping as their friends hoot and applaud. Others snap pictures with their phones.

"Par-tee! Par-tee! Par-tee!" shouts a young man wearing a Devil mask, a bright red satin shirt and a black cape.

The group takes up the chant. "Par-tee! Par-tee! Par-tee!" They've had a few drinks, but I think we'll get to Sausalito without anyone throwing up.

I wonder if Mr. Grainger would look at Luis' job differently if Grainger were the one assigned the job of cleaning the carpets after the antics of upchucked drunks.

I doubt that Mr. Grainger's job description mentions vomit.

For the 29th time today I check my phone to see if by some miracle there's a message from Emma. But the list...

"Ahhh!!!!!" Two cold hands suddenly grip my throat. I jump and cry out.

"My friend!" says a high, raspy voice, "Ever dance with the devil in the pale moonlight?"

"Let go of me!" I twist away, see a man in a Joker costume, his face hidden behind the plastic mask. I smell breath tainted with scotch and cigarettes.

"Neil!"

At the doorway to the front cabin stands a tall, slim woman with long too-black hair curled in ringlets. Her mask has gold satin around the eyes, and the nose and mouth beneath it are painted to look like cracked and weathered porcelain. The bright red mouth is expressionless, her eyes only shadows.

"Sorry, bro', sorry," the man says to me. "Just fooling around, bro'. Sorry."

The woman extends her arm to guide Neil the Super Villain back into the front cabin, long folds of purple fabric layered from her sleeves. He quietly brushes by her.

"I'm sorry," she tells me in an efficient tone. "We're here for an event, not to bother people." She wears a large black onyx ring in the shape of a spider, with crystal eyes that glisten when she moves her hand.

I rub my hair to see if it's still standing on end. "Who are you guys?"

"Just a social club," she says. "I'll make sure they don't get out of hand." She bows gracefully to me, then turns and returns to the front cabin.

I hear a boom box start to play, and the familiar opening notes of Michael Jackson's *Thriller*. I'm not sure where Alonzo is so I make my way up the stairs to see what's happening.

I emerge into the cold night air and see twelve of the masked passengers standing in formation between the benches on the top deck, tapping their feet in time to the music. A man and a woman at the stern each have video cameras to record the scene, and the man's rig looks big and professional.

I stop to watch the performance. The dancers lean on seat backs, sit down, jump up on seats, pivot in circles and jump down again. Other passengers come outside to watch.

One spectator lugs an oversized blue duffel bag, while the woman with him carries a young boy who has equally bright blue eyes. When the man sets down the heavy duffel the head of a yellow lab pops out.

"Jackson, look at the dancers!" the woman says to the toddler.

The boy's father looks over to see if I'm going to hassle them. Dogs have to be in carriers and the dog is in the duffel, so I just smile and nod to him. Hard to hassle a dog that looks like Zina.

The little boy watches the dancers thoughtfully from his mother's arms, not sure what to make of it all.

When the music stops the dancers hold their poses till the man with the big camera yells, "Cut!" and everybody cheers before rushing for their coats and capes to get warm.

I turn to a costumed woman who has a long, deep green velvet dress and short gray hair. "What's the name of your group?" I ask her.

Her mask covers her face down to the cheekbones, but allows me to see her smile between bright red lips. "We're just a social club!" she answers pleasantly.

By now the softly-lit towers of the Golden Gate Bridge are slipping behind the darkened headlands of Marin. The masked performers talk happily and sip hot coffee as we approach the pier in Sausalito.

We secure the lines and lift the steel gangplank into place, and the passengers hurry onto the dock. I have to get back and help Alonzo connect the hoses to refill the water tanks for tomorrow morning, but for now I let myself be carried along with the costumed group to see which way they go.

A large, dark blue bus with tinted windows is waiting in the parking lot, its engine throbbing. A card taped to the side window says "CHARTER." The woman with the cracked-patina mask leads her charges up the steps and into the warm bus, the costumed revelers still talking and laughing happily.

Two of the dancers are trailing the group, carrying the big boom box between them and struggling with their long skirts.

"Can I help?" I offer.

"Thanks!" the first girl says, holding out the handle on her side of the awkwardly-shaped machine. The feathers on her mask form the shape of a butterfly over her gold dress.

"Jessie!" the second girl whispers from behind her silver mask, but it is too late. I have taken the handle and she needs me to get the boom box to the bus.

"Where you guys headed?" I ask. This way they can't answer, "Just a social club."

"I dunno, they haven't told us," Jessie says.

Her frustrated partner remains silent.

We reach the bus and the driver unlocks the side panel for the heavy box. The broad compartment door slides open.

My heart jumps. Inside are three large trunks stenciled "Avanture

Video." The driver takes the boom box and slides it inside, but I can't take my eyes off those crates.

Avanture Video. Twice in one day.

I wonder if the big hat on the cameraman hides the dreadlocks of Dean, the beak-nosed engineer.

Dean the engineer. Twice in one day.

I pull out my phone to call Kreitzer and leave a message, but stop in my tracks when I see that I have my own missed call.

It's from Emma.

My God, it's from Emma!

She's calling me back for the first time in six days. Six days where I try to sound calm and Liam-like but steadily feel more and more helpless as the computer voice yet again tells me that there's no one there and to leave my name and number.

She's calling me back for the first time in six days, and I miss her call. Miss the chance to actually talk to her, to sound like she hopes I'll sound just one more time.

She calls me for the first time in six days, and I miss what could be my last chance to try to keep her from running away for good.

56.

Unpacked and Unrepentant

Wednesday, October 31 (Cont.)

"It's just... I'm really tired from having to study so late and then open for Manny so early in the morning..."

Emma's voice pauses, as it does at this point every time I replay the message.

It's been six days and then she calls me and I miss her call.

I play the message yet again. "I'm really tired from having to study so late and then open for Manny so early in the morning..." She doesn't pause. She hesitates.

There's a difference.

"I... We should talk. It would be good for us to talk. I'll come back down next Thursday. On the 8th. If I can. I'll do my best."

"If I can..." I know what those words mean.

"I'm sorry, Steve." I know what those words mean.

I sit in my little garage, the only light coming from the wall of aquariums. All the other walls are empty, their contents stacked and stuffed into the piles of cardboard boxes that almost fill the room.

The big giraffe-spotted *venustus* in the 210-gallon does not seem to notice that everything in my world is changing. He swims in place, front and center, to see if I have food. I'm holding my black cell phone instead of the yellow food bucket, but he waits patiently to see if I change my mind.

I'm running out of time.

Running out of time to pack the thousand little things still scattered in my garage, unpacked and unrepentant.

Running out of time to pack the best of Liam and the best of Steve into one human being and somehow act like having two heads is as natural as having two hands.

I survey the room, looking for a signal on where to start, to do what I can tonight so the problem isn't worse tomorrow.

Zina emerges from behind the boxes that surround her bed, stretching uncomfortably. She re-settles at my feet with a sigh.

I reach down and rub her back for a few minutes, then assemble another box and go into the bathroom to pack the sheets and towels and the medicine cabinet.

It's the best that I can do.

57.

The Case of

the Vanishing Volunteer

Thursday, November 1

My new $19 radio is in my jacket pocket and one earbud is in my right ear. As I empty the trash cans on the lower deck I look at my watch. Two minutes to go till 8:30.

It's Friday, and Phil Steen is going fishing for people who saw The Lady with the Joke Book in Her Purse. But for now all that's playing on my new radio is a weight-loss-pill commercial.

Finally I hear Mad say, "You're on the road with Phil Steen on the Dezert, KZRT in San Francisco!"

But then she launches into the traffic and weather report.

I'm on a ferry boat. I do not care about the traffic. I want to hear Phil and Mad's "The Case of the Vanishing Volunteer."

An older woman next to a window waves to me.

"Is that Alcatraz?" she asks, pointing to Angel Island.

"No," I tell her. "That's Angel Island. Alcatraz is smaller, has big buildings and a water tower on top."

"Oh. How long till we see Alcatraz?"

An enthusiastic man on the radio is telling me how I can save big money on insulated vinyl windows.

"Only a few minutes," I tell her.

Now the husband wants to talk to me. "Burt Lancaster was The Birdman of Alcatraz," he says. "Great movie, great characters."

I nod politely. The voice in my head says if I order now I'll save 25%.

"Movies back then weren't filled with all the profanity, the swear words every five seconds," he goes on, still looking squarely at me. His wife nods.

"That's true." I tell him, and resume walking towards the bow.

"Sir? Sir?" his wife calls after me.

I stop, turn around and come back to them, making sure to smile. "Yes, ma'am?"

I hear old style organ music, and Mad Turner saying, "And now for another exciting chapter of San Francisco's favorite soap opera, 'The Case of the Vanishing Volunteer!'"

The woman by the window smiles back at me.

"When we go by Alcatraz, would you mind taking a picture of my husband and me in front of the island?"

"Sure, I'd be happy to."

By the time I can re-focus Phil Steen is saying, "...woman who has such exquisite taste that she's been going around San Francisco promoting my new book..."

"You'll tell us when we get close to Alcatraz?" the woman asks.

I look out the windows. It won't be long. "Just watch for the little island with the big water tower," I tell her.

"...without telling me. But my savvy book publisher, who shall go nameless..."

"But can be found at RockinBooks.com," Mad comments.

"Yes, my savvy book publisher tells me that they have no budget for promoting my book, because they've spent it all on the national tour for the Real Matrons of Minneapolis..."

"But you will, you know. Just wave at us or something." The woman smiles at me expectantly.

Sometimes you just know it's not your day. I pull out the earbud and stuff it in my pocket.

"Let's start walking up there now," I tell the couple. "The best spot is outside on the bow as we go by the north end of the island."

"Thank you so much!" she says. They stand, preparing to follow me upstairs.

I notice how deliberately she makes sure to bring her purse.

* * *

"Our friend Dean has certainly earned a spot on the list, showing up twice in one day," I tell Mrs. Tarrow, then take another bite of pizza. "And he has links to Theatre Lab West and to Phil Steen. But when I call Kreitzer about it he just writes something down and says he's got it."

"That's all you can do, Steven. Just tell him what you see."

I go to the fridge, take down our chart and bring it to the breakfast bar.

> Knows Steven not good with questions.
> — Ferry? School? Classmate?
> Knows Steven's routine, could plant gun.
> — Ferry rider? Crew?
> Had motive to kill Supervisor Giantonio?
> — SoMa Triangle project? Other?
> Had motive to kill Candi Bonham?
> — Twin cowboys?
>
> Hired Candi to drop purse to get fingerprints
> — Woman, or has female partner
> — Not experienced in evidence

Moves in circles with the wealthy
Had stolen gun: Criminal record? Gang?

Carl Mathis: Parent, PR at Institute
Tommy Gonzalez: Former student
Tom Festane: Parent, ex-SoMa Triangle
Mary Anne Mathis: Parent, attorney
Eve Mortimer: Lost $ via SoMa Triangle
Dean @ Avanture: Knew Candi, reappears

"The problem," I tell her, "is that every name meets a few of our criteria, but none of them meets them all." Zina groans and changes her position at my feet.

Mrs. Tarrow takes another bite, waits, chews. "Murders always have a motive," she says, finally. "Once we find the motive the picture will become a lot more clear."

"How do we do that?" I ask her.

"Oh, I think Ken's already started the process."

I'm confused. "What process is that?"

She puts down her pizza, wipes her hands on her white cotton napkin. "Up till now the killer has been writing a script that makes you look like a murderer, trying to incriminate you," she tells me.

"And to try to make me act crazy, so I'll incriminate myself even though I'm not a criminal."

"Exactly," she says. "They've been writing the scripts to trap you. But now, with 'The Case of the Vanishing Volunteer,' that's all changed. Now *we're* the ones writing the script and trying to trap *them*."

58.

But You Never Kept Any for Yourself

Saturday, November 3 – Sunday, November 4

The days and nights of boxing up my books pay off, and they are soon stored in Mrs. Tarrow's garage, with a few favorites on a shelf in the living room.

The one 60-gallon tank that fits in the spare bedroom is moved in less than an hour. The fish inspect each rock and grain of sand as they try to figure out who moved all the furniture.

The rest of the tanks, however, are another story.

When you move aquariums you have to carry over half of each tank's water with the fish to keep them healthy, so their environment doesn't change dramatically all at once. And the same water has to stay with the same fish, no mix and match.

To make it harder still, the glass walls that can hold so much weight sitting on a shelf can hold almost nothing when the tank is moved. Lifting a tank that has more than a half inch of water in the bottom is risking disaster, not to mention a hernia.

It gets worse. The buckets we use to move the fish lose heat in the cool autumn air. Tropical fish like it warm and are vulnerable to infections if the temperature drops, so all these intricate steps have to be done quickly to avoid disaster.

Just writing about it makes me sore and tired. And worried.

Mrs. Tarrow persuades me to use professional movers the first day. There are too many steps, too many weird angles, too many places to slip and fall with something heavy.

At one point while I'm refilling the 210-gallon in its new space in the garage Leonard the Human Statue appears, newly liberated from his data entry gig. He has a bucket in each hand, a block of Styrofoam atop each one to discourage any attempted escapes. "Here's more for this tank," he tells me. "You've got Napoleon up there directing traffic."

"Who's that?" I ask, pouring water from the first bucket at a steady pace so I don't stir up too much sediment.

"Eli, the guy you said was so shy," Leonard says.

I laugh out loud, then catch myself. "I shouldn't be laughing. Eli knows everything there is to know about fish and how to move them."

Working side by side with Eli and Leonard is Linh, who quietly moves bucket after bucket until she has lugged the water from every 20-gallon tank. Luis is right there, too, carrying a zillion boxes so the movers can focus on the aquariums and furniture that need to go to the garage.

On Sunday Tommy Gonzalez and his girlfriend Rebecca come to help, and the kitchen cabinets all get boxed and taken down to storage.

Flowing through this process is Mrs. Tarrow, who seems to be everywhere at once. One moment she's tucking a few stray books onto a shelf, another she's unpacking my grandmother's cast iron pan so I'll have something familiar in the kitchen.

Each morning she has bagels and cream cheese and orange juice and bacon and waffles piled high on plates. Mid-day there's lemonade and grilled ham-and-cheese sandwiches and all sorts of fruit. On Sunday she barbecues burgers.

In the evenings we have to practically tie her down to let us order dinner from down the hill, but she finally relents.

Sunday night it's time to celebrate amid the ravaged pizza boxes. Luis has to go home to Leti and the kids, but Leonard, Eli, Tommy, Rebecca and Linh join Mrs. Tarrow and me to salute our victory.

As he reaches to refill his glass with wine Leonard asks Tommy, "So what kind of teacher was Steve when you were a kid?"

"Mr. Ondelle was the best," Tommy says. "He took me to my first baseball game ever, to see the Giants. It's because of him I'm going to college."

"Bravo," Mrs. Tarrow says, her water glass raised, and we all raise our glasses, too. Zina is curled up at her feet.

Leonard asks, "Did you get to see Professor Polymirth?"

"We were the first Polymirth scholars!" Tommy proclaims. "The first ones to translate 'To Be or Not to Be' so everyone could understand it!"

Leonard shakes his fist. "That's how you do theatre!"

"We had it all figured out," Tommy says. "Mr. Ondelle was going to get his Ph.D. and teach at a big university. He'd even bring his twin brother Professor Polymirth and do his crazy sh... stuff. We were all gonna graduate from high school and then we'd all go to whatever famous college he was at and we'd be his students all over again. Then we'd graduate from college and..." He looks expectantly at me. "You remember, Mr. Ondelle?"

"First you graduate from college, then we conquer the world," I recite. "I remember." Though it breaks my heart, I remember.

"You were gonna go to London, study Shakespeare and Ionesco and all those guys we read about."

Mrs. Tarrow turns and looks at me. "How do you feel, hearing Tommy say what a great teacher you were?"

I wish Emma were here so she could listen to all of this. But I just say, "I'm very proud of Tommy."

"I know, but that's not what I asked you," she says gently. "I asked how you felt when Tommy said you're a great teacher."

"It feels good," I tell her.

If it were Liam he'd tell her all about every feeling from heart to head and back again, going on and on and on. He'd tell her how he feels proud and broken at the same time. How he feels like he's let Tommy down even as the boy feels he's built Tommy up. How seeing Tommy fills one void in his life and rips the scab off another, how it brings both joy and searing pain.

But I am not like Liam. Not yet. So I say none of this.

"It's OK," Mrs. Tarrow says. "I just think you should be proud of you, too. Besides being proud of Tommy."

Tommy shakes his head and makes a strange sound in his throat. "Same old Mr. Ondelle," he says. "You gave us all this pride and confidence, but you never kept any for yourself."

59.

Second Best Place to Live in America!

Monday, November 5

I sit at the corner table at the Mexican place on Howard and wait for Luis and Paula. I'd love to use my break to go home and check water temperatures in the relocated tanks, but now that Paula is speaking to me again I don't want to screw it all up.

We're near Moscone Center and the room is filled with convention-goers. I try to read the badges dangling from their necks but all I can make out is, "and the Environment." Most wear jeans and T shirts, with a couple of men in suits and women in little black dresses.

I wonder if Candi would ever come here during conventions, eat with friends at one of these tables.

"Hey there."

I look up to see Paula smiling as she comes to the table and sits down. She wears a light blue sweater, jeans and boots. I realize I have seen her in a little black dress as well but choose not to dwell upon this thought.

"Hey there. Where's Luis?" I ask.

"We were just going out the door when they asked him for something. He asked me to go ahead so you wouldn't worry."

"No problem."

"Any word from Phil Steen?" she asks.

"No," I tell her.

"How'd the move go?"

"We did it. Turns out Eli is like an aquatic Napoleon. With him in command all the right fish are in the right tanks down the hill at Mrs. Tarrow's."

She raises one eyebrow. "Eli? You said he was really shy."

"With everything but fish, I guess."

"Reminds me of someone else I know." She gives me another grin and picks up her menu.

"Actually," I tell her, "the wildest story of all is from the ferry on Halloween night."

"Why am I not surprised?"

I tell her about the masked dancers, the costumed guy with the pro video rig, and the cache of Avanture Video equipment in the bus.

This last item makes her eyes go wide. "The tall guy has to have been what's-his-name, Dean from Avanture Video. And from Phil and Mad's!"

"He keeps turning up," I tell her.

"Paula! Paula Costa!" A guy in a blue striped shirt and khaki pants comes up to our table.

Paula looks startled, then stands to give him a hug. "Hi! What are you doing in San Francisco?"

"I'm here for the Green Building show!" His badge proudly announces, "Hi, my name is Brad!" He turns to me and says, "Hi, my name is Brad!"

I shake his hand.

He turns back to Paula. "You working here?"

"Blackman Planetarium, two blocks down, part time while they build the new Institute."

"I'm glad this one worked out. You teaching, too?"

"Just an adjunct job, at S.F. State. You still in Fort Collins?"

"Survey says, second best place to live in America!" Brad says. "At least if you're in construction."

"How long are you here?" Paula asks. My heart sinks when I hear her tone.

"Just till Friday, for the show. We're doing a big lighting job for Colorado State, so I have to get back. All halogen fixtures, computer controlled, really cool stuff."

She points to his left hand. "That's new!"

He touches his wedding ring, smiles. "Last summer. We both got lost in Wal-Mart and then we found each other."

"Congratulations!" Paula tells him. I look at her eyes and see it's not that simple.

"Thanks!" he says. "I never did find the apple jelly I was looking for, but I did find true love."

She just smiles.

He pauses just a little too long. "Hey, well, we have to be back at the booth in like 35 minutes. It's great to see you, Paula, I just wanted to say hi."

She gives him a hug goodbye. "Great to see you!"

He reaches back to shake my hand again.

"Nice to meet you," I say on cue.

Brad goes back to the front of the restaurant. Paula turns back to face me. I don't know whether to meet her eyes or pick up the menu.

"I'll be right back," she says and heads for the restroom.

So it's that bad.

Two minutes later Luis arrives at the table. "Sorry I'm late. They lost a tray of shells. Where's Paula?"

"In the bathroom."

He starts to pick up his menu, then looks at me and puts it down again. "What happened?"

"It's not me. A guy who's sitting over there. Old boyfriend with a new wedding ring."

Luis digests this. "She OK?"

"No."

He picks up his menu, looks back at the rear of the restaurant, puts it down again. "Damn shells."

Up front I can see Brad laughing with his friends.

Luis looks across at me. "You OK?"

"I guess," I tell him.

He gives me a long look. "So now you're all upset about Paula again."

"I know. It's not logical. It's just... It's not logical."

He's getting angry at me. "You doing this on purpose?"

"I know Emma is where... After all those nights wanting Paula to care about me..." I take a deep breath. "It still hurts to see her care for someone else."

Now there's no mistaking his anger. "*Cabrón, ese,* what's wrong with you? Whatever goes good for you, you try to screw it up! That girl Emma is in love with you, she's just scared! You got what you always wanted!"

"I know. I just have to... I know."

His voice stays soft but he's yelling at me angrily. "Then what the fuck you doing getting upset about someone else?!"

"I know."

"Stevie, you trying to fuck this up? That what you're trying to do? Make sure you always have some reason to be all serious and alone and sad?"

"No!" I practically yell at him. "I don't want to spend my life like that!"

Paula reappears, her composure restored. No trace remains that she's been upset.

The same cannot be said for Luis and me.

"What's with you guys? What happened?" she asks.

Luis does not answer. He just says, "Sorry I'm late."

I pretend to review the menu.

She looks back and forth at Luis, then at me, then back at Luis again. "You guys do what you want," she says, "but I'm having a margarita."

60.

It Has Been Haunting Me,
Sitting in the Closet

Three years ago, as seen from Wednesday, November 7

It is three years ago. But it is still like right now to me.

I look at myself in the mirror. I am wearing my Professor Polymirth costume for the first time since I walk away from teaching.

It has been haunting me, sitting in the closet. It's time to toss it or to put it back to work.

The black silk top hat and the tuxedo jacket with the long tails, worn over my white T-shirt. The translucent scarf that was a gift to Professor Polymirth from Tammy Keeler's mom.

Leonard the Human Statue stands back and looks at me.

"Not bad..." He leans his chin on his hand, thinking.

"I'd always feel confident portraying Professor Polymirth," I tell him. "That's what I need to get back."

Leonard smiles. "I don't think you lost your confidence. You just lost your audience."

"Which comes first, the confidence or the audience?"

He doesn't answer. "Baggy pants are cheap and they'll give you a *commedia dell'arte* look that gets laughs."

Some of my students struggle with reading the textbooks that are assigned to our grade level, but my silly twin brother Professor Polymirth helps them learn by acting out stories.

Teaching is something I know how to do.

I don't know how to do what Leonard does, entertaining people who are not required by law to sit with me all day in uncomfortable chairs.

I explain this once again to Leonard, but he says, "You keep saying how you wish you could do what I do. This is how actors get their confidence. We get up on stage and we just do it."

We just do it.

"Have you thought about your stage name?" Leonard asks.

"I think it's silly, but yes I've thought about it."

"It's a device," Leonard says, "just like Professor Polymirth. If someone asks your name you don't break character. You answer as the character."

"I guess."

"So, what's your character's name?"

I smile at him. "Well, the stage name is a lie about who I am, right?"

He rolls his eyes impatiently. "In a way."

"So if it's a lie about who I am, I take the L from 'lie' and the phrase 'I am' and that's it: Liam. My character's name is Liam."

"All right then, Liam," Leonard says, "let's see your pitch."

I take a deep breath, throw out my chest and begin.

"Ladies and gentlemen, there are many souvenirs of San Francisco. A keychain depicting the Golden Gate Bridge. A salt shaker shaped like Coit Tower. An Elvis tattoo that you don't remember getting but that wiggles its hips when you laugh."

Leonard nods his approval.

"But this is different!" I pull the little vial from my tuxedo coat. "The keychain, the salt shaker, they are replicas. What I have here is real, the true symbol of the City. It is... the fog."

"Keep your energy up," Leonard says. "You're just dying to share this."

I nod. "This is not replica fog, synthetic fog or reconstituted fog from concentrate. This is pure San Francisco ..."

More laughter. I shake my head, confused by memories.

"This fog is organic, non-allergenic, and features pure hydrogen and oxygen that are billions of years old!"

Now they're really laughing. I see Leonard standing in his Lincoln costume at the edge of the crowd, and the usually-serious 16th President laughs with them.

"They say you can't control the weather, but with this little miracle..." I lean down and roll the vial across the pavement. "Only you decide when the fog rolls in!"

A few groans mixed with the laughs, and it's time to do the close. I do my, "Pay me anything or nothing" bit and the crowd applauds.

A mother and her adult daughter hurry forward and each gives me $2 for a vial of fog. Another goes to a man in a Pittsburgh Steelers cap.

When the last vial is sold Abraham Lincoln approaches me. "You keep getting better and better," he says.

I shake my head. "Not with Emma."

Leonard the Human Statue looks at me very seriously. "The world will little note nor long remember that I am about to buy you lunch, but I'm going to do it anyway."

61.

A Thousand Rainy Fingers

Wednesday, November 7 (Cont.)

It is approaching 9:00 PM and the cloudy afternoon has become a rainy, windy evening. Worried passengers listen to the waves crashing on the bow, watch the spray rise in sheets to coat the main deck windows. And remember all the disaster movies they've ever seen.

Alonzo, Linh and I make a point of smiling and looking calm, our way of reassuring them that for the *Louis H. Baar* this is a day at the playground, not a threat.

When we finally reach Sausalito you can feel the sighs of relief as we slow to approach the dock. We secure the *Baar* for its eight hours of rest and I hurry up the ramp to the pier, locking the gate behind me. Cold rain blows in my face.

As I reach the newspaper racks at the edge of the parking lot I stop in my tracks. A dark figure steps from behind the ticket machines, hidden in a heavy black raincoat, a black hat pulled down over his face. He steps very close to me.

"Steven! I came to get you!"

It is Mrs. Tarrow. How can a five-foot-tall 70-something woman look like a huge hit man in the dark?

"It's too cold and wet for you to walk up the hill in this weather," she tells me.

"You scare the bleep out of me!" I tell her.

"Sorry, dear," she says in her matter-of-fact voice. "The car's over here." She leads the way to the old Volvo and we climb in. A thousand rainy fingers drum their nails on the metal roof.

"Thanks for coming to get me," I tell her.

"I made my German meat loaf. If you'd like some."

"That'll be great."

This is not about rain and wind and walking up the hill.

It is about Emma.

Mrs. Tarrow knows that this will be my second lonely Thursday without Emma, knows that for two weeks all I've heard is one brief voicemail, knows how Emma's silence weighs on my every step. So here is Mrs. Tarrow, with a warm car and a stick-to-your-ribs dinner.

As she pulls into the driveway I tell her, "If my aquariums weren't in the garage you could park inside and not get so wet when you get out of the car."

She ignores me.

We dash in the kitchen door and hang our wet raincoats to drip onto the tile. Zina spins in circles as she waits for us to rub her back. I bounce her rubber ball into the dining room so she can race in hot pursuit.

Mrs. Tarrow takes the meatloaf out of the oven, pulling tin foil off the baking dish. Only one small serving is missing.

She checks the temperature with one finger and says, "I'll just zap it in the microwave and we'll be set."

Two minutes later I'm in heaven, more specifically in the region of heaven reserved for home-made German-style meatloaf.

She leans against the breakfast bar and gives me a funny smile. "Do you mind if I ask you something?"

"Sure."

She hesitates, then rushes ahead. "Since Teri and Josh and Derek are back in Chicago for Thanksgiving this year, I'd still love to have a big turkey and a... I'd love to have lots of people at the table. I know Luis will be with his family. Do Leonard and Eli and your other friends have a place to go for Thanksgiving?"

"I don't think Leonard's going back east this year. Eli's like me, he never talks about his family. Tommy will be with his mom..."

"Would you mind asking them, the ones who may be here?"

"Sure."

She goes to the fridge, pretends to look for something so I can't see her expression. "Maybe you can ask Emma, invite her to come down."

I take a deep breath.

Another deep breath.

"You know she's not coming back, Mrs. Tarrow."

She straightens up, closes the refrigerator door and looks at me.

"I want my full house for Thanksgiving," she says softly. "How about you and I drive up to Sacramento to invite her?"

I race to think of an excuse, a way to avoid the humiliation of being rejected to my face instead of quietly forgotten from afar.

Mrs. Tarrow keeps looking at me, the way she does when I know she can read my every thought because I'm being me.

"Just think about it, Steven. It sounds like she's a wonderful girl and Thanksgiving dinner means a lot to me."

"I know," I tell her. "I know."

62.

They Already Knew
Who They Wanted to Win

Friday, November 9

"Well, if you weren't awake yet when we came on the air at 6:00 AM..."

"Hell, I work here and I wasn't awake yet when we came on the air at 6:00 AM," Mad interrupts.

Phil Steen laughs. "Well, I just hope you pushed the right buttons so we have this down."

"It's all there, Phil."

I listen impatiently. We're about to start boarding the 7:45 AM departure for Sausalito and they need to get to the point.

Phil says, "You're on the road with Phil Steen on The Dezert, KZRT in San Francisco, and if you missed it we are embroiled in a mystery here, a drama we call..."

Mad's voice, backed by dramatic music, says, "The Case of the Vanishing Volunteer!"

Phil keeps going. "The inspiring story of a brave soul who loves my new book so much that she has taken it upon herself to become my promoter."

"And what's wrong with that, I might ask?"

"Well, Mad, I'm glad you asked, because in fact my publisher's been too busy to promote my book. Even I have been too busy to promote my book. So when someone else steps up..."

"You're grateful."

"That's right."

"You want to thank her."

I think, "Mad, get on with it!" The passengers on the dock are inching towards the barrier, their biological time clocks telling them it's time to get on board.

"So we've been looking all over town, asking our listeners if anyone has heard or seen this woman who's been pushing my book so that I can invite her into the studio and thank her."

"And confirm that she's taking all her medications."

"Yes, that too," Phil agrees. "And today we got our first report from our detectives in the field. Mad, let's run that tape from just over 90 minutes ago."

There is a clicking sound, followed by Phil Steen's voice.

"Now I'm told that you have our first report in our 'Case of the Vanishing Volunteer' contest. May I get your name please?"

"My name is Anna," says the woman on the radio.

"OK, Anna, and where are you from?"

"I'm from Chicago, but now I live in Daly City."

"All right, Anna from the Windy City and Daly City, where did you see our mystery hack promoting my book?"

"It was back in August. Is that too long ago?"

"No, Anna, that's fine. Tell us, what did you see?"

"I was having lunch downtown with my sister for her birthday, and the woman at the table next to us had your book, and they were talking about it."

"That's great, Anna!" Phil proclaims. "Now, what can you tell us about her?"

"It's hard to remember after all this time."

"I'll help. Did she look more like Oprah Winfrey or more like Madonna?" Mad asks.

"I really don't... I... She had a really deep, raspy voice, like a man who smoked too much."

"So you remember her voice," Phil says, encouragingly. "What did she look like?"

"I don't really remember. She was big... Tall, I mean. I just remember wondering if she was... you know. A guy."

"A tall lady for a tall story," Mad says.

"You said they were discussing my book," Phil says. "What great things were they saying about it?"

"They, I mean... That's why I remembered it." Anna says. "The woman kept waving around the book, and I remembered you talking about it on your show and I recognized it."

"She was waving it around." Phil says.

"Yes, but she kept saying that the other person's job was to make sure the guy who needed the money got it."

"She's supposed to be selling my book," Phil says. "But now she wants copies given to the poor?"

"It was some kind of contest," Anna says. "But they already knew who they wanted to win."

"Really!" Mad says.

"I thought, is that illegal? Fixing a contest like that?"

Phil gets very serious. "Anna, you have to understand. This is the only promotion my book's been getting. My volunteer hack can't be breaking the law!"

"I don't..." Anna stammers. "She just wanted this guy to get the book and think it was an accident."

"So she couldn't just give him the book?"

"No, that was the thing. He had to find it for himself."

Phil sounds confused, but it's all becoming clear.

"So my secret fan is just leaving books lying around town for people to find?"

"I... It was strange to have a contest where you put the winning prize where only one person would find it."

"And the other woman, Anna? The woman my publicist hired to do all this?"

"I... I'm sorry. I don't... She was cute."

Candi Bonham's epitaph. "She was cute."

Phil asks, "Now I hope I'm not in trouble here, Anna. Did my publicist promise the woman any money?"

"She didn't promise, she gave her cash!"

"Oh, yes! I do so love cash!" Mad says.

Anna keeps going. "That part I remember! She handed over some bills. They looked big."

"Imagine it, ladies and gentlemen," Phil says. "This woman not only volunteers to promote my book, she pays other people cash from her own pocket to do it!"

Anna says, "That's it. That's all I remember."

"Well, Anna, you're our first 'Case of the Vanishing Volunteer' winner! Mad, what's Anna going to get?"

"Anna, your prize is... two tickets to our Oasis in the Dezert show at the Geary Auditorium on January 12!"

Anna squeals. "Thank you! I can't believe I won!"

Mad cuts in, "All right, Anna! It's your turn to do my job!"

Anna knows her line. "You're on the road with Phil Steen on the Dezert, KZRT FM!"

I know this is important. I know this is good news, to confirm that I am a target, that I'm chosen for some purpose.

I can't help but feel very alone.

The trample of the passengers sounds on the gangway. I won't be alone for long.

63.

Spaghetti is Good
for Meditation

Friday, November 9 (Cont.)

"Spaghetti is good for the soul," Mrs. Tarrow tells me.

I realize I've been looking at the same maelstrom of twirled noodles on my fork for what must be a long time. "Sorry," I tell her.

She smiles. "Actually, it's meditation that's good for the soul, and spaghetti is good for meditation."

I am still thinking about this statement when the doorbell rings. Zina rushes to the entryway as Mrs. Tarrow peers through the peephole. Before I can ask if she's sure it's safe she pulls open the door.

"Matt, how are you?" she proclaims to the Japanese man who is standing there with a teen-aged girl at his side. "Hi, Debbi!"

"Amanda, we're sorry to bother you," the man says, "but Debbi has something she needs to tell Mr. Ondelle and Mrs. Blount told us he used to live in the old garage and that he's staying with you. May we come in?"

"Of course!" She steps back and they come inside. He is tall and slim with short hair that is perfectly combed so every strand is in its appointed place. He reaches down and rubs Zina's back as she runs figure-eight's around the visitors.

"Debbi, it's nice to see you," Mrs. Tarrow says to the daughter, and then introduces them both to me. I ask them to call me Steve.

The girl is perhaps 15, younger than my grown-up students, but older than the kids in my old classes. It's hard to tell where the non-Japanese half of her comes from. Her long black hair is as perfectly parted as her father's.

"I... I'm sorry, Mr. Ond.... Steve..." Tears start to skip down her cheeks.

"What is it, dear?" Mrs. Tarrow asks. "What happened?"

"I... I was taking the shortcut by your house to get down the hill to the bus stop, and something was sticking out from under the big trash can with the pipes up the stairs..."

Suddenly every nerve in my body goes on alert. She's talking about the water barrel next to my garage.

Next to my former garage.

She reaches into her pocket and holds up a credit card. "I'm sorry. I saw it wasn't Mrs. Blount's name on the card or anyone else we knew, so I..." More tears now, and she rubs her eyes on the sleeve of her denim jacket.

"Did you buy anything with it," Mrs. Tarrow asks gently.

Debbi shakes her head. "No. I knew it was wrong. But I... It was weeks ago but I didn't know what to do with it and I was afraid to just throw it in the trash and so I just kept it and then Mom..."

"Maribel found it in a drawer," her dad explains. "Since it was found at Steve's place we thought that we should bring it back here, in case you know the owner."

Debbi hands the card to Mrs. Tarrow, who holds it by the edges, reads the name and lets out a deep sigh.

"We shouldn't be surprised," she says, and holds the card out for me to see.

The surface is scratched and one corner has started to peel, but the name is clearly legible. I already know what it will say, how Captain Kreitzer will react when I deliver it to him encased in a plastic sandwich bag.

The raised letters spell out, "Candace Bonham."

64.

It Is Like Here, but
There Is a Lake and Snow

Saturday, November 10

Siphon-haul-dump. Siphon-haul-dump.

It is a cool, foggy Saturday morning and I'm doing the top-row water changes I usually do each Friday night.

At least I have the time today. No calls to cover for a deckhand who's sick, no last-minute requests to take a shift for someone who's still partying at 6 AM.

Most times I welcome the diversion and the extra money. This time I welcome the chance to get back on schedule

Siphon-haul-dump.

Two more buckets into the barrel, at least twenty more to wrestle up to the trash-can-turned-water-tank before I'm done. To the tank that is now located up the hill from my aquariums instead of just outside my door.

A broad-shouldered young man with short brown hair emerges from my old home and carries a pair of empty take-out boxes to the recycling. He looks over and says, "Good morning."

He has an unusual accent. French, but with an unusual sound in the "ing" of "morning."

"Good morning," I respond.

I do not say, "You are living in my home and I am banished by my landlord because of you." That would be rude. So instead I think it but do not say it.

"Are you Steve?" he asks. "I am Patrice." He extends his hand. I shake it. "I am very sorry that you were made to move because I came. I did not know."

This is not what I want. I do not want him to be sorry. I want to be angry at him.

"I'm about to grill the bacon!" I turn and see Mrs. Tarrow at the bottom of the sixteen steps. She in turn sees Patrice and climbs the stairs to meet us.

"Hi. I'm Amanda Tarrow," she says, shaking his hand. Out of the corner of her eye she looks at me.

"Patrice Deschamps," he tells her. "Very nice to meet you. I am just saying to Steve that I am sorry that he had to move because I came."

"Mrs. Blount didn't tell you?" she asks.

"I met her the first time last night. My father arranged all of it. I just know that I have a place to live in Sausalito and I can drive from here to Berkeley and the pictures are like home."

"Ah," Mrs. Tarrow says. "And where are you from?"

"Switzerland, a place called Neuchâtel. It is like here, but there is a lake and snow."

That explains the accent. French-speaking Swiss sound different than French-speaking French.

"So you're going to school in Berkeley?" Mrs. Tarrow asks.

"Yes. The Haas School of Business, graduate school."

"That's wonderful, Patrice. Would you like to join us for some breakfast?"

Why is she doing this? This Patrice seems like a good guy, but I have already shared enough of my life with him without sharing my breakfast.

To my relief he says, "I cannot today, but thank you. Once I get everything arranged I would like to invite you to visit."

"That would be lovely!" Mrs. Tarrow says.

Patrice looks at me. "I would like to invite you, too, Steve. It is very strange, how things happened, and I'm very sorry."

I hate this. Why does he have to be a good guy?

We say our goodbyes and I bring my buckets down the stairs with Mrs. Tarrow. "Just leave them out here, please," she says as we enter the kitchen door.

I don't care if Patrice sends me an invitation encrusted with gold leaf. I'm not going back up there. Ever.

I wash up, then sit at the breakfast bar as Mrs. Tarrow puts the bacon on and Zina settles at my feet. When it's all sizzling furiously she glances over at me.

"Just remember," she says, "Ken may still find a way to trace who told his father that your garage would be a perfect home for his son."

"Maybe Patrice has a twin brother and a cowboy hat."

She ignores this and adjusts the heat beneath the bacon. "Jack would always say, 'Suspects will help you solve your case if you just let them. All you have to do is stir the pot!' That's exactly what Ken is doing with this radio event."

"I guess."

"It may make our killer nervous, having someone who saw the woman who hired Candi Bonham describe her in such detail on a big radio show, like the witness yesterday."

"Uh-huh," I tell her. So strange to see someone else walk out of my front door.

"If the woman's an accomplice she might not have known there'd be a murder. She could panic and call Ken."

"Uh-huh," I tell her.

Mrs. Tarrow cocks her head, leans over to get my attention. "Have you thought about Thanksgiving? About going up to see Emma?"

My stomach drops. "Yes."

"And..."

"I'm thinking about it."

65.

The Pen Tore at the Paper Instead of Writing on It

Monday, November 12

It's hard to climb 108 steps carrying a pizza box.

We take it for granted, the free hand just touching the rail.

We take it for granted that we can look down, see our feet, verify our point of contact with the world.

The mundane pizza box removes these safety nets. Carry it in one hand so I can look down and hold the rail and the pizza weighs more and more with every passing second. So I go back to two hands and now I'm climbing 108 steps without holding the rail, without seeing my feet, all while balancing a hot, viscous slab of melted cheese.

Like I say, it's harder than it looks.

Like a lot of things in life.

I finally reach the top of Excelsior Lane, follow the street to the narrow stairs that lead to the wrought iron gate and the path to Mrs. Tarrow's kitchen door.

Something's wrong. Her car is in the driveway. The lights inside should be blazing at dinnertime, whether I'm there or not. But the kitchen's dark.

I drop the pizza, unlock the door, hurry inside. Zina rushes up but stops before she reaches me, then runs back towards the faint light coming from the living room. The sound of... what? Someone struggling to breathe?

I race forward and switch on the light.

Mrs. Tarrow sits in her big chair in front of the TV. There is nothing on the screen. An oversized book is in her lap.

She is crying, softly.

I hesitate, then approach and kneel by the chair. "You OK?" I whisper. Zina stands immobile beside us, staring intently at her face.

"It's my own damn fool fault," Mrs. Tarrow says. "Bring me a tissue, will you please?"

I hurry to the bathroom, grab the box and bring it to her. She looks up, gives me a twisted smile.

"Thank you, dear."

She blows her nose twice, very loudly.

"Not very ladylike, am I, Steven?"

I put my hand on her shoulder. "I'm just glad you're OK."

She smiles, blows her nose again.

"What's going on?" I ask as gently as I can.

"I was foolish and I took out Jack's Memorial Book," she says, holding up the big binder in her lap. "We keep talking about Jack and about Ken Kreitzer, and what Ken wrote meant a lot to me, but I hadn't read it in a long time and I thought... I thought it was time I should read it again."

"Do you want me to put the book away?"

"No."

"OK." I don't know what to say so I just kneel there, my hand on her shoulder. Zina rests her head on the edge of the chair, her brown eyes locked on Mrs. Tarrow.

"Thank you, Steven," she says after a while.

"Scary moment with the kitchen lights out."

She looks over at the dining room. "I guess I lost track of time."

"I have the pizza, outside on the step. You want some?"

"In a little while, dear."

"OK."

More silence.

She looks up at me. "After I read what Ken wrote, I thought it would be good for you to read it, too. If you want to."

The book is already open on the right page, and she turns it sideways on her lap so I can read the passage.

Amid the signatures and short "Our deepest sympathies" and "Sorry for your loss" inscriptions there is a page filled with block lettering. It looks like the pen tore at the paper instead of writing on it. Discarded, blacked-out words are scattered along the way.

Dear Amanda,

I cannot imagine the sorrow you must feel. Whatever I can do to help, please ask.

It's nothing compared to what you and Teri are going through, but I've lost my father all over again. This father I knew and respected and loved. Jack demanded that I stop being one of the guys and become a Man, and taught me what that meant. In the process he made me a Police Officer.

Jack never wrote my initials KKK on the duty sheet. Obvious why not. He called me The Lonely Warrior, and wrote me down as TLW. The guys all know the code. I still use it.

Jack was pushing me when he coined that name, challenging me to come out of my shell. I did, and it made all the difference, but I will never fill the hole this leaves in my life.

I will always be Jack Tarrow's lonely warrior, because my life will never be the same as it was serving at his side.

You can count on me. I will never give you less than Jack gave me.

With love and sorrow,

Ken Kreitzer

"He sat at the reception and struggled and struggled to write that," she says. "It took him an hour. You can see the parts he blacked out so I couldn't see when a word was wrong. Other people wanted to sign but he wouldn't stop."

I try to picture Captain Kreitzer doing this. The image comes readily to life.

"Here, Steven, give me a hug," she says. "And this old lady will stop feeling sorry for herself and get things together in the kitchen."

I lean over and hug her. She seems so tiny and frail and yet whenever she gives me a hug she feels strong and agile. Zina nuzzles her, runs in a circle and then nuzzles her again.

"I've been thinking..." I tell Mrs. Tarrow.

She pulls back to look at me, a hopeful smile emerging. "Yes?"

A deep breath. "Can you go to Sacramento Wednesday? I have Trish's approval to take the day off."

Now her smile goes wall-to-wall. "I'll call my friends and ask them out for lunch," she says happily. "This will be fun!"

For her, maybe. For me it is pure terror, mixed with the last few broken shards of hope.

66.

Undecided as to Whether
I Should Be Allowed to Live

Wednesday, November 14

"Of course, Steven," Mrs. Tarrow is saying, "telling you not to worry is like telling the moon not to rise."

"Probably true," I mumble. "Thanks again for driving me."

"I wanted to see Anna Lise and Maria, and this gives me a great excuse."

I nod. "I just want her to come back."

"I know."

"I don't want her to see me and think I'm crazy. Like some kind of a nut who'll just show up and ambush her."

"I know."

"But if I don't do this then she'll never come back."

"That could very well be true."

We drive for a while in silence.

"Can I tell you something?" she asks me.

"Sure." I don't really mean it, and she knows it.

"I... what you said about not wanting to seem crazy started me thinking." She says.

"Uh huh."

She glances over at me. "I think you like to live in that place between normal and crazy. If you were normal you'd draw attention because you really are a wonderful young man. If you were crazy you'd draw attention because you were... crazy. But in between you don't draw attention. People don't expect a lot of you. You can hide."

I look in the side mirror again as the road curves slightly. The black Honda is still there, five or six cars back. "Honda's still there," I tell her.

"Lots of people own Hondas," she says.

I can't make out the driver. Since I first notice him a half hour ago he's been at that same distance. No closer, no farther. Just back a ways.

"What do you think about what I just said?" she asks me. I note that she has conveniently picked a location to ask me questions where I cannot just walk away.

"I guess."

"All your friends seem to believe you're a great person who can function perfectly well in society. The only person who doesn't seem to believe in you is you."

"Uh huh." If I weren't so worried about seeing Emma this discussion would tie me in knots. But I'm already tied in knots.

She looks up at a highway sign that reports that we are, indeed, heading towards Davis. "When we get closer I'll need you to navigate. Do you want to go to the bakery or to her apartment?"

"I don't know. She should be at work but I don't want to get her in trouble with Manny."

"I doubt he'd object to a friend saying hi and an old lady asking her to Thanksgiving dinner."

"I guess."

"We can take home an apple pie," she suggests. "He can't be upset if Emma's bringing in customers."

"I guess."

"Steven, do you know why I'm saying all these things to you now? Things that I know make you very uncomfortable?"

"Because you're driving 60 miles an hour and if I jump from the car I'll be killed."

She grins. "Well, yes, but besides that."

"Because you're trying to help me."

"That's true. That's always true."

"I know," I tell her.

"I'm saying things that may sound cruel because what I'm saying may be what Emma is thinking. I could be wrong, but..."

"It's worth thinking about ," I admit.

We see more signs for the exit that leads to Emma's school. Then signs for the exit that leads to Emma.

"Getting close now," Mrs. Tarrow says. "You need to decide where we're going and give me directions."

"She'll be at work. We should go to the bakery."

I pull out my phone and bring up the map. As we hit the off-ramp a calm lady's voice instructs us to turn right.

I check the mirror, then look back as we reach the green light. I can't see if the black Honda exits or not.

We make our way through the streets of West Sacramento. I think about Emma driving home on this street the night she meets me.

"Your destination is ahead, on the right," the calm voice announces.

"OK," my not-at-all-calm voice announces.

Mrs. Tarrow makes the turn on cue and we see the sign for the Gallienne Bakery at the next corner.

"There's a good spot just up there," she murmurs. As we pass the bakery I peer through the window but can't see if Emma's there.

Seconds later Mrs. Tarrow is expertly parallel parking the old
Volvo. I take a deep breath and climb out of the car.

"You ready?" she asks as she comes around to the curb.

Another deep breath. "Yes."

"Just remember, even if you won't admit it to yourself, you are a
wonderful young man. Even if she's frightened she knows how wonderful you really are."

"Yes, ma'am."

She gives me a big smile and tucks her hand in the crook of my
arm. Together we walk the half block back to the bakery.

The big front window proclaims, "Fine French Pastries" and,
"Wedding Cakes a Specialty."

We enter and bells above the front door chime happily. A large
man with broad shoulders and very short brown hair comes from the
back

"Morning," he says.. He has a French accent. Not Swiss French.
French French.

"Morning," I say.

Mrs. Tarrow looks at me and smiles.

The silence is getting awkward. "We're here to buy an apple pie," I
tell him.

He comes around the display case and goes to a tall cabinet in
the front corner, opposite two small wrought iron tables with chairs.
"Have to see what we've got left. Dutch apple's already gone. You
want regular or unsweetened? If I have it?"

"Regular," I answer.

He leans on the top of the case and scans it, then reaches down
and opens the door. "Last one." He scoops up a pie from the back of
the case, turns to bring it to the counter, his breathing audible as he
passes.

I'm building up the courage to ask if Emma is working today. But
before I can say the words she emerges from the back, wiping her
hands on her white apron. She wears jeans and a white T shirt.

She takes several flattened pink boxes from beneath the front counter and turns to carry them into the back when she sees me from the corner of her eye.

A smile comes to her face, only to be almost instantly erased by worry.

Now she forces the smile back again. "What are you doing here?"

"We're here to get an apple pie," I stammer.

"He told me your bakery is wonderful. Emma, I'm Amanda Tarrow and it's lovely to meet you."

The big man looks back and forth between us, and it doesn't take him long to figure it out. "You her friends from Sausalito?" It's hard to read whether a yes or no answer is the safer bet.

"Yes," I tell him.

"Manny, this is my friend Steve, and... well, you heard, this is Mrs. Tarrow."

"*Bonjour, monsieur Gallienne. Ça sent belle ici.*" Mrs. Tarrow says, surprising me.

"*Merci, madame. Bienvenue à Sacramento.*" He puts the pie down on the counter and shakes her hand, then turns to me.

"Nice to meet you," I say and extend my hand.

He looks down at my hand, then decides to shake it. "Manny Gallienne" is all he says.

Emma remains frozen behind the counter. She shudders, comes around to shake Mrs. Tarrow's hand. "It's nice to finally meet you."

"Yes, my dear, I really do exist," Mrs. Tarrow tells her with a smile. She turns to me. "You let her drive all this way?"

Mrs. Tarrow laughs, "I have cabin fever. I needed a road trip!"

Manny has watched all this from behind the counter. "You want anything else?" he asks. He clearly remains undecided as to whether I should be allowed to live.

"I get off at 1:30," Emma says to me softly. Can you come back then? I have to leave for class at 2:30."

I have her schedule memorized and know this isn't a great day, but it's the day I can get off work so it's the only day I've got. "Sure," I tell her.

"I'd also like a half dozen of these lemon drop cookies to take to my friends," Mrs. Tarrow says.

As Emma gets the cookies Manny assembles the pink box around the pie and seals it with a sticker emblazoned with a white shield and crossed swords. He tells Mrs. Tarrow, "She baked those cookies this morning."

Mrs. Tarrow beams. "Anna Lise and Maria will be thrilled! I have to tell them I know the pastry chef!"

"Manny's the only chef here," Emma says, resting her hand on his shoulder. "I'm just a half-baked Veterinary Physical Therapist."

67.

Two Strip Malls
and a Trailer Park

Wednesday, November 14 (Cont.)

We say goodbye and walk back towards the car. "You can text me after Emma goes to class and I'll pick you up," Mrs. Tarrow says matter-of-factly.

I'm still trying to figure out if what I'm about to do is going to make everything much worse.

As so often happens, Mrs. Tarrow reads my mind. "She was surprised. She'll be all right."

I persuade Mrs. Tarrow to go meet her friends so she won't be late. As she and the Volvo disappear I do what I so often do in San Francisco: I pick a direction and walk.

West Sacramento is like many towns. Older houses on shady streets. Two-story apartments behind walls of painted cinderblock.

Liquor stores on the corner with electric signs displaying lottery jackpots.

I see two different black Hondas driving past. One is driven by an old man and the other by a kid blasting his speakers. Neither appears to take any interest in me.

I realize I have time to walk by Emma's apartment and see her neighborhood, so I pull out my phone and orient myself. I'm only eight blocks away.

I pass an elementary school with overgrown grass fields. An old tin-roofed car repair shop and a storage place. Two strip malls and a trailer park.

In a few minutes I see the complex. Just as she described it, there are stucco walls and a pool shaped like Africa. I don't want neighbors reporting a strange guy lurking about, so I just wander past the mailboxes and look at Apartment 47.

There's "Kemmerer" on the mailbox, for her roommate Hope Kemmerer, who's usually at her boyfriend's place.

But below it is the name "Black" rather than "Hernandez."

My mind races with explanations. She's been divorced and is using her maiden name.

Could she have moved? No, I've sent her a postcard of Coit Tower with a little poem and she's received it.

A third roommate to split the bills? Leonard the Human Statue has lived on couches for weeks at a time.

She's in the Witness Protection program because her missing father...

Now I'm really getting silly.

It's time for me to start walking if I want to get back to the bakery by 1:30.

What am I going to say to Emma to persuade her to start coming back to San Francisco? I still haven't figured it out and I'm about to see her face to face.

"Mrs. Tarrow wants you to come over for Thanksgiving so please forget that you're falling out of love with me and come over anyway?"

"I know I'm struggling with how I am as Steve and how I act as Liam, but how about you ignore all that and come to Thanksgiving dinner so Mrs. Tarrow's happy?"

Yeah, Steve, great thinking.

1:30 comes as I walk the last block to the bakery and enter the front door. Emma is helping a woman who has little twin boys. Their hands are pressed against the glass as they ogle a shelf of cookies shaped like stars, rocket ships and cars.

Decisions made and their treats secured in a pure white bag, the boys rush for the door and I step aside to clear the way. Their mother thanks me.

"Cute kids," I tell her.

Emma looks at me across the counter, her face a mix of smile and trepidation. "Sorry I've been so busy,"

"No worries," I tell her. "You have time for a walk?"

"Just let me tell Manny."

She vanishes in the back and I can hear their voices but can't make out the words. At one point I hear him say, "...make sure you're OK."

I remember all her stories about Manny looking out for her. She's right, he's a good man.

A minute later she reappears without her apron and with a black sweater over her T-shirt.

As we walk out into the cool fall air she asks, "How did the move go?"

"Really well. Eli and Leonard and Linh and my students all helped a lot. And Mrs. Tarrow."

Step one complete. I said, "helped" instead of, "help" or, "have helped."

She nods. "It was nice to meet her."

We walk in silence for a while.

"Any news from Captain Kreitzer?" she asks me.

"He has more and more suspects. But nothing that makes any one of them stand out."

"I guess that's progress," she says. "Maybe the case will be solved soon."

"I hope so."

More awkward silence. I decide it's now or never.

"I'm here because I know..." Deep breath. "I know I make... I made things all confused and that if I don't do anything you'll never come back to see me again and that would..."

Must. Think. Like. Liam.

"That would break my heart because I'm in love with you and I want you to keep falling in love with me."

There. I said it.

Emma's eyes never leave the sidewalk. She pulls back her hair, lets it fall over her shoulders. Checks first her left and then her right fili-greed hoop earring. Checks the buttons on her sweater.

"Steve, I..." She stops, just stares straight ahead. Tears well at the corners of her eyes and she shakes her head, wipes them away.

"Look," I tell her, "I know you... you fell in love with Liam. With that side of me. I know it's hard to get used to the idea of... To the Steve side of me."

She wipes her eyes again. "I... I just felt like I knew you so well and then suddenly I realized I didn't know you much at all. I knew Liam, but I barely know Steve."

"I'm trying to figure it all out, too. But I'm afraid that I'll lose you because... It's hard. I'm doing better, but it takes time."

She starts walking again, eyes back on the sidewalk. "I just... I don't know what to do. Most of what you'd said about Steve wasn't very nice. Some days I'm convinced I should just give up. Some days I tell myself that if I try to get to know you, to get to know both sides of you, it'll be OK."

"What kind of day is today?" I ask her.

She keeps walking, keeps looking down. Then she looks back at me. "It's both," she says. "Every day it's both. I want to run away and I want to try."

"Mrs. Tarrow was hoping you could come down for Thanksgiving next week," I tell her. "Her daughter's not here and we want to fill up the house for her." I pause. "I'd really love it if you could come."

She bites her lip, looks down again.

"I can sleep in the living room or even out in the garage with my fish," I tell her. "It's not... It's not about that."

Finally she smiles. "I know."

"So can you come?"

She shakes her head, as if arguing with herself. "OK!" she says.

My heart wants to explode. She's actually coming!

"That's it," she says. "Decided. I'll come for Thanksgiving."

"That's fantastic!" I tell her. "Mrs. Tarrow's going to be thrilled!"

"She's so sweet," Emma says. "She's like a tiny, gentle version of Manny."

I laugh at this. "Hey," I ask her, "Is everything OK? I walked over to your apartment, and..."

"You did what???" She looks horrified.

Now I've done it. Just at my moment of triumph, of joy, I unlock the key to disaster all over again.

Same old Steve.

"I... " There's no way to turn back now. "To pass the time... I've always wanted to see where you live."

"Did you knock on the door?"

"No. When you're at work there's no point."

She laughs sadly.

"Is everything OK? Your name's not on the mail slot."

She looks me in the eye and takes a deep breath. "When tuition went up last year I had to move out."

"Why not tell me?"

"Because I was ashamed."

She's seen my garage. What could she be ashamed of compared to that? "What... Where are you living?" I ask her.

She takes another deep breath. "I'll show you."

We turn back towards the bakery. I'm thrilled at her decision to come down for Thanksgiving. I'm worried about what upsets her about where she's living.

When we get back to Gallienne's she leads me to the delivery entrance in the back. Her familiar freshly-washed white Camry is parked beside the bakery wall. She opens the metal door and leads me down a hallway.

At the far end of the corridor I can see the wide floor of the bakery, with work tables and ovens and mixers. She opens a door on the right, then stands back so I can look inside.

It is a small storeroom, with floor-to-ceiling shelves on the left side and an aisle in the middle. Instead of flour and sugar the shelves hold Emma's possessions.

One shelf has been taken out to create a desk space where her computer sits, with a pad of paper and sheaves of notes at its side. Her big brown purse dangles from a hook on the end closest to the door.

Familiar clothes hang on a rod in the back. The sweater with the embroidered flowers that I like so much. The blouse she wore the day we met. A bright red dress.

Packed everywhere are books and binders. Mostly textbooks, but an assortment of other things from mystery novels to poetry. A mirror hangs on the back wall.

The right side of the room holds a narrow futon with a dark brown frame and a burgundy-colored cushion. A single pillow rests against the back wall.

"Please don't tell anyone Manny let me do this," Emma pleads. "I don't want him to get in trouble."

"This is just as good a spot as my garage," I tell her. "All you need is an aquarium."

This time she can't help but laugh. A little.

Manny appears at the end of the hall, framed in the narrow passageway. He gives me a long glare.

68.

I Don't Know Why
I Tell Him This

Saturday, November 17

"Dad, I'm excited. And I'm scared. Emma's coming down to Mrs. Tarrow's for Thanksgiving dinner next Thursday."

It is a cool autumn day, with a stiff breeze that cuts between the buildings and stings your ears.

"It's the first time she's... I haven't seen her since I told her about Liam and then Mrs. Tarrow and I drive up there and I invite her down and I tell her I don't want her to give up on me and she says she'll come."

I have to slow down. I'm starting to talk like Jenni Mathis.

Three men and a woman cut through the courtyard, coming from Spear St. They look familiar, probably from the ferry.

"Mom, it's your birthday, we should go where you want to eat," a young man says.

"I didn't think Organia would be closed," the woman answers. "I'm still deciding what I want."

"How about the glass atrium place? You loved that place when we were kids," another young man suggests. An older man, apparently the father, agrees.

"I love their brunch," the woman says. "Let's go there."

I wait for them to move away. "Dad, you'd be proud of me," I whisper to my father. "For not backing down. For telling Emma how I really feel."

I don't know why I tell him this, since I have few memories of him telling people how he really feels.

It's the best that I can do.

69.

You Can Have
New Memories, Too

Thursday, November 22 — Thanksgiving

If I concentrate I can recall images from when I'm a little boy.

People in the living room watching football on TV and yelling. Women in the kitchen wearing aprons over nice dresses and the smell of pumpkin pie.

I think back to when my mother is still my mother, the few frames I can still see in that long-lost film. When she can look at me through the black-framed lenses of her glasses and not through the vortex at the bottom of a glass of vodka.

I think back to when my father is still alive.

But my father is not alive.

I open my eyes to see things as they really are.

In the kitchen Mrs. Tarrow is spreading butter beneath the skin of the turkey, as Emma holds the bird steady in the pan. They both look very serious and very satisfied.

I realize my fingers are still cold from lifting the big bird from the sink and patting it dry.

Emma.

Seeing her there is like a mirage. I know what it means when she starts having reasons she can't come back each Thursday. It means it's over. The tree is falling in the forest, even if the sound waves haven't reached me yet.

Yet here she is.

Mrs. Tarrow wears a dark red sweater and black pants with a necklace of black beads. Emma wears a bright red dress with a black flower pattern on the skirt. They swear to everyone that their perfectly coordinated looks are pure coincidence.

"Steve! They scored again!" It's Leonard calling me from the living room. I walk in to find him with Eli, fixated on the game.

Eli doesn't say anything, but looks happy. At least what passes for looking happy when Eli is concerned.

"What's up?" I ask him.

Eli looks over at me, still wearing his Giants baseball cap in football season. "I'm cool," he says.

Zina has followed me into the room, and she licks the potato chip salt off Eli's hands. Eli reaches down and hugs her. To my surprise Zina lets him do it.

"You gonna watch the game?" Leonard asks.

"In a little while," I tell him.

He cocks his head, looks at me more carefully. "You OK?"

"Yeah. Just... Lots of memories."

Leonard lowers his voice, nods towards the kitchen. "Dude, you can have new memories, too."

Eli looks at me, looks in the kitchen, looks back at me. He nods, the smallest of movements, but a nod.

I look through the arched opening to the dining room, and beyond there to the kitchen. Emma's heels are tucked against the wall by the door. She stands barefoot on the kitchen rug as she and Mrs. Tarrow secure the drumsticks with cooking twine.

The doorbell rings.

"I'll get it," I call to Mrs. Tarrow.

"Thank you!" she calls back. "We have our hands full here."

I open the door and stare into the face of Captain Kreitzer. He does not appear to be as surprised to see me as I am to see him.

In his hands is a large bouquet of brightly colored flowers.

"Hi, Steve," he says routinely. "Is Amanda free?"

"Sure, sure," I stammer. I step back to let him in and close the door.

He turns towards the kitchen, the floorboards squeaking beneath his heavy shoes. Mrs. Tarrow looks over her shoulder and sees him.

"Ken! What a wonderful surprise!" She rinses her hands and dries them quickly, then comes to give him a hug.

"We've been talking about you and it'd been a long time, so... I brought these." He hands her the flowers.

Emma has dried her hands and a beaming Mrs. Tarrow introduces her, saying, "This is Steve's friend, Emma."

They shake hands. Kreitzer says, "Nice to meet you."

She says, "I've heard a lot about you," then takes the flowers and goes off to find a vase.

He snorts. "I bet you have."

"Can you stay, Ken?" Mrs. Tarrow asks. "We have plenty of everything."

"I'm sorry, have to rush back," he says. "Actually got the day off with the family."

She smiles. "That's good. I'm glad."

"Smells great in here. Teri home?"

"No, odd-numbered year, my bad luck. So I invited all this good luck over instead."

Leonard has come in to see who rang the bell. Eli trails behind him with Zina. I introduce them to Kreitzer.

"This is great to see, Amanda, you with the big turkey and lots of friends. Does my heart good." Kreitzer gives her another hug. "Sorry I have to run."

"Ken, you drove all the way up here just to bring me flowers. How could I be anything but happy?"

He puts a big arm around her as they walk towards the door. He seems to be trying to figure out what to say, but nothing comes out so they just walk together.

"By the way," he finally tells her, "you were right. No charges on the credit card, and with the girl's help we were able to narrow down the dates. It was within a week of the time that Steve's friend found the gun on the ferry."

"They try to cover their tracks..." she says.

"And all they do is blaze a trail," Kreitzer recites. "Jack taught us very well."

One more hug and he's off. Mrs. Tarrow comes back to find that Emma already has the flowers in a vase and is bringing them to the dining room table.

"These are gorgeous!" Emma tells her.

"They are!" responds Mrs. Tarrow. "You like making stuffing?"

Emma grimaces. "I'd... I've never made it."

"No problem. Want to go watch football with the boys or get your hands all gooky?"

Emma looks at me, then back at Mrs. Tarrow. "I'll go for the gooky hands."

Mrs. Tarrow looks at me proudly. "She's still mine. You have to wait."

I think about how long I've waited.

I can wait a little longer.

70.

Are We Done Discussing Poison?

Thursday, November 22 – Thanksgiving (Cont.)

When we finally sit down to eat we have turkey and mashed potatoes and stuffing and corn on the cob and cranberry sauce and sweet peas and gravy and biscuits and butter and sweet potatoes and apple cider and wine and water and diet sodas.

Mrs. Tarrow sits happily at the head of the table, absorbing more warmth with every bite. She grows a half inch taller each time that someone asks for seconds.

Leonard raises his wine glass and toasts, "Here's to Mrs. Tarrow!" and I raise my glass of water in her honor.

"Oh, thank you all," she says. "Now toast Emma for doing so much of the work."

We all toast and clink glasses again.

"These flowers are wonderful," Emma says.

"Ken Kreitzer always wants to take care of me," Mrs. Tarrow says. "But Steven, my wish for this Thanksgiving is that he finds a way to help take care of things for you."

I wish I could bottle this moment, so I could drink from it when my troubles want to block out the sun.

Mrs. Tarrow must read my mind, because she adds, "He'll get them, Steven. He's stirring the pot."

"Like that quote of Jack's," I tell her.

She nods, then explains to the group, "My husband was an officer in the City. He loved to say, 'Why do all the work when the suspects will help us solve the case? All we have to do is stir the pot!'"

Eli speaks up. "You mean... Like the 'Case of the Vanishing Volunteer' contest on the radio?"

"Exactly," Mrs. Tarrow answers. "Ken's publicizing the facts of the case, which already brought us a witness who could describe the woman who hired Candi Bonham. There may be more witnesses out there. It could spook the guilty party, maybe spook them so badly they try to cover their tracks again and give us even more to work with."

Leonard has had a fair amount to drink, and now he raises his glass again. "Here's to stirring the pot!" Everyone toasts.

He raises his eyebrows, the classic sign that he's come up with a new idea. "Here's what we can do to help Captain Kreitzer. It's like Hamlet. We have a list..."

"Hamlet dies in the end," I tell him.

"We leave out that part, but we do it like Hamlet. The ghost tells Hamlet how Hamlet's uncle murdered his dad to steal the throne, not to mention stealing Hamlet's mom. Hamlet says 'The play's the thing wherein I'll catch the conscience of the King.'"

Emma says, "Tommy's always reminding Steve about when they studied Hamlet. And taking arms against a sea of troubles."

"Exactly!" Leonard conducts an invisible orchestra with his fork. "So here's the bit. Hamlet doctors a play they're putting on so it re-creates the murder. He knows that if his uncle's guilty the guy will panic and everyone will realize that he's the killer."

"But that's the middle of the story, not the climax," I tell him. "The rest of the play is about how Hamlet doesn't do anything about it, even though he knows who killed his father. That's why they all die in the end."

Leonard waves away any objections. "We'll just skip the part where everyone gets poisoned."

"Like *tetraodontidae*," Eli translates. I presume those are poisonous fish but don't want to interrupt.

Emma repeats, "The play's the thing wherein I'll catch the conscience of the King."

Leonard leans forward dramatically. "In Hamlet the plan works. The uncle gives himself away! And it can work for us, too!"

"Are we done discussing poison?" Mrs. Tarrow asks.

Leonard puts down his fork. "Yes, ma'am."

"Good," she says. "I'll get the pie."

* * *

Emma has to drive back to be ready for work in the morning, but she holds my hand as we walk down the stone stairs towards the old iron gate.

I don't have to look back to know that Mrs. Blount is at her window in the old white house, watching us from her lofty perch.

"I've... I've been thinking," she starts out. "I looked at the calendar in Mrs. Tarrow's kitchen."

"Uh-huh."

"I was thinking..." She glances over to meet my eyes. "Maybe the best thing to do is to give it some time."

My heart sinks.

She sees my expression. "Not like that. I... I'll come down next Thursday. I'll try to come every Thursday in December, try to see if we can make things work. And then we can talk again after Christmas. Does that sound OK?"

I can't believe it. Happy fireworks bang inside my brain. "Yes!" I tell her, then hesitate.

"What is it?" she asks me. "What's wrong?"

Must. Think. Like. Liam.

"I'm thinking that I very much want to kiss you right now."

She smiles, and for the first time in a long time I pull her close and feel the irreplaceable warmth of her lips.

PART IV.

JOURNAL FOUR

She sits on my bed looking at my leather-covered journals. Two volumes are stacked neatly at her left, three others at her right.

"This last one ends right before you and Leonard took your wild west rodeo on the road."

"Crazy times," I tell her. I look at my wall calendar, realize I'm close to a week behind on my water changes.

She leans forward to catch my eye, make sure I'm listening to her. "Now I know what you and Luis argued about that day."

"It's hard to... Sometimes you can have lots of feelings all at the same time and even though you know what's right you still have feelings that are wrong."

"Yes." She runs her fingertips along the spine of the third book, sets it on the stack at her right. Then she picks up the top book on the left.

"We don't have to talk about it," I tell her.

"It's OK," she says. "You were scared. Some of what you wrote... You could be sitting here with someone else."

I don't like to think about it.

I know she's right.

71.

Liam Always Defaults to Action

Monday, November 26

After the happy week of Thanksgiving comes a lonely week spent waiting for Thursday. The thought that Emma still might not return invites the shadows of self-doubt back into my life.

I try not to think about it, but it doesn't help.

To distract myself I think about how we can stir the pot. About, "The play's the thing wherein I'll catch the conscience of the King." I've been talking with Leonard the Human Statue and we have ideas.

But to put our plans into action I have to think like Liam. More than that, I have to be like Liam. The way that Emma hopes for me to be like Liam, with the Steve side of me still present and accounted for instead of disappearing for the day.

Liam always defaults to action. So I call Kreitzer and ask if we can go for another mid-day walk.

"So, what's up?" he asks after we meet behind the Ferry Building.

I set a course north along the Embarcadero, towards Fisherman's Wharf.

"I have a what-if for you," I tell him.

He controls the urge to roll his eyes. "Go ahead."

"Let's say that you have five people, and one of them steals $20 from you. If you and some actor friends put on a little play about someone stealing $20 from a wallet... If you did it five times, once in front of each person, maybe the thief would give themselves away."

"You reading Hamlet again?" he asks me.

Nothing surprises me with Kreitzer. Not even when he knows Shakespeare.

"You're a very busy guy," I tell him. "I don't think you want to hear about what my book club is reading."

He ponders this. "True enough."

A group of leather-coated motorcycle riders roars by along the waterfront, and I wait for them to pass so he can hear me again. The fourth guy in line is wearing brand new jeans and a price tag dangles from the belt loop above his right rear pocket.

"So if we wanted to put on this little play about the wallet and surprise our five friends," I tell Kreitzer, "we'd need to know where we might be likely to find them. I mean, we can't just stand outside their front doors in the morning."

He groans. "Uh-huh."

I give him my best disappointed teacher look. "Now we're just talking hypothetical situations here."

He rubs the scar on the back of his hand. "Let me guess. Tom Festane, Carl Mathis, Mary Anne Mathis, Eve Mortimer and..."

"Dean of the dreadlocks from Avanture Video."

Kreitzer shakes his head skeptically.

"He keeps showing up," I remind him.

"True enough," he admits. "And not Tommy Gonzalez or any of your other students?"

I shake my head skeptically. "No. Just hypothetically, of course."

He groans again. "Let me see what I can do."

72.

Only Now Do You Look Truly Silly

Tuesday, November 27

I look through the eyeholes of the plastic mask at Leonard's and my reflections in the bathroom mirror at the Palace Hotel. It's hard to see through this thing but I can take in enough to know we look completely silly.

$122.47 ought to get us farther than this.

"You OK, Steve?" Leonard asks.

"Just thinking we look completely silly."

"Oh, yeah? How about... now?!" With a flourish he brandishes his inflatable doll, her blonde bangs dangling across her eternally-surprised open mouth.

"OK, you're right," I tell him. "Only now do you look truly silly."

He pulls off his mask and gives me a Cheshire Cat grin under the wide brim of his cowboy hat. "Now you're talkin'!" he proclaims, and throws back his head to emit a raucous, insane laugh that echoes off the bathroom walls.

I imagine hotel security running down the grand corridor towards us from all directions, but perhaps insane laughs in the bathrooms of the Palace Hotel are more common than I think.

Nothing happens.

We deflate Leonard's doll and stuff it and the plastic masks into my old blue duffel bag. The cowboy hats won't fit so we leave them on. With our matching blue gingham shirts and cowboy boots we look like we're going to a highfalutin cattlemen's party somewhere in town.

We cross the Palace lobby and pass through the side door, then take the stairs down to street level.

Our plan is simple. Kreitzer and his team have explored every nuance of the relationships between everyone I've ever met and SoMa Triangle. And it's hard to put on a little play about voting patterns on the Board of Supervisors.

But the twin cowboys are a different story. Candi walks in on a pair of these rare individuals just days before she gets second billing in a double murder. Anyone who knows about the twin cowboys' sexual adventures at the Vergessen Hotel would recognize those twin characters named Vergessen if they met them on the street.

Even if the cowboys are fully clothed.

Enter the Leonard and Steve Shakespeare Company.

When we get to Yerba Buena Gardens, near the Institute of Science, Leonard asks, "Which way does he come from?"

I point towards Mission St. "According to the chart, that way." We are starting with Carl Mathis, for the simple reason that he is the first suspect for whom we've gotten a map of his usual haunts.

I look at my watch. No more than fifteen minutes to go. I text Luis in case he can take his lunch break from the Institute.

We inflate both plastic dolls and realign their matching blue gingham sundresses and their wigs, then place Leonard's cigar box on the pavement in front of us for tips.

Finally we put on the expressionless plastic masks. With their frozen faces and matte white complexion they're unnerving even without the big cowboy hats and inflatable women.

"Down by the Wharf this shtick might actually make some money," Leonard comments when we're done.

No sooner does he say it than two forty-something women with briefcases walk up to us.

"And who are you two supposed to be?" one asks with a broad smile.

"We're the Vergessen Twins from deep in the heart of cowboy country," Leonard answers in his best Texas twang. "And these here are our girlfriends, the Leaky sisters, Willah and Daisy May. They're nice folks but as girlfriends they, ah, suck."

The women look at the dolls' round, open mouths and burst out laughing.

Leonard the Human Statue is good at improvisation.

"Some girlfriends you got there," the woman says.

"I'm the lucky one," Leonard replies, pointing to the dolls. "His girlfriend is Daisy May, but my girl Willah here definitely will!"

Another laugh. "So what are the four of you going to do to get us to drop a dollar in the box?" the other woman asks, in the tone normally reserved for asking a man for a foot massage.

"Well, ma'am, we was thinking that given the questionable moral stature of our assemblage some folks would make a donation to have us not do nothin' here in this constitutionally-protected right-o'-way."

She turns to her friend and says, "Oh, no, we want to see exactly what you can do!"

So Leonard proceeds to grab his doll and do a fast-paced jig across the Yerba Buena Gardens lawn while singing *Thank God I'm a Country Boy* in a high-pitched voice, all while twirling his partner with an energy level that would put the traveling company of *Oklahoma!* to shame.

When he returns, breathing hard behind the mask, he meets the woman's eyes and says, "Or you could settle for some snappy repartay."

She laughs and shakes her head. "You win!" she says. They both open their purses to pull out dollar bills.

"What does he do?" asks the quiet woman, indicating me.

"Oh, it's very special," Leonard answers with a conspiratorial whisper. "He likes to watch!"

This earns an extra laugh and they move on.

I look around, hoping that we haven't missed Carl Mathis on his typical Tuesday routine. I don't see him, but I do see a short guy wearing sunglasses and a bright orange knit cap eating a sandwich at a table across the plaza by the Metreon.

Luis. Here to act as our spotter in case anything goes wrong.

A young couple from Sweden takes one look at us and has a passerby take their picture with the Vergessen Twins from Down in Cowboy Country. They drop a dollar in the box.

Still no Carl Mathis.

The people who stop to interact with the Vergessen Twins are fun, but through the too-small holes in my mask I try to watch the ones who ignore us. I study how they act, how they walk by.

They are the standard by which we can judge our five targets, the control group who will teach us how normal people react to twin street performers in cowboy hats with twin inflatable blondes.

Most of the un-sold and un-impressed just ignore us. One woman, offended by Leonard's entendre-laden patter, dispatches us with a curled lip and hurries on her way.

But not everyone just walks by. Another Leonard dance extravaganza with his Leaky sister, more coins and dollars in the box.

There he is, coming from Mission St.! It's Carl Mathis, the old church framing his tall, slim frame as he walks straight towards us.

I nudge Leonard and he nods, steps up and times his bit for Mathis' approach.

"Hello there!" Leonard proclaims. "We're the Vergessen Twins from the Midriff-T Ranch in the heart of Cowboy country, and these are our twin girlfriends, Kama and Sutra! They love their bucking broncos!"

Carl Mathis glances at the twin cowboys with their twin blondes, wrinkles his nose in disgust and keeps walking. No sign of stress, no change in his cadence. He walks away just as he approached, the same way that all the strangers do, with a dusting of contempt thrown in.

The thought crosses my mind that we could go 0-for-5 on this little project, not to mention feeling pretty stupid for wasting all this time and money. But that's not the way that Liam thinks.

We perform for ten more minutes to mask our true mission, then deflate the ladies and stuff them in the duffle, leaving the masks on until we get back to the Palace restroom. On the other side of the park Luis finishes his sandwich, tosses the wrapper in the trash and walks away.

I pick up the cigar box and hand it to Leonard. "At least you won't go home empty-handed."

"50-50," he says. "That's how them Vergessen Twins roll!"

"Keep it," I tell him. "You're the lead in this show."

He gives me a defiant look. "We'll talk when that credit card bill for the Leaky Sisters hits your mailbox."

73.

A Brilliant Mind,
A Wandering Mind

Wednesday, November 28

"Excuse me, but is your name Jacob?"

I've seen the young man several times on the *Louis H. Baar*, and each time I think I know him and go up to say hello. But each time there is no flicker of recognition, so I just walk on by.

But I need to be like Liam.

He straightens slightly from his slouched position by the window. "Yeah," he says.

"Jacob Johnson?"

He straightens up a little more.

"Yeah."

"I'm Steve Ondelle. Mr. Ondelle from school."

He looks at me, forces himself to focus. "Hey, Mr. Ondelle. Wassup?"

I hold out my hand. He looks at it for a moment, then realizes what I'm doing and shakes it. "It's great to see you again," I tell him.

"Sorry, Mr. Ondelle. Up too late last night." He rubs his eyes, pulls back his very long light brown hair.

Jacob Johnson. A kid some teachers dismiss as a goof-off. A favorite topic in the teacher's lounge.

I still believe that Jacob's a prodigy, complete with all the contradictions that prodigies possess.

A brilliant mind. A wandering mind.

The ability to make intuitive leaps. The ability to just lie there and do nothing.

The focus to do vast amounts of thoughtful work. The laziness to invent vast numbers of transparent excuses.

It's Jacob Johnson. All of the above.

"No worries," I say.

"I guess this isn't the scene you hoped for," he says. He's working himself more or less upright in the seat.

"Don't worry. I won't give you the lecture."

The first trace of a real smile. "What if Shakespeare... what was it? What if Shakespeare never completes a play? What if Galileo doesn't write down what he sees through the telescope? You had about fifty of 'em."

"At least fifty," I agree. I have to keep making up new ones because if I repeat myself Jacob Johnson will stop listening.

Of course, if I make it interesting Jacob Johnson can drink knowledge from a fire hose and transform it into concepts.

"What are you up to these days?" I ask him.

"You're gonna be pissed."

"Try me."

"I'm working for a startup in the City, online games. Part time. So I do odd jobs around town to make rent."

"Why would I be pissed?"

"I'm not going to college.'"

"What are you doing for the game company?"

"Production Assistant. Learning from the ground up."

"Sounds interesting."

He perks up a little. "I do all the grunt work, but whenever I have a question they'll answer it."

"Now that sounds very cool," I tell him. "Why am I going to be pissed?"

"It's just... the college thing."

"What is it I always tell you is most important?"

"You still don't ever use the past tense, do you?" he asks, his head cocked. "You're still doing your present tense or death thing."

"Yes, I am. What do I always tell you about dreams?"

His eyes roll. "Chase your dreams till they're too tired to keep running away."

"Professor Polymirth would give you an A," I tell him.

The defiant edge to his voice suddenly vanishes. "I still... You know I'm really sorry about what happened because I joked around with the Sam Spade thing," he says.

"It's all good," I tell him. "Everything happens for a reason."

He looks down, then forces his eyes back up to me. "It's cause everyone knew that Jim and I used to go up on the hill and smoke dope after school. That's why the rumors started. It... It really was my fault. If it'd been somebody else pretending to smoke... You know. Nobody would've cared, but some of the kids told their parents I was a big doper so you got... You know. You got caught in all the people hating on me."

I kneel down beside his seat, the way I'd do as his teacher back in school. "Thanks, Jacob," I tell him softly. "That means a lot to me. But I'm the one who decides to quit. You need to stop feeling guilty about something that's not your fault."

He hesitates. "So I guess I can talk to you again now."

"Is that why you're pretending you don't recognize me?"

"Yeah, I still felt bad about it. And I don't like getting lectured about going to college."

"Fair enough," I tell him. "I don't like people pretending I don't exist."

He gets that old Jacob Johnson smile. "Fair enough," he says. "Fair enough."

74.

Well, Jam My Zipper and Call Me Puddles!

Wednesday, November 28 (Cont.)

"You ready?" Leonard the Human Statue asks me from the next stall in the restaurant bathroom.

"As ready as I'm going to be," I reply.

"I'm comin' out!" He throws open the stall door, once again decked out in his cowboy outfit.

I more quietly open my door and step out. We look in the mirror.

"Damn!" Leonard says. "Them Vergessen twins are two fine lookin' cattle wranglers!"

Our expressionless white masks remain in my blue duffel bag, since pedestrians in Sausalito are less used to seeing cartoon characters on the street than their counterparts in San Francisco.

We walk back out through the restaurant and make our way

towards the front door. A little blue-eyed boy shouts, "Mama! Cowboys! Cowboys!" and we both wave to him as we go by.

If Tom Festane follows what's in the report, he'll walk down Bridgeway here in Sausalito sometime in the next half hour en route to his bank, his routine on the second and fourth Wednesday of each month.

I find myself wondering, if Kreitzer knows this much about Tom Festane, how much does he know about me?

"This is your turf," Leonard is saying. "Where should we set up?"

I look down the street, try to picture where he might park. "In front of the old fountain in Viña del Mar Park," I tell him. "That way we'll see him no matter which way he comes."

"Done," Leonard says, and we set out.

We reach the park and inflate our vinyl girlfriends, then put on our masks and set Leonard's donation box on the sidewalk in front of us. I hide my duffel bag behind a trash can.

Four young people approach us, each carrying a map and looking around for street signs.

"Howdy!" Leonard says happily. "We're the Vergessen Twins from down in cowboy country, and these are our girlfriends, Wanna and Woulda. You need any directions here in our fair city o' Sausalito?"

A young woman with long, straight brown hair examines us and laughs. "We're from Texas," she says, "and we don't got no cowboys like you down there."

"Ain't nobody nowhere's got cowboys like us, ma'am!" Leonard proclaims. "Just here in Sausalito, only place you'll find this much cowboy in just two pairs o' boots!"

"Where's Caledonia St.?" the man next to her asks, clearly unimpressed.

I point north, try to put on my own cowboy accent. "Caledonia forks off o' Bridgeway 'bout two blocks that way, mister!" I recite. "Just stay on the left side of this here street and you'll see the signs."

The man rolls his eyes but the woman drops some coins in the box and thanks us. They continue on their way.

"Just gettin' warmed up!" Leonard tells me.

Ten minutes and about three dollars later Festane appears on cue. He is slim, about 5'11, wearing business casual, and his pace is easy and relaxed.

I nudge Leonard and he whispers, "Showtime!"

"Howdy there!" he says as Festane reaches us. "We're the Vergessen Twins from the Bagel Plains down in cowboy country, and these are our dance partners Two-Step and One-Too-Many! You need any directions here in our fair city o' Sausalito?"

Festane stops, looks at us and laughs out loud. He adopts his own cowboy drawl. "Well, now I can't say that I do, pardner. But I might pay a dollar for that dance!"

"Happy to oblige!" Leonard answers, and prepares to set out with his Leaky sister.

"No, no!" Festane interrupts. "If you want that dollar I'm the one who'll be waltzin' with you."

"Well jam my zipper and call me Puddles!" Leonard says. "It would be a honor!"

They assume the classic ballroom position and Leonard starts reciting, "And, 1 2 3, 1 2 3..." as they waltz a full 360 degrees around the fountain. Passers-by gather and applaud when they return to the sidewalk, and they take a bow together.

Festane shakes Leonard's hand and says, "Thanks, I needed something goofy to brighten my day," then drops a five dollar bill in the box and goes on his way.

I watch him go. "Not exactly paralyzed with shock and fear, was he?" I tell Leonard.

He looks after Festane, nods his respect. "That guy's spent serious time in a dance studio. He knows how to move."

We perform ten more minutes to disguise our true intentions and then pack up. Still three more acts to go.

75.

The Stars of a

High School Horror Movie

Thursday, November 29

Luis walks with me as I do my chores and he commutes to work. I remember the rhythm of his boot heels clomping on the deck above me, miss that reassuring cadence.

"Last night on the phone she promises me she'll be there on the dock when we pull in," I tell him, looking off the bow towards San Francisco. "You'll finally get to meet her!"

He follows my gaze and laughs. "Stevie, we're not past Alcatraz. We can't see her from here!"

The crossing seems to take forever, and Luis distracts me with stories from the Institute. Two escaped penguins trying to break into the herring tank. A prankster who swaps a chicken bone for a rare

Australian fossil on display. Carl Mathis falling prey to a practical joker and issuing a press release announcing a new display of *E. coli*.

I tell him about our first two performances as the cowboy Vergessen Twins, and how Emma is joining us for Act III today.

Finally we approach the dock. "There she is!" I yell, and point her out. Luis sees her, too, leaning on the railing.

"Yo, Stevie..."

I wave and she waves back. "She's really here!" I tell Luis.

"Stevie! The bow line! Captain's gonna kill you!"

I come to my senses and hook the mooring rope, quickly securing the line and heading back inside to help Linh with the recycling so I can go.

Luis falls in step beside me, grinning.

* * *

Emma looks at Leonard and me as we stand at the Market St. end of the Palace Hotel's grand hallway. She laughs and says, "You look like the stars of a high school horror movie!"

"We ain't stars, we're super-stars!" Leonard brags.

We once again take up our station, inflate the dolls and straighten our cowboy hats. This time our impromptu stage is on Battery St. near the new headquarters of Talkami Inc.

Astride Mary Anne Mathis' routine Thursday route to the gym.

With a third conspirator today we have more options. If the sight of two such clever street performers leads Mary Anne Mathis to react in any way then Emma can follow her at a distance and see what she does next.

For this task she has donned dark glasses, an Alcatraz sweatshirt and a visitors map from the Palace concierge. Her hair is pinned up and covered with a floppy straw hat, and at any moment I expect her to ask us where to catch a cable car.

We are masked and accompanied by our blue gingham ladies. The late-lunch Financial District crowd stares and laughs. Two burly motorcycle cops shake their heads and chuckle as they roar by.

One has a scar shaped like the coastline of Peru on his elbow. I recognize it, realize he's one of the cops who watches Debbie Milovich and me play detective on behalf of Kreitzer, two months ago in North Beach.

Emma watches from half a block away on the other side of the street, pretending to be confused by the Palace's multicolored map.

Three college-age girls approach us. "Who are you guys supposed to be?" one asks.

"We're the Vergessen twins from Lake Datsabigun down in cowboy country," Leonard answers. "And these are our dance partners, Trudy and Untrudy."

"You guys should get a boom box so you've got some cowboy music," she advises. Her companions nod.

"Thank you! That's plum neighborly of you, ma'am," Leonard answers. Now bored, they move away.

There she is! Just stepping out of the passageway by the shops! Already wearing her pink and black workout gear.

"That's her!" I whisper to Leonard. She's with a slim older man with short grey hair who wears an expensive-looking suit, whom I recognize from his LinkedIn photo as her wealthy boss, Peter Polossov. You can read their conversation as she invites him to walk with her, he declines, then reverses himself and they turn and head this way.

I don't dare look at Emma but I hope she sees Leonard heft up his jeans with comic emphasis, our appointed signal.

Two middle aged women with Walgreens bags are between us and Mathis. On cue Leonard goes into his act.

"We're the Vergessen Twins from the concrete canyons of cowboy country," He proclaims. "And these are our girlfriends the Leaky sisters, who like all good cowgirls always want to go out for a ride!"

The women laugh but say nothing and keep walking. It's unclear whether Mathis heard us or not, as she remains in conversation with her companion.

Now Mathis and Polossov approach us, talking about something great that they have just received by Fed Ex. I adjust my mask to make sure I can see through these awkwardly-cut eye holes.

Leonard looks at them and touches the brim of his hat. "Howdy! We're the Vergessen Twins from the Queen-size lakebeds of cowboy country," he declares, "and these are our girlfriends the Leaky sisters, who love to strap on a saddle and go two-on-two!"

Mathis looks at the bizarre scene of the two masked cowboys with their twin inflatable blondes. In the space of a second she smiles at the comic image, does a double take as it all sinks in, and then has her face go blank as if we were never there. She keeps walking at the exact same pace.

That's it! No one else has reacted in that way. Not even close.

Candi surprising the twin cowboys and their twin blondes is not just a silly story.

She knows why Candi is dead.

And now she knows we know.

I look at Polossov. The color has drained from his face and he walks faster as he goes by. He looks away emphatically.

So he knows, too.

We do not follow them. An elderly couple approaches and Leonard starts again, hopefully loud enough for our departing targets to hear. "Howdy! We're the Vergessen Twins from the perky peaks of cowboy country," he shouts. "And these are our new friends, the Leaky Sisters. We were hoping to impress them but they found us deflating!"

The couple smiles and keeps walking.

* * *

Twenty minutes later we are back at the lobby in the Palace Hotel, our cowboy hats and dolls and masks safely packed away.

Emma has still not returned. No call, no text.

I'm freaking out.

"Dude, be cool," Leonard says. "We agreed she'd take her time to make sure they didn't spot her."

"I know."

"Did you see how Mathis reacted"" Leonard asks for the third time. "And the dude?"

"They get it."

Leonard can't stop. "Everybody else thinks twin cowboys named after the Vergessen Hotel are bizarre and funny. These two... it's like we're their worst nightmare!"

I nod in agreement. "I just want..."

OK, I can breathe again. Emma strides through the door from New Montgomery St., now wearing her own jacket and with her hair taken down to change her look. She sweeps past the registration desk and approaches with a big smile to give us each a hug.

"Sorry I didn't call," she says, holding up her phone. "Battery died."

"What did they do?" Leonard asks excitedly.

"Well," Emma says, 'they got around the corner and she didn't do much of anything."

"No reaction?" I ask her. "But when... I saw her!"

Emma smiles. "And then he started to freak out."

"I knew it!" Leonard says.

"You could see that she was telling him to act normal, but he kept turning to her and saying something and she kept shaking her head."

"Wow." It's all I can think of to say.

"She looked around a lot because he was acting so strange, so I watched them in the reflection of the bank window while I looked at my map," Emma says proudly.

"Gotta buy you a trenchcoat, girl!" Leonard tells her.

"Where did they go?" I ask, impatient.

Emma points in different directions as she talks, unable to control her excitement. "First they walked towards her gym, just like you said, but the guy was in such bad shape that she grabbed him by the shoulders, said like three words to him, and then they just circled back to their office. I had to come back the long way or they'd have seen me."

Leonard rubs his hands. "Don't you wish we could hear what they're saying to each other right now, behind closed doors?"

"You really got to them," Emma says.

This feels good. The puppet is finally messing with the puppeteers.

76.

Lost Inside the Maw
of Some Great Darkness

Fifteen years ago, as seen from Friday, November 30

It is very long ago.

My father and I are trying to watch the Giants game on the old TV. A narrow, luminescent white line cuts horizontally across the screen about two thirds of the way down. It never goes away.

"You know perfectly well that without me, if I didn't help pay... You need me to pay the mortgage."

"We both live here, Susan," my father says, his eyes remaining on the screen.

"If Jack Barquette didn't have that affair you'd still be working for him and we wouldn't have to do..." She makes a grand gesture, the wide sleeve of her robe waving gently from her flaccid arm. "We wouldn't have to do. These things."

"Uh-huh."

Tonight, for some reason, she is getting more angry instead of less. My father says nothing to set her off. I make no misstep she could interpret the wrong way. She even cheers with us when the Giants turn a big double play in the fourth.

But her fury grows, inning by inning.

"What would you do if I didn't give you the money you need, David? What would you do then?"

"Susan, we've discussed that all before."

"Well I want to discuss it again."

His eyes remain on the TV. "There's nothing to discuss."

"I could just take Steven with me and go and you'd just have to fig-ure it all out for yourself."

Now, as I think about it, I think she sees the look I give my father when she talks about leaving with me.

She knows that her threat of leaving still gets to me. It is planned to get to me, so she in turn will get to him. She remembers my tears that night, even longer ago.

I was very young. But I still remember.

I remember the sound of my cries, the feeling in my throat, my eyes, the emptiness and fear inside, my jaw aching, my stomach aching, my heart, my whole chest, standing there in the doorway and seeing the lights of the taxi as they go away and the cold air on my bare arms, the cold air sucking down my throat, feeling like suddenly the silence is so great and it's swallowing me up and I'm lost, being lost inside the maw of some great darkness and loneliness and I don't know where to grab to hold on but I have to grab somewhere, to hold onto something and then my father is holding me and saying it's all right, that she'll come back.

And she does come back. The next day.

But it's not all right. It's not the same. I never feel the same.

Not then.

Not now.

The darkness of that cold night never goes away.

I feel a hand touch my shoulder but I am very, very tired. I just want to sleep.

Wait, I'm not a little boy. I'm...

Now the hand pulls at my arm, tries to shake me.

I wake up all at once, look around the dark room.

I have no idea where I am.

I throw off the covers, sit up and search frantically for something familiar in the dim light.

"Steve! It's OK!"

That's Emma's voice. Emma is here.

"You had a nightmare. You're at Mrs. Tarrow's. Everything's OK."

I let out a deep breath, let every muscle in my body go limp.

Emma is here.

As I lie back down and pull up the covers my eyes adjust and I see her outline next to me. The gold "UCD" inscription on her T-shirt seem to glow in the dark.

"Sorry," I tell her. "Sorry if I woke you up."

"It's OK," she says. She rolls on her side, reaches out to put her hand on my chest. I try to calm my breathing.

"Do you remember what it was? The nightmare?"

I shake my head, hear the sound of my hair rubbing against the pillowcase. "It wasn't a nightmare. I was just... I was just thinking. I was asleep, but I was thinking. It wasn't like I was back there again."

"Back where?"

"At home. I was thinking... My parents used to have fights all the time. One night when I was little my mom kept threatening to leave and when my dad didn't freak out she called a taxi and went to a hotel."

She moves her hand to my shoulder, caresses it gently. "That must have been... I was terrified when my dad left."

I roll on my side, try to see her eyes in the dark. "My mom came back. It was never the same again for me, but she came back the next day."

"I don't like nightmares," she says.

"I don't have them very often," I tell her.

She reaches over, puts her arm around me and pulls herself close. I roll on my back and she puts her head on my shoulder and we hold each other.

I try to let myself relax. Let the feelings come. Let myself actually accept and embrace the caring of another person.

And, finally, to believe that all of it is real.

77.

We're Really
Stirring the Pot Now

Friday, November 30 (Cont.)

I don't think I've ever heard Captain Kreitzer babble. Not just grin. Not just laugh. He's all the way across that line to giggling with delight. I can hold the phone five feet from my ear and still hear him.

"You know this doesn't prove anything," he says finally. "They could have reacted because they're offended by inflatable dolls being brandished in public."

"Fully clothed inflatable dolls," I clarify.

"They could have a thing about gingham," he says.

Now I know he's playing with me. "I get what you're saying. But this is still a good thing."

"Yes, this is still a good thing."

"We're really stirring the pot now."

He laughs again. "Yes, exactly."

It's all starting to make sense to me. "So whatever it is about the twin cowboys that has him melting into a puddle, it can mean big problems for her."

"Exactly. The man with her was Peter Polossov, Mary Anne's boss. We think they've teamed up on dirty work before, but this is the first time they've been caught."

"Wow."

"We like it when suspects start to panic," he says, "even if we don't know what they're panicked about."

"And now we need to do to them what the killer's been trying to do to me with the gun and the credit card and the TSA and my house," I tell him. "Keep up the pressure. Give them more surprises. See if we can make them crack."

"It's a free country," Kreitzer says.

"It is."

He gives me his most serious tone. "But don't take chances. We don't want anyone else to get hurt."

"Can I bring up one more thing?" I ask him.

"Did you hear what I just said?"

"Yes."

"OK, what is it?" he says.

"Jack Tarrow's code for you on the old duty sheets, TLW. It occurs to me that 'Mimi from TLW' might not be Mimi from Theatre Lab West after all. Me-Me might be You-You from The Lonely Warrior."

He snorts. "No comment."

"Victoria Lee won't speak to you or your team but the Lee Agency's number is on Candi's phone bill and you have to track it down. If you use a subpoena you'll get the documents but alienate an office full of people who may have seen or heard something important. So you give someone else her phone number, someone crazy enough to call her on his own. Someone who's so worried about getting Luis' job back and about you arresting Tommy Gonzalez that he'll screw up the courage to go up there and talk to her."

I hear the papers shuffling on his desk. He says nothing.

"The twin cowboys with the twin blondes that are making Mathis and her boss freak out are a lucky coincidence because I don't stop with the Lee Agency, and I walk into that hair salon at the right moment. But it's Victoria Lee you can't get to. Everything else on the phone bill is already being scoured by your team."

More paper shuffling. No comment.

"You just don't seem like the kind of guy who puts perfume on your letters."

Another chuckle. "No, I'm not."

"You're not going to admit anything to me, are you?"

Still another chuckle.

78.

When It Does Come, the Call is Too Late

Monday, December 3

It's cold today. Not the freeze-solid cold like back east, but still an ache-in-your-bones cold. Unless you keep moving.

I stop at the little plaza on Spear St. to say hello to my father. Instead of a single white rose I have a mixed bouquet of brightly colored flowers. Today is ten years since the day he died.

He dies ten days before they send us home for Christmas break. So close to seeing him one more time before he goes.

There is no message at the dorm to tell me to get back while I still can, despite school policies for emergency visits home.

Despite my mailing home a copy of that policy underlined in red to make sure they'll let me know if the time comes.

When it does come, the call is too late. My mother simply says, "It's over."

My father's life, over.

A whole part of my life, over. With an empty space instead of words from which to set the scene for the next chapter.

I think again about going back, talking to the nice people who live in our old house and taking a cup of soil from the back yard where I'd play baseball with my father. I could grow something in it. Flowers that don't die after a few days.

But if you take soil from a garden all you have is dirt that's no longer connected to the ground.

If you take a person away from their home it becomes someone else's home. All you have when you go back is a person who's no longer connected to the ground.

"I know who I am," I whisper to the babbling fountain. I place the flowers on its marble ledge.

Out front on Spear St. a taxi blares its horn at a man in running shorts who steps into the street in front of him.

"I know who I am," I start again. "But I just... I have to prove to Emma that I can work out who I'm going to be."

The fear starts to grip me again, the fear of losing her. But I know that only makes things worse.

"I know I'll be OK if I just... She's here last Thursday and we have a great time and we actually spook Mary Anne Mathis and her boss so we think we know who's been behind all this. And then Emma decides to spend the night and she says she's coming again for the next three weeks and then we'll talk."

The fountain churns and bubbles, as it always does.

"I just... I know I'm not... I don't really know what to do, even though I know what I need to do. You know."

He does know, but he's no longer here. I'm talking to a marble fountain. Because it's ten years too late. It's all happening ten years too late.

It's the best that I can do.

79.

About Hollywood and Hubble

Wednesday, December 5

Today's 10:55 from Sausalito carries people of all shapes and sizes, at least fifty of whom wear matching *Phantom of the Opera* T shirts emblazoned with the tragic hero's portrait.

"So you guys are all big fans of the Phantom?" I ask a tall woman with jet-black hair who's standing in line at the snack bar. Her earrings reproduce the leaf-shaped pattern from the tughra of Emperor Suleiman the Magnificent.

"We're not just regular Phantom fans!" she proclaims. Her companions nod and giggle with her. "We all rode the bus from Fresno just to see him!"

"It's the mask," says the older, very thin woman beside her. "Men always look better when you can't see their faces!"

I have to laugh at that one. To my surprise I see Linh laughing, too.

Once we're moored in San Francisco I check the time on my phone and text Luis that I'll be a few minutes late for lunch.

I get a text back. It says, "Changed to pub on 5th."

Since I'm already late I decide to take transit instead of walking. An antique Muni train rounds the corner at the foot of Market, and I sprint to catch it.

Catching my breath, I drop into the old, hard wooden seat and text Luis, "Why the change?"

I get no answer. We trundle slowly down Market.

The train stops. We wait for passengers to depart and enter. Pull out. Stop. Over and over again.

"I'm never going to stop being a Dodger fan," a man behind me declares to his companions.

"That's obvious!" a woman replies. "And we love you anyway."

"Gail's right, Dave. No one wants you to stop cheering for the Dodgers," the other woman with him says. "It makes it fun having the rivalry in the family." I can only see her from the corner of my eye but I feel like I should recognize her.

"Well, I'm never going to stop watching my Dodgers," he insists.

We finally reach 5th St and I hop off and jog the two blocks down to Howard. The moment I walk into the pub I can tell that something is indeed very wrong.

She is trying to control herself but Paula is very upset.

"...like such a naive, trusting idiot," she is saying as I reach them. "It's so obvious he was lying all along." She brushes a tear from her cheek, now even angrier at herself for crying. An empty pint sits on the table, and as I join them the waitress brings her another.

"What's going on?" I slip into the chair next to Luis.

"They decided they didn't need another astronomer on the new team after all," Paula says. She spits out the words like a sip of curdled milk.

My jaw drops. "What?!"

"It's bullshit." Luis mutters.

"Bresham says that because he's given me a desk upstairs he's keeping his commitment, but if I have no hours and no shows... I have no income."

Luis seizes a breadstick from the basket, holds it up and looks at it angrily. He says nothing.

"I turned down the adjunct job at State so I could work on my grant proposals and this would have paid the rent," Paula says. Her eyes never leave the foamy top of her beer.

Luis bites the head off the breadstick, looks at the surviving piece as he chews.

Paula shakes her head. "I am so screwed."

"Why the change in plans?" I ask.

"I don't think he ever planned to keep me," she says. "I think he lied."

Luis looks over at me. "It's the Disneyland speech."

I'm confused. "The Disneyland speech is, what, four months ago? Why is he angry with you now?

She gives me a lonely smile. "I guess I slipped up a couple of times on the part where he wanted me to shut up about Hollywood and Hubble."

Luis and I look at each other.

She smiles. "OK, more than a couple of times."

Paula starts to laugh. Then Luis.

I feel awful, but I laugh with her anyway.

80.

Tangled Up Like the Cables Behind My Computer

Thursday, December 6

We have another hour before Emma has to leave to get back to Sacramento, before I have to start the second half of my shift.

It is mid-afternoon. The regulars at the sidewalk tables that line Columbus St. are drinking strong coffee and arguing in Italian, bundled up against the chilly gusts of wind that surge between the buildings.

"Let's look at that one," Emma says. "It's a long drive and I'll be starved if I don't get something now."

We look at the menu that says it offers authentic Neapolitan food. She looks at me, crinkles her nose.

We move on.

"So Kreitzer has a plan?"

"We're stirring the pot again. Trying to make them nervous enough to do something that proves they're guilty."

She shakes her head. "It would be wonderful if this whole thing would just be over."

"Amen," I tell her.

"I meant to ask," she says, a little too fast to sound natural. "Did you sell any fog this week?"

Here it comes. I could feel it building all afternoon.

And now it's here. That familiar, uncomfortable moment when...

"Did you hear my question?" she asks.

"Sorry... lost in thought," I tell her. "Yes, I sold fog three times this week. Earned enough to pay for a nice dinner the next time you come down."

"It's nice to hear the past tense again," she says. "Not much of that today."

"Sorry. I'm still adjusting."

She looks down at her dark brown boots, plays absently with one beaded earring. "I thought... I thought maybe you'd just keep talking, you know... Talking to me like you did before."

"I can just go into character and..."

"No!" She actually yells the word, then, embarrassed, lowers her voice. "I don't want to be with a character. I came here to be with you."

"I... It's all me. It's just... It's the difference between what I am and what I want to be."

"You're..." She waves her hands randomly in the air. "The way you think is all tangled up like the cables behind my computer."

"That's kind of how it feels," I answer.

We reach Vallejo St., wait for the light to change. Two blocks down is the police station where Captain Kreitzer first asks me his questions two months ago.

She pulls her purse strap higher on her shoulder, steers me to another menu. This one claims to represent the true flavors of Tuscany.

"I don't want a whole meal, just something light," she says. "All this stuff is... It's way too expensive."

We move on.

"Last week, when you had that nightmare?" she says. "When I woke you up you spoke normally. You used the past tense, the way that anyone else would do it."

"You're..." I try to think back. "Wow."

"I didn't want to say anything because I was hoping it would last. I didn't want to make you self-conscious."

"Thanks. That's... It's great that... I just wish I had realized what I was doing." I make sure to pronounce "had" and "was" and the "-ed" in "realized" carefully.

We wander up, look at yet another menu. This one features photos of big plates of classic seafood from Venice and Trieste.

She scans the images, adjusts the purse strap on her shoulder again. "I... I just can't seem to find something," she says, sadly. "I should just drop you off and get back on the road."

What do I say? What do you say when the first lines of a familiar scene ring out yet again, and you have no magic wand to stop them?

"I can just walk back if you need to get going," I tell her.

She shakes her head. "I'm sorry, I didn't mean to sound bitchy. I... I guess I'm still freaked out by everything."

"I don't blame you." I mean it when I tell her this.

She takes my arm, but it doesn't feel like it did before.

"Let's walk back to the car," she says, and forces out a smile.

81.

Three Things
Cannot Be Long Hidden

Friday, December 7

I stand atop a milk crate near the giant Christmas tree in Union Square, the donation box open at my feet.

"Ladies and Gentlemen!" I begin. "Christmas shoppers! I bring you good tidings for the Holidays!"

We've gotten lucky. The temperature is in the low 60's and a dull sun peers down from the soft blue sky.

"I present to you a poem, 'The Day Before Christmas'!" The passers-by pay no attention, but I concentrate on thinking like Liam and press on.

'Twas the day before Christmas, and all round the Square
Every shopper was rushing, over here, over there.

The purses were slung over shoulders with care
In the hope that pickpockets were not lurking there.

The children all wrestled, and some hit their heads,
While doses of sugar worked better than meds.
And Mom with her wine glass and I with my beer
Had not finished shopping, with Christmas so near.

But on this very corner there arose such a clatter
I put down my smartphone to check out the chatter.
I'd been watching the feed of the Niners' big game
And hoping they'd play well and wouldn't be lame.

Some shoppers have stopped to listen and I get a laugh for this.

The sun o'er our heads was hanging so low
That the foam on my brewski took on a faint glow,
When what to my wandering eyes should appear
But a truck painted red that was starting to veer.

With a little old driver, so lively and quick
He was wrinkled and thin, and with glasses quite thick.
More rapid than NASCAR his wheels leapt ahead
And he yelled, "Hey, watch out! Or you'll eat tire tread!"

"Hey lady, hey big dude, hey you with the blintzes,
Get onto the curb so you keep all your senses!
Get out of my way, now get away, all!
Or your Humpty Dumpty will have a great fall!"

He slammed on the brakes and the wheels did a-chatter
But, lucky for me, he had ABS standard.
As I first caught my breath and was turning around
He leapt from his truck... and then fell to the ground.

More people now. More laughter.

His eyes, how they twinkled! His dimples how merry!
His cheeks glowed like roses... in his bottle was sherry!

He had a round face and a big brown cigar
That smelled quite obnoxious to folks near and far.

"So what's the big hurry?" I walked up and said.
"Another six inches, I'd have ended up dead!"
He spoke not a word, but went straight to his truck,
And from an old tool chest he pulled out... a duck!

It was not any duck, or it all wouldn't matter.
'Twas my rubber ducky, though now a bit tattered.
My very best toy from my very best years,
Lost long ago and it caused many tears.

He sprang back to the cabin and the old engine roared,
I stood there in shock at the loss he'd restored.
Westward he sped, his bright eyes distending
As he raced off to find the next heart needing mending.

But I heard him exclaim, 'fore he drove on with flair,
"Think not about cost, but of how much you care!"

The shoppers applaud, and I sweep my top hat in a long, graceful arc as I bow. The crowd has grown to twenty or thirty people, the best yet that I've done with this new poem. As they disperse a number of them drop money in the box.

The last figure in the crowd is a tall man with a familiar square-shouldered silhouette. It's Captain Kreitzer.

"I thought I might find you here," he says.

I bow politely, trying to channel Liam as best I can. "Three things cannot be long hidden: the sun, the moon and the fog."

He nods. "Well said. You got five minutes to talk?"

"Sure."

He looks around. "Let's walk up Post St. Fewer people."

We cross the Square and start walking up the gentle slope into the Theatre District. The same path Paula and I walk on the night that Candi Bonham is found dead.

He looks down at his watch. "It's 1:40 now. If some people asked you to meet them nearby at 2:30 could you do it?"

"Sure," I tell him.

"So here's the deal. Go to the St. Francis Hotel lobby. Not the fancy one on Powell, the one by the registration desk in back, by the garage entrance. They have a little cafe in there where you can have some privacy. I'll see that the table in the back corner is clear for you."

"Another performance?" I ask.

"No," he says. "That's why I'm telling you now, so you know it's not your little friend at work again."

"Some friend," I tell him.

"Three men will come to see you. They will offer you gifts. You can accept their offer or tell them to shove it and rotate. Not my issue."

"How is it you know about all this?" I ask him.

He is distracted sending a text to someone on his phone, then looks up. "Sometimes you decide to give people a chance to do the right thing."

"OK. 2:30 it is. OK if I wear this?" I ask, indicating the top hat and tails.

"Free country. Steve or Liam, you can be whoever you want."

That's not the question, but I decide to let it go. I shake his hand, ready to head off to my mysterious meeting.

"By the way, you know the real quote, the real version of that line you used with me?" he asks.

"Which one?"

"It's a quotation from Buddha," Kreitzer says. "'Three things cannot be long hidden: the sun, the moon and the truth.'"

82.

Behind One of the Masks

Friday, December 7 (Cont.)

I decide that a tux and a top hat are not the ideal costume for a discreet meeting in an elegant cafe. I walk back to the St. Francis Hotel, change in the hotel's mezzanine restroom and emerge in jeans and my black wool jacket.

It's already 2:25, so I go down the grand staircase and enter the rear lobby. When I arrive at the little café the three men are already there.

One is a tall Black guy in his forties who wears a well-tailored suit. He looks like he's ready to go do something important.

The second is a white guy about the same age, but much shorter and much softer. He wears a Hawaiian shirt under a gray suit jacket, and both his jeans and his flip-flops are faded and worn.

I freeze in my tracks. The third man is the dreadlocked Dean from Avanture Video.

They stand to greet me and the man in the suit shakes my hand. "Jerry Cowan," he says. "Jerome Cowan Investigations."

"San Francisco Police?" I ask.

"Long ago. We're a private firm."

The man in the Hawaiian shirt now shakes my hand. "Lou Dodanos, Avanture Video."

"You know me," Dean says morosely.

I take the last chair at the little table and set my old blue duffel bag beside me. Lou and Dean share a small high-backed sofa across from us, while the well-dressed Cowan occupies a chair with carved wooden arms on my right.

The server, a woman in her twenties, has a black plastic brace on her left knee that's decorated with a Grateful Dead sticker. She takes our drink order.

I look at them.

They look at me.

Finally Cowan leans forward and says, "Listen, we came to share some things with you. We made some mistakes recently."

"Captain Kreitzer suggested this meeting?" I ask.

"Yes." Cowan answers.

More silence. If I don't say anything the three of them will apparently just sit there all day.

"So...?" I ask them.

Cowan clears his throat. He's the one who calls the shots. "Lou's been working on a pilot for a new TV reality show called 'Secret Lives of the Real City.'"

"I got friends in LA," Lou adds.

The drinks come. It doesn't take long for Dean to go through his Heineken, and Lou isn't far behind. Cowan and I just have water.

"The show's about everyday people who lead double lives. Lou asked me to join the production team and use my investigation, my research skills, to find people for the show."

"Lotta crazy people," Lou adds.

Cowan keeps going. "Women who are bank officers by day, then do 'theme parties' at night. A barker at a strip club on Broadway who's a preacher on the weekend. You get the idea."

"You gotta make it compelling. No nipples in the U.S. version, but it's gotta sell in Europe, too." Lou sounds very professorial.

I continue to sit in silence, though where this is going now seems obvious.

"Dean here recognized you as a street performer who sold these little bottles of fog, back when you came into his studio," Cowan says. "We found out you worked on the ferry, so your double life balanced out the more... sexually-oriented segments in the show."

Dean appears to be estimating the thread count in the heavy silk curtain that hangs beside our table. He says nothing.

"So you're following me," I tell him.

Cowan nods. "We've been taping you in public settings a few times a week for the last three months. Mostly out in the open, with our guys posing as tourists or news crews."

Lou says, "Not in the bathroom or nothing, so don't worry. You're gonna be..." but Cowan raises a hand to silence him.

"The guys filming the SoMa Triangle protests." I tell them.

"Yes." Cowan answers.

"The black Honda following Mrs. Tarrow's car on eastbound 80 from here to West Sacramento."

"Yes."

"I already know you staged the masquerade party on the ferry on Halloween."

Cowan's eyes narrow but he says nothing.

"We... we made a mistake." Cowan says. "We should have asked you first."

"Everybody wants to get on TV," Lou adds. "They'll do anything to get on our shows."

Cowan presses on. "We came to say we're sorry, and we won't use the tapes without your permission."

I look at Dean. "They're not tapes, they're digital files."

He raises his eyes and looks at me. "Dude, I swear, I didn't know about the purse and Phil's book and people trying to get you in trouble. Candi Bonham was my friend. When I saw you at the station and realized you were The Fog Seller dude I just... If I'd known about all that shit with the murders I'd never have, you know, I wouldn't have said anything to anybody."

"We hope you'll accept our apology," Cowan says.

What do I say to this? These guys follow me for weeks, freaking me out. Scaring Emma too. All for their stupid show.

Now Lou leans forward. "Hey, Steve, we're ready to offer you $5,000 to let us keep you in the show. Nothing sexy. Just you doing your fog thing and you on the ferry."

Five thousand dollars. When I work so hard to make fifty dollars why does five thousand from these guys sound so unimportant?

"And you and the dancers on the ferry that night, it's how we tie it all together, show how all your lives connect." Lou clearly thinks that Coppola, Spielberg and Scorsese will be impressed with this montage.

"No thanks," I tell them. "I don't need to be on TV."

Lou looks surprised. "Think about it, Steve. It's a lot of money."

"No, thanks."

He gives me a smile. "How about we make it six thousand. You can buy a lot of fish food with six thousand bucks."

"No, thanks." I don't ask how much they know about my fish, or how they know it.

Cowan cuts in. "Whatever you want, Steve. We'll do it your way. And we're very sorry."

"So what you're saying," I tell Cowan, "is that you'll stop following me, you won't use the video, and you hope I won't sue you or try to get you arrested."

Cowan folds his hands more tightly. "Yes." He hesitates. "Ask Ken Kreitzer. We served six years together. He'll tell you that my word is good, that I wouldn't... This just got out of hand."

I look at him, then at Dean, then at the Hawaiian-shirted producer sitting across from me. Lou meets my eyes and tries to look trustworthy.

He fails miserably.

* * *

The moment I clear the St. Francis Hotel lobby I call Kreitzer to hear what he has to say about all this.

He doesn't answer. I leave a message.

I call Emma but she's in class. I leave a message.

I call Mrs. Tarrow. She answers, which throws me off because I'm ready to talk to a recording, not a person.

"Just be careful, Steven," she says when I finish my story. "Stay vigilant. Just because we know they were following you doesn't mean someone else isn't following you, too."

"Thanks," I tell her. "For a minute there I've actually been feeling better."

"Sorry, dear," she says.

How can you be angry with a grandmotherly lady who says, "Sorry, dear"?

83.

Nets That Are 99% Loopholes

Friday, December 7 (Cont.)

"You remember the first time you sat in that chair?" Kreitzer asks me.

I look down at the chipped paint on the old steel legs, the worn linoleum floor. "Yes. You were wearing a red and black tie with a tiny stain near the tip."

He snorts. "You're just... No, I take it back. You're Steve Ondelle. It's probably true."

"So can you tell me what's behind The Three Stooges' apology?" I ask him.

Lieutenant Li knocks and enters.

"Our guys, the ones we have looking out for you," Kreitzer says. "They realized they weren't alone."

"So you arrested the guys from Avanture Video."

"No. We watched them watching you and tried to figure out who they were."

"Pretty obvious they weren't trained killers," Li says.

I have to admit he's right.

"Then one of our guys got video of Jerry Cowan taking video of you. I recognized him, called his office and asked what the hell he was doing in the middle of my murder investigation."

"What did he say?"

Kreitzer shakes his head. "He had no idea. Remember, we've kept your name out of the media. You've been through hell, but your friends, our department and the killer are the only ones who know."

"Jerry's a good guy," Li adds.

This ticks me off. "You want me to promise not to sue him?"

Li stops, looks at Kreitzer.

His boss ignores him. "You want to sue him, sue him. You can sub-poena the tapes we took and we'll give them to you."

"Sorry, Steve," Li says. "You do what you want to do."

Kreitzer stays serious. "And now, if you care to hear about it, we did finally get our big break in the murder case we're supposed to be investigating."

I wait as he pauses dramatically, realize I'm holding my breath.

"Peter Polossov, Mary Anne's boss, dropped in for a talk."

"Yes!!!"

"He'd been losing sleep over your twin cowboys performance. He decided to come in now as a witness so he didn't have to come in later as an accessory."

"So we've got her!" My heart is doing cartwheels. I can't believe it! We finally got her!

"On what charge?" Kreitzer asks calmly.

"Murder! Double murder!" I proclaim.

"Polossov says Mary Anne denied she knew anything about the killings, and denied it over and over again. She told him it's just a coincidence that Candi's murder saved his ass and that she'd never get involved in something that serious. Polossov himself hasn't committed any crime. Except maybe being a weasel."

I look at Kreitzer in disbelief.

"Here's the deal. Polossov was one of the twin cowboys at the Vergessen Hotel. It's a stunt his old college roommate pulled every few years, whenever he came to town for a convention. The buddy would get a suite, hire the girls, and buy different crazy hats each time. One year it was football helmets, another it was Viking horns. They even tried being identical Darth Vader's one time, but the helmets steamed up and they had to take them off."

Li chortles at this but Kreitzer keeps going.

"The friend handled everything, so there was never anything to document Polossov was there. Until they accidentally left a door unlocked..."

"And Candi walks in on them," I say.

Kreitzer nods. "Best guess is that when the hookers arrived the front door of the suite didn't latch behind them. The open door looked like a conference suite, so Candi walked right in. Not a big deal to be caught in *flagrante delecto* by a stranger... but one of Candi's many professions was being a masseur."

"Masseuse," Li corrects him.

"Whatever. It turns out that Polossov was one of Candi's clients for massages. And so was his wife. It wasn't a stranger who walked in on the twin cowboys."

"Candi recognizes him!" I say. Actually, I'm shouting again.

Kreitzer stands up, starts to pace. "Polossov panicked, because he's supposed to be a happily married guy. A wealthy happily married guy, whose wife Chloe is the majority shareholder in the company and manages the family trust and real estate holdings."

I'm listening carefully, trying to take it all in, trying to see the opening we need.

"Chloe Hylberg Polossov has a pre-nup with her husband, drafted by the Hylberg family attorneys," Kreitzer says.

"This being her second marriage and Polossov's third," Li adds.

Kreitzer nods. "That pre-nup is iron-clad, and it throws him from the family plane without a parachute if she divorces him for abuse, for an arrest... or for infidelity."

"The sad thing," I tell them, "is that all Candi tells the women at the salon is that the cowboys had matching hats."

Li shakes his head. "She called Polossov to discuss a deal."

"We don't know that," Kreitzer says.

"Candi calls Polossov?" I ask, disappointed.

Kreitzer hesitates. "She left a voicemail from a public phone and asked him to call her back at an assigned time."

"That's what started everything," Li says.

Kreitzer leans on the wall behind his desk. "They'd pulled this twin-hats stunt during Polossov's first two marriages and he never got caught, so he just kept right on rolling when he married Chloe Hylberg. When Candi called him from a public phone he realized he could lose everything. He had to get advice from someone he could trust, so he told Mary Anne Mathis, his right hand attorney at the firm."

"And his enforcer," Li adds.

Kreitzer looks down at his notepad. "Before they came to Talkami, Polossov and Mathis worked together at a law firm called Bolkmann and Young. Opposing witnesses in their civil cases would keep forgetting things under oath. The D.A.'s office couldn't prove there was any tampering, and when they left the case went cold."

I'm stunned. "So this may not be the first mission for the tall lady with the deep voice."

"Already working that angle," Li says.

Kreitzer says, "Mary Anne knew it wasn't just Polossov whose future was at stake if Candi called the wife and told an exciting tale of cowboy adventures. Talkami makes family software, and they have tight restrictions on their stock options, rules that require their execs to live as positive role models in the community. They're all paper millionaires who can't cash in till the company goes public or gets sold, and in the meantime they have to live squeaky clean lives."

I rub my forehead, try to take this all in. "But they're both already wealthy, right?"

Kreitzer shakes his head. "Mary Anne Mathis makes good money, but she's not a millionaire. Polossov had invested heavily in real estate and went bankrupt in 2008, and he married Chloe in 2009, three years after her first husband died."

"That explains the pre-nup," Li adds.

Kreitzer nods. "Polossov told us that if he's caught cavorting with hookers they can cite moral turpitude as a cause for termination, fire him and he loses the right to buy all his shares in the company. Then the wife can divorce him without a penny and he's lost it all."

"And Mary Anne's job and her stock options vanish with him," I tell them. It's making more and more sense.

"Exactly," Kreitzer says. "She's not exactly popular there. She'd lose everything."

"We checked," Li says. "Mary Anne Mathis has no assets except a 401K, her shares in Talkami and her house, and the house is mortgaged to the hilt and tied up in the divorce. We're talking three to five million dollars of Talkami shares if they go public next year, three to five million she'd lose if Polossov is sacked."

Kreitzer goes back to pacing. "I can't prove it, but I think Mary Anne heard Polossov's story and realized that both of them were about to become eligible for food stamps."

Li grins. "Not the kind of fringe benefit they're used to."

"I think she knew there wasn't much time," Kreitzer says, "so she had to improvise. Giantonio had been bringing Candi to charity events around town, so she'd seen them together. He was SoMa Triangle's big opponent, so a double murder didn't just eliminate Candi. It was an assassination that would rock City Hall, steal all the headlines and have us chasing all the wrong motives when we found your fingerprints on the purse."

"Because I'm not good with questions," I murmur.

"Exactly," Kreitzer says. "I think she got Candi accustomed to meeting at odd hours and getting paid in cash, so when Mathis showed up at the apartment door she knew she'd have no problem getting in."

"Her place was up on Nob Hill," Li adds. "The banging of the Cable Cars would cover the sound of the shots."

I shiver at the image of two helpless people being murdered. The blanks are filling in on Mrs. Tarrow's chart. "It all adds up," I tell them. "You have to be able to arrest her."

Kreitzer shakes his head.

"The life of a fisherman," Li says.

I look at him. "What does that mean?"

Kreitzer has returned to his seat and is looking at some papers. "Fishermen make a living with nets that are 99% loopholes."

Now I'm angry. "There has to be some way to arrest her!"

Kreitzer gives me a look. "We have a case, but it's a weak one, especially against a sophisticated defense. The maître' d' at a place on Montgomery says he thinks she was there that night or the night before and paid with cash. No one else remembers which night she was there either, which gives her an alibi we can't prove or disprove. She could muddy the water, create enough doubt to get a hung jury. They might even let her walk."

I shake my head. "There has to be something..."

Li looks at his boss and grins.

"Maybe there is," Kreitzer says. "Polossov has offered to do whatever we want him to do in return for immunity and confidentiality in the case, so his ass stays out of jail and his name stays out of the papers. And so he has some chance of begging his wife for a second chance and saving his marriage."

"And...?" I ask him

Kreitzer leans forward with an odd smile. "Are you and your actor friends up for one more performance?"

84.

And What Do I Get
if I Win?

Saturday, December 8

Mrs. Tarrow grins and takes another tiny sip of her amaretto. "Almost all filled in," she says proudly, setting the chart neatly on the breakfast bar.

I stop rinsing dishes and re-read it upside-down from where I stand at the sink.

Knows Steven not good with questions
— Daughter in Steven's class, on ferry
Knows Steven's routine.
— Commutes to SF, could plant gun
Had reason to kill Candi Bonham
— Boss cowboy twin, Could lose millions

Hired Candi to drop purse to get fingerprints

— Not experienced in evidence
— Civil attorney, not criminal
Had stolen gun — ???

Five names have been crossed out at the bottom of the list. Only one remains.

~~Carl Mathis: Parent, PR at Institute~~
~~Tommy Gonzalez: Former student~~
~~Tom Festane: Parent, ex-SoMa Triangle~~
Mary Anne Mathis: Parent, attorney
~~Eve Mortimer: Lost $ via SoMa Triangle~~
~~Dean @ Avanture: Knew Candi, reappears~~

"Mathis knows we've figured it out," I tell her. I go back to loading the dishwasher to dispel my nervous energy, with Zina supervising my work in case I drop something. "She's going to be suspicious of everyone and everything. She'll see how we're..."

"Don't be so sure of that," Mrs. Tarrow says. "When she was the one who knew what was coming and you didn't, everything felt like a surprise. You kept looking but you never saw the next blow before it hit you."

The purse, the gun in the bathroom, the hidden credit card, the TSA report, taking away my house... Mrs. Tarrow's right. A surprise, every time.

"And," she adds, "now you know that it's those silly TV people and not a murderer who's been following you everywhere. That has to be a relief."

"It is," I tell her, putting the big frying pan into the dishwasher and adjusting everything to make it fit.

She takes another sip of amaretto, watching my progress. "Well you don't look very happy about your tormentors being unmasked."

I shake my head. "I'm still worried about The Rabbit and The Pocket Watch. I think the odds are three-to-one she figures it out and we need a whole new plan."

She cocks her head skeptically.

"And I also think Kreitzer's going too far with this Phil Steen event. We're going to scare her off, not lure her in."

"We'll see," she says with a mischievous grin. "In fact, if you're so skeptical what's your bet on this little issue?"

"If I win..." I try to think. "If I win I get a single red rose to give to Emma. I need all the help I can get."

"She's been here every Thursday. Just like she said she would."

"When we're dressing up like twin cowboys and trapping Mary Anne Mathis it's wonderful," I tell her.

"I was so happy to see her that next morning," she says. "Your face, at breakfast... You looked different than I've ever seen you."

I nod. "But last week, when we don't have any adventures planned and we just hang around..."

"These things take time," Mrs. Tarrow says.

"I guess."

She brightens up again. "And what do I get if I win and our friend Ms. Mathis walks in with The Pocket Watch?"

I consider this. "A Thursday night dinner that Emma and I cook for you, all by ourselves."

"Now that, young man," she says, "is a deal!"

85.

The Dictionary That Translates How I Feel

Monday, December 10

This year Luis and Paula and I are starting a new tradition. We're having our very own Christmas party, at a dim sum restaurant on the edge of Chinatown.

Luis has been held up again, so Paula and I walk ahead to stake out a table. As usual, the little place is packed.

The hostess hurries forward, two fingers raised. "Two people!" she proclaims. "I put you at bar!"

Paula holds up three fingers. "One more is coming."

"Oh," she says, sadly. "Oh..." The silk frog buttons on her fire-engine-red satin blouse look like they're sad, too.

She looks around, sees something in the back and brightens again. "Right this way!"

With a graceful sweep of her arm she leads us to a narrow alcove behind the glittering aluminum Christmas tree. It holds a small table with three chairs, the hidden haven where the servers eat once the noontime rush is over.

Paula takes the seat at the back. I sit to her left, but a bristly branch of the artificial Christmas tree keeps brushing my arm.

I shift to the other chair, but a different branch now pokes me in the back. Paula starts to laugh.

"Sorry," she says. But I can tell she doesn't mean it.

I retreat to the first chair.

While we wait I tell her about the reality TV producers who've been following me, and that it's not a coven of hired killers out there in the darkness.

She breathes a huge sigh of relief. "Well, that's a nice Christmas present!"

I grimace. "Joseph and Mary get The Three Wise Men. I get The Three Stooges."

Still no Luis.

I look around and listen. We're the only ones in the restaurant who are speaking English.

"It seems like Captain Kreitzer will be able to arrest this woman soon," Paula says

A shiver goes through me. "I just want it to all be over."

"The things she's done, they've all backfired. She just made you more... Luis getting fired, the TSA interrogation, losing your home, those things made you more connected to the outside world instead of more withdrawn."

Inside I think, "I hope Emma agrees with you," but out loud I just murmur, "Thanks."

A young Chinese woman with a narrow face comes by with a cart and peers at us between the aluminum Christmas tree branches. "Prawn ball and sticky rice," she says, and points to two sets of bamboo containers.

Paula says, "No, thanks," and points to our empty chair.

The server moves on.

"Have you decided on your next move?" I ask Paula.

"No. I asked if the job they'd offered me at State was still open, but they'd filled it with a guy from Palomar."

Luis' job: lost.

Paula's job: lost.

She looks across the table and reads my mind. "I did it to myself, Steve. I kept pushing it. Bret's convinced that people know so little about science that we have to wow them with computer graphics or no one will come."

"He's wrong," I tell her.

She plants her elbows on the table, leans her head on her folded hands. "I just don't know any more. If he's right I need to get out of this business. No Ph.D. means no research jobs."

"My dad says that everything happens for a reason."

"I think that's true," Paula says. "This... I've got a lot of decisions to make and now some of them are easier."

I never know what to do when people confide in me, when they open up and share their real feelings.

No, Steve, that's not true. When I'm thinking like Liam, then I'm perfectly at ease. Happy to listen, happy to share, unafraid that I'll be seen as prying or poking or judgmental.

"You really have changed."

I bring my eyes back to Paula. "Excuse me?"

"You really have changed, since you met Emma. I mean, each time I see you I can see so much is different."

So strange, to be discussing Emma with Paula.

"Is it OK that I said that?" she asks.

"It's OK," I tell her. "I'm just... I don't know what scares me more, being portrayed as a murderer or trying to be what Emma wants me to be."

Paula nods. "I can see that."

"After Christmas, that's when we'll talk and she decides what she wants to do. Most of the time I..."

An older woman approaches with her cart. She leans over, tries to see us between the Christmas ornaments. She yells, "Steamed crab, rice noodle roll."

"Sorry, we're waiting for our..." The server does not wait for Paula to finish speaking, just moves on.

"So you're making lots of decisions," I say.

She knows I'm changing the subject back to her, but does not object.

"Lots of decisions." She gets a strange smile. "But I'm looking... I mean, I need a job, don't get me wrong. But I'm also looking for what you found. With Emma."

A hundred thoughts, dreams and all the wreckage of lost hopes flash through me. All I can manage to say is, "Uh-huh."

Good, Steve, Really thoughtful response.

"What told you... What was the moment when you knew Emma was the one?"

Is this really happening? Is beautiful Paula Costa really asking Steve Ondelle, the eternal awkward loner, about love?

"I don't know," I answer. "I just look at her and... It's like she has the only copy of the dictionary that translates how I feel. So when she's there I can talk about it. And she understands."

Paula shakes her head. "That's what everyone always tells me," she says. "It just happens. I have to figure out what I need to do so it can happen to me."

I try to say something, but no words come out.

"It's OK," she says. "I know the answer."

The older server comes back with a different cart that has just a few boxes stacked on it. "Beef heart and noodle," she says half-heartedly through the shiny silver branches.

I shake my head to decline this delicacy, then turn back to Paula. "What's that? What's the answer to how to find true love?"

"There is no answer," she says. "In the end you just have to decide."

Now I'm even more confused. "Decide...?"

She nods. "You can spend your life worrying that you'll never find love, or you can spend your life worrying that you'll love the wrong person. But you have to choose which worry is right for you."

"Now," I tell her, "you're starting to sound like me."

86.

The Rabbit Has Taken
His Pocket Watch

Tuesday, December 11

"The Rabbit Has Taken His Pocket Watch." It is Li's voice on the voicemail from last night. I've listened to it twenty times, and each time I feel both worried and excited all over again.

Those seven words mean that Act I has been completed, that our plan appears to be working.

And that Emma and I are half way to owing Mrs. Tarrow a hand-crafted home-cooked meal.

But first Kreitzer wants to turn up the pressure on Mary Anne Mathis. Just one more time.

I'm hoping it's not one time too many.

"I am so excited," Phil Steen is saying via my $19 radio, "because this Thursday at 7:00 PM we're going to present our first-ever KZRT The Dezert Stage Drama!"

"Like Hamlet?" Mad asks.

"Like nothing you've ever seen!" Phil answers. "We're taking over the stage at Theatre Lab West in San Francisco for the first performance of..."

The music plays and Mad delivers her echo-chamber version of the words, "The Case of the Vanishing Volunteer!"

"Yes, friends, we will be revealing the identity of my mysterious volunteer publicist..."

"Driven to distraction by her obsession with Phil Steen," Mad interjects.

"My obsessed publicist who spends her own money to hire a woman to give deserving people in San Francisco a free copy of my book."

Mad's echoing voice repeats, "*How Much is That Strange Man in the Window?*, available from Rockin' Books!"

"And... we'll explain why my very personal Good Samaritan carried out this bizarre plan!"

"Now you told me there's a dark side to this story, Phil," Mad says.

His tone gets very serious. "Yes, Mad, there is."

"Your mystery publicist wasn't out to help you."

"No, she wasn't." Phil admits.

"In fact, she was trying to cover up a crime."

"Well, Mad, now that you mention it, she was."

"And Phil, she didn't even like your book."

"Well I wouldn't go that far..."

"And the play on Thursday night, it tells the whole story?"

"Yes, Mad, it will. All the dirty lies, all the illicit sex, all the hidden truths about the seedy underworld of volunteer book promoters who turn to... murder!"

"Murder!"

"Yes, Mad, Murder," Phil says. And we'll show it all to you this Thursday night in our KZRT The Dezert Stage Drama, at 7:00 PM at Theatre Lab West. Ticket sales benefit the Boys and Girls Clubs of San Francisco, so come out this Thursday night for an evening of sex, lies, murder, Mad-ness and me!"

87.

Like She's Watching
Over My Shoulder

Thursday, December 13

After three days of waiting, Act II of the show begins today at 4:45.

For three days every radio and TV reporter in town has been interviewing Phil and Mad. For three days the story makes the front pages of all the big websites and what's left of the newspapers.

On the talk shows San Franciscans debate whether this is just another DJ publicity stunt or a genuine live on-stage accusation of murder.

Kreitzer's gruff, "No comment!" when asked if the performance is tied to the Supervisor's murder just feeds the speculation.

I look over at Leonard the Human Statue. His thick brown locks are gone, his hairline is receding, and the remaining close-cut hair is bleached to a dirty gray.

I look in the mirror and I, too, present a far different image. My skin has darkened from years in the sun and deep lines are etched around my eyes and mouth.

"Hold still, please."

"Sorry."

The woman continues hollowing my cheeks and neck with subtle highlights.

Or are those lowlights?

We are in the basement of Theatre Lab West, sitting in the same makeup chairs where Candi Bonham would prepare for her roles.

The thought keeps haunting me, like she's watching over my shoulder in the mirror.

If she is, I hope she's smiling.

Out of the corner of my eye I see the slim, dark-haired costume designer eyeing Leonard, comparing him to a photo I cannot see. She adjusts the shoulders on his jacket and again contemplates his silhouette.

"Shari, when you get a chance, I think his sideburns still need some touchup," she tells the makeup artist.

"OK," Shari answers. "Just give me a couple more minutes here."

Kreitzer has told us over and over again about the difference between entrapment and A Righteous Sting. We cannot suggest anything to anyone. We cannot invite anyone to do anything. All we can do is portray human beings doing what they want to do, and what happens next is whatever happens next.

"I think you're good to go," Shari tells me. "When you finish with Linda let me take one last look at you."

I get out of the makeup chair and return to the rack of clothes by the door.

"Linda, have you done... The next one is Eli Evers. Have you done him?" asks the makeup artist.

The costume designer shakes her head. "Not yet. I'll take him when you're done."

"I'll get him for you," I tell them. I walk out to the hallway, see Eli sitting on the stairs talking to Emma.

"You're up, Mr. Pacino!" I tell him.

He takes off his Giants cap, runs his fingers through his hair, tries to force a smile.

"You'll do great," Emma tells him.

"I'm cool," he murmurs. He shoots me a glance and goes into the makeup room, where Shari welcomes him by singing *Good Luck Will Rub Off if I Shake Hands with You* while brandishing her brush.

Eli laughs and climbs into the makeup chair.

I walk over to Emma, lean over, give her a kiss.

She kisses me back.

"I'm running out of exciting activities to plan for you on Thursdays," I tell her.

She rolls her eyes. "Three months ago I came to San Francisco looking for my father. Six weeks ago I was falling in love with a man who sells fog for a living. Now I'm playing Mrs. Tarrow's granddaughter in a police sting..."

I jump as I feel fingertips on my neck, but it is just Linda folding down the label in my shirt. "Sorry, darlin'," she tells me.

I view myself in the mirror as Linda tucks and pins my costume of torn green cotton pants, a belt that's four sizes too large and a pair of filthy hiking boots. A stained white T-shirt beneath a camouflage hoodie completes my ensemble.

Linda glances over at Emma in her black pants, white top and black blazer, sees that she's nervous.

"You look like a perfect granddaughter," Linda tells her.

Emma shivers. "I just want to get this over with."

Now Leonard walks up with the Theatre Lab West prop-master, who hands him a sleek pair of dark-rimmed glasses.

"Make sure you can walk normally while wearing 'em," the man tells him. "The shatterproof plastic distorts things a little."

"Thanks, Tim," Leonard says. "I'll practice. Can we test the audio down here in the catacombs?"

"Sure," Tim tells him. "Go stand on the landing and I'll walk back in here with Shari."

Leonard takes his position on the stairway and waits. For once he has no brass or pewter makeup, no silver-painted coat and pants. He is the archetype of a middle-aged businessman in an expensive charcoal-colored suit. He looks very important.

Tim the prop-master steps back into the concrete-walled makeup room, where Shari is now entertaining Eli with a cheerful rendition of *Supercalifragilisticexpialidocious*. Linda claps along with the music.

Holding up a small wireless microphone, Tim starts singing the Dick Van Dyke part to the song, in harmony with Shari's Julie Andrews, complete with the cockney accent.

I look up at where Leonard stands on the landing. He gives me a grinning thumbs up to confirm that the radio is working. Tim and Shari continue singing.

I can hear Eli laughing out loud as he watches their performance, his worries banished by the music.

This may not be the most traditional police sting in the history of San Francisco, but it certainly must be the most entertaining.

88.

Say
What You Need to Say,
While You Still Can

Thursday, December 13

I look at the phone hidden in my sleeve. 4:42 PM. Three minutes till the phone call.

I sit on the cold sidewalk on Market St. just south of Montgomery. Next to me is The Prophet of Market Street.

"Where did you learn to sing?" I ask him, wishing the time would pass more quickly.

"Church."

"Your dad a preacher?"

"Mother."

"Your mom's a preacher?"

He shakes his head. "Was. That's a word you need to start usin', son. 'Was.'"

"I'm working on it," I tell him.

"Need to say what you need to say, while you still can."

My earpiece crackles. "All units ready," Lieutenant Li tells us. "10-88. Repeat, 10-88. Launch the White Rabbit."

"You need to warm up?" I ask the Prophet.

"No. When I want to sing, I sing."

"You OK with singing now?"

"Don't want to see someone get hurt," he says. "That's what you said, so that's why I'm here."

He stands up, places his Styrofoam cup a couple of feet in front of him and begins:

Joshua fought the Battle of Jericho, Jericho, Jericho,
Joshua fought the Battle of Jericho
And the walls came tumblin' down!

I watch the Prophet as he belts out the lyrics in his beautiful deep voice, then steal a glance up Market St.

As it always does, a crowd has started to form around the Prophet. Two young men begin to clap in time with the song.

Up to the walls of Jericho
With a spear held in his hand,
"Now blow them horns," cried Joshua,
"This battle is in my hands!"

Joshua fought the Battle of Jericho, Jericho, Jericho,
Joshua fought the Battle of Jericho
And the walls came tumblin' down!

"Confirm when you have Alice," says the device in my ear, this time in Kreitzer's voice.

"Negative," says a man's voice. "No Alice yet."

"Monk, check on Alice." Kreitzer orders. "Now."

"10-4," says a woman's voice. "On my way. She was there at 16:30."

We have studied a wall filled with photos of Mary Anne Mathis. In a suit on her way to court. In jeans on her way to the mall. Mockups of what she'd look like with different hats and wigs and glasses. Even what she'd look like dressed as a man. Most of all, we're counting on her height. There aren't many women that tall and it's the one thing she can't disguise.

"White Rabbit crossing Pine St." says a male voice.

"Tell him to slow down," Kreitzer says. He's not happy.

"10-4," Li says.

"Hello?" This time it is Leonard's voice. "Oh, hi, Bill. Yes, I'm just walking over now." He pauses. "Oh, sure, no problem. We can push it back five minutes. I'll tell you all about it, but these new sunglasses suck."

"Keep the phone on your ear, White Rabbit," Li says. "We're still waiting for Alice."

The Prophet of Market Street is drawing more and more people, his powerful voice echoing off the buildings.

> Then the horns began to blow,
> The trumpets began to sound.
> Joshua commanded the children to shout
> And the walls came a-tumblin' down!

"This is Monk," says the woman's voice, and she sounds worried. "Alice is in Wonderland. Repeat, Alice is in Wonderland."

"Negative on Alice here," says a man. "Every exit covered, still negative on Alice."

"No Alice here," says the woman. "She was here at 16:30 and status now is negative. She is not here."

I hear Kreitzer say, "Shit!" under his breath. Either she's still somewhere in the building or she has eluded our watchers before the curtain even rises.

The Prophet of Market Street is belting out the last verse, with many in the crowd clapping along with him.

> Joshua fought the Battle of Jericho, Jericho, Jericho,

Joshua fought the Battle of Jericho
And the walls came tumblin' down!

He bows to the cheers that reward his final notes, his face calm and content as always.

"Negative on Alice," says a man's voice.

"White Rabbit, get moving." Kreitzer barks. "All units look for Alice, assume she's in Wonderland. All projects, execute."

"All projects?" Li asks, surprised.

"We've lost Alice. Get the damn rabbit moving!" Kreitzer commands.

"All projects execute!" Li shouts.

The people around us are oblivious to the drama playing out on the police radio. A few approach and drop money in the Prophet's cup.

"No worries, Bill, I'll cut the chatter and be there shortly!" Leonard's voice says happily through my earpiece.

Everything is going wrong, but we have to get our part right. If Mary Anne Mathis is heading south down Market St. our job is to slow her down, give the police more time to spot her and Leonard more time to stay ahead of her.

I stand up, lose my balance and then right myself, my hoodie shielding my face. "Do Eye on the Sparrow, Prophet!" I shout to him, half-swallowing the words to disguise my voice.

He turns, look at me and nods.

"Still negative on Alice." says the voice in my ear, his tone defensive.

The Prophet once again begins to sing.

Why would I be discouraged?
Why would the shadows come?
Why would my heart feel lonely
And long for heaven...

Suddenly his eyes go wide. His mouth opens but no sound comes out. He clutches his chest with his right hand and falls to his knees, and the crowd gasps. I step up to catch him in my arms as he falls backward, and I call out, "Get a doctor! Get a doctor!!!"

The Prophet moans, clutching his chest. His eyes are tightly closed.

"I'm a nurse," a woman says as she rushes up and kneels down beside me. She tries to open his mouth but he has clenched his teeth and she makes no progress. She places her fingers on his neck.

"Keep breathing for me, sir!" she says. "Give me nice strong breaths! Folks, step back please, we need room here!"

"I've got it, Carla," says a woman behind her, as she guides the growing crowd of onlookers a few feet back, overflowing the sidewalk.

"Thanks, Carolyn!" The nurse reaches down and untangles the Prophet's legs, and the two women pull him up so his back rests against a light-post.

Now there are sirens and soon a paramedic is beside her looking down at the Prophet, with two more men following with a stretcher. As planned, the ambulance has blocked the street and police close off the sidewalks to give them room to work.

"He's semi-conscious and I couldn't check for obstructions," Carla tells the paramedic, "but he's breathing and I'm getting a rapid pulse."

On cue, I start to back away.

The paramedic nods and turns to the men behind him. "Secure him so we can get him prepped and transport," he orders.

I slip farther away from the action as the paramedics gently lift The Prophet onto the stretcher and then wheel him to the waiting ambulance.

I take one more look. Still no face in the crowd that could be Mathis. I tuck my hoodie around my face, cross the street and head down the stairs into the Montgomery St. BART Station.

If Mary Anne Mathis is coming up Market St. she'll have to wait or retrace her steps. We have done our job.

I say a prayer that our other teams can say the same.

89.

Discussing Ugly Bridesmaids' Dresses

Thursday, December 13 (Cont.)

I do not take Muni or BART, but cross the Montgomery St. station to climb the stairs on the other side. I stay in character as a weathered man in a hoodie, shoulders slumped.

My earpiece has been silent as the teams carry out their diversions. Each blocks a different walking route between Mathis' office and Theatre Lab West, giving Leonard a buffer and helping Kreitzer's team to spot and then shadow Mathis before she can catch sight of him.

A heart attack on Market, an altercation and arrest on Battery St., a purse-snatching on Bush. In a big city it is all routine, even when three major streets are blocked by emergency vehicles in the same half hour.

Now the radio crackles on again. "This is Monk. I've checked all the rest rooms. Negative on Alice."

Li's voice says, "10-4, Monk."

Even with my head down as I walk, my eyes scan the streets around me. Stealing looks ahead, behind, in the front windows of cafes, at the opposite side's sidewalk.

No Mary Anne Mathis. No tall woman with a floppy hat.

As I approach Mission and New Montgomery there is in fact a tall woman in sunglasses with her hair tied back who has the right silhouette. But she is walking with two friends and laughing and discussing ugly bridesmaids dresses.

A corner of my mind wonders if it is the dresses or the bridesmaids that she thinks are ugly, but I suppress the thought. I turn right on 3rd St. to get back on the route to Theatre Lab West.

Step one in the plan is for the real Peter Polossov to call Mary Anne Mathis at 4:45 PM.

He'll tell her that Captain Kreitzer has asked him to come to Theatre Lab West tonight to discuss an investigation. He'll tell her that he's left the office and is already walking in that direction.

Phil Steen's event has been all over the media. Mary Anne Mathis almost certainly knows that tonight at Theatre Lab West they're planning to reveal the identity of The Lady with the Joke Book in Her Purse and the identity of the killer who hired her to cover up a crime.

She knows that if they get it right, the name they call will be hers.

She will not want the only man who knows her motive to join Kreitzer for such an event.

Polossov will ask for her advice as he walks towards the theatre from his office. We presume that she'll tell him to wait, to talk to her first.

He'll tell her that he's already running late and that he doesn't want to make things worse. That cooperating is the only answer.

We presume that she will want to rush out and follow him. That perhaps she will disguise herself.

That she will seek to prevent at any cost Polossov's talk with Captain Kreitzer at the theatre.

Because she does not know that their talk has already taken place.

Because she does not know that as he makes this call Peter Polossov is two miles away, standing safely in front of the police station on Vallejo St. with two officers at his side.

Because she does not know that the gray haired man wearing an identical suit and tie as he walks towards Theatre Lab West is really Leonard the Human Statue.

We think that we will be able to spot her as she leaves her building. To see through any disguise

But she has disappeared. Even as we think that we are outsmarting her, she is outsmarting us.

Keep your head down, Steve. Keep your footsteps short. Don't draw attention, just melt into the blur of San Francisco.

I look up to make sure no cars are coming as I cross Jessie St. and suddenly come face to face with the narrow, long-haired figure of Jacob Johnson, my old student. Ours eyes meet for an instant before I force them back to the pavement and keep walking in my shuffling gate.

"Mr. Ondelle?" he calls from behind me.

I try to keep walking, try to keep my rhythm just like the people who ignore our twin cowboys and their inflatable girlfriends.

I hear nothing else and presume he's gone. Though he could just as easily be following just a few paces behind me.

"Wonderland Units, report," Li says from inside my ear.

Several voices all respond with their numbers and the same answer: "Negative." Li acknowledges each report.

I reach Market and wait at the light to walk up Stockton St. I want to turn and look around to make sure Jacob is not trailing me, waiting to ask why I have become a weathered street person, but I don't dare look up.

In front of me is a fashionable young man who wears a double-breasted wool greatcoat over white capri-style pants and bright orange tennis shoes. A large black canvas bag, oversized sunglasses, a white baseball cap and a jet-black pony tail complete his look.

I have to admit, this guy has style. Not my style, but style.

The light changes and our cluster of pedestrians hurries across the street. There is no sign of Jacob.

My companion walks like he knows all eyes are on him and he's going to make it worth our trouble to watch.

Keep looking down, Steve. Stay in character. Keep your footsteps short...

The young man isn't wearing socks with his bright orange tennis shoes. He has a small tattoo on the side of his ankle in a flowery script. It takes me a while to read it, but since I have to keep my eyes down anyway I finally make it out. It says, "Jenni."

So maybe he's not gay after all, maybe he's...

Jenni.

I know someone with a daughter named Jenni.

I look again at the figure ahead of me. The height is about right. The black pony tail could be a wig. The coat hides the outline of the hips but it could... Could this attention-grabbing man be Mary Anne Mathis, walking in disguise right in front of where I'm walking in disguise?

I pretend to be distracted by something in a shop window, let him or her walk up Stockton half a block, the most direct route to Theatre Lab West. Then I pull out my cell phone and call Kreitzer. I glance around and breathe a sigh of relief. No sign of Jacob.

When Kreitzer answers I try to very calmly say, "I may have Alice half a block in front of me on Stockton St., about to cross O'Farrell, dressed as a man." I describe the outfit. "And he or she has the name Jenni tattooed on their right ankle."

I hear nothing on the phone, but over my earpiece I hear Kreitzer's voice shout, "Alice sighted!" He repeats my description, directs plainclothes officers and unmarked cars to look for her, alerts the team at TLW to be ready.

"I'll stay well back but try to follow her," I tell my cell phone, then realize Kreitzer has already hung up.

"Bill, I'm about to walk into Theatre Lab West for a meeting," Leonard says through the earpiece, "but while I'm out in front where people can see me from a block away I wanted to ask who you like in the playoffs this year."

"Be patient, White Rabbit," Li tells him. "We'll cue you when we see Alice reach the corner. All civilians, proceed to the back door if you want to see the show."

"We have her," a male voice says calmly. "Walking north on Stockton."

I take one last glance up the street. Bouncing happily like he doesn't have a care in the world, The Man Who May Be Mathis turns left on Geary St. In two minutes he or she will be approaching a man who looks just like Peter Polossov outside Theatre Lab West.

"Alice now heading west on Geary from Stockton, south sidewalk," the voice says.

Li answers, "10-4, Alice two blocks from Rabbit Hole."

They have her in sight, and since we only get one shot at this I hope to hell it's Mathis. Time to head for the alley.

"You know, Bill, the line here at the theatre is getting longer so I'm going to go in. Shall I call you tomorrow?" Leonard's heart must be racing, but he sounds bored with the proceedings.

"Give us ten more seconds, Mr. Rabbit," Li says. The time seems to drag on forever.

I have reached the corner of O'Farrell and turn right, allowing myself to walk faster than my character should be walking. The alley is just fifty yards ahead.

"Green light, White Rabbit!" Li shouts. "Into the rabbit hole!"

I imagine Leonard smiling as he enters the lobby and goes to the front window. Three patrons will immediately extend the line behind him, providing a buffer if she arrives too soon.

Li is trying to stay calm. "Rabbit hole, be ready for tea party in... 10, 9, 8, 7, 6..."

I imagine Mathis seeing Polossov enter the theatre, picture her hurrying the last few yards to reach the lobby quickly, to intervene and pull him away.

"5, 4, 3, 2... launch Tea Party!"

I picture her rushing into the lobby only to see Polossov disappear behind a door labeled "Staff Only." Her mind will be racing, trying to come up with a plan

A woman's voice in my earpiece says pleasantly, "The Tea Party has begun!"

I pump my fist in the air. I have spent days worrying about the trap we lay for Mathis, and now she has entered the first doorway.

Now I begin to worry about the trap she wants to lay for Leonard the Human Statue.

90.

When He Gets to 56
He Doesn't Like
What He Sees

Thursday, December 13 (Cont.)

I make my way through the alleyway behind Theatre Lab West, maneuver around the massive loading dock and reach the narrow metal door at the back corner of the building. Three officers are standing at the entrance. They stand aside to let me through.

I climb the three long, narrow flights of metal stairs, my boot heels echoing off-key, and pass through the door that leads to a small waiting area with mismatched folding chairs. I turn the corner, go through another door and head down the main hallway towards the control room, where we can watch all the proceedings on a massive monitor.

At least I'm trying to get to the control room. I've gone too far without seeing the double doors

This isn't the right hallway.

I double back towards the top of the stairs, round the corner to retrace my steps. But the door to the waiting room where I came in is locked.

Great. The show is about to begin and I've managed to get stuck in the catacombs above the stage.

I knock on the door. I wait.

I try calling Emma and then Mrs. Tarrow, but just get voicemail.

I send each of them a text, ask them to get someone to unlock the door I'm knocking on that's somewhere near the control room.

I knock again.

I wait.

At this rate I'm going to miss the show while everyone else is sitting there having...

I knock again.

Wait.

This isn't working.

Just around the corner to my right is another door, but it has one of those "Emergency Exit – Alarm will Sound" signs. This is not the time to be setting off alarms.

I look around, see a bright green exit sign with an arrow pointing to the right down at the end of the long corridor I just traversed. I set out once again down the hallway.

The door beneath the sign is locked, but as the green arrow promises there is a corridor to my right that goes up a flight of stairs. I climb the stairs, follow the corridor, see another exit sign ahead and continue walking.

The hallways are warm and I'm starting to sweat in the heavy hoodie, so I take it off and tie the sleeves around my waist.

I reach the end of this second corridor, turn right as directed by another green arrow sign and see a long corridor like the one I started in, with another exit sign above a door at the far end. If it's unlocked this will take me back towards the rear of the building, where I can find a stairway, start all over again and ask the officers for directions.

I hurry down the hallway and open the door beneath the exit sign.

Hallelujah! It's a stairway! I check and see that the door I'm exiting will lock behind me, so I roll up the hoodie and use it to prop the door open just in case I need to retrace my steps.

I hurry down three flights and push through the double doors to go back outside.

Only I'm not outside. I'm in a poorly lit classroom of some kind, with a single floor lamp to my left.

A voice to my left says, "What the..."

I turn to look at Leonard the Human Statue, dressed in an expensive suit and with his hair dyed gray.

Before I can speak the double door across the room opens and someone steps in and closes it behind them. I see the silhouette of the person but my eyes have not adapted to the low light and I can't make them out.

Alarms start to go off in my head but before I can react there are two loud bangs and flashes. First my mouth and then my chest explode in pain. I scream in agony as blood spatters across my shirt. My knees give way and I fall to the ground.

With pain scraping its ragged fingernails across my face and blood filling my mouth I realize what has happened. I've been shot, and if I don't hold still she's going to finish the job.

Three more loud bangs shake the room and Leonard groans and falls to the ground just a few feet away. I open one eye a millimeter and see a pool of blood spreading from beneath his body.

Hold still, Steve. If you want to live through this, hold still.

Footsteps slowly approach where Leonard and I have fallen.

The footsteps of the orange tennis shoes of The Man Who is Mary Anne Mathis.

Hold still. Hold your breath. Hold still.

She pauses. My mouth feels like I'm sucking a hot coal, but I have to lie still, have to hold my breath no matter how much my lungs scream for air.

Finally I hear her walk back towards the door she entered. I sneak a few short, silent breaths while her back is turned. I hear her push down on the metal bar but the door does not open. It is locked.

A moment of silence and I get one more good long breath. She crosses the room to the door I entered, giving our bodies a wide berth to avoid stepping in any blood. She pushes the metal bar.

This door, too is locked.

"Fuck!" she whispers. "Fuck!"

Hold your breath, Steve. Hold still.

She again avoids the pools of blood as she walks towards a side wall of the room. I can hear the door open, and after a moment she exits and lets it close behind her.

I open one eye half way, listen carefully, see the closed door. I take short, quiet breaths in case she returns.

"It's OK," Leonard whispers. "That door's locked so she can't get back in."

I let myself breathe, turn my head to see him sit up and take his own deep breaths. "What the fuck are you doing here, dude?"

"I... I got lost. I think I counted the floors wrong and came out on Two when I thought I was on One."

He wipes bright red blood on his shirt, looks over at me and gasps.

"Steve, your face! Are you OK?!"

I feel my mouth. My upper lip is badly split, and real blood is dripping down onto my T-shirt. "The first shot..." I realize I'm mumbling and spitting droplets of blood and rub my mouth, then recoil from the pain exploding from my gums and teeth.

"Shit. We have to get you to a doctor. Just let me... I'd better count to a hundred, just to be sure." He starts the countdown, still watching me as he whispers each number. Somewhere nearby an elevator whines.

Leonard's count has only gotten to 22 when we hear what sounds like a scream from somewhere far away. Another scream follows.

He looks at the door where Mathis exited, then looks at me. He keeps counting.

When he gets to 56 he doesn't like what he sees and says, "That's enough."

Leonard the Human Statue gets to his feet and pulls me up beside him. He opens a narrow slit in the door that our murderer used to leave the scene of the crime, then leads me through it.

My eyes are flooded by bright lights and Leonard guides me by the arm. He stops and my vision starts to adjust.

We are standing on a stage. In front of us Candi's co-workers at TLW sit in the first few rows of the theatre, admitted early to watch the preparations for the show. They appear stunned by the arrival of two men covered in blood.

They are watching the same stage where Paula and I watch *The Taming of the Shrew* the night of Candi's murder.

I look to my left and see The Man Who is Mary Anne Mathis being handcuffed. Kreitzer speaks to her slowly and carefully.

She nods to him, he asks something else, she nods again. A phalanx of officers leads her off backstage.

Mathis does not look back at the two blood-covered men she has tried to kill.

The staff members start to applaud, and Leonard says, "You need to take a bow... and then you need a doctor."

I try to ignore the pain shooting through my mouth, the woozy dizziness coming over me.

I bow. With a flourish, the way that Liam bows.

The small crowd cheers.

The floor reaches up to embrace me in soft and comforting darkness. I hear Leonard yelling something but it doesn't matter now.

91.

Do Everything in Slow Motion

Thursday, December 13 (Cont.)

The room is very very dark. I can hear the sound of a few people talking softly, far away.

Suddenly a loud electric wail slashes through the black. My head starts to hurt again.

Now drums pound like gunfire, vibrating the floor and the chair beneath me. My headache gets worse.

A spotlight floods the band on stage. Reflections shoot in all directions from chrome guitars and drums and mike stands.

Emma looks over, tries to examine my eyes. We're watching from the wings, sitting on uncomfortable folding chairs. I sip ice chips from a cup to sooth my stitches and settle my stomach.

"You OK?" she mouths to me

I nod and silently say, "OK" back to her.

I don't care how much it hurts. I'm not missing this.

Almost two hours have passed since the arrest of Mary Anne Mathis.

Enough time to be taken to the hospital in an ambulance, get five stitches on the inside of my upper lip, get my loose teeth deemed OK, get told I have a concussion and to rest and to do everything in slow motion for a few days.

Just enough time for Emma and me to be driven back in an SFPD car with its lights flashing so I can see the show.

Leonard the Human Statue paces behind us, too full of nervous energy to sit down. We are still in costume, still covered with stage blood from the squibs, with some of my real blood thrown in.

While we're at the hospital we learn that each team's little drama comes off as planned.

Mrs. Tarrow is walking with her granddaughter Emma when she has her purse snatched. Eli argues with a grizzled bike rider who pulls a knife to threaten him. The Prophet of Market Street has a heart attack.

Each piece of theatre blocks sidewalks and snarls traffic between Leonard the quarry and Mathis the hunter. As it turns out, it is Mrs. Tarrow's performance with Emma that alters Mathis' path, giving me the chance to spot her.

Kreitzer walks up, still grinning ear to ear, with Phil Steen and Mad at his side. "You ready for our big show?" he shouts over the pounding music.

I give him two thumbs up and try to grin. I've declined the Vicodin so I can enjoy the moment instead of just falling asleep, but the novocaine is starting to wear off and the stitches feel like tiny campfires inside my mouth.

Kreitzer, Phil and Mad all congratulate us, and as the song comes to an end they prepare to go on stage.

"San Francisco, are you ready to go on the road with Phil Steen on the Dezert, KZRT FM?" a too-loud voice shouts.

The crowd cheers.

"Here they are, Phil Steen and Mad Turner!"

They stride onto the stage, waving at the audience. "Hello, San Francisco!" Phil yells.

The crowd yells back.

Emma and I twist our chairs to watch the backstage monitor, with Kreitzer and Leonard standing behind us. Just this small effort makes my whole body ache.

Phil is saying, "Now, everyone, is my morning co-host Mad Turner not the most beautiful dominatrix in San Francisco?"

Mad wears a long black dress with the front of the sweeping skirt cut away to reveal black leggings and thigh-high leather boots. She bows to the applause and the whistles.

"Thanks to all of you for coming out tonight," Phil says, "to see our first-ever KZRT The Dezert Stage Drama!"

The music plays and Mad delivers her echo-chamber version of "The Case of the Vanishing Volunteer!"

Phil turns back to the audience. "You guys know, we've made a lot of jokes about my crazed volunteer publicist," he says. "But tonight's event is not a joke. It's tied to a major murder investigation by the SFPD."

"We can't tell you more than that for now," Mad adds, "and because of recent events I'm afraid we can't show you the stage play we prepared for tonight that showed how this case may have unfolded."

There is a soft moan of disappointment from the crowd.

Phil grins. "But we have something even better! We can show you a video of the amazing real-life conclusion to the story, which we recorded in this very theatre just two hours ago. Are you ready to see it?"

The crowd, which had gotten very quiet, now applauds.

"We're going to pick up the action in the lobby here at Theatre Lab West," Phil says. "Let's start the video!"

The large screen at the back of the stage comes to life. We see the stylish man who is Mary Anne Mathis enter the lobby just as a gray-haired man exits through a heavy wooden door. The image freezes.

"Our story starts when this young man..." Mad says, pointing up to Mary Anne, "follows this older gentleman into the theatre. The man in the suit enters a door marked 'Staff Only', so the guy following him... well, he can't follow him."

The action resumes and Mary Anne joins the line to buy a ticket. The phone rings and the agent answers it. "Theatre Lab West, can you hold, please?" she says.

The person on the other end of the line is apparently not interested in holding.

"I'm sorry, Captain. Yes, this is the front desk."

"He's already here, sir, he just came in. I sent him over to..."

More loud talk from the phone.

"Yes, sir," the woman says. "Yes, sir, of course."

She listens, then tells him, "When you come in, just go through the back of the lobby and follow the signs for Room 201."

The ticket agent looks up at the people in line, mouths the word, "Sorry," continues listening.

"Yes, sir," she tells Kreitzer. "I'll have someone tell him."

She hangs up and we see Leonard's friend Paul Strapp enter the lobby.

The ticket agent calls out, "Paul, can I ask a big favor?"

Paul turns, approaches the window. "Sure."

She scribbles something on a scrap of paper. "This gentleman is waiting in room 201 for a meeting. Could you go tell him the Captain will be fifteen minutes late?"

"No problem," Paul says, then turns and exits.

The Man who is Mary Anne Mathis listens to all this, looks at his watch.

The agent sells a ticket to the woman in front of Mary Anne and our high-fashion male suspect finally reaches the window.

"One for tonight," Mathis says pleasantly.

Without the tattoo I'd have been fooled. Mathis under-acts, presenting herself to the world as a relaxed, confident attention-hungry man with a high voice.

I wonder if she uses that same self-control to talk her way into Candi Bonham's apartment and murder two innocent people.

Ticket in hand, Mathis stands against the wall, takes out her cell phone and starts tapping the screen.

My hands would be trembling. Mary Anne's are steady.

The display pauses again and Phil steps forward. "Now let's recap what just happened. The young man just heard that his target is waiting in room 201 of the theatre and that he'll be alone for the next 15 minutes. Are you with me?"

Murmurs of "yes" come from the audience.

The video jumps ahead. Paul Strapp returns to the lobby, waves to the ticket agent as he exits through the front door.

"Thank you, Paul! You're a darling!" she calls after him.

"OK everyone," Mad says, "Now look for the young man."

Phil waits a beat. "I'll give you a clue. He's vanished. While we've been watching the conversation he's slipped through the Staff Only door. Let's see what happens next."

We cut to a different security camera as Mary Anne advances slowly down the corridor, reads the sign on the wall.

She turns right and a new camera shows her progress as her pace quickens down another long, straight corridor. At the end of the hallway is another sign with room numbers and arrows.

More cameras show her climbing the stairs, walking down the second floor corridor, and finally reaching a metal double door labeled "201."

There are gasps in the audience when she reaches into the black canvas bag and pulls out a small, strange-looking pistol.

"Yes," Mad says, "that's a gun. In fact, it's..."

"The Pocket Watch..." I murmur.

"It's a 7.65 millimeter Menz pistol."

The video continues. Mary Anne Mathis quietly opens the door marked 201 and slips through.

The camera view switches again, showing a wide shot of the classroom where Leonard is waiting for Mathis disguised as Polossov, all according to plan. When I enter Leonard has only a moment to look at me in shock before he sees Mary Anne enter the opposite door, gun raised and ready to fire.

We know what happens next. The sound I make when the squib hits me in the mouth is panicked and real. There are gasps in the audience as Leonard is shot and crumples to the ground.

Mathis walks forward, detours around the two bodies and the pools of blood.

"Yes, this guy just shot two men to death in cold blood," Phil tells the crowd.

Mathis tries two doors, finds both are locked, curses under her breath. She tries the third door, exits.

I lean forward, eager to see what happens before Leonard and I stagger onto the stage. Mathis enters a long corridor that is lined on either side with heavy curtains. She advances cautiously, her gun still at the ready.

Suddenly she hears the sound of pulleys and electric motors. We see Mathis panic as the massive curtains that line the hallway slowly rise towards the ceiling. The process is agonizing and seems to take forever.

There are no walls behind the curtains. With the layers of thick fabric gone, the video shows Mathis standing alone on the main stage at Theatre Lab West, near where Phil and Mad are standing now. One of her hands still holds the gun, out of sight inside her canvas bag.

She looks very small, very alone in the center of the wide, empty stage.

Mary Anne looks out at the audience. Looks to the wings on either side. Looks down at the side doors in the auditorium. Every exit is blocked by uniformed officers from the SFPD.

There is no way out.

Kreitzer calmly climbs the steps at the right of the stage.

Mathis drops the canvas bag with the gun in it. She looks out at the theatre. Not at the audience, just in that direction.

And then she tenses every muscle in her body. And then she screams.

It is a long, angry scream. Not a wail of self-pity or misery or woe. It is a scream of fury, long and deep and filled with more bile and hatred that most people will ever know.

When her breath is gone and the horrific sound has faded she takes a deep breath and screams her hatred yet again. It is anger so base and primitive and real that no one needs words to understand it.

And then Mary Anne Mathis is done. She walks towards Kreitzer with her hands clasped behind her neck.

Two officers rush forward and take her into custody. The image on the big screen fades and the crowd breaks into applause.

"As you've just seen," Phil tells the audience, "SFPD has captured the killer whom you just saw commit two murders."

"Phil, are you ready for more good news!" Mad asks.

"Why, yes, Magnificent Mad Turner, I am."

"I'm not sure how, but the two men who were shot were not killed," Mad announces. "We can't reveal their names, but let's thank the men who risked their lives to catch this suspect!"

"That's our cue," Leonard says. Emma helps me up, and he leads me onto the stage. Our entrance, covered in blood but miraculously returned to life, is greeted with applause and cheers.

We wave our thanks, and Leonard puts his arm around me and says, "You did it, dude."

I scan the theatre, let it all sink in. "You and me together," I tell him.

He shakes his head. "No, Steve. Think about it. You know what this means. You know exactly what it all means."

I look back at him. "It means Mary Anne Mathis is going to prison for the murders of Candi Bonham and Gerry Giantonio."

"Yes. And you know why they caught her, why justice is being served."

I grin. "Because we keep stirring the pot."

His voice is very low, very precise, with every word enunciated clearly. "Steve, this all happened because you stood your ground," he tells me. "This all happened because you took arms against a sea of troubles, and by opposing ended them."

92.

Answer Me with What You Want to Hear

Saturday, December 15

"You could have died," Emma tells me once again.

We're sitting at a little table at the front of the Gallienne Bakery in West Sacramento. Against his better judgment, Manny has gone into the back so she can talk to me alone.

"The pain-killers are actually pretty cool," I tell her.

"Don't joke about this."

"Yes, you're right. I was afraid she'd fire that last squib in my face to finish me off," I tell her. "If she'd shot me in the eye..."

"If you'd waited two more minutes I'd have seen your text and we'd have found you upstairs in that hallway."

"Would you have waited longer when the party was about to start?" I ask her with a smile.

"No. I'd have tried to find my way out on my own." She shivers. "And you didn't have the safety glasses and the bulletproof vest like Leonard did."

"Mrs. Tarrow kept reminding me while we were driving up here. About how I could have died just because I didn't stop to check the floor number when I came running down the stairs."

"That's what I want to talk about." She takes a sip of her tea. "That's why I asked if you could come."

My stomach starts to tighten up.

"Let's do one of your what-if's," she says. "What if you really were two people."

I sip my soda. "Uh huh."

"If one of you were going to die, who would you have chosen? To lose Steve? Or to lose Liam?"

"That's easy. I'd..."

"Wait!" She reaches over, gently covers my mouth. "Don't think about what I want to hear. Answer me with what *you* want to hear. For you."

I stop, try to think. I always choose to live as Steve or Liam as the fears of the day command. But I know that's the old way for me. To have a chance with Emma I have to decide once and for all who I want to be.

And I know that just as I can win this girl, this woman, I can also lose her.

93.

The One with the Gun
in His Locker

Monday, December 17

Kreitzer is on his cell phone. He points to the well-worn chair.

I sit down. I like sitting here now, in a place that once would frighten me to my bones.

"Yes, George Grainger please. This is Captain Kenneth Kreitzer of the San Francisco Police."

They explain something.

I notice that someone has cleaned the scuff marks off the front of the desk. In fact, the whole office has been cleaned, and a faint scent of lemon is present in the room.

"Yes, I know it's the week before Christmas. This is important."

More explanations.

"It's all right. I can wait."

Kreitzer looks over at me, a conspiratorial smile rippling his official reserve.

"You want some water?" he asks.

"No, I'm OK, thanks."

He taps his right foot. Rubs the scar on the back of his hand.

"You know I lost a bet on the Rabbit and the Pocket Watch," I tell him.

He snorts. "With who?"

"Mrs. Tarrow."

Another snort. "What did you expect?"

"Staging a fight and dropping a gun where Mary Anne Mathis would see it so soon after we surprise her with the twin cowboys... That should scare her away, not get her to take the bait," I tell him.

"Never underestimate the..."

He stops as someone new comes on the phone.

"Yes, I'm still here." He listens. "Captain Kenneth Kreitzer, K-R-E-I-T-Z-E-R." He listens some more. "No, it's OK. I'll wait."

"And if she took out the squibs and put in real bullets..."

He shakes his head. "The Pocket Watch was an antique 7.65 millimeter Menz from Germany. Only four places you can buy the ammo, all locked down. Plus a court order to intercept any package at her home or office."

"If she'd checked she'd have seen the squibs," I tell him.

"What'd you bet with Amanda Tarrow?"

"Emma and I have to make her a gourmet dinner."

"Good. She deserves a lot more than..."

They come back on the line, say something else.

"Thanks very much, no problem," Kreitzer answers, then rests the phone on his shoulder. Waits in silence for a moment, then looks back at me.

"I bet you'll count the floors on every stairway you climb the rest of your life," he says with a grin.

I feel for the stitches on the inside of my mouth with my tongue. At least they've stopped throbbing.

"Yeah, I think I will," I tell him.

Someone else comes onto the phone.

"Hello, Mr. Grainger," Kreitzer says. "Thanks for taking my call."

He listens, looks over at me, shakes his head as if to say "Blah, blah, blah."

"Good, good to hear it's a big family event. I'm calling to disclose some confidential information, now that we have an arrest in the Giantonio-Bonham case."

He listens for a moment.

"Right. This is off the record. That all right?"

Our illustrious GM apparently says yes.

"Good. So here's the deal. Your deckhand, Luis Deverro?"

Grainger says something.

"Right. The one with the gun in his locker. I can tell you now that when he placed the gun there he was carrying out procedures we defined to preserve the weapon as evidence when he found it on the *Louis H. Baar*. We wanted it to stay out of our custody to see if some-one else would come for it."

I smile at the careful wording Kreitzer uses to avoid lying and to avoid telling the truth. Grainger says something.

"Yes, I was trying to hint at it for you but couldn't tell you more at the time. Deverro violated your policies as part of our investigation. He'll probably get a commendation of some sort from the Mayor."

Grainger says something.

"Sure... sure. We could do that. We could make the commenda-tion for the Bay Area Transportation and Waterways District. I can talk to the Chief."

Grainger says something. Kreitzer rolls his eyes.

"But we need to give you time to get Deverro back on the payroll so it all looks like it was planned. So nothing can backfire."

Grainger says something.

"Right. For your cooperation with SFPD in breaking the case. Sure. Just call me when you've got Deverro back on duty, when his medical benefits are back in force, and I'll take it from there."

They exchange more details and Kreitzer hangs up. He exhales loudly.

"Any of your artistic friends do fancy calligraphy?" he asks.

I run down the list in my mind. "No."

"Shit. I'm going to have to call the Chief and get a real certificate."

"So Luis is getting his job back?" I ask him.

Another rare Kreitzer smile. "I gave Grainger a torch and he knew what to do with it."

"A torch?"

"Torches give you clear choices. You can grab the handle and be in the spotlight, or stick your fingers in the flames and get burned. This way Grainger gets a sound bite as a hero on TV and your friend Luis comes back to work."

"My God, it's really happening." Joy rushes over me. "We're getting Luis back on the *Louis H. Baar*! Thank you! Thank you so much for doing this!"

He stands up, reaches out and shakes my hand. "Thanks for everything you did. Couldn't have broken this one without you and your traveling Shakespeare Festival."

It's time for me to go. Before I turn away I tell him, "And thanks for believing I'm not a crazy man who murders people."

He looks at me for a long time. Then he says, "You're a good man, Steve. Strange, but good."

I stand there, surprised and silent. However hard it is for me to accept this, I can see that he believes it to be true.

94.

It Is a Gray So Dark
It Is Almost Black

Saturday, January 5

I look at my reflection in the little mirror in the sun visor of Emma's car. I am wearing my only suit, which I never wear. It is a gray so dark it is almost black, like one of my father's suits from my childhood. My tie is the red-yellow of the morning sun in mid-winter.

I do not recognize myself.

Emma glances over at me as she drives. Beneath her white cashmere sweater her white linen dress has lace across the shoulders and along the front. She wears an oversized pink wool hat, and has curled her hair so it spirals in waves as it flows down over her shoulders.

"Hey, you," she says.

"Hey, you," I reply. "Are you supposed to wear white to a funeral?"

"You wear white when you're happy, right?"

"I guess."

She smiles, red lipstick framing her white teeth "It's that kind of funeral."

The swollen lumps inside my mouth are getting smaller and smaller. Soon they'll be gone, the last reminders of how close I came to dying just three weeks ago.

I look over, watch Emma drive. Watch how her hands hold the wheel, how her hair moves as she looks to either side.

We pull up to the construction site for the Institute of Science, where a police officer waves us into the parking area.

"Nice day for a funeral!" he says as we drive by.

We lock the car and I look around, but don't see anyone. Emma takes my hand and says, "This way."

She leads me across the street and down the old steps that lead to the Music Concourse, the tree-lined park that lies between the Spreckels Museum and the Institute of Science.

An area that has changed little since my father's time.

"Good spot?" Emma asks me.

I look around. "Great spot," I tell her.

For January the day is warm and sunny, with the temperature in the mid-60's. Ahead of us is the old band shell, a half-dome behind a raised stage that faces rows of dark green benches.

The back rows are mostly empty, with a scattering of people sitting and talking or reading books.

The front benches hold a bizarre assortment of people, most of whom I know.

There is Captain Kreitzer in his dress uniform, sitting between Lieutenant Li and Mrs. Tarrow. She looks beautiful in her floral dress and her long black sweater. I see Luis with Leti and little David and Daniela, and Paula and Eli sitting with them. They all wave to us.

Linh and Alonzo are there, too, and Trish, and even more people from the Ferry Building and the *Louis H. Baar*. Paul Strapp sits behind them, with Linda, Tim and Shari from Theatre Lab West. I see Tommy Gonzalez and Rebecca, with Jacob sitting behind them.

There's Carla and Carolyn, the twins Cuca and Hermie and their brother Freddy, and Kim, Cheryl, Fred, Ralph, Judy, Beatrice, Carol, Kelli, Diane, Nora, Fernando, Lisa and more of my old students. And even Mr. Arce, my old Principal.

The crowd is full of bright colors and pure white. Everything but black for this funeral.

Leonard the Human Statue wears his Wizard of Oz Tin Man costume and bright silver makeup. With his conical metal hat he must be 6'6, and as he stands up on the stage he towers over us. He looks down and salutes me with his axe. I salute back.

Next to Leonard is a simple, jet black coffin, sitting on top of a folding table lined with a skirt of pleated black fabric. The coffin's side has been decorated with brightly colored images from Liam's costume, from top hat to scarf to a vial of San Francisco fog.

Emma guides me to the front row seat at the left, on the aisle, and sits beside me.

"The coffin's from the stage crew at Theatre Lab West," she whispers. "It's their thank-you for helping Candi."

Leonard raises his hands and everyone stops talking and sits down.

"Welcome!" he shouts, his voice amplified by the band shell. "We're here to honor the passing of Liam the Fog Seller!"

As the crowd applauds a figure emerges from the colonnade at the right, limping slightly. He is dressed in yellow pants and a white jacket over a white shirt, and wears a white straw hat. It is only when he reaches the center of the stage that I recognize The Prophet of Market Street.

He begins to sing, and the band shell makes his deep voice rumble across the concourse.

Amazing Grace, how sweet the sound,
That saved a wretch like me.
I once was lost but now am found,
Was blind, but now I see.

'Tis Grace that taught my heart to fear.
And Grace, my fears relieved.

How precious did that Grace appear
The moment I believed.

Through many dangers, toils and snares
We have all safely come.
'Tis Grace that brought us all right here,
and Grace will lead us home.

Amazing Grace, how sweet the sound,
That saved a wretch like me.
I once was lost but now am found,
Was blind, but now I see.

He looks down at me and smiles contentedly. "I told you once, young man, that you ain't killed nobody yet. You didn't like that much."

I nod my agreement.

"Now that you did what you need to do, now that we're at this funeral, I do believe that better days lie ahead." With that, he tips his hat, turns and walks off stage as everyone applauds.

Leonard steps forward again, his Tin Man costume glinting in the bright sunlight. He smiles down from behind his silver makeup. "There are a lot of great stories to tell about Liam the Fog Seller," he says. "But we realized there was one man who should speak for all of us, the man who understood Liam The Fog Seller best of all."

We all look around. I do not know what they have planned. Maybe Luis will say something to embarrass me, or Tommy will talk about old times back at school.

But neither Luis nor Tommy move.

I look back. Standing up behind us is Eli of the Coral Reef. Like me, he wears a suit he never wears.

He edges his way to the aisle and walks awkwardly towards the stage. I can see his hands are trembling.

He climbs the steps on the right and comes to the center of the stage. He looks down at an index card, then back up at us. The band shell makes his voice sound strong and loud.

"We're here to celebrate the life of Liam the Fog Seller," he begins. "He was someone I admired."

Eli takes a deep breath, looks back at Leonard, presses on.

"Liam was like the people on TV, except they have scripts when they talk, and Liam could make it up as he went along. I don't know how he did that."

"Magic!" Luis calls out. More laughter. Eli smiles.

"I... So that's what I wanted to say about Liam. He was great. May... May he rest in peace." He briefly rests his hand on the casket, then steps away again.

There are murmurs of, "Amen."

I'm trying to absorb every moment, every sound, every scent, every rustling of the leaves above us. This is all so strange. And all so wonderful.

"The... What I really wanted to talk about is Steve, Steve Ondelle. I mean, we all know that Steve is what was... who was inside Liam. Whatever Liam could do, he could do it because of Steve."

Someone in the back yells, "Yeah, Steve!"

"And Steve is shy, like me. And he's quiet, like me. And he loves fish, like me."

Now everyone laughs. Eli brightens even more.

"But every time I look at Steve, I know that he can be like Liam if he wants to. He just has to decide, and that... Steve can be whoever he decides he wants to be. And it makes me believe that maybe someday, if..."

He stops for a moment and I start to worry, but he takes a deep breath and keeps going.

"When I look at Steve I think that some day will come, if I keep trying, when I can be like Steve, and I can decide to be like Liam the Fog Seller, too."

"Amen," Leonard tells him, and more people repeat, "Amen."

"So I know this is supposed to be a funeral, and I don't want to mess things up," Eli says, "but having Liam die doesn't... I'm... I'm not sad. Because Steve's still here, and now Steve can just be Steve."

More "Yes" responses from the audience.

"The Institute of Science just closed down the aquarium so they can move to their new building," he says. "I'd spend hours there every day, so now I have a lot of free time. Steve keeps telling me that I should take up a new hobby."

That's true, though Eli never listens when I say it.

He reaches into his jacket pocket and pulls something out, still hidden in his hand. He forces a big smile and opens his hand to show us a glass vial filled with water.

"How can you remember your trip to San Francisco?" he begins, suddenly much louder. "Not with a toy Cable Car, because it's just a toy. Am I right?"

There are cheers and hoots. Emma looks at me in joyful surprise, as shocked as I am at Eli's transformation.

Eli beams as he strikes one of Liam's lecture poses, re-creating it perfectly. "No, no toys for you! You want the real thing, the heart and soul of San Francisco. Ladies and Gentlemen, I give you... San Francisco Bay!"

The group applauds. Eli looks right at me. "San Francisco Bay!" he proclaims. "This is not sniveling spring water that surrenders to life in a plastic bottle! This is the shaper of continents, the key to new worlds, real salt water! It controls everything in San Francisco... including the fog!"

Everyone is cheering. I can't believe it. I love it.

Eli holds up one finger, another Liam pose. "I have personally collected this real salt water from San Francisco Bay..."

This time I start to laugh, and I cannot stop. I feel Emma laughing just as hard beside me. This goes on for quite a while, and there is much joy all around us.

When Eli has finished and we all have recovered our senses Leonard comes back to the stage.

"Steve," he says, "It's time for you to say something."

Emma pushes me out of my seat and I slowly climb the short flight of stairs up to the stage, trying to think. From up here the concourse looks a mile long. More people have come to sit on the back benches, drawn by the music and the laughter.

I just stand there for a moment. I have no idea what to say. Everyone is quiet, so quiet I can hear the birds in the trees around the band shell.

I look over at Liam's colorfully decorated coffin.

I look down at the faces of my friends. I always think of myself as not having many friends, but here are all these people.

This is a new dance for me.

"Thank you for coming to say goodbye to Liam the Fog Seller," I tell them. "Thank you for coming to say hello to me. Thank you for being my friends."

From her seat in the front row Mrs. Tarrow nods. I know that's all I need to say.

It's the best that I can do.

PART V

JOURNAL FIVE

I stand outside the steel door at the back of the Gallienne Bakery in West Sacramento, California. Take a deep breath.

I knock on the cold metal surface. It hurts my knuckles but doesn't make much of a sound.

I wait. No answer.

I knock again.

The door opens and I am face to face with Emma.

"Hi." I hand her the flowers, red and white roses.

"Thank you," she says.

"I'm Steve Ondelle," I tell her. "I've worked on the Sausalito Ferry for the last five years, and before that I was a teacher. For the last three years I've made extra money as a street performer in San Francisco with the stage name of Liam, and I was just cleared by the police after a murderer tried to use me to cover up their crime."

"It's nice to meet you," she says, and smiles.

"I'd like to take you out to lunch," I tell her. "I'm parked up front."

"Oh," she says, a playful look in her eye. "Is it a white stretch limousine?"

"No, I'm afraid it's... I wasn't able to secure one of those."

"A black town car?"

I shake my head. "No, there were none available. It's a red compact I rented in San Francisco after I got my driver's license reinstated."

"My favorite color!"

"I'm glad. Would you like to go to lunch?"

"I'd love to," she says.

With the bouquet still in her hand she comes outside and pulls the steel door shut behind her. She wears a sleeveless summer dress with big pink flowers on a white background, a dress I have not seen before.

We walk up the driveway at the side of the bakery. Out of the corner of my eye I see Manny through the front window, standing by the counter, arms folded. He's frowning as he watches us go by.

After everything that's happened, I don't blame him.

"I hope you... I'm nervous about this first date," I tell her.

"That's OK," she says, and squeezes my hand. "I feel like I already know you."

The End

Acknowledgements

When you spend seven years writing a novel you have a lot of people to thank.

The Internet career expert Marta, whose writings help Luis with his job search, is in fact my wife Marta the Internet career expert. Without her faith, patience, feedback and encouragement this seven-year writing journey could never have been completed. Our sons, Michael and Christopher, and our daughter-in-law Ali, likewise gave me wonderful support.

Dr. Steven C. Young of Pomona College passed away before I completed this book, but I owe him an everlasting debt of gratitude for taking a student who loved to write and turning him into a Writer. It is a rare week when I do not use the lessons he taught me, either in my own work or in teaching others.

Pat FitzGerald of Sausalito gave me generous servings of her time and feedback, and in so doing helped me strengthen several key chapters of this book. I also received additional input from her team.

Veterinarian Dr. Terry Cosgrove and his wife Linda, long-time family friends, provided expert information for Emma's professional background as well as unflagging encouragement.

Attorney Baldwin Lee, another close family friend, gave me invaluable input about the different kinds of organizational structures that can be chosen by startups, and I also gained great perspectives on character from author Dr. Rick Hanson.

The Ferry *Louis H. Baar* is a fictional boat that is operated by a fictional agency, but it's named after a real person.

Louis H. "Bud" Baar, who passed away in 1992 at the age of 75, was a long-time Marin County Supervisor. He was one of the key local leaders who supported the creation of the Point Reyes National Seashore and the GGNRA, and who opposed offshore oil drilling in California.

Baar also served on the Marin County Transit District Board that in 1969 approved the return of ferry service to Sausalito after a hiatus of 28 years, making this fictional ferry's name most appropriate. He and his wife Bette were dear friends of our family and are both greatly missed.

Steve's garage as well as Mrs. Blount's and Mrs. Tarrow's houses all exist in the hills of Sausalito. I have changed their locations to place them side-by-side for dramatic purposes.

The Spear St. location of Steve's father's last office was an address where my father worked when I was growing up.

The California Institute of Science is a fictional organization, although I was inspired in the creation of its back story by the California Academy of Sciences' construction of a new facility in Golden Gate Park, which took place several years before the events depicted in this story.

Finally, the old South Windmill in Golden Gate Park is depicted in ruins in these pages, but in real life it had already been restored to its former glory by the time setting of this book, thanks to generous donations from the community.

Steve would be thrilled.

About the Author

Don Daglow set out to be a playwright, but turned out to be a game designer and novelist.

His creation of *Neverwinter Nights*, which ran for six years on AOL and was then expanded into a long series of hit game titles, earned a 2008 Technical Emmy® Award from the National Academy of Television Arts & Sciences.

Don wrote his first novel, a science fiction epic, at age 12. After studying theatre with Dr. Steven Young at Pomona College and earning his B.A. in Writing, Don won a National Endowment for the Humanities *New Voices* Playwriting Competition, and his work has also appeared in *The Magazine of Fantasy and Science Fiction*.

Don's family has lived in San Francisco and Marin for four generations, and his passion for this unique setting shines through in his writing. He works near the Sausalito Ferry, and he and his wife Marta have lived in three different Sausalito neighborhoods.

He currently serves as President of the Academy of Interactive Arts & Sciences Foundation and continues to create innovative new games, with over 100 titles to his credit.

14 99

20x

RECEIVED JUN 27 2018

CPSIA information can be obtained
at www.ICGtesting.com
Printed in the USA
LVHW03s1816200618
581384LV00005B/942/P

9 780996 781503